PENGUIN BOOKS

ENEMY OF GOD

Before becoming a full-time writer Bernard Cornwell worked as a television producer in London and Belfast. He now lives in Massachusetts with his American wife. He is the author of the hugely successful *Sharpe* series of historical novels.

Penguin publish his bestselling contemporary thrillers *Sea Lord*, *Wildtrack*, *Crackdown*, *Stormchild* and *Scoundrel*, and the historical novel *Redcoat*. Penguin also publish his myth-imbued Arthurian romance, *The Warlord Chronicles*, which consists of *The Winter King*, *Enemy of God* and *Excalibur*.

For more information about Bernard Cornwell's books, please visit his official website: www.bernardcornwell.net

D0995590

The Warlord Chronicles: II

Enemy of God

A NOVEL OF ARTHUR

BERNARD CORNWELL

PENGUIN BOOKS

PENGUIN BOOKS

Published by the Penguin Group
Penguin Books Ltd, 80 Strand, London WC2R 0RL, England
Penguin Group (USA) Inc., 375 Hudson Street, New York, New York 10014, USA
Penguin Group (Canada), 90 Eglinton Avenue East, Suite 700, Toronto, Ontario, Canada M4P 2Y3
(a division of Pearson Penguin Canada Inc.)
Penguin Ireland, 25 St Stephen's Green, Dublin 2, Ireland (a division of Penguin Books Ltd)
Penguin Group (Australia), 250 Camberwell Road, Camberwell, Victoria 3124, Australia
(a division of Pearson Australia Group Pty Ltd)
Penguin Books India Pvt Ltd, 11 Community Centre, Panchsheel Park, New Delhi – 110 017, India
Penguin Group (NZ), 67 Apollo Drive, Rosedale, Auckland 0632, New Zealand
(a division of Pearson New Zealand Ltd)
Penguin Books (South Africa) (Pty) Ltd, 24 Sturdee Avenue, Rosebank,
Johannesburg 2196, South Africa

Penguin Books Ltd, Registered Offices: 80 Strand, London WC2R 0RL, England

www.penguin.com

First published by Michael Joseph 1996
Published in Penguin Books 1997
Reissued in this edition 2011

001

Copyright © Bernard Cornwell, 1996
All rights reserved

The moral right of the author has been asserted

Printed in Great Britain by Clays Ltd, St Ives plc

ISBN: 978-1-405-93143-4

www.greenpenguin.co.uk

Enemy of God is for Susan Watt, its onlie begetter

FOREWORD

Enemy of God is the second novel of the Warlord series, and immediately follows the events described in *The Winter King*. In that book the King of Dumnonia and High King of Britain, Uther, dies and is succeeded by his lamed baby grandson, Mordred. Arthur, a bastard son of Uther's, is appointed one of Mordred's guardians and in time becomes the most important of those guardians. Arthur is determined to fulfil the oath he swore to Uther that Mordred, when he comes of age, will occupy Dumnonia's throne.

Arthur is also determined to bring peace to the warring British kingdoms. The major conflict is between Dumnonia and Powys, but when Arthur is invited to marry Ceinwyn, a Princess of Powys, it seems that war can be avoided. Instead Arthur elopes with the penniless Princess Guinevere and that insult to Ceinwyn brings on years of war that are ended only when Arthur defeats King Gorfyddyd of Powys at the Battle of Lugg Vale. Powys's throne then passes to Cuneglas, Ceinwyn's brother, who, like Arthur, wants peace between the Britons so that they can concentrate their spears against the common enemy, the Saxons (the Sais).

The Winter King, like the present book, was narrated by Derfel (pronounced Dervel), a Saxon slave boy who grew up in Merlin's household and became one of Arthur's warriors. Arthur sent Derfel to Armorica (today's Brittany) where he fought in the doomed campaign to preserve the British kingdom of Benoic against Frankish invaders. Among Benoic's refugees who return to Britain is Lancelot, King of Benoic, whom Arthur now wants to marry to Ceinwyn and place on the throne of Siluria. Derfel has fallen in love with Ceinwyn.

Derfel's other love is Nimue, his childhood friend who has become Merlin's helpmate and lover. Merlin is a Druid and the leader of the faction in Britain that wants to restore the island to its old Gods, to which end he is pursuing a Cauldron, one of the Thirteen Treasures of Britain, a quest which for Merlin and Nimue far outranks any battle against other kingdoms or invaders. Opposing Merlin are the Christians of Britain, one of whose leaders is Bishop Sansum who lost much of his power when he defied Guinevere. Sansum is now in disgrace and serving as Abbot of the Monastery of the Holy Thorn at Ynys Wydryn (Glastonbury).

The Winter King ended with Arthur winning the great battle at Lugg Vale. Mordred's throne is safe, the southern British kingdoms are allied and Arthur, though not a king himself, is their undisputed leader.

CHARACTERS

ADE	Mistress to Lancelot
AELLE	A Saxon king
AGRICOLA	Warlord of Gwent, who serves King Tewdric
AILLEANN	Once Arthur's mistress, mother of his twin sons Amhar and Loholt
AMHAR	Bastard son of Arthur and Ailleann
ARTHUR	Warlord of Dumnonia, guardian of Mordred
BALIN	One of Arthur's warriors
BAN	Once King of Benoic (a kingdom in Brittany), father of Lancelot
BEDWIN	Bishop in Dumnonia and chief councillor
BORS	Lancelot's cousin, his champion
BROCHVAEL	King of Powys after Arthur's time
BYRTHIG	Edling (Crown Prince) of Gwynedd, later King
CADOC	A Christian bishop, reputed saint, a recluse
CADWALLON	King of Gwynedd
CADWY	Rebellious prince in Isca
CALLYN	Champion of Kernow
CAVAN	Derfel's second-in-command
CEI	Arthur's childhood companion, now one of his warriors
CEINWYN	Princess of Powys, sister of Cuneglas
CERDIC	A Saxon king

ix

LEODEGAN	Exiled King of Henis Wyren, father to Guinevere and Gwenhwyvach
LIGESSAC	Traitor in exile
LOHOLT	Arthur's bastard son, twin to Amhar
LUNETE	Once Derfel's lover, now an attendant to Guinevere
MAELGWYN	Monk at Dinnewrac
MALAINE	Druid in Powys
MALLA	Sagramor's Saxon wife
MARK	King of Kernow, father of Tristan
MELWAS	Exiled King of the Belgae
MERLIN	The chief Druid of Dumnonia
MEURIG	Edling (Crown Prince) of Gwent, later King
MORDRED	King of Dumnonia, son of Norwenna
MORFANS	'The Ugly', one of Arthur's warriors
MORGAN	Arthur's elder sister, once Merlin's chief priestess
MORWENNA	Derfel's eldest daughter
NABUR	Christian magistrate in Durnovaria
NIMUE	Merlin's lover and chief priestess
NORWENNA	Mordred's mother, killed by Gundleus
OENGUS MAC AIREM	Irish King of Demetia, a land once called Dyfed
PEREDUR	Son to Lancelot and Ade
PYRLIG	Derfel's bard
RALLA	Merlin's servant, married to Gwlyddyn
SAGRAMOR	Arthur's Numidian commander, Lord of the Stones
SANSUM	Bishop in Dumnonia, later Derfel's superior at Dinnewrac
SCARACH	Issa's wife
SEREN	Derfel's second daughter
TANABURS	A Silurian Druid, killed by Derfel after Lugg Vale

PLACES

Names marked * are fictional

ABONA	Avonmouth, Avon
AQUAE SULIS	Bath, Avon
BENOIC	A kingdom, lost to the Franks, in Brittany (Armorica)
BODUAN	Garn Boduan, Gwynedd
BROCELIANDE	The surviving British kingdom in Armorica
BURRIUM	Gwent's capital. Usk, Gwent
CAER AMBRA*	Amesbury, Wiltshire
CAER CADARN*	South Cadbury, Somerset
CAER GEI*	Gwynedd's capital. North Wales
CAER SWS	Powys's capital. Caersws, Powys
CALLEVA	Silchester, Hampshire
CORINIUM	Cirencester, Gloucestershire
CWM ISAF	Near Newtown, Powys
DINNEWRAC*	A monastery in Powys
DOLFORWYN	Near Newtown, Powys
DUN CEINACH*	Haresfield Beacon, near Gloucester
DUNUM	Hod Hill, Dorset
DURNOVARIA	Dorchester, Dorset
ERMID'S HALL*	Near Street, Somerset
GLEVUM	Gloucester
HALCWM*	Salcombe, Devon
ISCA Dumnonia	Exeter, Devon
ISCA Siluria	Caerleon, Gwent
LINDINIS	Ilchester, Somerset

LLOEGYR	That part of Britian occupied by the Saxons, literally 'the lost lands'. In modern Welsh *Lloegr* means England
LLYN CERRIG BACH	The Lake of Little Stones, now Valley Airfield, Anglesey
LUGG VALE*	Mortimer's Cross, Hereford & Worcester
MAGNIS	Kenchester, Hereford & Worcester
NIDUM	Neath, Glamorgan
PONTES	Staines, Surrey
RATAE	Leicester
THE STONES	Stonehenge
THE TOR	Glastonbury Tor, Somerset
VENTA	Winchester, Hampshire
VINDOCLADIA	Roman Fort near Wimborne Minster, Dorset
YNYS MON	Anglesey
YNYS TREBES*	The lost capital of Benoic, Mont Saint-Michel, Brittany
YNYS WIT	Isle of Wight
YNYS WYDRYN	Glastonbury, Somerset

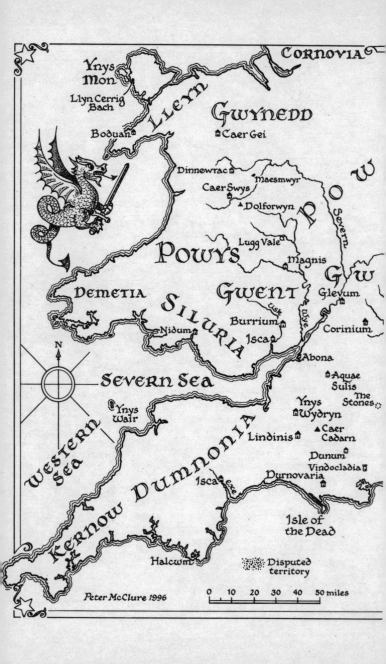

GERMAN
Sea

Ratae

LLOEGYR

London
Pontes
Thames

Caer
Ambra
Calleva

Venta
The Belgic
Lands

Ynys Wit

The Sea Palace

THE KINGDOMS
~ of ~
# BRITAIN
c. 495 AD

Wall of Hadrian
RHEGED
ELMET
CORNOVIA

POWYS

LLOEGYR

0   100 miles

PART ONE

The Dark Road

TODAY I HAVE BEEN thinking about the dead.

This is the last day of the old year. The bracken on the hill has turned brown, the elms at the valley's end have lost their leaves and the winter slaughter of our cattle has begun. Tonight is Samain Eve.

Tonight the curtain that separates the dead from the living will quiver, fray, and finally vanish. Tonight the dead will cross the bridge of swords. Tonight the dead will come from the Otherworld to this world, but we shall not see them. They will be shadows in darkness, mere whispers of wind in a windless night, but they will be here.

Bishop Sansum, the saint who rules our small community of monks, scoffs at this belief. The dead, he says, do not have shadowbodies, nor can they cross the sword bridge, but instead they lie in their cold graves and wait for the final coming of our Lord Jesus Christ. It is proper, he says, for us to remember the dead and to pray for their immortal souls, but their bodies are gone. They are corrupt. Their eyes have melted to leave dark holes in their skulls, worms liquefy their bellies, and mould furs their bones. The saint insists that the dead do not trouble the living on Samain Eve, yet even he will take care to leave a loaf of bread beside the monastery hearth this night. He will pretend it is carelessness, but all the same there will be a loaf of bread and a pitcher of water beside the kitchen ashes tonight.

I shall leave more. A cup of mead and a piece of salmon. They are small gifts, but all I can afford, and tonight I shall place them in the shadows by the hearth then go to my monk's cell and welcome the dead who will come to this cold house on its bare hill.

3

I shall name the dead. Ceinwyn, Guinevere, Nimue, Merlin, Lancelot, Galahad, Dian, Sagramor; the list could fill two parchments. So many dead. Their footsteps will not stir a rush on the floor nor frighten the mice that live in the monastery's thatched roof, but even Bishop Sansum knows that our cats will arch their backs and hiss from the kitchen corners as the shadows that are not shadows come to our hearth to find the gifts that deter them from working mischief.

So today I have been thinking about the dead.

I am old now, maybe as old as Merlin was, though not nearly so wise. I think that Bishop Sansum and I are the only men living from the great days and I alone remember them fondly. Maybe some others still live. In Ireland, perhaps, or in the wastes north of Lothian, but I do not know of them, though this much I do know: that if any others do live, then they, like me, cower from the encroaching darkness like cats shrinking from this night's shadows. All that we loved is broken, all that we made is pulled down and all that we sowed is reaped by the Saxons. We British cling to the high western lands and talk of revenge, but there is no sword that will fight a great darkness. There are times, too frequent now, when all I want is to be with the dead. Bishop Sansum applauds that wish and tells me it is only right that I should yearn to be in heaven at God's right hand, but I do not think I shall reach the saints' heaven. I have sinned too much and thus fear hell, but still hope, against my faith, that I will pass to the Otherworld instead. For there, under the apple trees of four-towered Annwn, waits a table heaped with food and crowded with the shadowbodies of all my old friends. Merlin will be cajoling, lecturing, grumbling and mocking. Galahad will be bursting to interrupt and Culhwch, bored with so much talk, will steal a larger portion of beef and think no one notices. And Ceinwyn will be there, dear lovely Ceinwyn, bringing peace to the turmoil roused by Nimue.

But I am still cursed by breath. I live while my friends feast, and as long as I live I shall write this tale of Arthur. I write at the behest of Queen Igraine, the young wife of King Brochvael of

4

Powys who is the protector of our small monastery. Igraine wanted to know all I can remember of Arthur and so I began to write these tales down, but Bishop Sansum disapproves of the task. He says Arthur was the Enemy of God, a spawn of the devil, and so I am writing the tales in my native Saxon tongue that the saint does not speak. Igraine and I have told the saint that I am writing the gospel of our Lord Jesus Christ in the enemy's language and maybe he believes us, or maybe he is biding his time until he can prove our falsehood and then punish me.

I write each day. Igraine comes frequently to the monastery to pray that God will grant her womb the blessing of a child, and when her prayers are done she takes the finished skins away and has them translated into British by the clerk of Brochvael's justice. I think she changes the story then, making it match the Arthur she wants rather than the Arthur who was, but perhaps that does not matter for who will ever read this tale? I am like a man building a wall of mud and wattle to resist an imminent flood. The darkness comes when no man will read. There will just be Saxons.

So I write about the dead and the writing passes the time until I can join them; the time when Brother Derfel, a humble monk of Dinnewrac, will again be Lord Derfel Cadarn, Derfel the Mighty, Champion of Dumnonia and beloved friend of Arthur. But now I am just a cold old monk scribbling memories with my one remaining hand. And tonight is Samain Eve and tomorrow is a new year. The winter is coming. The dead leaves lie in shining drifts against the hedgerows, there are redwings in the stubble, gulls have flown inland from the sea and woodcock gather under the full moon. It is a good season, Igraine tells me, to write of old things and so she has brought me a fresh pile of skins, a flask of newly mixed ink and a sheaf of quills. Tell me of Arthur, she says, of golden Arthur, our last and best hope, our king who never was a king, the Enemy of God and the scourge of Saxons. Tell me of Arthur.

*

5

A field after battle is a dreadful thing.

We had won, but there was no elation in our souls, just weariness and relief. We shivered about our fires and tried not to think of the ghouls and spirits that stalked the dark where the dead of Lugg Vale lay. Some of us slept, but none slept well for the nightmares of battle's end harried us. I woke in the black hours, startled out of sleep by the memory of a spear thrust that had so nearly skewered my belly. Issa had saved me, pushing the enemy's spear away with the edge of his shield, but I was haunted by what had so nearly happened. I tried to sleep again, but the memory of that spear thrust kept me awake, and so at last, shivering and weary, I stood and drew my cloak about me. The vale was lit by guttering fires, and in the dark between the flames there drifted a miasma of smoke and river mist. Some things moved in the smoke, but whether they were ghosts or the living I could not tell.

'You can't sleep, Derfel?' A voice spoke softly from the doorway of the Roman building where the body of King Gorfyddyd lay.

I turned to see it was Arthur who watched me. 'I can't sleep, Lord,' I admitted.

He picked his way through the sleeping warriors. He wore one of the long white cloaks that he liked so much and, in the fiery night, the garment seemed to shine. There was no mud on it, or any blood, and I realized he must have kept the cloak bundled safe for something clean to wear after battle. The rest of us would not have cared if we had ended the fight stark naked so long as we lived, but Arthur was ever a fastidious man. He was bare-headed and his hair still showed the indentations where the helmet had clasped his skull. 'I never sleep well after battle,' he said, 'not for a week at least. Then comes a blessed night of rest.' He smiled at me. 'I am in your debt.'

'No, Lord,' I said, though in truth he was in my debt. Sagramor and I had held Lugg Vale all that long day, fighting in the shield-wall against a vast horde of enemies, and Arthur had failed to rescue us. A rescue had come at last, and victory with it, but of all Arthur's battles Lugg Vale was the nearest to a defeat. Until the last battle.

'I, at least, will remember the debt,' he said fondly, 'even if you do not. It is time to make you wealthy, Derfel, you and your men.' He smiled and took my elbow to lead me to a bare patch of earth where our voices would not disturb the restless sleep of the warriors who lay closer to the smoking fires. The ground was damp and rain had puddled in the deep scars left by the hoofs of Arthur's big horses. I wondered if horses dreamed of battle, then wondered if the dead, newly arrived in the Other-world, still shuddered at the memory of the sword stroke or spear blow that had sent their souls across the bridge of swords. 'I suppose Gundleus is dead?' Arthur interrupted my thoughts.

'Dead, Lord,' I confirmed. The King of Siluria had died earlier in the evening, but I had not seen Arthur since the moment when Nimue had pinched out her enemy's life.

'I heard him screaming,' Arthur said in a matter-of-fact voice.

'All Britain must have heard him screaming,' I answered just as drily. Nimue had taken the King's dark soul piece by piece, all the while crooning her revenge on the man who had raped her and taken one of her eyes.

'So Siluria needs a King,' Arthur said, then stared down the long vale to where the black shapes drifted in the mist and smoke. His clean-shaven face was shadowed by the flames, giving him a gaunt look. He was not a handsome man, but nor was he ugly. Rather he had a singular face; long, bony and strong. In repose it was a rueful face, suggesting sympathy and thoughtfulness, but in conversation it was animated by enthusiasm and a quick smile. He was still young then, just thirty years old, and his short-cropped hair was untouched by grey. 'Come,' he touched my arm and gestured down the vale.

'You'd walk among the dead?' I pulled back aghast. I would have waited till dawn had chased the ghouls away before venturing away from the protective firelight.

'We made them into the dead, Derfel, you and I,' Arthur said, 'so they should fear us, should they not?' He was never a superstitious man, not like the rest of us who craved blessings, treasured amulets and watched every moment for omens that might warn against dangers. Arthur moved through that spirit world like a blind man. 'Come,' he said, touching my arm again.

So we walked into the dark. They were not all dead, those things that lay in the mist, for some called piteously for help, but Arthur, normally the kindest of men, was deaf to the feeble cries. He was thinking about Britain. 'I'm going south tomorrow,' he said, 'to see Tewdric.' King Tewdric of Gwent was our ally, but he had refused to send his men to Lugg Vale, believing that victory was impossible. The King was in our debt now, for we had won his war for him, but Arthur was not a man to hold a grudge. 'I'll ask Tewdric to send men east to face the Saxons,' Arthur went on, 'but I'll send Sagramor as well. That should hold the frontier through the winter. Your men,' he gave me a swift smile, 'deserve a rest.'

The smile told me that there would be no rest. 'They will do whatever you ask,' I answered dutifully. I was walking stiffly, wary of the circling shadows and making the sign against evil with my right hand. Some souls, newly ripped from their bodies, do not find the entrance to the Otherworld, but instead wander the earth's surface looking for their old bodies and seeking revenge on their killers. Many of those souls were in Lugg Vale that night and I feared them, but Arthur, oblivious of their threat, strolled carelessly through the field of death with one hand holding up the skirts of his cloak to keep it free of the wet grass and thick mud.

'I want your men in Siluria,' he said decisively. 'Oengus Mac Airem will want to plunder it, but he must be restrained.' Oengus was the Irish King of Demetia who had changed sides in the battle to give Arthur victory and the Irishman's price was a share of slaves and wealth from the dead Gundleus's kingdom. 'He can take a hundred slaves,' Arthur decreed, 'and one third of Gundleus's treasury. He's agreed to that, but he'll still try to cheat us.'

'I'll make sure he doesn't, Lord.'

'No, not you. Will you let Galahad lead your men?'

I nodded, hiding my surprise. 'So what do you want of me?' I asked.

'Siluria is a problem,' Arthur went on, ignoring my question. He stopped, frowning as he thought about Gundleus's kingdom. 'It's been ill-ruled, Derfel, ill-ruled.' He spoke with a deep distaste. To the rest of us corrupt government was as natural as snow in winter or flowers in the springtime, but Arthur was genuinely horrified by it. These days we remember Arthur as a warlord, as the shining man in polished armour who carried a sword into legend, but he would have wanted to be remembered as nothing but a good, honest and just ruler. The sword gave him power, but he gave that power to the law. 'It isn't an important kingdom,' he continued, 'but it will make endless trouble if we don't put it right.' He was thinking aloud, trying to anticipate every obstacle that lay between this night after battle and his dream of a peaceful united Britain. 'The ideal answer,' he said, 'would be to divide it between Gwent and Powys.'

'Then why not do that?' I asked.

'Because I have promised Siluria to Lancelot,' he said in a voice that brooked no contradiction. I said nothing, but just touched Hywelbane's hilt so that the iron would protect my soul from the evil things of this night. I was gazing southwards to where the dead lay like a tide-rill by the tree fence where my men had fought the enemy all that long day.

There had been so many brave men in that fight, but no Lancelot. In all the years that I had fought for Arthur, and in all the years that I had been acquainted with Lancelot, I had yet to see Lancelot in the shield-wall. I had seen him pursuing beaten fugitives, and seen him lead captives off to parade them before an excited crowd, but I had never seen him in the hard, sweaty, clanging press of struggling shield-walls. He was the exiled King of Benoic, unthroned by the horde of Franks that had erupted out of Gaul to sweep his father's kingdom into oblivion, and not once, so far as I knew, had he ever carried a spear against a Frankish war-band, yet bards throughout the length and breadth of Britain sang of his bravery. He was Lancelot, the King without land, the hero of a hundred fights, the sword of the Britons, the handsome lord of sorrows, the paragon, and all of that high reputation was made by song and none of it, so far as I knew, with a sword. I was his enemy, and he mine, but both of us were friends of Arthur and that friendship kept our enmity in an awkward truce.

Arthur knew my hostility. He touched my elbow so that we both walked on south towards the tide-rill of the dead. 'Lancelot is Dumnonia's friend,' he insisted, 'so if Lancelot rules Siluria then we shall have nothing to fear from it. And if Lancelot marries Ceinwyn, then Powys will support him too.'

There, it was said, and now my hostility was brittle with anger, yet still I said nothing against Arthur's scheme. What could I say? I was the son of a Saxon slave, a young warrior with a band of men but no land, and Ceinwyn was a Princess of Powys. She was called *seren*, the star, and she shone in a dull land like a spark of the sun fallen into mud. She had been betrothed to Arthur, but had lost him to Guinevere, and that loss had brought on the war that had just ended in the slaughter of Lugg Vale. Now, for peace, Ceinwyn must marry Lancelot, my enemy, while I, a mere nothing, was in love with her. I wore her brooch and I carried her image in my thoughts. I had even sworn an oath to protect her, and she had not spurned the oath. Her acceptance had filled me with an insane hope that my love for her was not hopeless, but it was. Ceinwyn was a Princess and she must marry a King, and I was a slave-born spearman and would marry where I could.

So I said nothing about my love for Ceinwyn, and Arthur, who was disposing of Britain in this night after his victory, suspected nothing. And why should he? If I had confessed to him that I was in love with Ceinwyn he would have thought it as outrageous an ambition as a dunghill rooster wanting to mate with an eagle. 'You know Ceinwyn, don't you?' he asked me.

'Yes, Lord.'

'And she likes you,' he said, only half as a question.

'So I dare to think,' I said truthfully, remembering Ceinwyn's pale, silvery beauty and loathing the thought of it being given into Lancelot's handsome keeping. 'She likes me well enough,' I went on, 'to have told me she has no enthusiasm for this marriage.'

'Why should she?' Arthur asked. 'She's never met Lancelot. I don't expect enthusiasm from her, Derfel, just obedience.'

I hesitated. Before the battle, when Tewdric had been so desperate to end the war that threatened to ruin his land, I had gone on a peace mission to Gorfyddyd. The mission had failed, but I had talked with Ceinwyn and told her of Arthur's hope that she should marry Lancelot. She had not rejected the idea, but nor had she welcomed it. Back then, of course, no one believed Arthur could defeat Ceinwyn's father in battle, but Ceinwyn had considered that unlikely possibility and had asked me to request one favour of Arthur if he should win. She wanted his protection, and I, falling so hard in love with her, translated that request as a plea that she should not be forced into a marriage she did not want. I told Arthur now that she had begged his protection. 'She's been betrothed too often, Lord,' I added, 'and too often disappointed, and I think she wants to be left alone for a time.'

'Time!' Arthur laughed. 'She hasn't got time, Derfel. She's nearly twenty! She can't stay unmarried like a cat that won't catch mice. And who else can she marry?' He walked on a few paces. 'She has my protection,' he said, 'but what better protection could she want than to be married to Lancelot and placed on a throne? And what about you?' he asked suddenly.

'Me, Lord?' For a moment I thought he was proposing that I should marry Ceinwyn and my heart leapt.

'You're nearly thirty,' he said, 'and it's time you were married. We'll see to it when we're back in Dumnonia, but for now I want you to go to Powys.'

'Me, Lord? Powys?' We had just fought and defeated Powys's army and I could not imagine that anyone in Powys would welcome an enemy warrior.

Arthur gripped my arm. 'The most important thing in the next few weeks, Derfel, is that Cuneglas is acclaimed King of Powys. He thinks no one will challenge him, but I want to be sure. I want one of my men in Caer Sws to be a witness to our friendship. Nothing more. I just want any challenger to know that he will have to fight me as well as Cuneglas. If you're there and if you're seen to be his friend then that message will be clear.'

'So why not send a hundred men?' I asked.

'Because then it will look as if we're imposing Cuneglas on Powys's throne. I don't want that. I need him as a friend, and I don't want him returning to Powys looking like a defeated man. Besides,' he smiled, 'you're as good as a hundred men, Derfel. You proved that yesterday.'

I grimaced, for I was always uncomfortable with extravagant compliments, but if the praise meant that I was the right man to be Arthur's envoy in Powys then I was happy, for I would be close to Ceinwyn again. I still treasured the memory of her touch on my hand, just as I treasured the brooch she had given me so many years before. She had not married Lancelot yet, I told myself, and all I wanted was a chance to indulge my impossible hopes. 'And once Cuneglas is acclaimed,' I asked, 'what do I do then?'

'You wait for me,' Arthur said. 'I'm coming to Powys as soon as I can, and once we've settled the peace and Lancelot is safely betrothed, we'll go home. And next year, my friend, we'll lead the armies of Britain against the Saxons.' He spoke with a rare relish for the business of making war. He was good at fighting, and he even enjoyed battle for the unleashed thrills it gave his usually so careful soul, but he never sought war if peace was available because he mistrusted the uncertainties of battle. The vagaries of victory and defeat were too unpredictable, and Arthur hated to see good order and careful diplomacy abandoned to the chances of battle. But diplomacy and tact would never defeat the invading Saxons who were spreading westwards across Britain like vermin. Arthur dreamed of a well-ordered, lawfully governed, peaceful Britain and the Saxons were no part of that dream.

'We'll march in the spring?' I asked him.

'When the first leaves show.'

'Then I would ask one favour of you first.'

'Name it,' he said, delighted that I should want something in return for helping to give him victory.

'I want to march with Merlin, Lord,' I said.

He did not answer for a while. He just stared down at the damp ground where a sword lay with its blade bent almost double. Somewhere in the dark a man moaned, cried out, then was silent. 'The Cauldron,' Arthur said at last, his voice heavy.

'Yes, Lord,' I said. Merlin had come to us during the battle and pleaded that both sides should abandon the fight and follow him on a quest to find the Cauldron of Clyddno Eiddyn. The Cauldron was the greatest Treasure of Britain, the magical gift of the old Gods, and it had been lost for centuries. Merlin's life was dedicated to retrieving those Treasures, and the Cauldron was his greatest prize. If he could find the Cauldron, he told us, he could restore Britain to her rightful Gods.

Arthur shook his head. 'Do you really think the Cauldron of Clyddno Eiddyn has stayed hidden all these years?' he asked me. 'Through all the Roman years? It was taken to Rome, Derfel, and it was melted down for pins or brooches or coins. There is no Cauldron!'

'Merlin says there is, Lord,' I insisted.

'Merlin has listened to old women's tales,' Arthur said angrily. 'Do you know how many men he wants to take on this search for his Cauldron?'

'No, Lord.'

'Eighty, he told me. Or a hundred. Or, better still, two hundred! He won't even say where the Cauldron is, he just wants me to give him an army and let him march it away to some wild place. Ireland, maybe, or the Wilderness. No!' He kicked the bent sword, then prodded a finger hard into my shoulder. 'Listen, Derfel, I need every spear I can muster next year. We're going to finish the Saxons once and for ever, and I can't lose eighty or a hundred men to the chase of a bowl that disappeared nearly five hundred years ago. Once Aelle's Saxons are defeated you can chase this nonsense if you must. But I tell you it is a nonsense. There is no Cauldron.' He turned and began to walk back to the fires. I followed, wanting to argue with him, but I knew I could never persuade him for he would need every spear he could muster if he was to defeat the Saxons, and he would do nothing now that would weaken his chances of victory in the spring. He smiled at me as if to compensate for his harsh refusal of my request. 'If the Cauldron does exist,' he said, 'then it can stay hidden another year or two. But in the meantime, Derfel, I plan to make you rich. We shall marry you to money.' He slapped my back. 'One last campaign, my dear Derfel, one last great slaughter, then we shall have peace. Pure peace. We won't need any cauldrons then.' He spoke exultingly. That night, among the dead, he really did see peace coming.

We walked towards the fires that lay around the Roman house where Ceinwyn's father, Gorfyddyd, lay dead. Arthur was happy that night, truly happy, for he saw his dream coming true. And it all seemed so easy. There would be one more war, then peace for evermore. Arthur was our warlord, the greatest warrior in Britain, yet that night after battle, among the shrieking souls of the smoke-wreathed dead, all he wanted was peace. Gorfyddyd's heir, Cuneglas of Powys, shared Arthur's dream. Tewdric of Gwent was an ally, Lancelot would be given the kingdom of Siluria and together with Arthur's Dumnonian army the united Kings of Britain would defeat the invading Saxons. Mordred, under Arthur's protection, would grow to assume Dumnonia's throne and Arthur would retire to enjoy the peace and prosperity his sword had given Britain.

Thus Arthur disposed the golden future.

But he did not reckon on Merlin. Merlin was older, wiser and subtler than Arthur, and Merlin had smelt the Cauldron out. He would find it, and its power would spread through Britain like a poison.

For it was the Cauldron of Clyddno Eiddyn. It was the Cauldron that broke men's dreams.

And Arthur, for all his practicality, was a dreamer.

In Caer Sws the leaves were heavy with the last ripeness of summer.

I had travelled north with King Cuneglas and his defeated men and so I was the only Dumnonian present when the body of King Gorfyddyd was burned on Dolforwyn's summit. I saw the flames of his balefire gust huge in the night as his soul crossed the bridge of swords to its shadowbody in the Otherworld. The fire was surrounded by a double ring of Powys's spearmen who carried flaming torches that swayed together as they sang the Death Lament of Beli Mawr. They sang for a long time and the sound of their voices echoed from the near hills like a choir of ghosts. There was much sorrow in Caer Sws. So many in the land had been made widows and orphans, and on the morning after the old King was burned and when his balefire was still sending a pyre of smoke towards the northern mountains, there was still more sorrow when the news of Ratae's fall arrived. Ratae had been a great fortress on Powys's eastern frontier, but Arthur had betrayed it to the Saxons to buy their peace while he fought against Gorfyddyd. None in Powys knew of Arthur's treachery yet and I did not tell them.

I did not see Ceinwyn for three days, for they were the days of mourning for Gorfyddyd and no women went to the balefire. Instead the women of Powys's court wore black wool and were shut up inside the women's hall. No music was played in the hall, only water was given for drink and their only food was dry bread and a thin gruel of oats. Outside the hall the warriors of Powys gathered for the new King's acclamation and I, obedient to Arthur's orders, tried to detect whether any man would challenge Cuneglas's right to the throne, but I heard no whisper of opposition.

At the end of the three days the door of the women's hall was thrown open. A maidservant appeared in the doorway and scattered rue on the hall's threshold and steps, and a moment later a billow of smoke gushed from the door and we knew the women were burning the old king's marriage bedding. The smoke swirled from the hall's door and windows, and only when the smoke had dissipated did Helledd, now Queen of Powys, come down the steps to kneel before her husband, King Cuneglas of Powys. She wore a dress of white linen which, when Cuneglas raised her, showed muddy marks where she had knelt. He kissed her, then led her back into the hall. Black-cloaked Iorweth, Powys's chief Druid, followed the King into the women's hall, while outside, ringing the hall's wooden walls in ranks of iron and leather, the surviving warriors of Powys watched and waited.

They waited while a choir of children chanted the love duet of Gwydion and Aranrhod, the Song of Rhiannon, and then every long verse of Gofannon's March to Caer Idion, and it was only when that last song was finished that Iorweth, now robed in white and carrying a black staff tipped with mistletoe, came to the door and announced that the days of mourning were at last over. The warriors cheered and broke from the ranks to seek their own women. Tomorrow Cuneglas would be acclaimed on Dolforwyn's summit and if any man wanted to challenge his right to rule Powys then the acclamation would provide that chance. It would also be my first glimpse of Ceinwyn since the battle.

Next day I stared at Ceinwyn as Iorweth performed the rites of acclamation. She stood watching her brother and I gazed at her in a kind of wonder that any woman could be so lovely. I am old now, so perhaps my old man's memory exaggerates Princess Ceinwyn's beauty, but I do not think so. She was not called the *seren*, the star, for nothing. She was of average height, but very slightly built and that slenderness gave her an appearance of fragility that was, I later learned, a deception, for Ceinwyn had, above all things, a will of steel. Her hair, like mine, was fair, only hers was pale gold and sun-bright while mine was more like the colour of dirty straw. Her eyes were blue, her demeanour was demure and her face as sweet as honey from a wild comb. That day she was dressed in a blue linen gown that was trimmed with the black-flecked silver-white fur of a winter stoat, the same dress she had worn when she had touched my hand and taken my oath. She caught my eye once and smiled gravely and I swear my heart checked in its beating.

The rites of Powys's kingship were not unlike our own. Cuneglas was paraded about Dolforwyn's stone circle, he was given the symbols of kingship, and then a warrior declared him King and dared any man present to challenge the acclamation. The challenge was answered by silence. The ashes of the great balefire still smoked beyond the circle to show that a King had died, but the silence about the stones was proof that a new King reigned. Then Cuneglas was presented with gifts. Arthur, I knew, would be bringing his own magnificent present, but he had given me Gorfyddyd's war sword that had been found on the battlefield and I now gave it back to Gorfyddyd's son as a token of Dumnonia's wish to have peace with Powys.

After the acclamation there was a feast in the lone hall that stood on Dolforwyn's summit. It was a meagre feast, richer in mead and ale than in food, but it was a chance for Cuneglas to tell the warriors his hopes for his reign.

He spoke first of the war that had just ended. He named the dead of Lugg Vale, and promised his men that those warriors had not died in vain. 'What they achieved,' he said, 'is peace between the Britons. A peace between Powys and Dumnonia.' That caused some growls among the warriors, but Cuneglas stilled them with a raised hand. 'Our enemy,' he said, and his voice was suddenly hard, 'is not Dumnonia. Our enemy is the Saxon!' He paused, and this time no one growled in dissent. They just waited in silence and watched their new King, who was in truth no great warrior, but a good and honest man. Those qualities seemed obvious on his round, guileless young face to which he had vainly attempted to add dignity by growing long, plaited moustaches that hung to his breast. He might be no warrior, but he was shrewd enough to know that he had to offer these warriors the chance of war, for only by war could a man earn glory and wealth. Ratae, he promised them, would be retaken and the Saxons punished for the horrors they had inflicted on its inhabitants. Lloegyr, the Lost Lands, would be reclaimed from the Saxons, and Powys, once the mightiest of Britain's kingdoms, would once again stretch from the mountains to the German Sea. The Roman towns would be rebuilt, their walls raised to glory again and the roads repaired. There would be farmland, booty and Saxon slaves for every warrior in Powys. They applauded that prospect, for Cuneglas was offering his disappointed chieftains the rewards that such men always sought from their kings. But, he went on after raising a hand to still the cheering, the wealth of Lloegyr would not be reclaimed by Powys alone. 'Now,' he warned his followers, 'we march alongside the men of Gwent and beside the spearmen of Dumnonia. They were my father's enemies, but they are my friends and that is why my Lord Derfel is here.' He smiled at me. 'And that is why,' he continued, 'under the next full moon, my dear sister will pledge her betrothal to Lancelot. She will rule as Queen in Siluria and the men of that country will march with us, and with Arthur and with Tewdric, to rid the land of Saxons. We shall destroy our true enemy. We shall destroy the Sais!'

This time the cheers were unstinted. He had won them over. He was offering them the wealth and power of old Britain and they clapped their hands and stamped their feet to show their approval. Cuneglas stood for a while, letting the acclamation continue, then he just sat and smiled at me as if he recognized how Arthur would have approved of all he had just said.

I did not stay on Dolforwyn for the drinking that would go on all night, but instead walked back to Caer Sws behind the ox-drawn wagon that carried Queen Helledd, her two aunts and Ceinwyn. The royal ladies wanted to be back in Caer Sws by sunset and I went with them, not because I felt unwelcome among Cuneglas's men, but because I had found no chance to talk with Ceinwyn. So, like a moonstruck calf, I joined the small guard of spearmen who escorted the wagon homewards. I had dressed carefully that day, wanting to impress Ceinwyn, and so I had cleaned my mail armour, brushed the mud from my boots and cloak, then woven my long fair hair into a loose plait that hung down my back. I wore her brooch on my cloak as a sign of my allegiance to her.

I thought she would ignore me, for all through that long walk back to Caer Sws she sat in the wagon and stared away from me, but at last, as we turned the corner and the fortress came into sight, she turned and dropped off the wagon to wait for me beside the road. The escorting spearmen moved aside to let me walk beside her. She smiled as she recognized the brooch, but made no reference to it. 'We were wondering, Lord Derfel,' she said instead, 'what brought you here.'

'Arthur wanted a Dumnonian to witness your brother's acclamation, Lady,' I answered.

'Or did Arthur want to be sure that he would be acclaimed?' she asked shrewdly.

'That too,' I admitted.

She shrugged. 'There's no one else who could be King here. My father made certain of that. There was a chieftain called Valerin who might have challenged Cuneglas for the kingship, but we hear Valerin died in the battle.'

'Yes, Lady, he did,' I said, but I did not add that it had been I who had killed Valerin in single combat by the ford at Lugg Vale. 'He was a brave man, and so was your father. I am sorry for you that he's dead.'

She walked in silence for a few paces as Helledd, Powys's Queen, watched us suspiciously from the ox-cart. 'My father,' Ceinwyn said after a while, 'was a very bitter man. But he was always good to me.' She spoke bleakly, but shed no tears. Those tears had all been wept already and now her brother was King and Ceinwyn faced a new future. She hitched up her skirts to negotiate a muddy patch. There had been rain the night before and the clouds to the west promised more soon. 'So Arthur comes here?' she asked.

'Any day now, Lady.'

'And brings Lancelot?' she asked.

'I would think so.'

She grimaced. 'The last time we met, Lord Derfel, I was to marry Gundleus. Now it is to be Lancelot. One King after another.'

'Yes, Lady,' I said. It was an inadequate, even a stupid answer, but I had been struck by the exquisite nervousness that ties a lover's tongue. All I ever wanted was to be with Ceinwyn, but when I found myself at her side I could not say what was in my soul.

'And I am to be Queen of Siluria,' Ceinwyn said, without any relish at the prospect. She stopped and gestured back down the Severn's wide valley. 'Just past Dolforwyn,' she told me, 'there's a little hidden valley with a house and some apple trees. And when I was a little girl I always used to think the Otherworld was like that valley; a small, safe place where I could live, be happy and have children.' She laughed at herself and began walking again. 'All across Britain there are girls who dream of marrying Lancelot and being a Queen in a palace, and all I want is a small valley with its apple trees.'

'Lady,' I said, nerving myself to say what I really wanted to say, but she immediately guessed what was on my mind and touched my arm to hush me.

'I must do my duty, Lord Derfel,' she said, warning me to guard my tongue.

'You have my oath,' I blurted out. It was as near to a confession of love as I was capable of at that moment.

'I know,' she said gravely, 'and you are my friend, are you not?'

I wanted to be more than a friend, but I nodded. 'I am your friend, Lady.'

'Then I will tell you,' she said, 'what I told my brother.' She looked up at me, her blue eyes very serious. 'I don't know that I want to marry Lancelot, but I have promised Cuneglas that I will meet him before I make up my mind. I must do that, but whether I shall marry him, I don't know.' She walked in silence for a few paces and I sensed she was debating whether to tell me something. Finally she decided to trust me. 'After I saw you last,' she went on, 'I visited the priestess at Maesmwyr and she took me to the dream cave and made me sleep on the bed of skulls. I wanted to discover my fate, you see, but I don't remember having any dreams at all. But when I woke the priestess said that the next man who wanted to marry me would marry the dead instead.' She gazed up at me. 'Does that make sense?'

'None, Lady,' I said and touched the iron on Hywelbane's hilt. Was she warning me? We had never spoken of love, but she must have sensed my yearning.

'It makes no sense to me either,' she confessed, 'so I asked Iorweth what the prophecy meant and he told me I should stop worrying. He said the priestess talks in riddles because she's incapable of talking sense. What I think it means is that I should not marry at all, but I don't know. I only know one thing, Lord Derfel. I will not marry lightly.'

'You know two things, Lady,' I said. 'You know my oath holds.'

'I know that too,' she said, then smiled at me again. 'I'm glad you're here, Lord Derfel.' And with those words she ran on ahead and scrambled back into the ox-cart, leaving me to puzzle over her riddle and to find no answer that could give my soul peace.

Arthur came to Caer Sws three days later. He came with twenty horsemen and a hundred spearmen. He brought bards and harpists. He brought Merlin, Nimue and gifts of the gold taken from the dead in Lugg Vale, and he also brought Guinevere and Lancelot.

I groaned when I saw Guinevere. We had won a victory and made peace, yet even so I thought it cruel of Arthur to bring the woman for whom he had spurned Ceinwyn. But Guinevere had insisted on accompanying her husband and so she arrived in Caer Sws in an ox-drawn wagon that was furnished with furs, hung with dyed linens and draped with green branches to signify peace. Queen Elaine, Lancelot's mother, rode in the cart with Guinevere, but it was Guinevere, not the Queen, who commanded attention. She stood as the cart pulled slowly through Caer Sws's gate and she remained standing as the oxen drew her to the door of Cuneglas's great hall, where once she had been an unwanted exile and to which she now came like a conqueror. She wore a robe of linen dyed gold, she wore gold about her neck and on her wrists, while her springing red hair was trapped by a circle of gold. She was pregnant, but the pregnancy did not show beneath the precious gold linen. She looked like a Goddess.

Yet if Guinevere looked a Goddess, Lancelot rode into Caer Sws like a God. Many folk assumed he must be Arthur for he looked magnificent on a white horse draped with a pale linen cloth that was studded with small golden stars. He wore his white-enamelled scale armour, his sword was scabbarded in white and a long white cloak, lined with red, hung from his shoulders. His dark, handsome face was framed by the gilded edges of his helmet that was now crested with a pair of spread swan's wings instead of the sea-eagle wings he had worn in Ynys Trebes. People gasped when they saw him and I heard the whispers hurry through the crowd that this was not Arthur after all, but King Lancelot, the tragic hero of the lost kingdom of Benoic and the man who would marry their own Princess Ceinwyn. My heart sank at the sight of him, for I feared his magnificence would dazzle Ceinwyn. The crowd hardly noticed Arthur, who wore a leather jerkin and a white cloak and seemed embarrassed to be in Caer Sws at all.

That night there was a feast. I doubt Cuneglas could have felt much welcome for Guinevere, but he was a patient, sensible man who, unlike his father, did not choose to take offence at every imagined slight, and so he treated Guinevere like a Queen. He poured her wine, served her food and bent his head to talk with her. Arthur, seated on Guinevere's other side, beamed with pleasure. He always looked happy when he was with his Guinevere, and there must have been a keen pleasure for him to see her treated with such ceremony in the very same hall where he had first glimpsed her standing among the lesser folk at the back of the crowd.

Arthur paid most of his attentions to Ceinwyn. Everyone in the hall knew how he had spurned her once and how he had broken their betrothal to marry the penniless Guinevere, and many men of Powys had sworn they could never forgive Arthur that slight, yet Ceinwyn forgave him and made her forgiveness obvious. She smiled on him, laid a hand on his arm and leaned close to him, and later in the feast, when mead had melted away all the old hostilities, King Cuneglas took Arthur's hand, then his sister's, and clasped them together in his and the hall cheered to see that sign of peace. An old insult was laid to rest.

A moment later, in another symbolic gesture, Arthur Ceinwyn's hand and led her to a seat that had been left e beside Lancelot. There were more cheers. I watched stony as Lancelot stood to receive Ceinwyn, then as he sat beside her and poured her wine. He took a heavy golden bracelet from his wrist and presented it to her, and though Ceinwyn made a show of refusing the generous gift, she at last slipped it onto her arm where the gold gleamed in the rush light. The warriors on the hall floor demanded to see the bracelet and Ceinwyn coyly lifted her arm to show the heavy band of gold. I alone did not cheer. I sat as the sound thundered about me and as a heavy rain beat on the thatch. She had been dazzled, I thought, she had been dazzled. The star of Powys had fallen before Lancelot's dark and elegant beauty.

I would have left the hall there and then to carry my misery into the rainswept night, but Merlin had been stalking the floor of the hall. At the beginning of the feast he had been seated at the high table but he had left it to move among the warriors, stopping here and there to listen to a conversation or to whisper in a man's ear. His white hair was drawn back from his tonsure into a long plait that he had bound in a black ribbon, while his long beard was similarly plaited and bound. His face, dark as the Roman chestnuts that were such a delicacy in Dumnonia, was long, deeply lined and amused. He was up to mischief, I thought, and I had shrunk down in my place so that he would not work that mischief on me. I loved Merlin like a father, but I was in no mood for more riddles. I just wanted to be as far from Ceinwyn and Lancelot as the Gods would let me go.

I waited until I thought Merlin was on the far side of the hall and that it was safe for me to leave without him spotting me, but it was just at that moment that his voice whispered in my ear. 'Were you hiding from me, Derfel?' he asked, then he gave an elaborate groan as he settled on the floor beside me. He liked pretending that his great age had made him feeble, and he made a great play of massaging his knees and groaning at the pain in his joints. Then he took the horn of mead out of my hand and took ... 'Behold the virgin Princess,' he said, gesturing with ... empty ... towards Ceinwyn, 'going to her grisly fate. Let's ... scratched between the plaits of his beard as he thought ... t his next words. 'A half month till the betrothal? Marriage a week or so later, then a handful of months till the child kills her. No chance of a baby coming out of those little hips without splitting her in two.' He laughed. 'It will be like a pussy cat giving birth to a bullock. Very nasty, Derfel.' He peered at me, enjoying my discomfort.

'I thought,' I responded sourly, 'that you had made Ceinwyn a charm of happiness?'

'So I did,' he said blandly, 'but what of it? Women like having babies and if Ceinwyn's happiness consists of being ripped into two bloody halves by her firstborn then my charm will have worked, will it not?' He smiled at me.

' "She will never be high," ' I said, quoting Merlin's prophecy that he had uttered in this very hall not a month before, ' "and she will never be low, but she will be happy." '

'What a memory for trivia you do have! Isn't the mutton awful? Under-cooked, you see. And it's not even hot! I can't abide cold food.' Which did not stop him stealing a portion from my dish. 'Do you think that being Queen of Siluria is high?'

'Isn't it?' I asked sourly.

'Oh, dear me, no. What an absurd idea! Siluria's the most

wretched place on earth, Derfel. Nothing but grubby valleys, stony beaches and ugly people.' He shuddered. 'They burn coal instead of wood and most of the folk are black as Sagramor as a result. I don't suppose they know what washing is.' He pulled a piece of gristle from his teeth and tossed it to one of the hounds that scavenged among the feasters. 'Lancelot will soon be bored by Siluria! I can't see our gallant Lancelot enduring those ugly, coal-blackened slugs for very long, so, if she survives childbirth, which I doubt, poor little Ceinwyn will be left all alone with a heap of coal and a squalling baby. That'll be the end of her!' He seemed pleased at the prospect. 'Have you ever noticed, Derfel, how you find a young woman in the height of her beauty, with a face to snatch the very stars out of their heavens, and a year later you discover her stinking of milk and infant shit and you wonder how you could ever have found her beautiful? Babies do that to women, so look on her now, Derfel, look on her now, for she will never again be so lovely.'

She was lovely, and worse, she seemed happy. She was robed in white this night and about her neck was hung a silver star looped on a silver chain. Her golden hair was bound by a fillet of silver, and silver raindrops hung from her ears. And Lancelot, that night, looked as striking as Ceinwyn. He was said to be the handsomest man in Britain, and so he was if you liked his dark, thin, long, almost reptilian face. He was dressed in a black coat striped with white, wore a gold torque at his throat and had a circle of gold binding his long black hair that was oiled smooth against his scalp before cascading down his back. His beard, trimmed to a sharp point, was also oiled.

'She told me,' I said to Merlin, and knowing as I spoke that I revealed too much of my heart to that wicked old man, 'that she isn't certain about marrying Lancelot.'

'Well, she would say that, wouldn't she?' Merlin answered carelessly, beckoning to a slave who was carrying a dish of pork towards the high table. He scooped a handful of ribs into the lap of his grubby white robe and sucked greedily on one of them. 'Ceinwyn,' he went on when he had sucked most of the rib bare, 'is a romantic fool. She somehow convinced herself she could marry where she liked, though the Gods alone know why any girl should think that! Now, of course,' he said with his mouth full of pork, 'everything changes. She's met Lancelot! She'll be dizzy with him by now. Maybe she won't even wait for the marriage? Who knows? Maybe, this very night, in the secrecy of her chamber, she'll tup the bastard dry. But probably not. She's a very conventional girl.' He said the last three words disparagingly. 'Have a rib,' he offered. 'It's time you were married.'

'There is no one I want to marry,' I said sulkily. Except Ceinwyn, of course, but what hope did I have against Lancelot?

'Marriage has nothing to do with wanting,' Merlin said scornfully. 'Arthur thought it was, and what a fool for women Arthur is! What you want, Derfel, is a pretty girl in your bed, but only a fool thinks the girl and the wife have to be the same creature. Arthur thinks you should marry Gwenhwyvach.' He said the name carelessly.

'Gwenhwyvach!' I said too loudly. She was Guinevere's younger sister and was a heavy, dull, pale-skinned girl whom Guinevere could not abide. I had no particular reason to dislike Gwenhwyvach, but nor could I imagine marrying such a drab, soulless and unhappy girl.

'And why ever not?' Merlin asked in pretended outrage. 'A good match, Derfel. What are you, after all, but the son of a Saxon slave? And Gwenhwyvach is a genuine Princess. No money, of course, and uglier than the wild sow of Llyffan, but think how grateful she'll be!' He leered at me. 'And consider Gwenhwyvach's hips, Derfel! No danger there of a baby getting stuck. She'll spit the little horrors out like greased pips!'

I wondered if Arthur had really proposed such a marriage, or whether it was Guinevere's idea? More likely it was Guinevere. I watched her as she sat arrayed in gold beside Cuneglas and the triumph on her face was unmistakable. She looked uncommonly beautiful that night. She was ever the most striking-looking woman in Britain, but on that rainy feast night in Caer Sws she seemed to glow. Maybe that was because of her pregnancy, but the likelier explanation was that she was revelling in her ascendancy over these people who had once dismissed her as a penniless exile. Now, thanks to Arthur's sword, she could dispose of these people just as her husband disposed of their kingdoms. It was Guinevere, I knew, who was Lancelot's chief supporter in Dumnonia, and Guinevere who had made Arthur promise Lancelot Siluria's throne, and Guinevere who had decided that Ceinwyn should be Lancelot's bride. Now, I suspected, she wanted to punish me for my hostility to Lancelot by making her inconvenient sister into my lumpen bride.

'You look unhappy, Derfel,' Merlin provoked me.

I did not rise to the provocation. 'And you, Lord?' I asked. 'Are you happy?'

'Do you care?' he asked airily.

'I love you, Lord, like a father,' I said.

He hooted at that, then half choked on a sliver of pork, but was still laughing when he recovered. 'Like a father! Oh, Derfel, what an absurdly emotional beast you are. The only reason I raised you was because I thought you were special to the Gods, and maybe you are. The Gods do sometimes choose the strangest creatures to love. So tell me, loving would-be son, does your filial love extend to service?'

'What service, Lord?' I asked, though I knew well enough what he wanted. He wanted spearmen to go and seek the Cauldron.

He lowered his voice and leaned closer to me, though I doubt anyone could have heard our conversation in the loud, drunken hall. 'Britain,' he said, 'suffers from two sicknesses, but Arthur and Cuneglas recognize only one.'

'The Saxons.'

He nodded. 'But Britain without the Saxons will still be diseased, Derfel, for we risk losing the Gods. Christianity spreads faster than the Saxons, and Christians are a bigger offence to our Gods than any Saxon. If we don't restrain the Christians then the Gods will desert us utterly, and what is Britain without her Gods? But if we harness the Gods and restore them to Britain,

27

then the Saxons and the Christians will both vanish. We attack the wrong disease, Derfel.'

I glanced at Arthur who was listening intently to something Cuneglas was saying. Arthur was not an irreligious man, but he carried his beliefs lightly and bore no hatred in his soul for men and women who believed in other Gods, yet Arthur, I knew, would hate to hear Merlin talk of fighting against the Christians. 'And no one listens to you, Lord?' I asked Merlin.

'Some,' he said grudgingly, 'a few, one or two. Arthur doesn't. He thinks I'm an old fool on the edge of senility. But what about you, Derfel? Do you think I'm an old fool?'

'No, Lord.'

'And do you believe in magic, Derfel?'

'Yes, Lord,' I said. I had seen magic work, but I had seen it fail too. Magic was difficult, but I believed in it.

Merlin leaned even closer to my ear. 'Then be at Dolforwyn's summit this night, Derfel,' he whispered, 'and I will grant you your soul's desire.'

A harpist struck the chord that would summon the bards for the singing. The warriors' voices died away as a chill wind gusted rain through the open door and flickered the small flames of the tallow candles and the grease-soaked rush lights. 'Your soul's desire,' Merlin whispered again, but when I looked to my left he had somehow vanished.

And in the night the thunder growled. The Gods were abroad and I was summoned to Dolforwyn.

I left the feast before the giving of gifts, before the bards sang and before the drunken warriors' voices swelled in the haunting Song of Nwyfre. I heard the song far behind me as I walked alone down the river valley where Ceinwyn had told me of her visit to the bed of skulls and of the strange prophecy that made no sense.

I wore my armour, but carried no shield. My sword, Hywelbane, was at my side and my green cloak was about my shoulders. No man walked the night lightly, for night belonged

28

to ghouls and spirits, but I had been summoned by Merlin so I knew I would be safe.

My path was made easy for there was a road that led east from the ramparts towards the southern edge of the range of hills where Dolforwyn lay. It was a long walk, four hours in the wet dark, and the road was black as pitch, but the Gods must have wanted me to arrive for I neither lost the road, nor met any dangers in the night.

Merlin, I knew, could not be far ahead of me, and though I was two lifetimes younger than he, I neither caught up with him nor even heard him. I just heard the fading song and afterwards, when the singing had faded into the dark, I listened to the rill of the river running over the stones and the patter of rain falling in the leaves and the scream of a hare caught by a weasel and the shriek of a badger calling for her mate. I passed two crouching settlements where the dying glow of fires showed through the low openings beneath the bracken thatch. From one of those huts a man's voice called out in challenge, but I called to him that I was travelling in peace and he quieted his barking dog.

I left the road to find the narrow track that twisted up Dolforwyn's flank and I feared the darkness would make me lose my way under the oaks that grew thick on the hill's side, but the rain clouds thinned to let a wan moonlight drift through the wet heavy leaves and show me the stony path that climbed sunwise up the royal hill. No man lived here. It was a place of oaks, stone and mystery.

The path led from the trees into the wide open space of the summit where the lone feasting hall stood and where the circle of standing stones marked where Cuneglas had been acclaimed. This summit was Powys's most sacred place, yet for most of the year it stood deserted, used only at high feasts and at times of great solemnity. Now, in the wan moonlight, the hall stood dark and the hilltop seemed empty.

I paused at the edge of the oaks. A white owl flew above me, its stubby body rushing on short wings close to my helmet's wolf-tailed crest. The owl was an omen, but I could not tell whether the omen was good or evil and I was suddenly afraid. Curiosity had drawn me here, but now I sensed the danger. Merlin would not offer me my soul's desire for nothing, and that meant I was here to make a choice, and it was a choice I suspected I would not want to make. Indeed, I feared it so much that I almost turned back into the dark of the trees, but then a pulse on the scar of my left hand held me in place.

The scar had been put there by Nimue and whenever the scar throbbed I knew that my fate was gone from my choosing. I was oath-sworn to Nimue. I could not go back.

The rain had stopped and the clouds were tattered. There was a cold wind beating the treetops, but no rain. It was still dark. Dawn could not be far off, but as yet no hint of light rose across the eastern hills. There was only the glimmering wash of moonlight that turned the stones of Dolforwyn's royal circle into silvered shapes in the dark.

I walked towards the stone circle and the sound of my heart seemed louder than the footfall of my heavy boots. Still no one appeared and for a moment I wondered if this was some elaborate jest on Merlin's part, but then, in the centre of the stone ring, where the single stone of Powys's kingship lay, I saw a gleam that was brighter than any reflection of misted moonlight from rain-glossed rock.

I moved closer, my heart thumping, then stepped between the circle's stones and saw that the moonlight was reflecting from a cup. A silver cup. A small silver cup which, when I came close to the royal stone, I saw was filled with a dark, moon-glossed liquid.

'Drink, Derfel,' Nimue's voice said in a whisper that barely carried above the sound of the wind in the oaks. 'Drink.'

I turned, looking for her, but could see no one. The wind lifted my cloak and flapped some loose thatch on the hall's roof. 'Drink, Derfel,' Nimue's voice said again, 'drink.'

I looked up into the sky and prayed to Lleullaw that he would preserve me. My left hand, that was now throbbing in pain, was clasped tight about Hywelbane's hilt. I wanted to do the safe thing, and that, I knew, was to walk away and go back to the warmth of Arthur's friendship, but the misery in my soul had brought me to this cold bare hill and the thought of Lancelot's hand resting on Ceinwyn's slender wrist made me look down to the cup.

I lifted it, hesitated, then drained it.

The liquid tasted bitter so that I shuddered when it was all gone. The rank taste stayed in my mouth and throat as I carefully laid the cup back on the king's stone.

'Nimue?' I called almost beseechingly, but there was no answer except for the wind in the trees.

'Nimue!' I called again, for my head was reeling now. The clouds were churning black and grey, and the moon was splintering into spikes of silvered light that slashed up from the distant river and shattered in the thrashing dark of the twisting trees. 'Nimue!' I called as my knees gave way and as my head spun in lurid dreams. I knelt by the royal stone that suddenly loomed as large as a mountain before me, then I fell forward so heavily that my sprawling arm sent the empty cup flying. I felt sick, but no vomit would come, there were just dreams, terrible dreams, shrieking ghouls of nightmare that screamed inside my head. I was crying, I was sweating and my muscles were twitching in uncontrollable spasms.

Then hands seized my head. My helmet was dragged from my hair, then a forehead was pressed against mine. It was a cool white forehead and the nightmares skittered away to be replaced by a vision of a long, naked white body with slender thighs and small breasts. 'Dream, Derfel,' Nimue soothed me, her hands stroking my hair, 'dream, my love, dream.'

I was crying helplessly. I was a warrior, a Lord of Dumnonia, beloved of Arthur and so in his debt after the last battle that he would grant me land and wealth beyond my dreams, yet now I wept like an orphaned child. My soul's desire was Ceinwyn, but Ceinwyn was being dazzled by Lancelot and I thought I could never know happiness again.

'Dream, my love,' Nimue crooned, and she must have swept a black cloak over both our heads for suddenly the grey night vanished and I was in a silent darkness with her arms about my neck and her face pressed close to mine. We knelt, cheek beside each other's cheek, with my hands shuddering spasmodically and helplessly on the cool skin of her bare thighs. I let my body's twitching weight lean on her slender shoulders and there, in her arms, the tears ended, the spasms faded and suddenly I was calm. No vomit edged my throat, the ache in my legs was gone and I felt warm. So warm that the sweat still poured off me. I did not move, I did not want to move, but just let the dream come.

At first it was a wondrous dream for it seemed I had been given the wings of a great eagle and I was flying high above a land I did not know. Then I saw it was a terrible land, broken by great chasms and by tall mountains of jagged rock down which small streams cascaded white towards dark peaty lakes. The mountains seemed to have no end, nor any refuge, for as I coasted above them on the wings of my dream, I saw no houses, no huts, no fields, no flocks, no herds, no souls, but only a wolf running between the crags and the bones of a deer lying in a thicket. The sky above me was as grey as a sword, the mountains below were dark as dried blood and the air beneath my wings as cold as a knife in the ribs.

'Dream, my love,' Nimue murmured, and in the dream I swept low on my wide wings to see a road twisting between the dark hills. It was a road of beaten earth, broken by rocks, that picked its cruel way from valley to valley, sometimes climbing to bleak passes before it dropped again to the bare stones of another valley floor. The road edged black lakes, cut through shadowed chasms, skirted snow-streaked hills, but always led towards the north. How it was the north I did not know, but this was a dream in which knowledge needs no reason.

The dream wings dropped me down to the road's surface and suddenly I was flying no longer, but climbing the road towards a pass in the hills. The slopes on either side of the pass were steep

32

black slabs of slate running with water, but something told me the road's end lay just beyond the black pass and that if I could just keep walking on my tired legs I would cross the crest and find my soul's desire at the farther side.

I was panting now, my breath coming in agonized gasps as I dreamed my way up the last few paces of the road and there, suddenly, at the summit, I saw light and colour and warmth.

For the road dropped beyond the pass to a coastline where there were trees and fields, and beyond the coast was a glittering sea in which an island lay, and in the island, shining in the sudden sun, was a lake. 'There!' I spoke aloud for I knew the island was my goal, but just when it seemed I was given a renewed energy to run down the road's last miles and plunge into that sunlit sea, a ghoul sprang into my path. It was a black thing in black armour with a mouth spitting black slime and a black-bladed sword twice as long as Hywelbane in its black-clawed hand. It screamed a challenge at me.

And I screamed too, and my body stiffened in Nimue's embrace.

Her arms gripped my shoulders. 'You have seen the Dark Road, Derfel,' she whispered, 'you have seen the Dark Road.' And suddenly she pulled away from me and the cloak was whipped from my back and I fell forward onto Dolforwyn's wet grass as the wind swirled cold about me.

I lay there for long minutes. The dream had passed and I wondered what the Dark Road had to do with my soul's desire. Then I jerked aside and vomited, and after that my head felt clear again and I could see the fallen silver cup beside me. I picked it up, rocked back onto my haunches and saw that Merlin was watching me from the far side of the royal stone. Nimue, his lover and priestess, was beside him, her thin body swathed in a vast black cloak, her black hair held in a ribbon and her golden eye shining in the moonlight. The eye in that socket had been prised out by Gundleus, and for that injury he had paid a thousandfold.

Neither spoke, but just watched as I spat the last vomit from my mouth, cuffed at my lips, shook my head, then tried to stand. My body was still weak, or else my skull was still reeling, for I could not raise myself and so, instead, I knelt beside the stone and leaned on my elbows. Small spasms still made me twitch from time to time. 'What did you make me drink?' I asked, putting the silver cup back on the rock.

'I made you drink nothing,' Merlin answered. 'You drank of your own free will, Derfel, just as you came here of your own free will.' His voice, that had been so mischievous in Cuneglas's hall, was now cold and distant. 'What did you see?'

'The Dark Road,' I answered obediently.

'It lies there,' Merlin said, and pointed north into the night.

'And the ghoul?' I asked.

'Is Diwrnach,' he said.

I closed my eyes for I knew now what he wanted. 'And the island,' I said, opening my eyes again, 'is Ynys Mon?'

'Yes,' Merlin said. 'The blessed isle.'

Before the Romans came and before the Saxons were even dreamed of, Britain was ruled by the Gods and the Gods spoke to us from Ynys Mon, but the island had been ravaged by the Romans who had cut down its oaks, destroyed its sacred groves and slaughtered its guardian Druids. That Black Year had occurred more than four hundred years before this night, yet Ynys Mon was still sacred to the few Druids who, like Merlin, tried to restore the Gods to Britain. But now the blessed island was a part of the kingdom of Lleyn, and Lleyn was ruled by Diwrnach, the most terrible of all the Irish Kings who had crossed the Irish Sea to take British land. Diwrnach was said to paint his shields with human blood. There was no King in all Britain more cruel or more feared, and it was only the mountains that hemmed him in and the smallness of his army that kept him from spreading his terror south through Gwynedd. Diwrnach was a beast that could not be killed; a creature that lurked at the dark edge of Britain and, by common consent, he was best left unprovoked. 'You want me,' I said to Merlin, 'to go to Ynys Mon?'

'I want you to come with us to Ynys Mon,' he said, indicating Nimue, 'with us and a virgin.'

'A virgin?' I asked.

'Because only a virgin, Derfel, can find the Cauldron of Clyddno Eiddyn. And none of us, I think, qualifies,' he added the last words sarcastically.

'And the Cauldron,' I said slowly, 'is on Ynys Mon.' Merlin nodded and I shuddered to think of such an errand. The Cauldron of Clyddno Eiddyn was one of the thirteen magical Treasures of Britain that had been dispersed when the Romans had laid waste Ynys Mon, and Merlin's final ambition of his long life was to reassemble the Treasures, but the Cauldron was his real prize. With the Cauldron, he claimed, he could control the Gods and destroy the Christians, and that was why, with a bitter tasting mouth and a belly rank with sourness, I was kneeling on a wet hilltop in Powys. 'My job,' I said to Merlin, 'is to fight the Saxons.'

'Fool!' Merlin snapped. 'The war against the Sais is lost unless we regain the Treasures.'

'Arthur doesn't agree.'

'Then Arthur is a fool as great as you. What do the Saxons matter, fool, if our Gods have deserted us?'

'I am sworn to Arthur's service,' I protested.

'You are sworn to my bidding too,' Nimue said, holding up her left hand to show the scar that matched mine.

'But I want no man on the Dark Road,' Merlin said, 'who does not come willingly. You must choose your loyalty, Derfel, but I can help you choose.'

He swept the cup off the rock and put in its place a heap of the rib bones that he had taken from Cuneglas's hall. He knelt, picked up one bone and placed it in the centre of the royal stone. 'That is Arthur,' he said, 'and this,' he took another bone, 'is Cuneglas, and this,' he laid a third bone so that it made a triangle with the first two, 'we shall speak of later. This,' he laid a fourth bone across one of the triangle's corners, 'is Tewdric of Gwent, and this is Arthur's alliance with Tewdric, and this is his alliance with Cuneglas.' The second triangle was thus formed on top of the first and the two now resembled a crude, six pointed star. 'This is Elmet,' he began the third layer that was parallel with the first, 'and this is Siluria, and this bone,' he held up the last, 'is the alliance of all those kingdoms. There.' He leaned back and gestured at the precarious tower of bones standing at the stone's centre. 'You see, Derfel, Arthur's careful scheme, though I tell you, I promise you, that without the Treasures the scheme will fail.'

He fell silent. I stared at the nine bones. All of them, except for the mysterious third bone, were still hung with scraps of meat, tendon and gristle. It was just that third bone that had been scraped clean and white. I touched it very gently with my finger, taking care not to disturb the fragile balance of the squat tower. 'And what is the third bone?' I asked.

Merlin smiled. 'The third bone, Derfel,' he said, 'is the marriage between Lancelot and Ceinwyn.' He paused. 'Take it.'

I did not move. To take the third bone would be to collapse Arthur's fragile network of alliances that were his best, indeed his only hope of defeating the Saxons.

Merlin sneered at my reluctance, then he took hold of the third bone, but he did not pull it free. 'The Gods hate order,' he snarled at me. 'Order, Derfel, is what destroys the Gods, so they must destroy order.' He pulled the bone out and the pile immediately collapsed into chaos. 'Arthur must restore the Gods, Derfel,' Merlin said, 'if he is to bring peace to all Britain.' He held the bone out to me. 'Take it.'

I did not move.

'It is just a pile of bones,' Merlin said, 'but this bone, Derfel, is your soul's desire.' He held the clean bone towards me. 'This bone is Lancelot's marriage to Ceinwyn. Snap this bone in two, Derfel, and the marriage will never happen. But leave this bone whole, Derfel, and your enemy will take your woman to his bed and maul her like a dog.' He thrust the bone towards me again, and again I did not take it. 'You think your love for Ceinwyn isn't written all over your face?' Merlin asked derisively. 'Take it! Because I, Merlin of Avalon, grant you, Derfel, power of this bone.'

I took it, the Gods help me, but I took it. What else could I do? I was in love and I took that cleansed bone and I placed it in my pouch.

'It won't help you,' Merlin mocked me, 'unless you break it.'

'It may not help me anyway,' I said, at last discovering that I could stand.

'You are a fool, Derfel,' Merlin said, 'But you are a fool who is good with a sword and that is why I need you if we're to walk the Dark Road.' He stood. 'It's your choice now. You can break the bone and Ceinwyn will come to you, that I promise, but you will then be sworn to the Cauldron's quest. Or you can marry Gwenhwyvach and waste your life battering Saxon shields while the Christians connive to take Dumnonia. I leave the choice to you, Derfel. Now close your eyes.'

I closed my eyes and dutifully kept them closed for a long time, but at last, when no more instructions were given, I opened them.

The hilltop was empty. I had heard nothing, but Merlin, Nimue, the eight bones and the silver cup were all gone. Dawn showed in the east, the birds were loud in the trees and I had a clean-picked bone in my pouch.

I walked downhill to the road beside the river, but in my head I saw the other road, the Dark Road that led to Diwrnach's lair, and I was frightened.

WE HUNTED BOAR THAT morning and Arthur deliberately sought my company as we walked out of Caer Sws. 'You left early last night, Derfel,' he greeted me.

'My belly, Lord,' I said. I did not want to tell him the truth, that I had been with Merlin, for then he would have suspected that I had not yet abandoned the Cauldron's quest. It was better to lie. 'I had a sour belly,' I explained.

He laughed. 'I never know why we call them feasts,' he said, 'for they're nothing but an excuse to drink.' He paused to wait for Guinevere, who liked to hunt and who was dressed this morning in boots and leather trews that were strapped tight to her long legs. She hid her pregnancy beneath a leather jerkin over which she wore a green cloak. She had brought a brace of her beloved deerhounds and she handed me their leashes so that Arthur could carry her through the ford that lay beside the old fortress. Lancelot offered the same courtesy to Ceinwyn who cried out in evident delight as Lancelot swept her into his arms. Ceinwyn was also dressed in men's clothes, but hers were not cut close and subtle like Guinevere's. Ceinwyn had probably borrowed whatever hunting clothes her brother did not want and the baggy, over-long garments made her look boyish and young beside Guinevere's sophisticated elegance. Neither woman carried a spear, but Bors, Lancelot's cousin and his champion, carried a spare weapon in case Ceinwyn wanted to join a kill. Arthur had insisted that the pregnant Guinevere should not carry a spear. 'You must take care today,' he said as he restored her to her feet on the Severn's southern bank.

'You worry too much,' she said, then took the hounds' leashes from me and pushed a hand through her thick, springing red hair as she turned back to Ceinwyn. 'Become pregnant,' she said, 'and men think you're made of glass.' She fell into step beside Lancelot, Ceinwyn and Cuneglas, leaving Arthur to walk beside me towards the leafy valley where Cuneglas's huntsmen had reported plenty of game. There might have been fifty of us hunters altogether, mostly warriors, though a handful of women had chosen to come and two score of servants brought up the rear. One of those servants sounded a horn to tell the huntsmen at the valley's far end that it was time to drive the game down towards the river and we hunters hefted our long, heavy boar spears as we spread out into a line. It was a cold late summer's day, cold enough to cloud our breath, but the rain had cleared and the sun shone on fallow fields laced with a morning mist. Arthur was in high spirits, revelling in the day's beauty, his own youth and the prospect of a hunt. 'One more feast,' he said to me, 'then you can go home and rest.'

'One more feast?' I asked dully, my mind fuddled with tiredness and from the lingering effects of whatever Merlin and Nimue had given me to drink on Dolforwyn's peak.

Arthur clapped my shoulder. 'Lancelot's betrothal, Derfel. Then back to Dumnonia. And to work!' He sounded delighted at the prospect and he enthusiastically told me his plans for the coming winter. There were four broken Roman bridges that he wanted rebuilt, then the kingdom's stonemasons would be sent to finish the royal palace at Lindinis. Lindinis was the Roman town close to Caer Cadarn, the place of Dumnonia's royal acclamations, and Arthur wanted to make it the new capital. 'There are too many Christians in Durnovaria,' he said, though he hastily, and typically, added that he had nothing personal against Christians.

'It's just, Lord,' I said drily, 'that they have something against you.'

'Some do,' he admitted. Before the battle, when Arthur's cause had seemed utterly lost, a party opposed to Arthur had grown bold in Dumnonia and that party had been led by the

39

Christians, the same Christians who had the guardianship of Mordred. The immediate cause of their hostility had been a loan that Arthur had forced from the church to pay for the campaign that ended in Lugg Vale, and that loan had sparked a bitter enmity. It was odd, I thought, how the church preached the merits of poverty, but never forgave a man for borrowing its money.

'I wanted to talk to you of Mordred,' Arthur said, explaining why he had sought my company on this fine morning. 'In ten years,' Arthur went on, 'he'll be old enough to take the throne. That's not long, Derfel, not long at all, and he needs to be raised well in those ten years. He must be taught letters, he must learn to use a sword and he must learn responsibility.' I nodded agreement, though not with any enthusiasm. The five-year-old Mordred would doubtless learn all the things Arthur wanted, but I did not see what business it was of mine. Arthur had other ideas. 'I want you to be his guardian,' he said, surprising me.

'Me!' I exclaimed.

'Nabur cares more about his own advancement than he does about Mordred's character,' Arthur said. Nabur was the Christian magistrate who was the child King's present guardian, and it was Nabur who had plotted most vigorously to destroy Arthur's power; Nabur and, of course, Bishop Sansum. 'And Nabur is no soldier,' Arthur went on. 'I pray that Mordred will rule in peace, Derfel, but he needs the skills of war, all kings do, and I can think of no one better than you to train him.'

'Not me,' I protested. 'I'm too young!'

Arthur laughed at that objection. 'The young should be raised by the young, Derfel,' he said.

A distant horn sounded to signal that game had been started from the valley's end. We hunters entered the trees and stepped over the tangles of briar and the dead trunks that were thick with fungi. We advanced slowly now, listening for the terrifying sound of a boar crashing through the brush. 'Besides,' I went on, 'my place is in your shield-wall, not in Mordred's nursery.'

'You'll still be in my shield-wall. You think I would lose you, Derfel?' Arthur said with a grin. 'I don't want you tied to Mordred, I just want him in your household. I need him to be raised by an honest man.'

I shrugged that compliment away, then thought guiltily of the clean, unbroken bone in my pouch. Was it honest, I wondered, to use magic to change Ceinwyn's mind? I looked at her, and she glanced my way and gave me a shy smile. 'I have no household,' I said to Arthur.

'But you will, and soon,' he said. Then he held up a hand and I froze, listening to the sounds ahead of us. Something heavy was trampling in the trees and we both instinctively crouched with our spears held a few inches above the ground, but then we saw that the frightened beast was a fine stag with good antlers and we relaxed as the animal pounded past. 'We'll hunt him tomorrow, maybe,' Arthur said, watching the stag run past. 'Give your hounds a run in the morning!' he shouted to Guinevere.

She laughed and came down the hill towards us, her hounds straining at their leashes. 'I should like that,' she said. Her eyes were bright and her face flushed by the cold. 'The hunting's better here than in Dumnonia,' she said.

'But not the land,' Arthur said to me. 'There's an estate north of Durnovaria,' he went on, 'that is Mordred's by right and I plan to make you its tenant. I'll grant you other land, too, for your own, but you can make a hall on Mordred's land and raise him there.'

'You know the estate,' Guinevere said. 'It's the one north of Gyllad's holding.'

'I know it,' I said. The estate had good river land for crops and fine uplands for sheep. 'But I'm not sure I know how to raise a child,' I grumbled. The horns sounded loud ahead and the huntsmen's hounds were baying. Cheers sounded far to our right, signifying that someone had found quarry, though our part of the wood was still empty. A small stream tumbled to our left and the wooded ground climbed to our right. The rocks and twisted tree roots were thick with moss.

Arthur dismissed my fears. 'You won't raise Mordred,' he said, 'but I do want him raised in your hall, with your servants, your manners, your morals and your judgments.'

'And,' Guinevere added, 'your wife.'

A snapping of a twig made me look uphill. Lancelot and his cousin Bors were there, both standing in front of Ceinwyn. Lancelot's spear shaft was painted white and he wore tall leather boots and a cloak of supple leather. I looked back to Arthur. 'The wife, Lord,' I said, 'is news to me.'

He clasped my elbow, the boar hunt forgotten. 'I plan to appoint you Dumnonia's champion, Derfel,' he said.

'The honour is above me, Lord,' I said cautiously, 'besides, you are Mordred's champion.'

'Prince Arthur,' Guinevere said, for she liked to call him Prince even though he was bastard born, 'is already chief of the Council. He can't be champion as well, not unless he's expected to do all Dumnonia's work?'

'True, Lady,' I said. I was not averse to the honour, for it was a high one, though there was a price. In battle I would have to fight whatever champion presented himself for single combat, but in peace it would mean wealth and status far above my present rank. I already had the title of Lord and the men to uphold that rank and the right to paint my own device on these men's shields, but I shared these honours with two score other Dumnonian war leaders. To be the King's champion would make me the foremost warrior of Dumnonia, though how any man could claim that status while Arthur lived, I could not see. Nor, indeed, while Sagramor lived. 'Sagramor,' I said carefully, 'is a greater warrior than I, Lord Prince.' With Guinevere present I had to remember to call him Prince once in a while, though it was a title he disliked.

Arthur waved my objection aside. 'I am making Sagramor Lord of the Stones,' he said, 'and he wants nothing more.' The lordship of the Stones made Sagramor into the man who guarded the Saxon frontier and I could well believe that the black-skinned, dark-eyed Sagramor would be well content with such a belligerent appointment. 'You, Derfel,' he prodded my chest, 'will be the champion.'

'And who,' I asked drily, 'will be the champion's wife?'

'My sister Gwenhwyvach,' Guinevere said, watching me closely.

I was grateful that I had been forewarned by Merlin. 'You do me too much honour, Lady,' I said blandly.

Guinevere smiled, satisfied that my words implied acceptance. 'Did you ever think, Derfel, that you would marry a Princess?'

'No, Lady,' I said. Gwenhwyvach, like Guinevere, was indeed a Princess, a Princess of Henis Wyren, though Henis Wyren was no more. That sad kingdom was now called Lleyn and was ruled by the dark Irish invader, King Diwrnach.

Guinevere yanked the leashes to subdue her excited hounds. 'You can be betrothed when we return to Dumnonia,' she said. 'Gwenhwyvach has agreed.'

'There is one obstacle, Lord,' I said to Arthur.

Guinevere yanked on the leashes again, quite unnecessarily, but she hated all opposition and so she took out her frustration on the hounds instead of on me. She did not dislike me at that time, but nor did she particularly like me either. She knew of my aversion for Lancelot, and that doubtless prejudiced her against me, but she would not have thought my dislike significant, for she doubtless dismissed me as merely one of her husband's war leaders; a tall, dull, flaxen-haired man who lacked the civilized graces that Guinevere so valued. 'An obstacle?' Guinevere asked me dangerously.

'Lord Prince,' I said, insisting on talking to Arthur and not to his wife, 'I am oath-sworn to a lady.' I thought of the bone in my pouch. 'I have no claim on her, nor can I expect anything from her, but if she does claim me then I am obligated to her.'

'Who?' Guinevere demanded immediately.

'I can't say, Lady.'

'Who?' Guinevere insisted again.

'He doesn't need to say,' Arthur defended me. He smiled. 'How long can this lady claim your loyalty?'

'Not long, Lord,' I said, 'only days now.' For once Ceinwyn was betrothed to Lancelot then I could consider my oath to her voided.

'Good,' he said vigorously, and smiled at Guinevere as though inviting her to share his pleasure, but Guinevere was scowling instead. She detested Gwenhwyvach, finding her graceless and boring, and she desperately wanted to marry her sister out of her life. 'If all goes well,' Arthur said, 'you can be married in Glevum at the same time that Lancelot marries Ceinwyn.'

'Or are you demanding these few days,' Guinevere asked acidly, 'to conjure up reasons why you should not marry my sister?'

'Lady,' I said earnestly, 'it would be an honour to marry Gwenhwyvach.' That, I think, was the truth, for Gwenhwyvach would doubtless prove an honest wife, though whether I would prove a good husband was another matter, for my only reason for marrying Gwenhwyvach would be the high rank and great wealth she would bring as her dowry; but those, for most men, were the purpose of marriage. And if I could not have Ceinwyn, what did it matter who I married? Merlin ever warned us against confusing love and marriage, and though the advice was cynical, there was truth there. I was not expected to love Gwenhwyvach, just to marry her, and her rank and dowry were my rewards for fighting that long bloody day in Lugg Vale. If those rewards were tinged with Guinevere's mockery, they were still a rich gift. 'I will marry your sister gladly,' I promised Guinevere, 'so long as the keeper of my oath does not call on me.'

'I pray she does not,' Arthur said with a smile, then whipped round as a shout sounded uphill.

Bors was crouched with his spear. Lancelot was beside him, but was glancing down the slope towards us, perhaps worried that the animal would escape through the gap between us. Arthur gently pushed Guinevere back, then gestured for me to climb the hill and plug the gap.

'Two of them!' Lancelot called to us.

'One will be a sow,' Arthur called, then ran a few paces upstream before starting to climb uphill. 'Where?' he asked. Lancelot pointed with his white-shafted spear, but I could still see nothing in the bushes.

'There!' Lancelot said petulantly, prodding his spear towards a tangle of briars.

Arthur and I climbed another few feet and then at last we could see the boar deep inside the undergrowth. He was a big old beast with yellow tusks, small eyes and humps of muscle under his dark scarred hide. That muscle could move him at lightning speed and make him hook his sword sharp tusks with a fatal skill. We had all seen men die from tusk wounds, and nothing made a boar more dangerous than to be cornered with a sow. All hunters prayed for a boar charging in open ground so that they could use the beast's own speed and bulk to drive the spear into his body. Such a confrontation demanded nerve and skill, but not nearly so much nerve as when a man had to charge the boar.

'Who saw him first?' Arthur asked.

'My Lord King did.' Bors indicated Lancelot.

'Then he's yours, Lord King.' Arthur graciously waived the honour of the kill to Lancelot.

'He is my gift to you, Lord,' Lancelot answered. Ceinwyn was standing behind him, biting her lower lip and with eyes wide. She had taken the spare spear from Bors, not because she hoped to use it, but to spare him the burden, and she held the weapon nervously.

'Put the hounds on him!' Guinevere joined us. Her eyes were bright and her face animated. She was, I think, often bored in Dumnonia's great palaces and the hunting field gave her an excitement she craved.

'You'll lose both dogs,' Arthur warned her. 'This pig knows how to fight.' He moved cautiously forward, judging how best to provoke the beast, then he stepped sharply ahead and beat hard down on the bushes with his spear as though to offer the boar a path out of its sanctuary. The beast grunted, but did not move, not even when the spear blade flashed down within inches of its snout. The sow was behind the boar, watching us.

'It's done this before,' Arthur said happily.

'Let me take him, Lord,' I said, suddenly anxious for him.

'You think I've lost my skill?' Arthur asked with a smile. He beat the bushes again, but the briars would not lie flat, nor would the boar move. 'The Gods bless you,' Arthur said to the beast, then he shouted a challenge and jumped into the tangle of thorns. He leapt to one side of the path he had crudely beaten and as he landed he rammed the spear hard forward, aiming its glittering blade at the boar's left flank just forward of its shoulder.

The boar's head seemed to twitch, only a slight twitch, but it was enough to deflect the spear blade off the tusk so that it slashed a bloody and harmless cut down the animal's flank, and then it charged. A good boar can come from a still stance into instant madness with its head down and tusks ready to gut upwards, and this beast was already past Arthur's spearhead when it charged and Arthur was trapped by the brambles.

I shouted to distract the boar and plunged my own spear into its belly. Arthur was on his back, his spear abandoned, and the boar was on top of him. The hounds howled and Guinevere was shouting at us to help. My spear was deep in the beast's belly and its blood spurted up to my hands as I levered up and over to roll the wounded beast off my Lord. The creature weighed more than two full sacks of grain, and its muscles were like iron ropes that twitched my spear. I gripped hard and pushed up, but then the sow charged and swept my feet away from under me. I fell, and my weight pulled the spear shaft down and thus brought the boar back onto Arthur's belly.

Arthur had somehow gripped both the beast's tusks and, using all his strength, was now forcing its head away from his chest. The sow vanished, plunging downhill towards the stream. 'Kill him!' Arthur shouted, though he was half laughing as well. He was just inches from death, but he was loving the moment. 'Kill him!' he called again. The boar's back legs were thrusting, its spittle was spattering Arthur's face and its blood was soaking his clothes.

I was on my back, my face lacerated with thorns. I scrambled to my feet and reached for my jerking, twisting spear that was still buried in the great brute's belly, but then Bors plunged a knife into the boar's neck and I saw the enormous strength of the animal begin to ebb as Arthur managed to force the squat, stinking, bloody head away from his ribs. I seized my spear and twisted the blade, searching for the animal's life blood deep in its guts as Bors stabbed a second time. The boar suddenly pissed on Arthur, gave one last desperate lunge of its huge neck and then abruptly slumped down. Arthur was awash in its blood and urine, and half buried under its bulk.

He cautiously let go of the tusks, then dissolved into helpless laughter. Bors and I took a tusk each and, with a concerted heave, hauled the corpse away from Arthur. One of the tusks had caught in Arthur's jerkin and it ripped the cloth as we tugged it away. We dropped the beast into the brambles, then helped Arthur to his feet. The three of us stood grinning, our clothes muddied and torn and covered with leaves, twigs and the blood of the boar. 'I'll have a bruise there,' Arthur said, tapping his chest. He turned to Lancelot, who had not moved to help during the struggle. There was the briefest pause, then Arthur bowed his head. 'You gave me a noble gift, Lord King,' he said, 'and I took it most ignobly.' He wiped his eyes. 'But I enjoyed it all the same. And we shall all enjoy it at your betrothal feast.' He looked at Guinevere and saw that she was pale, almost trembling, and immediately he crossed to her. 'Are you ill?'

'No, no,' she said, and she put her arms about him and leaned her head against his bloodied chest. She was crying. It was the first time I had ever seen her cry.

Arthur patted her back. 'There was no danger, my love,' he said, 'no danger. I just made a hash of the killing.'

'Are you hurt?' Guinevere asked, pulling away from him and cuffing away her tears.

'Only scratched.' His face and hands were lacerated by

thorns, but he was otherwise unwounded except for the bruise caused by the tusk. He stepped away from her, picked up his spear and gave a whoop. 'I haven't been put on my back like that in a dozen years!'

King Cuneglas came running, worried about his guests, and the huntsmen arrived to truss and carry the corpse away. They must all have noted the comparison between Lancelot's unstained clothes and our dishevelled and bloody state, but no one remarked on it. We were all excited, pleased to have survived and eager to share the story of Arthur holding the brute away from his body by its tusks. The story spread and the sound of men's laughter rang loud among the trees. Lancelot alone did not laugh. 'We must find you a boar now, Lord King,' I said to him. We were standing a few paces from the excited crowd that had gathered to watch as the huntsmen gralloched the beast to give Guinevere's hounds a meal of its guts.

Lancelot gave me a sidelong, considering glance. He disliked me every scrap as much as I disliked him, but suddenly he smiled. 'A boar,' he said, 'would be better than a sow, I think.'

'A sow?' I asked, smelling an insult.

'Didn't the sow charge you?' he asked, then opened his eyes guilelessly wide. 'Surely you don't think I was referring to your marriage!' He offered me an ironic bow. 'I must congratulate you, Lord Derfel! To marry Gwenhwyvach!'

I forced my anger down, and made myself look into his narrow mocking face with its delicate beard, dark eyes, and long hair oiled as black and shining as a raven's wing. 'And I must congratulate you, Lord King, on your betrothal.'

'To *Seren*,' he said, 'the star of Powys.' He gazed at Ceinwyn who stood with her hands clasped to her face as the huntsmen's knives ripped out the long coils of the boar's intestines. She looked so young with her bright hair drawn up at the nape of her neck. 'Doesn't she look charming?' Lancelot asked me in a voice like the purr of a cat. 'So vulnerable. I never believed the stories of her beauty, for who would expect to find such a jewel among

48

Gorfyddyd's whelps? But she is beautiful, and I am so very fortunate.'

'Yes, Lord King, you are.'

He laughed and turned away. He was a man in his glory, a King come to take his bride, and he was also my enemy. But I had his bone in my pouch. I touched it, wondering if the struggle with the boar had broken the rib, but it was still whole, still hidden and just waiting for my pleasure.

Cavan, my second-in-command, came to Caer Sws on the eve of Ceinwyn's betrothal and brought with him forty of my spearmen. Galahad had sent them back, reckoning that his work in Siluria could be completed by the twenty remaining men. The Silurians, it seems, had glumly accepted their country's defeat and there had been no unrest at the news of their King's death, merely a docile submission to the exactions of the victors. Cavan told me that Oengus of Demetia, the Irish King who had brought Arthur victory at Lugg Vale, had taken his allotted portion of slaves and treasure, stolen as much again, and had then gone home, and the Silurians were evidently happy enough that the renowned Lancelot was now to be their King. 'And I reckon the bastard's welcome to the place,' Cavan said when he found me in Cuneglas's hall where I spread my blanket and took my meals. He scratched at a louse in his beard. 'Scrubby place, Siluria.'

'They breed good warriors,' I said.

'Fighting to get away from home, I wouldn't wonder.' He sniffed. 'What clawed your face, Lord?'

'Thorns. Fighting a boar.'

'I thought you might have got married when I wasn't watching you,' he said, 'and that was her wedding gift.'

'I am to be married,' I told him as we walked out of the hall into Caer Sws's sunlight, and I described Arthur's proposal to make me Mordred's champion and his own brother-in-law. Cavan was pleased at the news of my imminent enrichment for he was an Irish exile who had sought to turn his skills with spear

49

and sword into a fortune in Uther's Dumnonia, but somehow the fortune had kept slipping away across the throwboard. He was twice my age, a squat man, broad-shouldered, grey-bearded and with hands thick with the warrior rings we forged from the weapons of defeated enemies. He was delighted that my marriage would mean gold and he was tactful about the bride who would bring that metal. 'She isn't a beauty like her sister,' he said.

'True,' I admitted.

'In fact,' he said, abandoning tact, 'she's as ugly as a sack of toads.'

'She is plain,' I conceded.

'But plain ones make the best wives, Lord,' he declared, never having been married himself, though never lonely either. 'And she'll bring us all wealth,' he added happily, and that, of course, was the reason I would marry poor Gwenhwyvach. My common sense could not put faith in the pork rib in my pouch, and my duty to my men was to reward them for their fidelity, and those rewards had been few in the last year. They had lost virtually all their possessions at the fall of Ynys Trebes and had then struggled against Gorfyddyd's army at Lugg Vale; now they were tired, they were impoverished and no men had ever deserved more of their lord.

I greeted my forty men who were waiting to be assigned quarters. I was glad to see Issa among them, for he was the best of my spearmen: a young farm boy of huge strength and undying optimism who protected my right side in battle. I embraced him, then expressed my regrets that I had no gifts for them. 'But our reward is coming soon,' I added, then glanced at the two dozen girls they must have attracted in Siluria, 'though I'm glad to see most of you have already found some rewards for yourselves.'

They laughed. Issa's girl was a pretty dark-haired child of perhaps fourteen summers. He introduced her to me. 'Scarach, Lord.' He named her proudly.

'Irish?' I asked her.

She nodded. 'I was a slave, Lord, to Ladwys.' Scarach spoke the tongue of Ireland; a language like ours, but different enough, like her name, to mark her race. I guessed she had been captured by Gundleus's men in a raid on King Oengus's lands in Demetia. Most Irish slaves came from such settlements on Britain's west coast though none, I suspected, were ever captured from Lleyn. No one but a fool ventured uninvited into Diwrnach's territory.

'Ladwys!' I said. 'How is she?' Ladwys had been Gundleus's mistress, a dark, tall woman whom Gundleus had secretly married, though he had been ready enough to disown the marriage when Gorfyddyd had offered him the prospect of Ceinwyn's hand.

'She's dead, Lord,' Scarach said happily. 'We killed her in the kitchen. I put a spit in her belly.'

'She's a good girl,' Issa said eagerly.

'Evidently,' I said, 'so look after her.' His last girl had deserted him for one of the Christian missionaries who wandered Dumnonia's roads, but somehow I doubted that the redoubtable Scarach would prove such a fool.

That afternoon, using lime from Cuneglas's stores, my men painted a new device on their shields. The honour of carrying my own device had been granted to me by Arthur on the eve of the battle at Lugg Vale, but we had been given no time to change the shields which, till now, had all carried Arthur's symbol of the bear. My men expected me to choose a wolf's mask as our symbol, to echo the wolf-tails that we had begun to wear on our helmets in the forests of Benoic, but I insisted that we each painted a five-pointed star. 'A star!' Cavan growled in disappointment. He wanted something fierce, with claws and beak and teeth, but I insisted on the star. '*Seren*,' I said, 'for we are the stars of the shield-wall.'

They liked that explanation, and none suspected the hopeless romanticism that lay behind my choice. So we first laid a coat of black pitch on the round, leather-covered willow-board shields, then painted the stars in lime, using a scabbard to get the edges straight, and when the limewash had dried we applied a varnish made of pine resin and egg-white that would protect the stars from rain for a few months. 'It's different,' Cavan grudgingly allowed when we admired the finished shields.

'It's splendid,' I said, and that night, when I dined in the circle of warriors who ate on the floor of the hall, Issa stood behind me as shield-bearer. The varnish was still wet, but that only made the star seem brighter. Scarach served me. It was a poor meal of barley gruel, but Caer Sws's kitchens could provide no better for they were busy preparing the next night's great feast. Indeed the whole compound was busy with those preparations. The hall had been decorated with boughs of dusk-red beech, the floor had been swept and strewn with new rushes, and from the women's quarters we heard tales of dresses being made and delicately embroidered. At least four hundred warriors were now in residence at Caer Sws, most of them quartered in crude shelters thrown up on the fields outside the ramparts, and the warriors' women, children and dogs thronged the fort. Half the men belonged to Cuneglas, the other half were Dumnonians, but despite the recent war there was no trouble, not even when the news spread that Ratae had fallen to Aelle's Saxon horde because of Arthur's treachery. Cuneglas must have suspected that Arthur had purchased Aelle's peace by some such means and he accepted Arthur's oath-promise that the men of Dumnonia would extract vengeance for the dead of Powys who lay in the ashes of the captured fortress.

I had seen neither Merlin nor Nimue since the night on Dolforwyn. Merlin had left Caer Sws, but Nimue, I heard, was still in the fortress and was staying hidden in the women's quarters where, rumour said, she was much in the Princess Ceinwyn's company. That seemed unlikely to me because Nimue and Ceinwyn were so very different. Nimue was a few years older than Ceinwyn and she was dark and intense and forever trembling on the narrow divide between madness and anger, while Ceinwyn was fair and gentle and, as Merlin had told me, so very conventional. I could not imagine that either woman had much to say to the other, and so I assumed that the rumours were false and that Nimue was with Merlin who, I believed, had gone to find the men who would carry their swords into Diwrnach's dreaded land to seek the Cauldron.

But would I go with him? On the morning of Ceinwyn's betrothal I walked northwards into the great oaks that lapped around Caer Sws's wide valley. I sought a particular place and Cuneglas had told me where to find it. Issa, loyal Issa, came with me, but he had no idea what business took us into the dark, deep wood.

This land, the heart of Powys, had been lightly touched by the Romans. They had built forts here, like Caer Sws, and they had left a few roads that arrowed along the river valleys, but there were no great villas or towns like those that gave Dumnonia its gloss of a lost civilization. Nor, here in Cuneglas's heartland, were there many Christians; the worship of the old Gods survived in Powys without the rancour that soured religion in Mordred's realm, where Christian and pagan vied for royal favour and the right to erect their shrines in the holy places. No Roman altars had replaced Powys's Druid groves and no Christian churches stood by its holy wells. The Romans had cut down some of the shrines, but many had been preserved and it was to one of those ancient holy places that Issa and I came in the leafy twilight of the midday forest.

It was a Druid shrine, a grove of oaks deep within a massive wood. The leaves above the shrine had yet to fade to bronze, but soon they would turn and fall onto the low stone wall that lay in a semicircle at the grove's centre. Two niches had been made in the wall and two human skulls were set in the niches. Once there had been many such places in Dumnonia, and many more had been remade after the Romans had left. Too often, though, the Christians would come and break the skulls, pull down the dry-stone walls and cut down the oaks, but this shrine in Powys might have stood among these deep woods for a thousand years. Little scraps of wool had been pushed between the stones as markers for the prayers that folk offered in this grove.

53

It was silent in the oaks; a heavy silence. Issa watched from the trees as I walked to the centre of the semicircle where I unstrapped Hywelbane's heavy belt.

I laid the sword on the flat stone that marked the shrine's centre and took from my pouch the clean white rib bone that gave me power over Lancelot's marriage. This I placed beside the sword. Last of all I put down on the stone the small golden brooch that Ceinwyn had given me so many years before. Then I lay down flat in the leaf mould.

I slept in hope of a dream that would tell me what to do, but no dream came. Maybe I should have sacrificed some bird or beast before I slept, a gift that might have provoked a God to grant me the answer I sought, but no answer came. There was just silence. I had put my sword and the power of the bone into the hands of the Gods, into the keeping of Bel and Manawydan, of Taranis and Lleullaw, but they ignored my gifts. There was only the wind in the high leaves, the scratching of squirrel claws on the oak branches and the sudden rattle of a woodpecker.

I lay still when I woke. There had been no dream, but I knew what I wanted. I wanted to take the bone and snap it in two, and if that gesture meant walking the Dark Road into Diwrnach's kingdom, then so be it. But I also wanted Arthur's Britain to be whole and good and true. And I wanted my men to have gold and land and slaves and rank. I wanted to drive the Saxons from Lloegyr. I wanted to hear the screams of a broken shield-wall and the blare of war horns as a victorious army pursued a shattered enemy to ruin. I wanted to march my starry shields into the flat eastern land that no free Briton had seen in a generation. And I wanted Ceinwyn.

I sat up. Issa had come to sit close beside me. He must have wondered why I stared so fixedly at the bone, but he asked no questions.

I thought of Merlin's small, squat tower of bones that represented Arthur's dream and wondered if that dream would really collapse if Lancelot did not marry Ceinwyn. The marriage was hardly the clasp that held Arthur's alliance together; it was merely a convenience to give Lancelot a throne and Powys a stake in Siluria's royal house. If the marriage never happened then the armies of Dumnonia and Gwent and Powys and Elmet would still march against the Sais. All that I knew, and all that was true, yet I also sensed that the bone could somehow jar Arthur's dream. The moment I snapped the bone in two I became sworn to Merlin's search, and that search promised to bring enmity to Dumnonia; the enmity of the old pagans who so hated the upstart Christian religion.

'Guinevere,' I suddenly said the name aloud.

'Lord?' Issa asked in puzzlement.

I shook my head to show that I had nothing more to say. Indeed, I had not meant to speak Guinevere's name aloud, yet I had suddenly understood that to break the bone would do more than encourage Merlin's campaign against the Christian God, it would also make Guinevere into my enemy. I closed my eyes. Could my Lord's wife be an enemy? And what if she were? Arthur would still love me, and I him, and my spears and starry shields were worth more to him than all Lancelot's fame.

I stood and retrieved the brooch, the bone and the sword. Issa watched as I pulled a thread of green-dyed wool from my cloak and jammed it between the stones. 'You were not at Caer Sws,' I asked him, 'when Arthur broke his betrothal to Ceinwyn?'

'No, Lord. I heard about it, though.'

'It was at the betrothal feast,' I said, 'just like the one we'll attend tonight. Arthur was sitting at the high table with Ceinwyn beside him and he saw Guinevere at the back of the hall. She was standing in a shabby cloak with her hounds beside her and Arthur saw her there and nothing was ever the same again. The Gods alone know how many men died because he saw that head of red hair.' I turned back to the low stone wall and saw there was an abandoned nest inside one of the mossy skulls. 'Merlin tells me that the Gods love chaos,' I said.

'Merlin loves chaos,' Issa said lightly, though there was more truth in his words than he knew.

'Merlin loves it,' I agreed, 'but most of us fear chaos and

that's why we try to make order.' I thought of the carefully ordered pile of bones. 'But when you have order, you don't need Gods. When everything is well ordered and disciplined then nothing is unexpected. If you understand everything,' I said carefully, 'then there's no room left for magic. It's only when you're lost and frightened and in the dark that you call on the Gods, and they like us to call on them. It makes them feel powerful, and that's why they like us to live in chaos.' I was repeating the lessons of my childhood, the lessons given to us on Merlin's Tor. 'And now we have a choice,' I told Issa. 'We can live in Arthur's well-ordered Britain or we can follow Merlin to chaos.'

'I'll follow you, Lord, whatever you do,' Issa said. I do not think he understood what I was saying, but he was content to trust me anyway.

'I wish I knew what to do,' I confessed. How easy it would be, I thought, if the Gods just walked Britain as they used to. Then we could see them, hear them and talk to them, but now we were like blindfolded men seeking a clasp-pin in a thorn thicket. I strapped the sword back into its place, then tucked the unbroken bone safe back in the pouch. 'I want you to give a message to the men,' I told Issa. 'Not to Cavan, for I'll talk to him myself, but I want you to tell them that if anything strange happens this night, they are released from their oaths to me.'

He frowned at me. 'Released from our oaths?' he asked, then shook his head vigorously. 'Not me, Lord.'

I hushed him. 'And tell them,' I went on, 'that if something strange does happen, and it may not, then loyalty to my oath could mean fighting against Diwrnach.'

'Diwrnach!' Issa said. He spat and made the symbol against evil with his right hand.

'Tell them that, Issa,' I said.

'So what might happen tonight?' he asked me anxiously.

'Maybe nothing,' I said, 'maybe nothing at all,' because the Gods had given me no sign in the grove and I still did not know what I would choose. Order or chaos. Or neither, for maybe the

56

bone was nothing but a piece of kitchen scrap and its breaking would do nothing except symbolize my own shattered love for Ceinwyn. But there was only one way to find out, and that was to break the bone. If I dared.

At Ceinwyn's betrothal feast.

Of all the feasts of those late summer nights the betrothal feast of Lancelot and Ceinwyn was the most lavish. Even the Gods seemed to favour it, for the moon was full and clear, and that was a wonderful omen for a betrothal. The moon rose shortly after sunset, a silver orb that loomed huge above the peaks where Dolforwyn lay. I had wondered if the feast would be held in Dolforwyn's hall, but Cuneglas, seeing the huge number to be fed, had decided to keep the celebrations inside Caer Sws.

There were far too many guests for the King's hall, and so only the most privileged were allowed inside its thick wooden walls. The rest sat outside, grateful that the Gods had sent a dry night. The ground was still wet from the rain earlier in the week, but there was plenty of straw for men to make dry seats. Pitch-soaked torches had been tied to stakes and, moments after the moonrise, those torches were lit so that the royal compound was suddenly bright with leaping flames. The wedding would be held in the daylight so that Gwydion, the God of light, and Belenos, the God of the sun, would grant their blessing, but the betrothal was given to the moon's blessing. Every now and then a burning wisp from a torch would float to earth to set alight a patch of straw and there would be bellows of laughter, screaming children, barking dogs and a flurry of panic until the fire was extinguished.

Over a hundred men were guests inside Cuneglas's hall. Tapers and rush lights were clustered together to flicker weird shadows in the high, beamed thatch where the sprays of beech leaves were now mixed with the year's first clusters of holly berries. The hall's one table was set on the dais beneath a row of shields and each shield had a taper below it to illuminate the device painted on the leather. At the centre was Cuneglas's royal shield of Powys with its spread-winged eagle, and on one side of the eagle was Arthur's black bear and on the other Dumnonia's red dragon. Guinevere's device of a moon-crowned stag was hung next to the bear, while Lancelot's sea-eagle flew with a fish in its claws next to the dragon. No one was present from Gwent, but Arthur had insisted that Tewdric's black bull be hung, along with Elmet's red horse and the fox mask of Siluria. The royal symbols marked the great alliance; the shield-wall that would batter the Saxons back to the sea.

Iorweth, Powys's chief Druid, announced the moment when he was certain that the last rays of the dying sun had vanished into the far Irish Sea, and then the guests of honour took their places on the dais. The rest of us were already seated on the hall's floor where men were calling for more of Powys's famously strong mead that had been specially brewed for this night. Cheers and applause greeted the honoured guests.

Queen Elaine came first. Lancelot's mother was dressed in blue with a gold torque at her throat and a golden chain binding the coils of her grey hair. A huge roar welcomed Cuneglas and Queen Helledd next. The King's round face beamed with pleasure at the prospect of this night's celebration in honour of which he had tied small white ribbons to his dangling moustaches. Arthur came in sober black, while Guinevere, following him to the dais, was splendid in her gown of pale gold linen. It was cut and stitched cunningly so that the precious fabric, skilfully dyed with soot and hive-gum, seemed to cling to her tall, straight body. Her belly barely betrayed her pregnancy and a murmur of appreciation for her beauty sounded among the watching men. Small gold scales had been sewn into the gown's cloth so that her body appeared to glint as she slowly followed Arthur to the centre of the dais. She smiled at the lust she knew she had provoked, and that she wanted to provoke, for this night Guinevere was determined to outshine whatever Ceinwyn wore. A circlet of gold held Guinevere's unruly red hair in place, a belt of golden chain links was looped around her waist, while in honour of Lancelot she wore at her neck a golden brooch depicting a sea-eagle. She kissed Queen Elaine on both cheeks, kissed Cuneglas on one, bobbed her head to Queen Helledd, then sat at Cuneglas's right hand while Arthur slipped into the empty chair beside Helledd.

Two seats remained, but before either was filled Cuneglas stood and rapped the table with his fist. Silence fell, and in the silence Cuneglas mutely gestured towards the treasures that were arrayed on the edge of the dais in front of the linen hanging from the table.

The treasures were the gifts Lancelot had brought for Ceinwyn and their magnificence caused a storm of acclamation in the hall. We had all inspected the gifts and I had listened sourly as men extolled the King of Benoic's generosity. There were torques of gold, torques of silver and torques made of a mixture of gold and silver, so many torques that they merely served as the foundation on which the greater gifts were piled. There were Roman hand mirrors, flasks of Roman glass and piles of Roman jewels. There were necklaces, brooches, ewers, pins and clasps. There was a king's ransom in glittering metal, in enamel, coral and precious gems and all of it, I knew, had been rescued from burning Ynys Trebes when Lancelot, disdaining to carry his sword against the rampaging Franks, had fled on the first ship to escape the city's slaughter.

The applause for the gifts was still sounding when Lancelot arrived in his glory. Like Arthur he was dressed in black, but Lancelot's black clothes were hemmed by strips of rare gold cloth. His black hair had been oiled and sleeked back so that it lay close to his narrow skull and flat against his back. The fingers of his right hand glittered with rings of gold while his left was dull with warrior rings, none of which, I sourly assumed, he had earned in battle. Around his neck he wore a heavy gold torque with finials glinting with bright stones, and on his breast, in Ceinwyn's honour, he wore her royal family's symbol of the spread-winged eagle. He wore no weapons, for no man was allowed to bring a blade into a King's hall, but he wore the enamelled sword belt that had been a gift from Arthur. He acknowledged the cheers with a raised hand, kissed his mother on the cheek, kissed Guinevere on the hand, bowed to Helledd, then sat.

The one chair remained empty. A harpist had begun to play, her plangent notes scarcely audible above the buzz of talk. The smell of roasting meat wafted into the hall, where slave girls carried round the jugs of mead. Iorweth the Druid bustled up and down the hall making a corridor between the men seated on the rush-strewn floor. He pushed men aside, bowed to the King when the corridor was made, then gestured with his staff for silence.

A great cheer erupted from the crowd outside.

The guests of honour had entered the hall from the rear, stepping straight from the night's shadows onto the dais, but Ceinwyn would make her entrance through the large door at the front of the hall and to reach that door she had to walk through the throng of guests waiting in the fire-lit compound. The cheer we heard was the sound of those guests applauding her progress from the women's hall, while inside the King's hall we waited for her in expectant silence. Even the harpist lifted her fingers from the strings to watch the door.

A child entered first. It was a small girl dressed in white linen who walked backwards up the aisle made by Iorweth for Ceinwyn's passage. The child strewed dried petals of spring flowers on the newly laid rushes. No one spoke. Every eye was fixed on the door except for mine, for I was watching the dais. Lancelot gazed at the door, a half smile on his face. Cuneglas kept cuffing tears from his eyes, so great was his happiness. Arthur, the maker of peace, beamed. Guinevere alone was not smiling. She just looked triumphant. She had once been scorned in this hall and now she was disposing of its daughter in marriage.

I watched Guinevere as, with my right hand, I took the bone from my pouch. The rib felt smooth in my grasp and Issa, standing behind me with my shield, must have wondered what significance that piece of kitchen waste carried in this moon-bright night of gold and fire.

I looked at the hall's great door just as Ceinwyn appeared and, in the instant before the cheers began in the hall, there was a gasp of astonishment. Not all the gold in Britain, not all the Queens of old, could have outshone Ceinwyn that night. I did not even need to look at Guinevere to know that she had been utterly outwitted on this night of beauty.

This, I knew, was Ceinwyn's fourth betrothal feast. She had come here once for Arthur, but he had broken that oath under the spell of Guinevere's love, and afterwards Ceinwyn had been betrothed to a Prince from distant Rheged, but he had died of a fever before they could marry; then, not long ago, she had carried the betrothal halter to Gundleus of Siluria, but he had died screaming under Nimue's cruel hands, and now, for the fourth time, Ceinwyn carried the halter to a man. Lancelot had given her a hoard of gold, but custom demanded that she return to him the gift of a common ox halter as a symbol that from this day on she would submit to his authority.

Lancelot stood as she entered and the half smile spread into a look of joy, and no wonder, for her beauty was dazzling. At her other betrothals, as befitted a Princess, Ceinwyn had come in jewels and silver, in gold and finery, but this night she wore only a simple bone-white gown that was belted with a pale blue cord that hung by the dress's simple skirt to end in tassels. No silver decked her hair, no gold showed at her throat, she wore no precious jewels anywhere, just the linen dress and, about her pale blonde hair, a delicate blue wreath made from the last dog-violets of summer. She wore no shoes, but stepped barefoot among the petals. She displayed no sign of royalty or any symbol of wealth, but had just come to the hall dressed as simply as any peasant girl, and it was a triumph. No wonder men gasped, and no wonder they cheered as she paced slow and shy between the guests. Cuneglas was weeping for happiness, Arthur led the applause, Lancelot smoothed his oiled hair and his mother beamed her approval. For a moment Guinevere's face was unreadable, but then she smiled, and it was a smile of pure triumph. She might have been outshone by Ceinwyn's beauty, but this night was still Guinevere's night and she was seeing her old rival being consigned to a marriage of her own devising.

I saw that smirk of triumph on Guinevere's face and maybe it was her gloating satisfaction that made up my mind. Or maybe it was my hatred for Lancelot, or my love for Ceinwyn, or maybe Merlin was right and the Gods do love chaos for, in a sudden surge of anger, I gripped the bone in both my hands. I did not think of the consequences of Merlin's magic, of his hatred for the Christians or the risk that we would all die pursuing the Cauldron in Diwrnach's realm. I did not think of Arthur's careful order, I was only aware that Ceinwyn was being given to a man I hated. I, like the other guests on the floor, was standing and watching Ceinwyn between the heads of the warriors. She had reached the great central oak pillar of the high hall where she was surrounded and besieged by the wolfish din of cheers and whistles. I alone was silent on the floor. I watched her and I placed my two thumbs at the centre of the rib and gripped its ends between my fists. Now, Merlin, I thought, now, you old rogue, let me see your magic now.

I snapped the rib. The noise of its splintering was lost among the cheers.

I pushed the rib's broken halves into the pouch, and I swear my heart was hardly beating as I watched the Princess of Powys who had stepped from the night with flowers in her hair.

And who now suddenly stopped. Just beside the pillar hung with berries and leaves, she stopped.

From the moment Ceinwyn had entered the hall she had kept her eyes on Lancelot and they were on him still and a smile was still on her face, but she stopped and her sudden stillness caused a slow puzzled silence to fall across the hall. The child scattering petals frowned and looked about for guidance. Ceinwyn did not move.

Arthur, smiling still, must have thought she had been overcome by nerves for he beckoned her encouragingly. The halter in her hands trembled. The harpist struck one uncertain chord, then lifted her fingers from the strings, and as her notes died away in the silence I saw a black-cloaked figure come from the crowd beyond the pillar.

It was Nimue, her one gold eye reflecting the flames in the puzzled hall.

Ceinwyn looked from Lancelot to Nimue and then, very slowly, she held out a white-sleeved arm. Nimue took her hand and looked into the Princess's eyes with a quizzical expression. Ceinwyn paused for a heartbeat, then gave the smallest nod of consent. Suddenly the hall was urgent with talk as Ceinwyn turned away from the dais and, following Nimue's lead, plunged into the crowd.

The talk died away for no one could find any explanation for what was now happening. Lancelot, left standing on the dais, could only watch. Arthur's mouth had dropped open while Cuneglas, half risen from his seat, stared incredulously as his sister threaded the crowd that edged aside from Nimue's fierce, scarred and derisive face. Guinevere looked ready to kill.

Then Nimue caught my eye and smiled and I felt my heart beating like a trapped wild thing. Then Ceinwyn smiled at me and I had no eyes for Nimue, only for Ceinwyn, sweet Ceinwyn, who was carrying the ox halter through the crowd of men towards my place in the hall. The warriors edged aside, but I seemed made of stone, unable to move or to speak as Ceinwyn, with tears in her eyes, came to where I stood. She said nothing, but just held the halter in offering to me. A babble of astonishment brewed all around us, but I ignored the voices. Instead I fell to my knees and took the halter, then I seized Ceinwyn's hands and pressed them against my face that, like hers, was wet with tears.

The hall was erupting in anger, in protest and amazement, but Issa stood over me with his shield raised. No man carried an edged weapon into a king's hall, but Issa was holding the shield with its five-pointed star as though he would beat down any man who challenged the astonishing moment. Nimue, on my other side, was hissing curses into the hall, daring any man to challenge the Princess's choice.

Ceinwyn knelt so that her face was close to mine. 'You swore an oath, Lord,' she whispered, 'to protect me.'

'I did, Lady.'

'I release you from the oath if that is your wish.'

'Never,' I promised.

She pulled away slightly. 'I will marry no man, Derfel,' she warned me softly, her eyes on mine. 'I will give you everything but marriage.'

'Then you give me everything I could ever want, Lady,' I said, my throat full and my eyes blurred with tears of happiness. I smiled and gave her back the halter. 'Yours,' I said.

She smiled at that gesture, then dropped the halter into the straw and kissed me softly on the cheek. 'I think,' she whispered mischievously in my ear, 'that this feast will go better without us.' Then we both stood and, hand in hand, and ignoring the questions and protests and even some cheers, we walked into the moonlit night. Behind us was confusion and anger, and in front of us was a crowd of puzzled people through whom we walked side by side. 'The house beneath Dolforwyn,' Ceinwyn said, 'is waiting for us.'

'The house with the apple trees?' I asked, remembering her telling me about the little house that she had dreamed of as a child.

'That house,' she said. We had left the crowd gathered about the hall doors and were walking towards Caer Sws's torchlit gate. Issa had rejoined me after retrieving our swords and spears, and Nimue was at Ceinwyn's other side. Three of Ceinwyn's servants were hurrying to join us, as were a score of my men. 'Are you certain of this?' I asked Ceinwyn as though, somehow, she could turn back the last few minutes and restore the halter to Lancelot.

'I am more certain,' Ceinwyn said calmly, 'than of anything I ever did before.' She gave me an amused glance. 'Did you ever doubt me, Derfel?'

'I doubted myself,' I said.

She squeezed my hand. 'I am no man's woman,' she said,

'only my own,' and then she laughed with pure delight, let go of my hand and broke into a run. Violets fell from her hair as she ran for sheer joy across the grass. I ran after her, while behind us, from the astonished hall's doorway, Arthur called for us to come back.

But we ran on. To chaos.

NEXT DAY I TOOK a sharp knife and trimmed the snapped ends of the two bone fragments, and then, working very carefully, I made two long narrow troughs in Hywelbane's wooden handgrips. Issa walked to Caer Sws and fetched back some glue that we heated over the fire and, once we were sure that the two troughs exactly matched the shape of the bone fragments, we coated the troughs with the glue, then pushed the two scraps into the sword's hilt. We wiped off the excess glue, then bound the strips with bands of sinew to set them firmly into the wood. 'It looks like ivory,' Issa said admiringly when the job was done.

'Strips of pig bone,' I said dismissively, though in fact the two scraps did look like ivory and gave Hywelbane a rich appearance. The sword was named for its first owner, Merlin's steward Hywel, who had taught me my weapons.

'But the bones are magic?' Issa asked me anxiously.

'Merlin's magic,' I said, but I did not explain any further.

Cavan came to me at midday. He knelt on the grass and bowed his head, but he did not speak, nor did he need to speak for I knew why he had come. 'You are free to go, Cavan,' I told him. 'I release you from your oath.' He looked up at me, but the business of being freed of an oath was too heavy for him to say anything, so I smiled. 'You're not a young man, Cavan,' I said, 'and you deserve a lord who will offer you gold and comfort instead of a Dark Road and uncertainty.'

'I have a mind, Lord,' he found his voice at last, 'to die in Ireland.'

'To be with your people?'

'Yes, Lord. But I cannot go back a poor man. I need gold.'

'Then burn your throwboard,' I advised him.

He grinned at that, then kissed Hywelbane's hilt. 'No resentment, Lord?' he asked me anxiously.

'No,' I said, 'and if you ever need my help, send word.'

He stood and embraced me. He would go back to Arthur's service and take with him half my men, for only twenty stayed with me. The others feared Diwrnach, or else were too eager to find riches, and I could not blame them. They had earned honour, warrior rings and wolf-tails in my service, but little gold. I gave them permission to keep the wolf-tails on their helmets, for those they had earned in the terrible fights in Benoic, but I made them paint out the newly made stars on their shields.

The stars were for the twenty men who stayed with me, and those twenty were the youngest, the strongest and the most adventurous of my spearmen and, the Gods know, they needed to be, for by snapping the bone I had committed them to the Dark Road.

I did not know when Merlin would summon us and so I waited in the small house to which Ceinwyn had led us in the moonlight. The house lay north and east of Dolforwyn in a small valley so steep that the shadows did not flee from the stream until the sun was halfway up its climb in the morning sky. The valley's steep sides were shrouded by oaks, though around the house was a patchwork of tiny fields where a score of apple trees had been planted. The house had no name; nor even did the valley, it was simply called Cwm Isaf, the Lower Valley, and it was now our home.

My men built huts among the trees on the valley's southern slope. I did not know how I was to provide for twenty men and their families, for Cwm Isaf's little farm would have been hard pressed to feed a fieldmouse, let alone a warrior band, but Ceinwyn had gold and, as she promised me, her brother would not let us starve. The farm, she told me, had belonged to her father, one of the thousands of scattered tenancies that had supported Gorfyddyd's wealth. The last tenant had been a cousin of Caer

Sws's candleman, but he had died before Lugg Vale and no other tenant had yet been chosen. The house itself was a poor thing, a little rectangle of stone with a roof thickly thatched with rye-straw and bracken that desperately needed repair. There were three chambers inside. One, the central room, had been for the farm's few beasts, and that room we swept clean to give ourselves a living space. The other rooms were sleeping chambers, one for Ceinwyn and the other one for me.

'I have promised Merlin,' she had said that first night in explanation of the two sleeping chambers.

I felt my flesh crawl. 'Promised him what?' I asked.

She must have blushed, but no moonlight came into deep Cwm Isaf and so I could not see her face, but only feel the pressure of her fingers in mine. 'I have promised him,' she said slowly, 'that I will stay a virgin till the Cauldron is found.'

I had begun to understand then just how subtle Merlin had been. How subtle and wicked and clever. He needed a warrior to protect him while he travelled into Lleyn and he needed a virgin to find the Cauldron, and so he had manipulated us both. 'No!' I protested. 'You can't go into Lleyn!'

'Only a virgin can discover the Cauldron,' Nimue had hissed at us from the dark. 'Would you have us take a child, Derfel?'

'Ceinwyn cannot go to Lleyn,' I insisted.

'Quiet,' Ceinwyn had hushed me. 'I promised. I made an oath.'

'Do you know what Lleyn is?' I asked her. 'You know what Diwrnach does?'

'I know,' she said, 'that the journey there is the price I pay for being here with you. And I promised Merlin,' she said again. 'I made an oath.'

And so I slept alone that night, but in the morning, after we had shared a scanty breakfast with our spearmen and servants, and before I put the bone scraps into Hywelbane's hilt, Ceinwyn walked with me up Cwm Isaf's stream. She listened to my passionate arguments why she should not travel the Dark Road, and she dismissed them all by saying that if Merlin was with us then who could prevail against us?

'Diwrnach could,' I said grimly.

'But you're going with Merlin?' she asked me.

'Yes.'

'Then don't prevent me,' she insisted. 'I will be with you, and you with me.' And she would hear no more argument. She was no man's woman. She had made up her mind.

And then, of course, we spoke of what had happened in the last few days and our words tumbled out. We were in love, smitten just as hard as Arthur had been smitten by Guinevere, and we could not hear enough of the other's thoughts and stories. I showed her the pork bone and she laughed when I told her how I had waited till the last moment to snap it in two.

'I really didn't know if I dared turn away from Lancelot,' Ceinwyn admitted. 'I didn't know about the bone, of course. I thought it was Guinevere who made up my mind.'

'Guinevere?' I asked, surprised.

'I couldn't bear her gloating. Is that awful of me? I felt as though I was her kitten, and I couldn't bear it.' She walked on in silence for a while. Leaves drifted down from the trees that were still mostly green. That morning, waking to my first dawn in Cwm Isaf, I had seen a martin fly away from the thatch. He did not come back and I guessed we would not see another till the spring. Ceinwyn walked barefoot beside the stream, her hand in mine. 'And I've been wondering about that prophecy of the skull bed,' she went on, 'and I think it means I'm not supposed to marry. I've been betrothed three times, Derfel, three times! And three times I lost the man, and if that isn't a message from the Gods, what is?'

'I hear Nimue,' I said.

She laughed. 'I like her.'

'I couldn't imagine the two of you liking each other,' I confessed.

'Why ever not? I like her belligerence. Life is for the taking, not for submission, and all my life, Derfel, I've done what people told me to do. I've always been good,' she said, giving the

69

word 'good' a wry stress. 'I was always the obedient little girl, the dutiful daughter. It was easy, of course, for my father loved me and he loved so few people, but I was given everything I ever wanted and in return all they ever wanted of me was that I should be pretty and obedient. And I was very obedient.'

'Pretty, too.'

She dug an elbow into my ribs as reproof. A flock of pied wagtails flew up from the mist that shrouded the stream ahead of us. 'I was always obedient,' Ceinwyn said wistfully. 'I knew I would have to marry where I was told to marry, and that didn't worry me because that's what kings' daughters do, and I can remember being so happy when I first met Arthur. I thought that my whole lucky life would go on for ever. I had been given such a good man, and then, suddenly, he vanished.'

'And you didn't even notice me,' I said. I had been the youngest spearman in Arthur's guard when he came to Caer Sws to be betrothed to Ceinwyn. It was then that she had given me the small brooch I still wore. She had rewarded all Arthur's escort, but never knew what a fire she started in my soul that day.

'I'm sure I did notice you,' she said. 'Who could miss such a big, awkward, straw-haired lump?' She laughed at me, then let me help her over a fallen oak. She wore the same linen dress she had worn the previous night, though now the bleached skirt was soiled with mud and moss. 'Then I was betrothed to Caelgyn of Rheged,' she continued her tale, 'and I wasn't quite so sure I was lucky any more. He was a sullen beast, but he promised to bring father a hundred spearmen and a bride-price of gold and I convinced myself I would be happy all the same, even if I did have to live in Rheged, but Caelgyn died of the fever. Then there was Gundleus.' She frowned at that memory. 'I realized then that I was just a throwpiece in a game of war. My father loved me, but he would even let me go to Gundleus if that meant more spears to carry against Arthur. That was when I first understood that I would never be happy unless I made my own happiness, and it was just then that you and Galahad came to see us. Remember?'

'I remember.' I had accompanied Galahad on his failed

mission of peace and Gorfyddyd, as an insult, had made us dine in the women's hall. There in the candlelight, as a harpist played, I had talked to Ceinwyn and given her my oath to protect her.

'And you cared whether I was happy,' she said.

'I was in love with you,' I confessed. 'I was a dog howling at a star.'

She smiled. 'And then came Lancelot. Lovely Lancelot. Handsome Lancelot, and everyone told me I was the luckiest woman in Britain, but do you know what I sensed? That I would just be another possession to Lancelot, and he seems to have so many already. But I still wasn't sure what I should do, then Merlin came and talked to me, and he left Nimue and she talked and talked, but I already knew I didn't want to belong to any man. I've belonged to men all my life. So Nimue and I made an oath to Don and I swore to Her that if She gave me the strength to take my own freedom then I would never marry. I will love you,' she promised me, looking up into my face, 'but I will not be any man's possession.'

Maybe not, I thought, but she, like me, was still Merlin's gaming piece. How busy he had been, he and Nimue, but I said nothing of that, nor of the Dark Road. 'But you will be Guinevere's enemy now,' I warned Ceinwyn instead.

'Yes,' she said, 'but I always was, right from the moment when she decided to take Arthur away from me, but I was just a child then and I didn't know how to fight her. Last night I struck back, but from now on I'll just stay out of sight.' She smiled. 'And you were to marry Gwenhwyvach?'

'Yes,' I confessed.

'Poor Gwenhwyvach,' Ceinwyn said. 'She was always very good to me when they lived here, but I remember every time her sister came into the room she'd run away. She was like a big plump mouse and her sister was the cat.'

Arthur came to the lower valley that afternoon. The glue holding the scraps of bone was still drying in Hywelbane's hilt as his warriors filled the trees on Cwm Isaf's southern slope that faced our small house. The spearmen did not come to threaten us, but had merely diverted themselves from their long march home to comfortable Dumnonia. There was no sign of Lancelot, nor of Guinevere, as Arthur walked alone across the stream. He carried no sword or shield.

We met him at our door. He bowed to Ceinwyn, then smiled at her. 'Dear Lady,' he said simply.

'You are angry with me, Lord?' she asked him anxiously.

He grimaced. 'My wife believes I am, but no. How can I be angry? You only did what I once did, and you had the grace to do it before the oath was given.' He smiled at her again. 'You have, perhaps, inconvenienced me, but I deserved that. May I walk with Derfel?'

We followed the same path that I had taken that morning with Ceinwyn, and Arthur, once he was out of sight of his spearmen, put an arm about my shoulders. 'Well done, Derfel,' he said quietly.

'I am sorry if it hurt you, Lord.'

'Don't be a fool. You did what I once did and I envy you the newness of it. It just changes things, that's all. It is, as I said, inconvenient.'

'I won't be Mordred's champion,' I said.

'No. But someone will. If it was up to me, my friend, I would take you both home and make you champion and give you all I had to give, but things cannot always be as we want.'

'You mean,' I said bluntly, 'that the Princess Guinevere will not forgive me.'

'No,' Arthur said bleakly. 'Nor will Lancelot.' He sighed. 'What shall I do with Lancelot?'

'Marry him to Gwenhwyvach,' I said, 'and bury them both in Siluria.'

He laughed. 'If only I could. I'll send him to Siluria, certainly, but I doubt Siluria will hold him. He has ambitions above that small kingdom, Derfel. I'd hoped that Ceinwyn and a family would keep him there, but now?' He shrugged. 'I would have done better to give the kingdom to you.' He took his arm from about my shoulders and faced me. 'I do not release you from your oaths, Lord Derfel Cadarn,' he said formally, 'you are still my man and when I send for you, you will come to me.'

'Yes, Lord.'

'That will be in the spring,' he said. 'I am sworn to three months' peace with the Saxons and I will keep that peace, and when the three months are up the winter will keep our spears stacked. But in the spring we march and I shall want your men in my shield-wall.'

'They will be there, Lord,' I promised him.

He raised both hands and put them on my shoulders. 'Are you also sworn to Merlin?' he asked, staring into my eyes.

'Yes, Lord,' I admitted.

'So you'll chase a Cauldron that doesn't exist?'

'I shall seek the Cauldron, yes.'

He closed his eyes. 'Such stupidity!' He dropped his hands and opened his eyes. 'I believe in the Gods, Derfel, but do the Gods believe in Britain? This isn't the old Britain,' he said vehemently. 'Maybe once we were a people of one blood, but now? The Romans brought men from every corner of the world! Sarmatians, Libyans, Gauls, Numidians, Greeks! Their blood is mingled with ours, just as it seethes with Roman blood and mixes now with Saxon blood. We are what we are, Derfel, not what we once were. We have a hundred Gods now, not just the old Gods, and we cannot turn the years back, not even with the Cauldron and every Treasure of Britain.'

'Merlin disagrees.'

'And Merlin would have me fight the Christians just so his Gods can rule? No, I won't do it, Derfel.' He spoke angrily. 'You can look for your imaginary Cauldron, but don't think I'll play Merlin's game by persecuting Christians.'

'Merlin,' I said defensively, 'will leave the fate of the Christians to the Gods.'

'And what are we but the Gods' implements?' Arthur asked. 'But I won't fight other Britons just because they worship another God. Nor will you, Derfel, so long as you're oath-sworn.'

'No, Lord.'

He sighed. 'I do hate all this rancour about Gods. But then, Guinevere always tells me I am blind to the Gods. She says it's my one fault.' He smiled. 'If you're sworn to Merlin, Derfel, then you must go with him. Where will he take you?'

'To Ynys Mon, Lord.'

He stared at me in silence for a few heartbeats, then shuddered. 'You go to Lleyn?' he asked incredulously. 'No one comes alive from Lleyn.'

'I shall,' I boasted.

'Make sure you do, Derfel, make sure you do.' He sounded gloomy. 'I need you to help me beat the Saxons. And after that, maybe, you can return to Dumnonia. Guinevere isn't a woman to hold grudges.' I doubted that, but said nothing. 'So I shall summon you in the spring,' Arthur went on, 'and pray you survive Lleyn.' He put an arm through mine and walked me back towards the house. 'And if anyone asks you, Derfel, then I have just reproved you angrily. I have cursed you, even struck you.'

I laughed. 'I forgive you the blow, Lord.'

'Consider yourself reproved,' he said, 'and consider yourself,' he went on, 'the second luckiest man in Britain.'

The luckiest in the world, I thought, for I had my soul's desire.

Or I would have it, the Gods preserve us, when Merlin had his.

I stood and watched the spearmen go. Arthur's banner of the bear showed briefly in the trees, he waved, hoisted himself onto his horse's back and then was gone.

And we were alone.

So I was not in Dumnonia to see Arthur's return. I should have liked that, for he rode back a hero to a country that had dismissed his chances of survival and had plotted to replace him by lesser creatures.

Food was scarce that autumn, for the sudden flare of war had depleted the new harvest, but there was no famine and Arthur's men collected fair taxes. That sounds like a small improvement, but after the recent years it caused a stir in the land. Only the rich paid taxes to the Royal Treasury. Some paid in gold, but most paid in grain and leather and linen and salt and wool and dried fish that they, in turn, had demanded from their tenants. In the last few years the rich had paid little to the King and the poor had paid much to the rich, so Arthur sent spearmen to inquire of the poor what tax had been levied of them and used their answers to make his own levy of the rich. From the proceeds he returned a third of the yield back to the churches and magistrates so that they could distribute the food in the winter. That action alone told Dumnonia that a new power had come to the land, and though the wealthy grumbled, none dared raise a shield-wall to fight Arthur. He was the warlord of Mordred's kingdom, the victor of Lugg Vale, the slaughterer of Kings, and those who opposed him now feared him.

Mordred was moved into the care of Culhwch, Arthur's cousin and a crude, honest warrior who probably took small interest in the fate of a small and troublesome child. Culhwch was too busy suppressing the revolt that had been started by Cadwy of Isca deep in Dumnonia's west, and I heard that he led his spears in a swift campaign across the great moor, then south into the wild land on the coast. He ravaged Cadwy's heartland, then stormed the rebellious Prince in the old Roman stronghold of Isca. The walls had decayed and the veterans of Lugg Vale swarmed over the town's ramparts to hunt the rebels through the streets. Prince Cadwy was caught in a Roman shrine and there dismembered. Arthur ordered parts of his body to be displayed in Dumnonia's towns, and his head, with its easily recognizable blue tattoos on the cheeks, to be sent to King Mark of Kernow who had encouraged the revolt. King Mark sent back a tribute of tin ingots, a tub of smoked fish, three polished turtle shells that had washed up on the shores of his wild country and an innocent disavowal of any complicity in Cadwy's rebellion.

Culhwch, in capturing Cadwy's stronghold, found letters there that he sent to Arthur. The letters were from the Christian party in Dumnonia and had been written before the campaign that ended in Lugg Vale, and they revealed the full extent of the plans to rid Dumnonia of Arthur. The Christians had disliked Arthur ever since he had revoked High King Uther's rule that the church was to be exempt from taxes and loans, and they had become convinced that their God was leading Arthur to a great defeat at Gorfyddyd's hands. It was the prospect of that almost certain defeat that had encouraged them to put their thoughts into writing, and those same writings were now in Arthur's keeping.

The letters revealed a worried Christian community who wanted Arthur's death, but also feared the incursion of Gorfyddyd's pagan spearmen. To save themselves and their riches they had been ready to sacrifice Mordred, and the letters encouraged Cadwy to march on Durnovaria during Arthur's absence, kill Mordred and then yield the kingdom to Gorfyddyd. The Christians promised him help, and hoped that Cadwy's spears would protect them once Gorfyddyd ruled.

Instead it brought them punishment. King Melwas of the Belgae, a client King who had sided with the Christians who opposed Arthur, was made the new ruler of Cadwy's land. It was hardly a reward, for it took Melwas far away from his own people to a place where Arthur could keep him under close watch. Nabur, the Christian magistrate who had held Mordred's guardianship, and who had used that guardianship to raise the party that opposed Arthur and who was the writer of the letters suggesting Mordred's murder, was nailed to a cross in Durnovaria's amphitheatre. These days, of course, he is called a saint and martyr, but I only remember Nabur as a smooth, corrupt liar. Two priests, another magistrate and two landowners were also put to death. The last conspirator was Bishop Sansum, though he had been too clever to let his name be put into writing, and that cleverness, together with his strange friendship for Arthur's maimed pagan sister, Morgan, saved Sansum's life. He swore undying loyalty to Arthur, put a hand on a crucifix and swore he had never plotted to kill the King, and so remained as the guardian of the shrine of the Holy Thorn at Ynys Wydryn. You could bind Sansum in iron and hold a sword to his throat, and still he would slither free.

Morgan, his pagan friend, had been Merlin's most trusted priestess until the younger Nimue usurped that position, but Merlin and Nimue were both far away and that left Morgan as virtual ruler of Merlin's lands in Avalon. Morgan, with her gold mask hiding her fire-ravaged face and her black robe shrouding her flame-twisted body, assumed Merlin's power and it was she who finished the rebuilding of Merlin's hall on the Tor, and she who organized the tax-collectors in the northern part of Arthur's land. Morgan became one of Arthur's most trusted advisers; indeed, after Bishop Bedwin died of a fever that autumn, Arthur even suggested, against all precedence, that Morgan be named as a full councillor. No woman had ever sat on a King's Council in Britain and Morgan might well have been the first, but Guinevere made sure she was not. Guinevere would let no woman be a councillor if she could not be one herself, and besides, Guinevere hated anything that was ugly and, the Gods know, poor Morgan was grotesque even with her gold mask in place. So Morgan stayed in Ynys Wydryn, while Guinevere supervised the building of the new palace at Lindinis.

It was a gorgeous palace. The old Roman villa that Gundleus had burned was rebuilt and extended so that its cloistered wings enclosed two great courtyards where water flowed in marble channels. Lindinis, close to the royal hill of Caer Cadarn, was to be Dumnonia's new capital, though Guinevere took good care that Mordred, with his twisted left foot, was allowed nowhere near the place. Only the beautiful were allowed in Lindinis, and in its arcaded courtyards Guinevere assembled statues from villas and shrines throughout Dumnonia. There was no Christian shrine there, but Guinevere made a great dark hall for the women's Goddess Isis, and she provided a lavish suite of rooms where Lancelot could stay when he visited from his new kingdom in Siluria. Elaine, Lancelot's mother, lived in those rooms and she, who had once made Ynys Trebes so beautiful, now helped Guinevere make Lindinis's palace into a shrine of beauty.

Arthur, I know, was rarely at Lindinis. He was too busy preparing for the great war against the Saxons, to which end he began re-fortifying the ancient earth citadels in southern Dumnonia. Even Caer Cadarn, deep in our heartland, had its wall strengthened and new timber fighting platforms poised on its ramparts, but his greatest work was at Caer Ambra, just a half hour's walk east of the Stones, which was to be his new base against the Sais. The old people had made a fort there, but all that autumn and winter the slaves toiled to steepen the ancient earth walls and to make new palisades and fighting platforms on their summits. More forts were strengthened south of Caer Ambra to defend the lower parts of Dumnonia against the southern Saxons led by Cerdic, who were sure to attack us while Arthur assaulted Aelle in the north. Not since the Romans, I dare say, had so much British earth been dug or timber split, and Arthur's honest taxes could never pay for half that labour. He therefore made a levy on the Christian churches that were plentiful and powerful in southern Britain, the same churches that had supported Nabur and Sansum's effort to topple him. That levy was eventually repaid, and it protected the Christians from the ghastly attentions of the Saxon heathens, but the Christians never forgave Arthur, nor did they notice that the same levy was taken from the handful of pagan shrines that still possessed wealth.

Not all the Christians were Arthur's enemies. At least a third of his spearmen were Christians and those men were as loyal as any pagan. Many other Christians approved of his rule, but most of the leaders of the church let their greed dictate their loyalty and they were the ones who opposed him. They believed that their God would one day return to this earth and walk among us like a mortal man, but He would not come again until all pagans had been converted to His faith. The preachers, knowing that Arthur was a pagan, hissed curses at him, but Arthur ignored their words as he made his ceaseless tours of southern Britain. One day he would be with Sagramor on Aelle's border, the next he would be fighting one of Cerdic's war-bands as it probed deep into the river valleys of the south, and then he would ride north through Dumnonia and across Gwent to Isca where he would argue with local chieftains about the number of spearmen who could be raised from western Gwent or eastern Siluria. Thanks to Lugg Vale Arthur was now far more than Dumnonia's chief lord and Mordred's protector; he was Britain's warlord, the undisputed leader of all our armies, and no King dared refuse him, nor, in those days, wanted to.

But all this I missed, for I was in Caer Sws and I was with Ceinwyn and I was in love.

And waiting for Merlin.

Merlin and Nimue came to Cwm Isaf just days before the winter solstice. Dark clouds were pressing close above the bare oak tops on the ridges, and the morning frost had lingered well into the afternoon. The stream was a patchwork of ice ledges and trickling water, the fallen leaves were crisp and the valley's soil as hard as stone. We had a fire in the central chamber so our house was warm enough, though it was choking with the smoke that billowed about the untrimmed beams before finding the small hole in the roof's ridge. Other fires smoked from the shelters that my spearmen had made across the valley; stout little huts with walls of earth and stone supporting roofs of timber and bracken. We had made a beast shed behind the house where a bull, two cows, three sows, a boar, a dozen sheep and a score of chickens were penned at night to protect them from the wolves. We had plenty of wolves in our woods and their howling echoed at every dusk, and at night we would sometimes hear them scrabbling beyond the beast shed. The sheep would bleat piteously, the hens would set up a cackling panic, and then Issa, or whoever else stood guard, would shout and hurl a firebrand into the wood's edge and the wolves would skitter away. One morning, going early to fetch water from the stream, I came face to face with a big old dog wolf. He had been drinking, but as I stepped out of the bushes he raised a grey muzzle, stared at me, then waited for my salute before he loped silently upstream. It was, I decided, a good omen and, in those days as we waited for Merlin, we counted the omens.

We also hunted the wolves. Cuneglas gave us three brace of long-haired wolfhounds that were bigger and shaggier than the famous Powysian deerhounds like those Guinevere kept in Dumnonia. The sport kept my spearmen active and even Ceinwyn liked those long cold days in the high woods. She wore leather breeches, high boots and a leather jerkin, and hung a hunter's long knife at her waist. She would braid her fair hair into a knot at the back of her head, then scramble up rocks and down gullies and over dead trees behind her brace of hounds who were leashed on long horsehair ropes. The simplest way to hunt wolves was with a bow and arrow, but as few of us possessed that skill we used the dogs, war spears and knives, and by the time Merlin returned we had a pile of pelts stacked in Cuneglas's store hall. The King had wanted us to move back to Caer Sws, but Ceinwyn and I were as happy as our anticipation of Merlin's ordeal allowed us and so we stayed in our small valley and counted the days.

And we were happy in Cwm Isaf. Ceinwyn took a ridiculous pleasure in doing all the things that till now had been done for her by servants, though strangely she was never able to wring a chicken's neck and I always used to laugh when she killed a hen. She had no need to do it, for any one of the servants could have killed the fowl and my spearmen would do anything for Ceinwyn, but she insisted on sharing the work, though when it came to killing hens, ducks or geese she could not make herself do it properly. The only method she ever devised was to lay the poor creature down on the earth, put a small foot on its neck and then, with her eyes tight closed, give the head one quick decisive tug.

She was more successful with the distaff. Every woman in Britain, save for the very richest, was forever with a distaff and spindle, for spinning wool into thread was one of those endless jobs that will presumably last until the sun has made its last turn about the earth. As soon as one year's fleeces had been turned into yarn, so the next year's fleeces came to the storehouses and the women would collect their apronfuls, wash and comb the wool, then start spinning the thread again. They spun when they walked, they spun as they talked, they spun whenever there was no other task needing their hands. It was monotonous, mindless work, but not unskilled; at first Ceinwyn could only produce pathetic little tatters of wool, but she became better, though never as quick as those women who had spun the wool since the very first day their hands were big enough to hold the distaff. She would sit of an evening, telling me about her day, and her left hand would turn the staff and her right would flick the weighted spindle that hung from the distaff to elongate and twist the emerging thread. When the spindle reached the floor she would wind the thread around it, fix the spooled yarn with the bone clip on the spindle's top and then start spinning again. The wool she made that winter was often lumpy, or else fragile, but I loyally wore one of the shirts she made from that thread until it fell apart.

Cuneglas visited us often, though his wife, Helledd, never came. Queen Helledd was truly conventional and she disapproved deeply of what Ceinwyn had done. 'She thinks it brings disgrace on the family,' Cuneglas told us cheerfully. He became, like Arthur and Galahad, one of my dearest friends. He was, I think, lonely in Caer Sws, for other than Iorweth and some of the younger Druids he had few men with whom he could talk of anything but hunting and war, and so I replaced the brothers he had lost. His older brother, who should have become King, had been killed in a fall from a horse, the next son had died of a fever and the youngest had been killed fighting the Saxons. Cuneglas, like me, deeply disapproved of Ceinwyn's going on the Dark Road, but he told me that nothing short of a sword blow would ever stop her. 'Everyone always thinks she's so sweet and kind,' he told me, 'but there's a will of iron there. Stubborn.'

'Can't kill chickens.'

'I can't even imagine her trying!' he laughed. 'But she is happy, Derfel, and for that I thank you.'

It was a happy time, one of the happiest of all our happy times, but always shadowed by the knowledge that Merlin would come and demand the fulfilment of our oaths.

He came on a frosty afternoon. I was outside the house, using a Saxon war axe to split newly chopped logs that would fill our house with smoke, and Ceinwyn was inside, hushing a squabble that had risen between her maidservants and the fiery Scarach, when a horn sounded across the valley. The horn was a signal from my spearmen that a stranger approached Cwm Isaf and I lowered the axe in time to see Merlin's tall figure striding among the trees. Nimue was with him. She had stayed a week with us after the night of Lancelot's betrothal and then, without a word of explanation, had slipped away one night, but now, dressed in black beside her lord in his long white robe, she returned.

Ceinwyn came from the house. Her face was smudged with soot and her hands bloodied from a hare she had been jointing. 'I thought he was bringing a war-band,' she said, her blue eyes fixed on Merlin. That was what Nimue had told us before she left; that Merlin was raising the army that would protect him on the Dark Road.

'Maybe he's left them at the river?' I suggested.

She pushed a lock of hair away from her face, adding a smudge of blood to the soot. 'Aren't you cold?' she asked, for I had been stripped to the waist as I chopped the wood.

'Not yet,' I said, though I pulled on a wool shirt as Merlin leapt long legged over the stream. My spearmen, anticipating news, trailed from their huts to follow him, but they stayed outside the house when he ducked his tall figure under our low lintel.

He offered us no greeting, but just went past us into the house. Nimue followed him, and by the time Ceinwyn and I entered they were already squatting beside the fire. Merlin held his thin hands to the blaze, then seemed to give a long sigh. He said nothing, and neither of us wanted to ask his news. I, like him, sat at the fire's edge while Ceinwyn put the half jointed hare into a bowl then wiped her hands free of blood. She waved Scarach and the servants out of the house, then sat beside me.

Merlin shivered, then seemed to relax. His long back was bowed as he hunched forward with his eyes closed. He stayed thus for a long time. His brown face was deeply lined and his beard a startling white. Like all Druids he shaved the front part of his skull, but now that tonsure was smothered with a fine layer of short white hair, evidence that he had been a long time on the road without a razor or a bronze mirror. He looked so old that day, and hunched by the fire he even looked feeble.

Nimue sat opposite him, saying nothing. She did rise once to take Hywelbane from its nail hooks in the main beam and I saw her smile as she recognized the two strips of bone set into the handle. She unsheathed the blade, then held it into the smokiest part of the fire, and once the steel was covered in soot she carefully scratched an inscription into the soot with a piece of straw. The letters were not like these I write now, that both we and the Saxons employ, but were older magical letters, mere strokes slashed by bars, that only the Druids and sorcerers used. She propped the scabbard against the wall and hung the sword back on its nails, but did not explain the significance of what she had written. Merlin ignored her.

He opened his eyes suddenly, and the appearance of feebleness was replaced by a terrible savagery. 'I put a curse,' he said slowly, 'on the creatures of Siluria.' He flicked his fingers towards the fire and a puff of brighter flame hissed in the wood. 'May their crops be blighted,' he growled, 'their cattle barren, their children crippled, their swords blunted and their enemies triumphant.' It was, for him, a mild enough curse, but there was a hissing malevolence in his voice. 'And on Gwent,' he went on,

83

'I give a murrain, and frosts in summer and wombs shrivelled to dry husks.' He spat into the flames. 'In Elmet,' he said, 'the tears will make lakes, plagues will fill graves, and rats shall rule their houses.' He spat again. 'How many men will you bring, Derfel?'

'All I have, Lord.' I hesitated to admit how few that was, but I finally gave him the answer, 'Twenty shields.'

'And those of your men who are still with Galahad?' He gave me a quick glance from beneath his bushy white eyebrows. 'How many of those?'

'I have heard nothing from them, Lord.'

He sneered. 'They form a palace guard for Lancelot. He insists on it. He makes his brother into a doorkeeper.' Galahad was Lancelot's half-brother and as unlike him as any man could be. 'It is a good thing, Lady,' Merlin looked at Ceinwyn, 'that you did not marry Lancelot.'

She smiled at me. 'I think so, Lord.'

'He finds Siluria tedious. I can't blame him for that, but he'll seek Dumnonia's comforts and be a snake in Arthur's belly.' He smiled. 'You, my Lady, were supposed to be his plaything.'

'I had rather be here,' Ceinwyn said, gesturing at our rough stone walls and smoke-stained roof beams.

'But he'll try to strike at you,' Merlin warned her. 'His pride climbs higher than Lleullaw's eagle, Lady, and Guinevere is cursing you. She killed a dog in her temple of Isis and draped its pelt on a crippled bitch that she gave your name.'

Ceinwyn looked pale, made the sign against evil and spat into the fire.

Merlin shrugged. 'I have countered the curse, Lady,' he said, then stretched his long arms and bent his head back so that his ribboned plaits almost touched the rush-covered floor behind him. 'Isis is a foreign Goddess,' he said, 'and her power is feeble in this land.' He brought his head forward again, then rubbed his eyes with his long hands. 'I have come empty-handed,' he said bleakly. 'No man in Elmet would step forward, and none elsewhere. Their spears, they say, are dedicated to Saxon bellies. I offered them no gold, I offered no silver, only a fight on behalf of the Gods, and they offered me their prayers, then let their womenfolk talk to them of children and hearths and cattle and land and so they slunk away. Eighty men! That's all I wanted. Diwrnach can field two hundred, maybe a handful more, but eighty would have sufficed, yet there were not even eight men who would come. Their Lords are sworn to Arthur now. The Cauldron, they tell me, can wait till Lloegyr is ours again. They want Saxon land and Saxon gold and all I offered them was blood and cold on the Dark Road.'

There was a silence. A log collapsed in the fire to spring a constellation of sparks toward the blackened roof. 'Not one man offered a spear?' I asked, shocked at the news.

'A few,' he said dismissively, 'but none I would trust. None worthy of the Cauldron.' He paused, then looked tired again. 'I am struggling against the lure of Saxon gold and against Morgan. She opposes me.'

'Morgan!' I could not hide my astonishment. Morgan, Arthur's eldest sister, had been Merlin's closest companion until Nimue usurped her place, and though Morgan hated Nimue I did not think that hatred extended to Merlin.

'Morgan,' he said flatly. 'She has spread a tale through Britain. The tale says that the Gods oppose my quest and that I am to be defeated, and that my death will embrace all my companions. She dreamed the tale and folk believe her dreams. I am old, she says, and feeble, and loose-witted.'

'She says,' Nimue spoke softly, 'that a woman will kill you, not Diwrnach.'

Merlin shrugged. 'Morgan plays her own game and I don't yet understand it.' He rooted about in a pocket of his gown and brought out a handful of dried knotted grasses. Each knotted stem looked alike to me, but he sorted through them and selected one that he held towards Ceinwyn. 'I release you from your oath, Lady.'

Ceinwyn glanced at me, then looked back to the knot of grass. 'Will you still take the Dark Road, Lord?' she asked Merlin.

'Yes.'

'But how will you find the Cauldron without me?'

He shrugged, but offered no answer.

'How will you find it with her?' I asked, for I still did not understand why a virgin must find the Cauldron, or why that virgin should have to be Ceinwyn.

Merlin shrugged again. 'The Cauldron,' he said, 'was ever under the guard of a virgin. One guards it now, if my dreams tell me correctly, and only another virgin can reveal its hiding-place. You will dream it,' he said to Ceinwyn, 'if you are willing to come.'

'I shall come, Lord,' Ceinwyn said, 'as I promised you.'

Merlin pushed the grass knot back into the pocket before rubbing his face again with his long hands. 'We leave in two days,' he announced flatly. 'You must bake bread, pack dried meat and fish, sharpen your weapons, and make sure you have furs against the cold.' He looked at Nimue. 'We shall sleep at Caer Sws. Come.'

'You can stay here,' I offered.

'I must speak to Iorweth.' He stood, his head level with the rafters. 'I release you both from your oaths,' he said very formally, 'but pray you will come anyway. But it will be harder than you know and harder than you fear in your worst dreams, for I have pledged my life on the Cauldron.' He looked down at us and his face was immensely sad. 'The day we step on the Dark Road,' he told us, 'I shall begin to die, for that is my oath, and I have no certainty that the oath will bring me success, and if the search fails then I shall be dead and you will be alone in Lleyn.'

'We shall have Nimue,' Ceinwyn said.

'And she is all you will have,' Merlin said darkly, then ducked out of the door. Nimue followed him.

We sat in silence. I put another log on the fire. It was green, for all our firewood was fresh-cut unseasoned timber which was why it smoked so badly. I watched the smoke thicken and swirl about the rafters, then took Ceinwyn's hand. 'Do you want to die in Lleyn?' I chided her.

'No,' she said, 'but I want to see the Cauldron.'

I stared into the fire. 'He will fill it with blood,' I said softly.

Ceinwyn's fingers caressed mine. 'When I was a child,' she said, 'I heard all the tales of old Britain, how the Gods lived among us and everyone was happy. There was no famine then, and no plagues, just us and the Gods and peace. I want that Britain back, Derfel.'

'Arthur says it can never return. We are what we are, not what we once were.'

'So who do you believe?' she asked. 'Arthur or Merlin?'

I thought a long time. 'Merlin,' I finally said, and perhaps that was because I wanted to believe in his Britain where all our sorrows would be magically taken away. I loved the idea of Arthur's Britain too, but that would take war and hard work and a trust that men would behave well if they were treated well. Merlin's dream demanded less and promised more.

'They we'll go with Merlin,' Ceinwyn said. She hesitated, watching me. 'Are you worried by Morgan's prophecy?' she asked.

I shook my head. 'She has power,' I said, 'but not like his. And not like Nimue, either.' Nimue and Merlin had both suffered the Three Wounds of Wisdom, and Morgan had only endured the wound to the body, never the wound to the mind or the wound to pride; but Morgan's prophecy was a shrewd tale, for in some ways Merlin was defying the Gods. He wanted to tame their caprices and in return give them a whole land dedicated to their worship, but why would the Gods want to be tamed? Maybe they had chosen Morgan's lesser power to be their instrument against Merlin's meddling, for what else could explain Morgan's hostility? Or maybe Morgan, like Arthur, believed that Merlin's quest was a nonsense, an old man's hopeless search for a Britain that had vanished with the coming of the Legions. For Arthur there was only one fight, and that was to hurl the Saxon Kings from Britain, and Arthur would have supported his sister's whispering tale if that meant no British spears were to be wasted against Diwrnach's blood-painted shields. So perhaps Arthur was using his sister to make certain that no precious Dumnonian lives were to be thrown away in Lleyn. Except for my life, and my men's lives, and my beloved Ceinwyn's life. For we were oath-sworn.

But Merlin had released us from our oaths and so I tried one last time to persuade Ceinwyn to stay in Powys. I told her how Arthur believed that the Cauldron no longer existed, how it must have been stolen by the Romans and taken to that great sink of treasure, Rome, and melted down to make hair-combs or cloak-pins or coins or brooches. All that I told her, and when I was done she smiled and asked me once again who I believed, Merlin or Arthur.

'Merlin,' I said again.

'And so do I,' Ceinwyn said. 'And I'm going.'

We baked bread, packed food and sharpened our weapons. And the next night, the eve of our going on Merlin's quest, the first snow fell.

Cuneglas gave us two ponies that we loaded with food and furs, then we slung our star-painted shields on our backs and took the northern road. Iorweth gave us a blessing and Cuneglas's spearmen accompanied us for the first few miles, but once we had passed the great ice wastes of the Dugh bog that lay beyond the hills north of Caer Sws those spearmen stepped aside and we were alone. I had promised Cuneglas that I would protect his sister's life with my own and he had embraced me, then whispered in my ear. 'Kill her, Derfel,' he said, 'rather than let Diwrnach have her.'

There were tears in his eyes and they almost made me change my mind. 'If you order her not to go, Lord King,' I said, 'she might obey.'

'Never,' he said, 'but she is happier now than she has ever been. Besides, Iorweth tells me you will return. Go, my friend.' He had stepped back. His parting gift had been a bag of gold ingots that we stowed on one of the ponies.

The snowy road led north into Gwynedd. I had never been

to that kingdom before and found it a crude, hard place. The Romans had come here, but only to dig lead and gold. They had left few marks on the land and given it no law. The folk lived in squat, dark huts that huddled together inside circling stone walls from which dogs snarled at us and on which the skulls of wolves and bears were mounted to deter the spirits. Cairns marked the summits of hills and every few miles we would find a pole struck into the road's verge and hung with dead men's bones and ribbons of tattered cloth. There were few trees, the streams were frozen and snow blocked some of the passes. At night we sheltered in the huddled houses where we paid for our warmth with slivers of gold chopped from Cuneglas's ingots.

We dressed in furs. Ceinwyn and I, like my men, were swathed in lice-ridden wolf-pelts and deerskins, but Merlin wore a suit made from the coat of a great black bear. Nimue had grey otter skins that were much lighter than our furs, but even so she seemed not to feel the cold as the rest of us did. Nimue alone carried no weapons. Merlin had his black staff, a fearsome thing in battle, while my men had spears and swords and even Ceinwyn carried a light spear and had her long-bladed hunting knife scabbarded at her waist. She wore no gold and the folk who gave us shelter had no conception of her rank. They did notice her bright hair and assumed that she, like Nimue, was one of Merlin's adepts. Merlin they loved, for they all knew of him and they brought their crippled children to be touched by his hand.

It took us six days to reach Caer Gei where Cadwallon, King of Gwynedd, was spending the winter. The caer itself was a hilltop fort, but under the fort's shoulder there was a deep valley with tall trees growing from its steep sides and in the valley a wooden palisade circling a timber hall, some store-rooms and a score of sleeping huts, all of them ghosted white with snow and with long icicles hanging from their eaves. Cadwallon proved to be a sour old man while his hall was merely one third the size of Cuneglas's hall and the press of warriors meant that its earth floor was already packed tight with beds. A space was grudgingly made for us and a corner screened for Nimue and Ceinwyn. That night Cadwallon gave us a feast, a poor thing of salted mutton and stewed carrots, but the best his stores could provide. He did generously offer to take Ceinwyn off our hands by making her his eighth wife, but he seemed neither offended nor disappointed when she refused. His seven existing wives were dark, sullen women who shared a round hut where they squabbled and persecuted each other's children.

It was a wretched place, Caer Gei, though a royal one, and it was hard to believe that Cadwallon's father, Cunedda, had been the High King before Uther of Dumnonia. Gwynedd's spears had fallen on lean times since those great days. It was hard to believe, too, that it was here, beneath the high peaks that were now brilliant with ice and snow, that Arthur had been raised. I went to see the house where his mother had been given shelter after Uther had rejected her and found it to be an earth-walled hall about the same size as our house in Cwm Isaf. It stood among fir trees whose boughs were bent low by snow, and it looked north towards the Dark Road. The house was now home to three spearmen, their families and livestock. Arthur's mother had been half sister to King Cadwallon who was thus Arthur's uncle, though Arthur's birth had been illegitimate and the relationship could hardly be expected to yield many spears for Arthur's spring campaign against the Saxons. Cadwallon, indeed, had sent men to fight against Arthur at Lugg Vale, but that gift of men had been a precaution to keep Powys's friendship rather than because the King of Gwynedd hated Dumnonia. Most of the time Cadwallon's spears faced north towards Lleyn.

The King summoned Byrthig, his Edling, to the feast so that he could tell us of Lleyn. Prince Byrthig was a short, squat man with a scar running from his left temple across his broken nose and down into his thick beard. He had only three teeth, which made his efforts to chew meat lengthy and messy. He would use his fingers to chafe the meat against his one front tooth, thus abrading the food into shreds that he washed down with mead, and the laborious work had left his bristling black beard filthy with meat juices and half chewed scraps. Cadwallon, in his gloomy manner, offered him as a husband to Ceinwyn and again seemed unmoved by her gentle refusal.

Diwrnach, Prince Byrthig told us, had his home at Boduan, a fort that lay far to the west in the peninsula of Lleyn. The King was one of the Irish Lords Across the Sea, but his war-band, unlike that of Oengus of Demetia, was not composed of men from a single Irish tribe but was a collection of fugitives from every tribe. 'He welcomes whatever comes across the water, and the more murderous they are, the better,' Byrthig told us. 'The Irish use him to rid themselves of their outlaws and there have been many of those of late.'

'The Christians,' Cadwallon grumbled in curt explanation, then spat.

'Lleyn is Christian?' I asked in surprise.

'No,' Cadwallon snapped as though I should have known better. 'But Ireland is bowing to the Christian God. Bowing in droves, and those who can't stand that God flee to Lleyn.' He pulled a scrap of bone from his mouth and inspected it gloomily. 'We'll have to fight them soon,' he added.

'Diwrnach's numbers increase?' Merlin asked.

'So we hear, though we hear little enough,' Cadwallon replied. He looked up as the heat in the hall melted a swathe of snow from the sloping roof. There was a scraping rumble, then a soft crash as the mass slid off the thatch.

'Diwrnach,' Byrthig explained, his voice made sibilant by his ravaged teeth, 'asks only to be left alone. If we do not disturb him, he will only occasionally disturb us. His men come to take slaves, but we have few people left in the north now, and his men will not travel far, but if his war-band grows too large for Lleyn's crops then he will seek new land somewhere.'

'Ynys Mon is famous for its crops,' Merlin said. Ynys Mon was the big island that lay off Lleyn's northern coast.

'Ynys Mon could feed a thousand,' Cadwallon agreed, 'but

only if its people are spared to plough and reap, and its people are not spared. No one is. Any Briton with sense left Lleyn years ago, and the ones who are left crouch in terror. So would you if Diwrnach came visiting to search for what he wants.'

'Which is?' I asked.

Cadwallon looked at me, paused, then shrugged. 'Slaves,' he said.

'In which,' Merlin asked silkily, 'you pay him tribute?'

'A small price for peace,' Cadwallon dismissed the accusation.

'How much?' Merlin demanded.

'Forty a year,' Cadwallon finally admitted. 'Mostly orphaned children and maybe some prisoners. He's happiest, though, with girls.' He looked broodingly at Ceinwyn. 'He has an appetite for girls.'

'Many men do, Lord King,' Ceinwyn answered drily.

'But not like Diwrnach's appetite,' Cadwallon warned her. 'His wizards have told him that a man armed with a shield covered with the tanned skin of a virgin girl will be invincible in battle.' He shrugged. 'Can't say I've ever tried it myself.'

'So you send him children?' Ceinwyn said accusingly.

'Do you know any other kind of virgin?' Cadwallon retorted.

'We think he's touched by the Gods,' Byrthig said, as though that explained Diwrnach's appetite for virgin slaves, 'for he seems mad. One of his eyes is red.' He paused to grind a piece of grey mutton on his front tooth. 'He covers his shields in skin,' he went on when the meat had been reduced to a tissue, 'then paints them with blood and that's why his men call themselves the Bloodshields.' Cadwallon made the sign against evil. 'And some men say he eats the girls' flesh,' Byrthig went on, 'but we don't know that; who knows what the mad do?'

'The mad are close to the Gods,' Cadwallon growled. He was plainly terrified of his northern neighbour, and no wonder, I thought.

'Some of the mad are close to the Gods,' Merlin said. 'Not all.'

'Diwrnach is,' Cadwallon warned him. 'He does what he

wants, to whom he wants, how he wants and the Gods keep him safe while he does it.' Again I made the sign against evil, and suddenly wished I was back in far Dumnonia where there were lawcourts and palaces and long Roman roads.

'With two hundred spears,' Merlin said, 'you could scour Diwrnach from Lleyn. You could wash him into the sea.'

'We tried once,' Cadwallon said, 'and fifty of our men died of the flux in one week, and another fifty were shivering in their own excrement, and always his howling warriors circled us on ponies and their long spears showered out of the night. When we reached Boduan there was only a great wall hung with dying things that bled and screamed and twisted on their hooks and none of my men would scale that horror. Nor would I,' he admitted. 'And if I had, what then? He would have fled to Ynys Mon and it would have taken me days and weeks to find the ships to follow him over the water. I have neither the time, the spearmen, nor the gold to scour Diwrnach into the sea, so I give him children instead. It's cheaper.' He shouted for a slave to bring him more mead, then gave Ceinwyn a sour glance. 'Give her to him,' he said to Merlin, 'and he might give you the Cauldron.'

'I will give him nothing for the Cauldron,' Merlin snapped. 'Besides, he does not even know the Cauldron exists.'

'He does now,' Byrthig put in. 'All Britain knows why you go north. And do you think his wizards don't want to find the Cauldron?'

Merlin smiled. 'Send your spearmen with me, Lord King, and we shall take both the Cauldron and Lleyn.'

Cadwallon snorted at that proposal. 'Diwrnach, Merlin, teaches a man to be a good neighbour. I will let you travel my land, for I fear your curse if I don't, but not one man of mine will go with you, and when your bones are buried in Lleyn's sands I shall tell Diwrnach that your trespass was none of my doing.'

'Will you tell him by which road we travel?' Merlin asked, for we faced two roads now. One led around the coast and was the usual winter road north, while the other was the Dark Road that most men reckoned was impassable in winter. Merlin hoped that by using the Dark Road we could surprise Diwrnach and be gone from Ynys Mon almost before he knew we had even come.

Cadwallon smiled for the only time that night. 'He knows already,' the King said, then glanced at Ceinwyn, the brightest figure in that smoke-dark hall. 'And doubtless he looks forward to your coming.'

Did Diwrnach know we planned to use the Dark Road? Or was Cadwallon guessing? I spat anyway, to protect us all from evil. The solstice was due, the long night of the year when life ebbs, hope is bleak and the demons have dominion of the air, and that was when we would be on the Dark Road.

Cadwallon thought us fools, Diwrnach waited for us, and we wrapped ourselves in fur and slept.

The sun shone next morning, making the surrounding peaks into dazzling spikes of whiteness that hurt our eyes. The sky was almost clear and a strong wind blew snow from the ground to make clouds of glittering specks that wafted across the white land. We loaded the ponies, accepted the grudging gift of a sheepskin from Cadwallon, then marched towards the Dark Road that began just north of Caer Gei. It was a road without settlements, without farms, without a soul to offer us shelter; nothing but a rugged path through the wild mountain barrier that protected Cadwallon's heartland from Diwrnach's Blood-shields. Two poles marked the beginning of the road and both were topped by rag-draped human skulls from which long icicles clinked in the wind. The skulls faced north towards Diwrnach, two talismans to keep his evil beyond the mountains. I saw Merlin touch an iron amulet that hung around his neck as we passed between the twin skulls and remembered his dreadful promise that he would begin to die the moment we reached the Dark Road. Now, as our boots squeaked and crunched through the road's undisturbed layer of snow, I knew that oath of death had begun its work. I watched him, but saw no signs of distress as, all that day, we climbed into the hills, sliding on snow and trudging in a cloud of our own misting breath. We slept that night in an abandoned shepherd's hut that still blessedly had a ragged roof of old timbers and decaying straw with which we built a fire that flickered feebly in the snowy darkness.

Next morning we had gone no more than a quarter mile when a horn sounded above and behind us. We stopped, turned, and shaded our eyes to see a dark line of men cresting a hill down which we had slithered the previous evening. There were fifteen of them, all with shields, swords and spears, and when they saw they had gained our attention they half ran and half slid down the treacherous slope of snow. Their progress made great cloudy plumes that drifted westwards on the wind.

My men, without orders from me, formed a line, unstrapped their shields and lowered their spears so that they formed a shield-wall across the road. I had given Cavan's responsibilities to Issa and he growled at them to stand firm, but no sooner had he spoken than I recognized the curious device painted on one of the approaching shields. It was a cross, and that Christian symbol was carried by only one man I knew. Galahad.

'Friends!' I called to Issa, then broke into a run. I could see the approaching men clearly now, and they were all from those of my men who had been left in Siluria and forced to serve as Lancelot's palace guard. Their shields still bore the device of Arthur's bear, but Galahad's cross led them. He was waving and shouting, and I was doing the same, so that neither of us heard a word the other spoke until we had already met and embraced. 'Lord Prince,' I greeted him, then embraced him again, for of all the friends I ever had in this world he was the best.

He had fair hair and a face as broad and strong as his half-brother Lancelot's was narrow and subtle. Like Arthur he invited trust on sight, and if all Christians had been like Galahad I think I would have taken the cross in those early days. 'We slept all night across the ridge,' he gestured back up the road, 'and half froze, while you must all have rested there?'

He pointed towards the wisp of smoke still drifting from our fire.

'Warm and dry,' I said, and then, when the newcomers had greeted their old companions, I embraced them all and gave their names to Ceinwyn. One by one they knelt and swore her loyalty. They had all heard how she had fled her betrothal feast to be with me, and they loved her for that and now held their naked sword blades for her royal touch. 'What of the other men?' I asked Galahad.

'Gone to Arthur.' He grimaced. 'None of the Christians came, sadly. Except me.'

'You think this is worth a pagan Cauldron?' I asked, gesturing towards the cold road ahead.

'Diwrnach lies at the road's end, my friend,' Galahad said, 'and I hear he is a King as evil as anything that ever crawled from the devil's pit. A Christian's task is to fight evil, so here I am.' He greeted Merlin and Nimue, and then, because he was a Prince and so of equal rank to Ceinwyn, embraced her. 'You are a fortunate woman,' I heard him whisper.

She smiled and kissed his cheek. 'More fortunate now that you are here, Lord Prince.'

'That's true, of course.' Galahad stepped back and looked from her to me, and from me to her. 'All Britain speaks of you two.'

'Because all Britain is stuffed with idle tongues,' Merlin snapped in a surprising burst of shrewishness, 'and we have a journey to make when you two have finished gossiping.' His face was pinched and his temper short. I put it down to age and the hard road we walked in cold weather, and tried not to think of his death-oath.

The journey through the mountains took us two more days. The Dark Road was not long, but it was hard and it climbed up steep hills and went through gaping valleys where the smallest sound echoed hollow and cold from the ice-locked walls. We found an abandoned settlement to spend the second night on the road, a place of round stone huts that were huddled inside a wall the height of a man on which we set three guards to watch the glittering moonlit slopes. There was no fuel for a fire and so we sat close together and sang songs and told tales and tried not to think of the Bloodshields. Galahad gave us news of Siluria that night. His brother, he told us, had refused to occupy Gundleus's old capital at Nidum because it was too far from Dumnonia and had no comforts other than a decaying Roman barrack block, so he had moved Siluria's government to Isca, the huge Roman fort that lay beside the Usk at the very edge of Siluria's territory and just a stone's throw from Gwent. It was as close as Lancelot could get to Dumnonia while still staying in Siluria. 'He likes mosaic floors and marble walls,' Galahad said, 'and there's just enough of them at Isca to keep him satisfied. He's gathered every Druid in Siluria there.'

'There are no Druids in Siluria,' Merlin growled. 'None that are any good, anyway.'

'Those who call themselves Druids, then,' Galahad said patiently. 'He has two he particularly values and he pays them to make curses.'

'On me?' I asked, touching the iron on Hywelbane's hilt.

'Among others,' Galahad said, glancing at Ceinwyn and making the sign of the cross. 'He'll forget in time,' he added, trying to reassure us.

'He'll forget when he's dead,' Merlin said, 'and even then he'll carry a grudge across the bridge of swords.' He shivered, not because he feared Lancelot's enmity, but because he was cold. 'Who are these so-called Druids he particularly values?'

'Tanaburs's grandsons,' Galahad said, and I felt an icy hand creep round my heart. I had killed Tanaburs, and though I had possessed the right to take his soul, it was still a brave fool who killed a Druid and Tanaburs's dying curse still hovered about me.

We went slowly the next day, our pace held back by Merlin. He insisted he was well and refused any assistance, but his step faltered too often, his face looked yellow and haggard, and his breath came in short, harsh gasps. We had hoped to be over the last pass by nightfall, but we were still climbing towards it as the short day's light faded. All afternoon the Dark Road had twisted uphill, though to call it a road was a mockery for it was nothing but a stony, dreadful path that crossed and re-crossed a frozen stream where the ice hung thick from the ledges of the frequent small waterfalls. The ponies kept slipping and sometimes refused to move at all; it seemed we spent more time supporting them than leading them, but as the last light drained cold into the west we reached the pass and it was just as I had seen it in my shivering dream on Dolforwyn's summit. It was just as bleak, just as cold, though with no black ghoul barring the Dark Road that now dropped steeply onto Lleyn's narrow coastal plain and then ran north to the shore.

And beyond that shore lay Ynys Mon.

I had never seen the blessed isle. I had heard of it all my life and known of its power and lamented the destruction worked on it by the Romans in the Black Year, but I had never seen it except in the dream. Now, in the winter's dusk, it looked nothing like that lovely vision. It was not sunlit, but shadowed by cloud, so that the big isle looked dark and menacing, a threat made worse by the sullen glint of black pools that broke its low hills. The isle was almost free of snow, though its rocky edges were fretted white by a grey and miserable sea. I fell to my knees at the sight of the island, we all did except for Galahad, and even he finally went on one knee as a mark of respect. As a Christian he some-times dreamed of going to Rome or even to far-off Jerusalem, if such a place really existed, but Ynys Mon was our Rome and our Jerusalem, and we were now in sight of its holy soil.

We were also now in Lleyn. We had crossed the unmarked border and the few settlements on the coastal plain beneath us were the holdings of Diwrnach. The fields were lightly covered with snow, smoke rose from huts, but nothing human seemed to move in that dark space and all of us, I think, were wondering how we were to go from the mainland to the island. 'There are ferrymen on the straits,' Merlin said, reading our thoughts. He alone of us had been to Ynys Mon, but it had been many years ago and long before he had ever known that the Cauldron still existed. He had gone there when Leodegan, Guinevere's father, had ruled the land in the days before Diwrnach's ragged ships had come from Ireland to sweep Leodegan and his motherless daughters out of their kingdom. 'In the morning,' Merlin said, 'we shall walk to the shore and pay our ferrymen. By the time Diwrnach knows we have reached his land, we shall already have gone.'

'He'll follow us to Ynys Mon,' Galahad said nervously.

'And we shall be gone again,' Merlin said. He sneezed. He looked wretchedly cold. His nose was running, his cheeks were pale and from time to time he shivered uncontrollably, but he found some dusty herbs in a small leather pouch and he swallowed them with a handful of melted snow and insisted he was well.

He looked much worse next morning. We had spent that night in a cleft of the rocks where we had not dared light a fire, despite Nimue's charm of concealment that she had worked with the help of a polecat's skull we had found higher up the road. Our sentries had watched the coastal plain where three small glints of fire betrayed the presence of life, while the rest of us had clung together in the deep rocks where we shivered and cursed the cold and wondered if morning would ever dawn. It came at last with a seeping, leprous light that made the distant isle look darker and more menacing than ever. But Nimue's charm seemed to have worked, for no spearmen guarded the Dark Road's ending.

Merlin was shaking now and was much too weak to walk, and so four of my spearmen carried him in a litter made of cloaks and spears as we slid and edged our way down to the first small wind-bent trees in the hedgerows of Lleyn. The road was sunken here and its ruts were frosted hard where it twisted between hunched oaks, thin hollies and the small neglected fields. Merlin was moaning and shuddering, and Issa wondered if we should turn back. 'To cross the mountains again,' Nimue said, 'would surely kill him. We go on.'

We came to a fork in the road and there found our first sign of Diwrnach. It was a skeleton, bound together with horsehair ropes and hung from a pole so that its dry bones rattled in the brisk west wind. Three crows had been nailed to the post below the human bones and Nimue sniffed their stiffened bodies to decide what kind of magic had been imbued into their deaths. 'Piss! Piss!' Merlin managed to say from his litter. 'Quick, girl! Piss!' He coughed horribly, then turned his head to spit the sputum towards the ditch. 'I won't die,' he said to himself, 'I will not die!' He lay back as Nimue squatted by the pole. 'He knows we're here,' Merlin warned me.

'Is he here?' I asked, crouching beside him.

'Someone is. Be careful, Derfel.' He closed his eyes and sighed. 'I am so old,' he said softly, 'so horribly old. And there's badness here, all about us.' He shook his head. 'Get me to the island, that's all, just reach the island. The Cauldron will cure all.'

Nimue finished, then waited to see which way the steam from her urine blew, and the wind took it towards the right-hand fork and that omen decided our path. Before we set off Nimue went to one of the ponies and found a leather bag from which she took a handful of elf bolts and eagle stones that she distributed among the spearmen. 'Protection,' she explained as she laid a snake stone in Merlin's litter. 'Onwards,' she ordered us.

We walked all morning, our pace slowed by the need to carry Merlin. We saw no one and that absence of life put a dreadful fear into my men for it seemed as though we had come to a land of the dead. There were rowan and holly berries in the hedge-rows, and thrushes and robins in the branches, but there were no cattle, no sheep and no men. We did see one settlement from which a wisp of smoke blew in the wind, but it was far off and no one appeared to be watching us from its circling wall.

Yet men were in this dead land. We knew that when we paused to rest in a small valley where a stream trickled slug-gishly between icy banks under a grove of small, black, wind-bent oaks. The intricate branches were each delicately limned with a white frost and we rested beneath them until Gwilym, one of the spearmen who was standing guard at the rear, called to me.

I went to the oaks' edge to see that a fire had been set on the lower slope of the mountains. There were no flames visible, just a thick gruel of grey smoke that boiled fiercely before being snatched away by the west wind. Gwilym pointed to the smoke with his spear-blade, then spat to avert its evil.

Galahad came to stand beside me. 'A signal?' he asked.

'Probably.'

'So they know we're here?' He crossed himself.

'They know.' Nimue joined us. She was carrying Merlin's heavy black staff and she alone seemed to burn with energy in this cold, dead place. Merlin was sick, the rest of us were besieged by fear, but the deeper we pierced into Diwrnach's black land the fiercer Nimue became. She was nearing the Cauldron, and the lure of it was like a fire in her bones. 'They're watching us,' she said.

'Can you hide us?' I asked, wanting another of her concealment spells.

She shook her head. 'This is their land, Derfel, and their Gods are powerful here.' She sneered as Galahad made the sign of the cross a second time. 'Your nailed God won't defeat Crom Dubh,' she said.

'He's here?' I asked fearfully.

'Or one like him,' she said. Crom Dubh was the Black God, a crippled and malevolent horror who gave dark nightmares. The other Gods, it was said, avoided Crom Dubh, which suggested we were alone in his power.

'So we're doomed,' Gwilym said flatly.

'Fool!' Nimue hissed at him. 'We're only doomed if we fail to find the Cauldron. Then we'd all be doomed anyway. Are you going to watch that smoke all morning?' she asked me.

We walked on. Merlin could not speak any longer and his teeth chattered, even though we piled him with furs. 'He's dying,' Nimue told me calmly.

'Then we should find shelter,' I said, 'and build a fire.'

'So we can all be warm while we're slaughtered by Diwrnach's spearmen?' She scoffed at the idea. 'He's dying, Derfel,' she explained, 'because he's close to his dream and because he made his bargain with the Gods.'

'His life for the Cauldron?' Ceinwyn, walking on my other side, asked the question.

'Not quite,' Nimue admitted. 'But while you two were setting up your little house,' she made that statement sarcastically, 'we went to Cadair Idris. We made a sacrifice there, the old sacrifice, and Merlin pledged his life, not for the Cauldron, but for the search. If we find the Cauldron, he'll live, but if we fail then he dies and the shadow-soul of the sacrifice can claim Merlin's soul for all time.'

I knew what the old sacrifice was, though I had never heard of it being made in our time. 'Who was the sacrifice?' I asked.

'No one you knew. No one we knew. Just a man.' Nimue was dismissive. 'But his shadow-soul is here, watching us, and it wants us to fail. It wants Merlin's life.'

'What if Merlin dies anyway?' I asked.

'He won't, you fool! Not if we find the Cauldron.'

'If I find it,' Ceinwyn said nervously.

'You will,' Nimue said confidently.

'How?'

'You'll dream,' Nimue said, 'and the dream will lead us to the Cauldron.'

And Diwrnach, I realized when we reached the straits dividing the mainland from the island, wanted us to find it. The signal fire told us his men had been watching us, but they had neither shown themselves nor tried to stop our journey, and that suggested Diwrnach knew of our quest and wanted it to succeed so that he could take the Cauldron for himself. There could be no other reason why he was making it so easy for us to reach Ynys Mon.

The straits were not wide, but the grey water swirled and sucked and foamed as it swept through the channel. The sea ran fast in those narrows, twisting itself into sullen whirlpools or else breaking white on hidden rocks, but the sea was not as frightening as the far shore that stood so utterly empty and dark and bleak, almost as if it waited to suck our souls away. I shivered as I looked at that distant grassy slope and could not help thinking of the far-off Black Day when the Romans had stood on this same rocky shore and that far bank had been thick with Druids who had hurled their dread curses at the foreign soldiers. The curses had failed, the Romans had crossed, and Ynys Mon had died, and now we stood in the same place in a last, desperate attempt to wind back the years and spool back the centuries of sadness and hardship so that Britain would be restored to its blessed state before the Romans came. It would be Merlin's Britain then, a Britain of the Gods, a Britain without Saxons, a Britain full of gold and feasting halls and miracles.

We walked east towards the narrowest part of the straits and there, rounding a point of rock and beneath the earth loom of a deserted fortress, we found two boats hauled up on the pebbles of a tiny cove. A dozen men waited with the boats, almost as though they had expected us. 'The ferrymen?' Ceinwyn asked me.

'Diwrnach's boatmen,' I said, and touched the iron in Hywelbane's hilt. 'They want us to cross,' I said, and I was afraid because the King was making it so easy for us.

The sailors were quite unafraid of us. They were squat, hard-looking creatures with fish scales sticking to their beards and their thick woollen clothes. They carried no weapons other than their gutting knives and fish-spears. Galahad asked if they had seen any of Diwrnach's spearmen, but they simply shrugged as if his language made no sense to them. Nimue spoke to them in her native Irish and they responded politely enough. They claimed to have seen no Bloodshields, but did tell her that we must wait until the tide had reached its height before we could cross. Only then, it seemed, were the straits safe for boats.

We made Merlin a bed in one of the boats, then Issa and I climbed to the deserted fort and stared inland. A second pyre of smoke blew skyward from the valley of twisted oaks, but otherwise nothing had changed and no enemies were in sight. But they were there. You did not need to see their blood-daubed shields to know that they were close. Issa touched his spearblade. 'It seems to me, Lord,' he said, 'that Ynys Mon would be a good place to die.'

I smiled. 'It would be a better place to live, Issa.'

'But our souls will surely be safe if we die on the blessed isle?' he asked anxiously.

'They will be safe,' I promised him, 'and you and I will cross the bridge of swords together.' And Ceinwyn, I promised myself, would be just a pace or two ahead of us, for I would kill her myself before any of Diwrnach's men could lay their hands on her. I drew Hywelbane, its long blade still smeared with the soot in which Nimue had written her charm, and I held its tip to Issa's face. 'Make me an oath,' I ordered him.

He went on one knee. 'Say it, Lord.'

'If I die, Issa, and Ceinwyn still lives, then you must kill her with one sword stroke before Diwrnach's men can take her.'

He kissed the sword's tip. 'I swear it, Lord.'

At high tide the swirling currents died away so that the sea lay still except for the wind-fretted waves that had floated the two boats up from the shingle. We lifted the ponies on board, then took our places. The boats were long and narrow and, as soon as we had settled amidst the sticky fishing nets, the boatmen gestured that we were to bail out the water that seeped between the tarred planks. We used our helmets to scoop the cold sea back to its place and I prayed to Manawydan, the sea God, that he would preserve us as the boatmen put their long oars between the tholes. Merlin shivered. His face was whiter that I had ever seen it, but touched by a nauseous yellow and smeared by flecks of foam that dribbled from the corners of his lips. He was not conscious, but muttered odd things in his delirium.

The boatmen chanted a strange song as they pulled on their oars, but fell silent when they reached the middle of the straits.

They paused there and one man in each boat gestured back towards the mainland.

We turned. At first I could only see the dark strip of the shore beneath the snow-white and slate-black loom of the mountains beyond, but then I saw a ragged black thing moving just beyond the stony beach. It was a banner, mere fluttering strips of rags tied to a pole, but an instant after it appeared a line of warriors showed themselves above the strait's bank. They laughed at us, their cackling coming clear through the cold wind above the sound of the lapping sea. They were all mounted on shaggy ponies and all were dressed in what appeared to be torn strips of ragged black cloth that caught the breeze and fluttered like pennants. They carried shields and the hugely long war spears that the Irish favoured, and neither the shields nor the spears frightened me, but there was something about their tattered, long-haired wildness that struck a sudden chill through me. Or perhaps that chill came from the sleet that had begun to spit on the west wind to dimple the sea's grey surface.

The ragged, dark riders watched as our boats grounded on Ynys Mon. The boatmen helped us lift Merlin and the ponies safe ashore, then they ran their boats back into the sea.

'Shouldn't we have kept the boats here?' Galahad asked me.

'How?' I asked. 'We'd have to divide the men, some to guard the boats and some to go with Ceinwyn and Nimue.'

'So how do we get off the island?' Galahad asked.

'With the Cauldron,' I adopted Nimue's confidence, 'all things will be possible.' I had no other answer to give him and dared not tell him the truth. That truth was that I felt doomed. I felt as though the curses of those ancient Druids were even now congealing around our souls.

We struck north from the beach. Gulls screamed at us, whirling around us in the flying sleet as we climbed up from the rocks into a bleak moorland broken only by outcrops of stone. In the old days, before the Romans came to destroy Ynys Mon, the land had been thick with sacred oaks amongst which the greatest mysteries of Britain were performed. The news of those rituals governed the seasons in Britain, Ireland, and even Gaul, for here the Gods had come to earth, and here the link between man and the Gods had been strongest before it had been sundered by the short Roman stabbing swords. This was holy ground, but it was also difficult ground, for after just an hour's walking we came to a vast bog that seemed to bar our path into the island's interior. We ranged along the bog's edge, seeking a path, but there was none; so, as the light began to fade, we used our spear-shafts to discover the firmest passage through the spiky tussocks of grass and the sucking, treacherous patches of marsh. Our legs were soaked in freezing mud and the sleet found its way inside our furs. One of the ponies became stuck and the other began to panic, so we unloaded both beasts, distributed their remaining burdens amongst ourselves, then abandoned them.

We struggled on, sometimes resting on our circular shields that served like shallow coracles to support our weight until, inevitably, the brackish water seeped over their edges and forced us to stand again. The sleet became harder and thicker, whipped by a rising wind that flattened the marsh grass and drove the cold deep into our bones. Merlin was shouting strange words and thrashing his head from side to side, while some of my men were weakening, sapped by the cold as well as by the malevolence of whatever Gods now ruled this ruined land.

Nimue was the first to reach the bog's far side. She leapt from tussock to tussock, showing us a path, and finally reached firm ground where she jumped up and down to show us that safety was close. Then, for a few seconds, she froze before pointing Merlin's staff back the way we had come.

We turned to see that the dark riders were with us, only now there were more of them; a whole horde of tattered Bloodshields was watching us from the bog's far side. Three ragged banners were hoisted above them, and one of those banners was lifted in ironic salute before the riders turned their ponies eastwards. 'I should never have brought you here,' I said to Ceinwyn.

'You didn't bring me, Derfel,' she said. 'I came of my own

will.' She touched a gloved finger to my face. 'And we shall leave the same way, my love.'

We climbed up from the bog to find, beyond a low crest, a landscape of small fields that lay between lumpish moors and sudden rock outcrops. We needed a refuge for the night and found it in a settlement of eight stone huts that were circled by a wall the height of a spear. The place was deserted, though people clearly lived there for the small stone huts were swept clean and the ashes in the hearth were still just warm to the touch. We stripped the turf roof off one hut and cut the roof timbers into shreds with which we made a fire for Merlin, who was now shivering and raving. We set a guard, then stripped off our furs and tried to dry our sopping boots and wet leggings.

Then, as the very last of the light seeped from the grey sky, I went to stand on the wall and searched all about the landscape. I saw nothing.

Four of us stood guard for the first part of the night, then Galahad and another three spearmen watched through the rest of that rainy darkness and not one of us heard anything other than the wind and the crackle of the fire in the hut. We heard nothing, we saw nothing, yet in the morning's first wan light there was a newly severed head of a sheep dripping blood on one part of the wall.

Nimue angrily pushed the sheep's head off the wall's coping, then screamed a challenge towards the sky. She took a pouch of grey powder and scattered it on the fresh blood, and afterwards she rapped the wall with Merlin's staff and told us the malevolence had been countered. We believed her because we wanted to believe her, just as we wanted to believe that Merlin was not dying. But he was deathly pale, breathing shallowly and making no sound. We tried to feed him with the last of our bread, but he clumsily spat the crumbs out. 'We must find the Cauldron today,' Nimue said calmly, 'before he dies.' We gathered our burdens, hoisted our shields onto our backs, picked up our spears and followed her northwards.

Nimue led us. Merlin had told her all he knew of the sacred

isle and that knowledge took us northwards all morning long. The Bloodshields appeared soon after we had left our shelter and, now that we neared our goal, they became bolder so that at any one time there were always a score in sight and sometimes three times that number. They formed a loose ring about us, but took care to stay well outside the range of our spears. The sleet had stopped with the dawn, leaving just a cold, damp wind that bent the grass on the moors and lifted the black tatters of the dark riders' cloaks.

It was just after midday that we came to the place Nimue called Llyn Cerrig Bach. The name means the 'lake of little stones' and it was a dark sheet of shallow water, surrounded by bogs. Here, Nimue said, the old Britons had held their most sacred ceremonies, and here too, she told us, our search would begin; but it seemed a bleak place in which to seek the greatest Treasure of Britain. To the west was a small, shallow neck of the sea beyond which lay another island, to the south and north were just farmlands and rocks, and to the east there rose a very small steep hill that was crowned with a group of grey rocks like a score of other such outcrops we had passed that morning. Merlin lay as if dead. I had to kneel beside him and put my ear close to his face to hear the tiny scratching of each laboured breath. I laid my hand on his forehead and found it was cold. I kissed his cheek. 'Live, Lord,' I whispered to him, 'live.'

Nimue told one of my men to plant a spear in the ground. He forced the point into the hard soil, then Nimue took a half dozen cloaks and, by hanging them from the spear's butt and weighting their hems with stones, she formed a kind of tent. The dark riders made a ring about us, but stayed far enough away so that they could not interfere with us, nor we with them.

Nimue groped under her otter skins and brought out the silver cup from which I had drunk on Dolforwyn and a small clay bottle stoppered with wax. She ducked under the tent and beckoned Ceinwyn to follow.

I waited and watched as the wind chased black ripples across the lake, then suddenly Ceinwyn screamed. She screamed again, terribly, and I started towards the tent, only to be stopped by Issa's spear. Galahad, who as a Christian was not supposed to believe in any of this, stood beside Issa and shrugged at me. 'We've come this far,' he said. 'We should see it to the end.'

Ceinwyn screamed again, and this time Merlin echoed the noise by uttering a faint and pathetic moan. I knelt beside him and stroked his forehead and tried not to think what horrors Ceinwyn dreamed inside the black tent.

'Lord?' Issa called to me.

I twisted round to see that he was looking southwards to where a new group of riders had joined the Bloodshields' ring. Most of the newcomers were on ponies, but one man was mounted on a gaunt black horse. That man, I knew, had to be Diwrnach. His banner flew behind him; a pole on which was mounted a crosspiece and from the crosspiece there hung two skulls and a clutch of black ribbons. The King was cloaked in black and his black horse was hung with a black saddle cloth, and in his hand was a great black spear that he raised vertically into the air before riding slowly forward. He came alone and when he was fifty paces from us he unslung his round shield and ostentatiously turned it about to show that he did not come looking for a fight.

I walked to meet him. Behind me Ceinwyn gasped and moaned inside the tent about which my men made a protective ring.

The King was dressed in black leather armour beneath his cloak and wore no helmet. His shield looked flaky with rust and I supposed the flakes had to be the layers of dried blood, just as its leather covering had to be the flayed skin of a slave girl. He let the grim shield hang beside his long black sword scabbard as he curbed his horse and rested the great spear's butt on the ground. 'I am Diwrnach,' he said.

I bowed my head to him. 'I am Derfel, Lord King.'

He smiled. 'Welcome to Ynys Mon, Lord Derfel Cadarn,' he said, and doubtless he wanted to surprise me by knowing my full name and title, but he astonished me more by being a good-looking man. I had expected a hook-nosed ghoul, a thing from nightmare, but Diwrnach was in early middle age and had a broad forehead, a wide mouth and a short clipped black beard that accentuated his strong jawline. There was nothing mad about his appearance, but he did have one red eye and that was enough to make him fearsome. He leaned his spear against his horse's flank and took an oatcake from a pouch. 'You look hungry, Lord Derfel,' he said.

'Winter is a time for hunger, Lord King.'

'But you will not refuse my gift, surely?' He broke the oatcake into halves and tossed one half to me. 'Eat.'

I caught the oatcake, then hesitated. 'I am sworn not to eat, Lord King, till my purpose is finished.'

'Your purpose!' he teased me, then slowly put his half of the oatcake into his mouth. 'It wasn't poisoned, Lord Derfel,' he said when it was eaten.

'Why should it be, Lord King?'

'Because I am Diwrnach and I kill my enemies in so many ways.' He smiled again. 'Tell me about your purpose, Lord Derfel.'

'I come to pray, Lord King.'

'Ah!' he said, drawing the sound out as if to suggest that I had cleared up all the mystery. 'Are prayers said in Dumnonia so very ineffective?'

'This is holy ground, Lord King,' I said.

'It is also my ground, Lord Derfel Cadarn,' he said, 'and I believe strangers should seek my permission before they dung its soil or piss on its walls.'

'If we have offended you, Lord King,' I said, 'then we apologize.'

'Too late for that,' he said mildly. 'You are here now, Lord Derfel, and I can smell your dung. Too late. So what shall I do with you?' His voice was low, almost gentle, suggesting that here was a man who would see reason very easily. 'What shall I do with you?' he asked again, and I said nothing. The ring of dark riders was unmoving, the sky was leaden with cloud and

Ceinwyn's moans had subsided to small whimpers. The King lifted his shield, not in threat but because its weight rested uncomfortably on his hip, and I saw with horror that the skin of a human arm and hand hung from its lower edge. The wind stirred the fat fingers of the hand. Diwrnach saw my horror and smiled. 'She was my niece,' he said, then he stared past me and another slow smile showed on his face. 'The vixen is out of the covert, Lord Derfel,' he said.

I turned to see that Ceinwyn had come out from under the tent. She had discarded her wolfskins and was dressed in the bone-white dress she had worn to her betrothal feast, its hems still soiled by the mud she had kicked onto the linen when she had run away from Caer Sws. She was barefoot, her golden hair had been unloosed and to me it seemed she was in a trance. 'The Princess Ceinwyn, I believe,' Diwrnach said.

'Indeed, Lord King.'

'And still a maid, I hear?' the King asked. I said nothing in answer. Diwrnach leaned forward to ruffle his horse's ears fondly. 'It would have been courteous of her, do you not think, to have greeted me when she arrived in my country?'

'She too has prayers to say, Lord King.'

'Then let us hope they work.' He laughed. 'Give her to me, Lord Derfel, or else you will die the slowest of deaths. I have men who can take the skin from a man inch by inch until he is nothing but a thing of raw flesh and blood and yet still he can stand. He can even walk!' He patted his horse's neck with a black-gloved hand, then smiled on me again. 'I have choked men on their own dung, Lord Derfel, I have pressed them beneath the stones, I have burned them, I have buried them alive, I have bedded them down with vipers, I have drowned them, I have starved them and I have even frightened them to death. So many interesting ways, but just give the Princess Ceinwyn to me, Lord Derfel, and I will promise you a death as swift as a bright star's fall.'

Ceinwyn had started to walk westwards and my men had snatched up Merlin's litter, their cloaks, weapons and bundles, and were now going with her. I looked up at Diwrnach. 'One day, Lord King,' I said, 'I will put your head in a pit and bury it in slave dung.' I walked away from him.

He laughed. 'Blood, Lord Derfel!' he shouted after me. 'Blood! It's what the Gods feed on, and yours will make a rich brew! I'll make your woman drink it in my bed!' And with that he kicked back his spurred boots and wheeled his horse towards his men.

'Seventy-four of them,' Galahad told me as I caught up with him. 'Seventy-four men and spears. And we are thirty-six spears, one dying man and two women.'

'They won't attack yet,' I reassured him. 'They'll wait till we've discovered the Cauldron.'

Ceinwyn must have been freezing in her thin dress and without any boots, but she was sweating as if it was a summer's day as she staggered across the grass. She was finding it difficult to stand, let alone walk, and she was twitching just as I had twitched on Dolforwyn's summit after drinking from the silver cup; but Nimue was beside her, talking to her and supporting her, but also, oddly, tugging her away from the direction she wanted to take. Diwrnach's dark riders were keeping pace with us, a moving ring of Bloodshields that moved across the island in a loose, wide circle that was centred on our small party.

Ceinwyn, despite her dizziness, was almost running now. She seemed barely conscious and was mouthing words I could not catch. Her eyes looked empty. Nimue constantly dragged her to one side, making her follow a sheep path that twisted north about the knoll that was crowned with grey stones, but the closer we came to those high and lichen-covered rocks the more Ceinwyn resisted until Nimue was forced to use all her wiry strength to keep her on the narrow path. The front edge of the ring of dark riders had already gone past the steep knoll so that it, like us, lay within their circle. Ceinwyn was whimpering and protesting, then she began to hit at Nimue's hands, but Nimue held her hard and dragged her on, and all the while Diwrnach's men moved with us.

Nimue waited until the path was at its closest point to the steep crest of rocks, then at last she let Ceinwyn run free. 'To the rocks!' she shrieked. 'All of you! To the rocks! Run!'

We ran. I saw then what Nimue had done. Diwrnach dared not touch us until he knew where we were going and if he had seen Ceinwyn heading for the rocky knoll he would surely have sent a dozen spearmen to garrison its summit, then sent the rest of his men to capture us. But now, thanks to Nimue's cleverness, we would have the steep jumble of huge boulders to protect us, the same boulders, if Ceinwyn was right, that had protected the Cauldron of Clyddno Eiddyn through more than four and a half centuries of gathering darkness. 'Run!' Nimue screamed, and all about us the ponies were being whipped inwards as the ring of dark riders closed to cut us off.

'Run!' Nimue shrieked again. I was helping to carry Merlin, Ceinwyn was already clambering up the rocks and Galahad was shouting at men to find themselves places where they could stand amidst the stones and use their spears. Issa stayed with me, his spear ready to cut down any dark rider who came close. Gwilym and three others snatched Merlin from us and carried him to the foot of the rocks just as the two leading Bloodshields reached us. They shrieked a challenge as they kicked their ponies up the hill, but I knocked the first man's long spear aside with my shield then swung my own spear so that its steel blade cracked like a club across the pony's skull. The beast screamed and fell sideways and Issa slid his spear into the rider's belly while I slashed my spear back at the second rider. His spear-shaft clattered on mine, then he was past me, but I managed to seize a handful of his long tattered ribbons and so dragged him backwards off the small beast. He flailed at me as he fell. I put a boot on his throat, raised the spear and rammed it hard down at his heart. There was a leather breastplate beneath his ragged tunic, but the spear cut through both and suddenly his black beard was frothing with a bloody foam.

'Back!' Galahad shouted at us, and Issa and I tossed our shields and spears to the men already safe on the high rocks' summit, then clambered up ourselves. A black-shafted spear clattered on the rocks beside me, then a strong hand reached down, grasped my wrist and hauled me up. Merlin had been similarly dragged up the rocks, then unceremoniously dropped in the summit's centre where, like a cup crowned by the ring of vast boulders, there was a deep stony hollow. Ceinwyn was in that hollow, scrabbling like a frantic dog at the little stones that filled the cup. She had vomited and her hands obliviously scratched among the mix of vomit and small cold stones.

The knoll was ideal for defence. Our enemy could only climb the rocks with hands and feet, while we could shelter in the clefts of the summit's crown to deal with them as they appeared. A few tried to reach us, and those men screamed as the blades slashed into their faces. A shower of spears was thrown at us, but we held our shields aloft and the weapons clattered harmlessly away. I put six men down in the central hollow and they used their shields to shelter Merlin, Nimue and Ceinwyn while the other spearmen guarded the summit's outer rim. The Blood-shields, their ponies abandoned, made one more rush and for a few moments we were busy stabbing and lunging. One of my men took a spear cut on his arm during that brief fight, but otherwise we were unhurt, while the dark riders carried four dead and six wounded men back to the knoll's foot. 'So much,' I told my men, 'for shields made of virgins' skins.'

We waited for another attack, but none came. Instead Diwrnach walked his horse up the slope alone. 'Lord Derfel?' he called in his deceptively pleasant voice and, when I showed my face between two rocks, he offered me his placid smile. 'My price has risen,' the King said. 'Now, in return for your swift death, I demand the Princess Ceinwyn and the Cauldron. It is the Cauldron that you've come for, is it not?'

'It is all Britain's Cauldron, Lord King,' I said.

'Ah! And you think I would be an unworthy guardian?' He shook his head sadly. 'Lord Derfel, you do insult a man so very easily. What was it to be? My head in a pit being dunged by slaves? What a paltry imagination you do have. Mine, I fear, sometimes seems excessive, even to me.' He paused and glanced towards the sky as if judging how much daylight remained. 'I have few enough warriors, Lord Derfel,' he went on in his reasonable voice, 'and I do not want to lose any more of them to your spears. But sooner or later you must come out of the rocks and I shall wait for you, and as I wait I shall let my imagination rise to new heights of achievement. Give the Princess Ceinwyn my greetings, and tell her I so look forward to a closer acquaintance.' He raised his spear in mocking salute, then rode back to the ring of dark riders who now had the knoll entirely surrounded.

I let myself down into the bowl in the knoll's centre and saw that whatever we found here would prove too late for Merlin; death was plain on his face. His jaw was hanging open and his eyes were as empty as the space between the worlds. His teeth chattered once to show he was still alive, but that life was a thread now and it was fraying fast. Nimue had taken Ceinwyn's knife and was scratching and clawing at the small stones that filled the hollow of the summit, while Ceinwyn, her face looking exhausted, had slumped against a rock where she shivered and watched as Nimue dug. Whatever trance had possessed Ceinwyn had now passed and I helped her clean the mess from her hands, found her suit of wolfskins and covered her over.

She pulled on her gloves. 'I had a dream,' she whispered to me, 'and saw the end.'

'Our end?' I asked in alarm.

She shook her head. 'Ynys Mon's end. There were lines of soldiers, Derfel, in Roman skirts and breastplates and bronze helmets. Great hunting lines of soldiers and their sword arms were bloody to their shoulders because they just killed and killed. They came through the forests in a great line, just killing. Arms going up and down, and all the women and children running away, only there was nowhere to run and the soldiers just closed on them and chopped them down. Little children, Derfel!'

'And the Druids?'

'All dead. All but three, and they brought the Cauldron here. They'd made a pit for it already, you see, before the Romans crossed the water, and they buried it here, then covered it with stones from the lake, and after that they put ashes on the stones and lifted fire with their bare hands so that the Romans would think nothing could be buried here. And when that was done they walked singing into the woods to die.'

Nimue hissed in alarm, and I twisted around to see that she had uncovered a small skeleton. She fumbled among her otter skins and brought out a leather bag that she tore open to take out two dried plants. They had spiky leaves and small, faded golden flowers and I knew she was placating the dead bones with a gift of asphodel. 'It was a child they buried,' Ceinwyn explained the smallness of the bones, 'the guardian of the Cauldron and the daughter of one of the three Druids. She had short hair and a fox-skin bracelet on her wrist, and they buried her alive so she would guard the Cauldron till we found it.'

Nimue, the dead soul of the Cauldron's guardian placated by the asphodel, dragged the girl's bones from the small stones, then attacked the deepening hole with her knife and snapped at me to come and help her. 'Dig with your sword, Derfel!' she ordered, and I obediently thrust Hywelbane's tip into the pit.

And found the Cauldron.

At first it was just a glimpse of dirty gold, then a sweep of Nimue's hand showed a heavy golden rim. The Cauldron was much bigger than the hole we had made and so I ordered Issa and another man to help make it wider. We scooped the stones out with our helmets, working in a desperate haste for Merlin's soul was flickering out the very last of his long life. Nimue was panting and weeping as she attacked the tight packed stones that had been brought to this summit from the sacred lake of Llyn Cerrig Bach.

'He's dead!' Ceinwyn cried. She was kneeling beside Merlin.

'He is not dead!' Nimue spat between clenched teeth, then she seized the golden rim with both her hands and began to tug at the Cauldron with all her strength. I joined her, and it seemed impossible that the huge vessel could be moved with all the weight of stones that still pressed into its deep belly; but somehow, with the Gods' help, we shifted that great thing of gold and silver out of its dark pit.

And thus we brought the lost Cauldron of Clyddno Eiddyn into the light.

It was a great bowl as wide as a man's outstretched hands and as deep as the blade of a hunting knife. It was made of thick uneven silver, stood on three short golden legs and was decorated with lavish traceries of gold. Three golden hoops were fixed to its rim so that it could be hung above a fire. It was the greatest Treasure of Britain and we ripped it from its grave, shedding stones, and I saw how the gold that decorated it was shaped into warriors and Gods and deer. But we had no time to admire the Cauldron, for Nimue frantically scattered the last stones from its belly and placed it back in the hole before tearing the black furs from Merlin's body. 'Help me!' she screamed, and together we rolled the old man into the pit and down into the belly of the great silver bowl. Nimue tucked his legs inside the golden rim and laid a cloak over him. Only then did Nimue lean back against the boulders. It was freezing, but her face was shining with sweat.

'He's dead,' Ceinwyn said in a small, frightened voice.

'No,' Nimue insisted tiredly, 'no, he's not.'

'He was cold!' Ceinwyn protested. 'He was cold and there was no breath.' She clung to me and began weeping softly. 'He's dead.'

'He lives,' Nimue said harshly.

It had begun to rain again; a small, spitting, wind-hurried rain that slicked the stones and beaded our bloodied spear-blades. Merlin lay shrouded and unmoving in the Cauldron's pit, my men watched the enemy across the tops of the grey stones, the dark riders ringed us and I wondered what madness had brought us to this miserable place at the dark cold end of Britain.

'So what do we do now?' Galahad asked.

'We wait,' Nimue snapped, 'we just wait.'

I will never forget the cold of that night. Frost made crystals on the rock and to touch a spear-blade was to leave a scrap of skin frozen to the steel. It was so bitterly cold. The rain turned to snow at dusk, then stopped, and after the snow's passing the wind dropped and the clouds sailed off to the east to reveal an enormous moon rising full above the sea. It was a moon full of portent; a great swollen silver ball that was hazed by a shimmer of distant cloud above an ocean crawling with black and silver waves. The stars had never seemed so bright. The great shape of Bel's chariot blazed above us, eternally chasing the constellation we called the trout. The Gods lived among the stars and I sent a prayer winging up through the cold air in the hope that it would reach those far bright fires.

Some of us dozed, but it was the shallow sleep of weary, cold and frightened men. Our enemies, ringing the knoll with their spears, had made fires. Ponies brought the Bloodshields fuel and the flames burned vast in the night to spew sparks into the clear sky.

Nothing moved in the Cauldron's pit where Merlin's cloaked body was shadowed from the moon by the loom of high rock where we took turns to watch the riders' shapes against the fires. At times a long spear would fly out of the night and its head would glitter in the moonlight before the weapon clattered harmlessly against the stones.

'So what will you do with the Cauldron now?' I asked Nimue.

'Nothing till Samain,' she said dully. She lay crumpled near the heap of discarded bundles that had been thrown into the summit's hollow, her feet resting on the spoil we had scrabbled so desperately from the pit. 'Everything has to be right, Derfel. The moon must be full, the weather right and all the thirteen Treasures assembled.'

'Tell me of the Treasures,' Galahad said from the hollow's farther side.

Nimue spat. 'So you can mock us, Christian?' she challenged him.

Galahad smiled. 'There are thousands of folk, Nimue, who mock you. They say the Gods are dead and that we should put our faith in men. We should follow Arthur, they say, and they believe your search for cauldrons and cloaks and knives and horns is so much nonsense that died with Ynys Mon. How many Kings of Britain would send you men for this search?' He stirred, trying to find some comfort in this cold night. 'None, Nimue, none, because they mock you. It's all too late, they say. The Romans changed everything and sensible men say that your Cauldron is as dead as Ynys Trebes. The Christians say you are doing the devil's work, but this Christian, dear Nimue, carried his sword to this place and for that, dear lady, you owe me at least civility.'

Nimue was not used to being reprimanded, except perhaps by Merlin, and she stiffened at Galahad's mild rebuke, but then at last she relented. She pulled Merlin's bearskin about her shoulders and hunched forward. 'The Treasures,' she said, 'were left to us by the Gods. It was long ago, when Britain was quite alone in all the world. There were no other lands; just Britain and a wide sea that was covered by a great mist. There were twelve tribes of Britain then, and twelve Kings and twelve feasting halls and just twelve Gods. Those Gods walked as we do on the land and one of them, Bel, even married a human; our Lady here,' she gestured towards Ceinwyn, who was listening as avidly as any of the spearmen, 'is descended from that marriage.'

She paused as a shout sounded from the ring of fires, but the shout presaged no threat and silence fell on the night again as Nimue went on with her tale. 'But other Gods who were jealous of the twelve who ruled Britain came from the stars and tried to take Britain from the twelve Gods, and in the battles the twelve tribes suffered. One spear stroke from a God could kill a hundred people, and no earthly shield could stop a God's sword, so the twelve Gods, because they loved Britain, gave the twelve tribes twelve Treasures. Each Treasure was to be kept in a royal hall and the presence of the Treasure would keep the spears of the Gods from falling on the hall or any of its people. They were not grand things. If the twelve Gods had given us splendid things then the other Gods would have seen them, guessed their purpose and stolen them for their own protection. So the twelve gifts were just common things: a sword, a basket, a horn, a chariot, a halter, a knife, a whetstone, a sleeved coat, a cloak, a dish, a throwboard and a warrior ring. Twelve ordinary things, and all the Gods asked of us was that we should cherish the twelve Treasures, to keep them safe and offer them honour, and in return, as well as having the protection of the Treasures, each tribe could use its gift to summon their God. They were allowed one summons a year, only one, but that summons gave the tribes some power in the terrible war of the Gods.'

She paused and pulled the furs tighter about her thin shoulders. 'So the tribes had their Treasures,' she went on, 'but Bel, because he loved his earthly girl so very much, gave her a thirteenth Treasure. He gave her the Cauldron and he told her that whenever she began to grow old she had only to fill the Cauldron with water, immerse herself, and she would be young again. Thus, in all her beauty, she could walk beside Bel for ever and ever. And the Cauldron, as you saw, is splendid; it is gold and silver, lovely beyond anything man can make. The other tribes saw it and were jealous, and in this way the wars of Britain began. The Gods warred in the air and the twelve tribes warred on earth, and one by one the Treasures were captured, or else they were bartered for spearmen, and in their anger the Gods withdrew their protection. The Cauldron was stolen, Bel's lover grew old and died, and Bel placed a curse on us. The curse was the existence of other lands and other peoples, but Bel promised us that if one Samain we drew the twelve Treasures of the twelve tribes together again and made the proper rites, and filled the thirteenth Treasure with the water that no man drinks but without which no man can live, then the twelve Gods would come to our aid again.' She stopped, shrugged and looked at

Galahad. 'There, Christian,' she said, 'that is why your sword came here.'

There was a long silence. The moonlight slid down the rocks, creeping ever nearer to the pit where Merlin lay beneath the thin cover of a cloak.

'And you have all twelve Treasures?' Ceinwyn asked.

'Most,' Nimue said evasively. 'But even without the twelve, the Cauldron has immense power. Vast power. More power than all the other Treasures together.' She looked belligerently across the pit towards Galahad. 'And what will you do, Christian, when you see that power?'

Galahad smiled. 'I shall remind you that I carried my sword in your quest,' he said softly.

'We all did. We are the warriors of the Cauldron,' Issa said quietly, displaying a streak of poetry I had not suspected in him, and the other spearmen smiled. Their beards were frosted white, their hands were wrapped in strips of cloth and fur and their eyes looked hollow, but they had found the Cauldron and the pride of that achievement filled them, even if, at first light, they must face the Bloodshields and the dawning knowledge that we were all doomed.

Ceinwyn leaned against me, sharing my wolfskin cloak. She waited till Nimue was sleeping, then tipped her face up to mine. 'Merlin's dead, Derfel,' she said in a small sad voice.

'I know,' I said, for there had been neither motion nor sound from the Cauldron's pit.

'I felt his face and hands,' she whispered, 'and they were cold as ice. I put my knife blade beside his mouth and it didn't cloud. He's dead.'

I said nothing. I loved Merlin because he had stood to me as a father and I could not truly believe he had died at this moment of his triumph, but nor could I find the hope to see his life's soul again. 'We should bury him here,' Ceinwyn said softly, 'inside his Cauldron.' Again I did not speak. Her hand found mine. 'What shall we do?' she asked.

Die, I thought, but still I said nothing.

'You will not let me be taken?' she whispered.

'Never,' I said.

'The day I met you, Lord Derfel Cadarn,' she said, 'was the best day of my life,' and that made my tears come, but whether they were tears of joy or a lament for all that I would lose in the next cold dawn, I do not know.

I fell into a shallow sleep and dreamed I was trapped in a bog and surrounded by dark riders who were magically able to move across the soaking land, and then I found I could not raise my shield arm and I saw the sword coming down on my right shoulder and I woke with a start, reaching for my spear, only to see that it was Gwilym who had inadvertently touched my shoulder as he clambered up the rock to take over guard duty. 'Sorry, Lord,' he whispered.

Ceinwyn slept in the crook of my arm and Nimue was huddled on my other side. Galahad, his fair beard whitened by frost, was snoring gently and my other spearmen either dozed or else lay in cold stupefaction. The moon was almost above me now, its light slanting down to show the stars painted on my men's stacked shields and on the stony side of the pit we had scrabbled in the summit's hollow. The mist that had shimmered the moon's swollen face when it had hung just above the sea was gone and now it was a pure, hard, clear, cold disc etched as sharp as a newly minted coin. I half remembered my mother telling me the name of the man in the moon, but I could not pin the memory down. My mother was a Saxon and I had been in her belly when she had been captured in a Dumnonian raid. I had been told she was still alive in Siluria, but I had not seen her since the day the Druid Tanaburs had snatched me from her arms and tried to kill me in the death pit. Merlin had raised me after that, and I had become a Briton, a friend of Arthur and the man who had taken the star of Powys from her brother's hall. What an odd thread of life, I thought, and how sad that it would be cut short here on Britain's sacred isle.

'I don't suppose,' Merlin said, 'that there is any cheese?'

I stared at him, thinking I must still be dreaming.

'The pale sort, Derfel,' he said anxiously, 'that crumbles. Not the hard dark yellow stuff. I can't abide that hard dark yellow cheese.'

He was standing in the pit and peering earnestly at me with the cloak that had covered his body now hanging about his shoulders like a shawl.

'Lord?' I said in a tiny voice.

'Cheese, Derfel. Did you not hear me? I am hungry for cheese. We did have some. It was wrapped in linen. And where is my staff? A man lies down for a small sleep and immediately his staff is stolen. Is there no honesty left? It's a terrible world. No cheese, no honesty and no staff.'

'Lord!'

'Stop shouting at me, Derfel. I'm not deaf, just hungry.'

'Oh, Lord!'

'Now you're weeping! I do hate blubbing. All I ask is a morsel of cheese and you start weeping like a child. Ah, there's my staff. Good.' He plucked it from beside Nimue and used it to hoist himself out of the pit. The other spearmen were awake now and gaping at him. Then Nimue stirred and I heard Ceinwyn gasp. 'I suppose, Derfel,' Merlin said as he began rummaging in the piled bundles to find his cheese, 'that you've landed us in a predicament? Surrounded, are we?'

'Yes, Lord.'

'Outnumbered?'

'Yes, Lord.'

'Dear me, Derfel, dear me. And you call yourself a lord of warriors? Cheese! Here it is. I knew we had some. Wonderful.'

I pointed a tremulous finger at the pit. 'The Cauldron, Lord.' I wanted to know whether the Cauldron had performed a miracle, but I was too confused with wonder and relief to be coherent.

'And a very nice Cauldron it is, Derfel. Capacious, deep, full of the qualities one wants in a cauldron.' He bit a hunk of the cheese. 'I am famished!' He took another bite, then settled back against the rocks and beamed at us all. 'Outnumbered and surrounded! Well, well! Whatever next?' He crammed the last of the cheese into his mouth then brushed the crumbs from his hands. He bestowed a special smile on Ceinwyn, then held out a long arm for Nimue. 'All well?' he asked her.

'All well,' she said calmly as she settled into his embrace. She alone did not seem surprised by his appearance or by his evident health.

'Except that we're surrounded and outnumbered!' he said mockingly. 'What shall we do? Usually the best thing to do in an emergency is to sacrifice someone.' He peered expectantly about the stunned circle of men. His face had recovered its colour and all his old mischievous energy had returned. 'Derfel, perhaps?'

'Lord!' Ceinwyn protested.

'Lady! Not you! No, no, no, no, no. You've done enough.'

'No sacrifice, Lord,' Ceinwyn pleaded.

Merlin smiled. Nimue appeared to have gone to sleep in his arm, but for the rest of us there could be no more sleep. A spear clattered on the lower rocks and the sound made Merlin hold his staff out to me. 'Climb to the top, Derfel, and hold my staff to the west. To the west, remember, not the east. Try and do something right for a change, will you? Of course, if you want a job done properly then you should always do it yourself, but I don't want to wake Nimue. Off you go.'

I took the staff and clambered up the rocks to stand on the highest point of the knoll and there, following Merlin's instructions, I pointed it towards the distant sea.

'Don't prod with it!' Merlin called up to me. 'Point it! Feel its power! It isn't an ox goad, boy, it's a Druid's staff!'

I held the staff westward. Diwrnach's dark riders must have scented magic, for his own sorcerers suddenly howled and a pack of spearmen scuttled up the slope to hurl their weapons at me.

'Now,' Merlin called as the spears fell beneath me, 'give it power, Derfel, give it power!' I concentrated on the staff, but truly felt nothing, though Merlin seemed satisfied with my effort. 'Bring it down now,' he said, 'and get some rest. We have a fair walk to make in the morning. Is there any more cheese? I could eat a sackful!'

We lay in the cold. Merlin would not discuss the Cauldron, nor his illness, but I sensed the change of mood in all of us. We were suddenly hopeful. We would live, and it was Ceinwyn who first saw the way of our salvation. She prodded my side, then pointed up at the moon, and I saw that what had been a clear, clean shape was now hazed by a torque of shimmering mist. That misty torque looked like a ring of powdered gems, so hard and bright did those tiny points shine about the full silver moon.

Merlin did not care about the moon, he was still talking of cheese. 'There used to be a woman in Dun Seilo who made the most wonderful soft cheese,' he told us. 'She wrapped it in nettle leaves as I remember, then insisted it spent six months sitting in a wooden bowl that had been steeped in ram's urine. Ram's urine! Some people do possess the most absurd superstitions, but all the same her cheese was very good.' He chuckled. 'She made her poor husband collect the urine. How did he do it? I never liked to ask. Grasp it by the horns and tickle, do you think? Or maybe he used his own and never told her. I would have done. Is it getting warmer, do you think?'

The glittering ice mist about the moon had faded, but the fading had not made the moon's edges any duller. Instead they were being diffused by a gentler mist that was now being wafted on a small west wind that was indeed warmer. The bright stars were hazed, the crystal frost on the rocks was melting to a wet sheen and we had all stopped shivering. Our spear-points could be touched again. A fog was forming.

'The Dumnonians, of course, insist their cheese is the very finest in Britain,' Merlin said earnestly, as though none of us had anything better to do than listen to a lecture on cheese, 'and, admittedly, it can be good, but too often it is hard. I remember Uther broke a tooth once on a piece of cheese from a farm near Lindinis. Clean in two! Poor fellow was in pain for weeks. He never could abide having a tooth pulled. He insisted I work some magic, but it's a strange thing, magic never works with teeth. Eyes, yes, bowels, every time, and even brains sometimes, though there's few enough of those in Britain these days. But teeth? Never. I must work on that problem when I have some time. Mind you, I do enjoy pulling teeth.' He smiled extravagantly, showing off his own rare set of perfect teeth. Arthur was similarly blessed, but the rest of us were plagued by toothaches.

I looked up to see that the topmost rocks were almost hidden by the fog that was thickening by the minute. It was a Druid's fog, brewing dense and white beneath the moon and smothering the whole of Ynys Mon in its thick cloak of vapour.

'In Siluria,' Merlin said, 'they serve a pale bowl of slops and call it cheese. It's so repellent that even the mice won't eat it, but what else does one expect of Siluria? Was there something you wished to say to me, Derfel? You look excited.'

'Fog, Lord,' I said.

'What an observant man you are,' he said admiringly. 'So perhaps you would pull the Cauldron from the pit? It's time we went, Derfel, it's time we went.'

And so we did.

PART TWO

The Broken War

'No!' Igraine protested, when she looked at the last parchment in the pile.

'No?' I asked politely.

'You can't just leave the story there!' she said. 'What happened?'

'We walked out, of course.'

'Oh, Derfel!' She threw the parchment down. 'There are scullions who know how to tell a tale better than you! Tell me how it happened, I insist!'

So I told her.

It was near dawn and the fog lay like a fleece so thick that when we managed to descend the rocks and assemble on the grass at the top of the knoll we were in danger of losing each other by taking just one step. Merlin made us form a chain, each person holding the cloak of the one in front, and then, with the Cauldron tied to my back, we crept downhill in single file. Merlin, with his staff held at arm's length, led us clean through the surrounding Bloodshields and not one of them saw us. I could hear Diwrnach shouting at them, telling them to spread out, but the dark riders knew it was a wizard's fog and they preferred to stay close by their fires; yet those first few steps were the most dangerous part of our journey.

'But the stories,' my Queen insisted, 'say that you all disappeared. Diwrnach's men claimed that you flew off the island. It's a famous story! My mother told it to me. You can't just say that you walked away!'

'But we did,' I said.

'Derfel!' she reprimanded me.

'We neither disappeared,' I said patiently, 'nor did we fly, whatever your mother might have told you.'

'So what happened then?' she asked, still disappointed in my pedestrian version of the tale.

We walked for hours, following Nimue who possessed an uncanny ability to find her way in darkness or fog. It was Nimue who had led my war-band on the night before Lugg Vale, and now, in that thick winter fog in Ynys Mon, she led us to one of the great grassy hummocks that had been made by the Old People. Merlin knew the place, indeed he claimed to have slept there years before, and he ordered three of my men to pull away the stones that blocked the entrance which lay between two curving banks of grassy earth that jutted out like horns. Then, one by one, on our hands and knees, we crawled into the mound's black centre.

The mound was a grave and it had been made by piling huge rocks to make a central passageway off which branched six smaller chambers, and when the whole thing was done the Old People had roofed the corridor and chambers with stone slabs, then piled earth above the stones. They did not burn their dead as we did, or leave them in the cold earth like Christians, but placed them in the stone chambers where they still lay, each with treasures: horn cups, deer antlers, stone spearheads, flint knives, a bronze dish and a necklace of precious pieces of jet that were strung on a decayed thread of sinew. Merlin insisted we should not disturb the dead for we were their guests, and we huddled together in the central passage and left the bone-chambers alone. We sang songs and told tales. Merlin told us how the Old People had been the guardians of Britain before the British came and there were places, he said, where they still lived. He had been to those deep lost valleys in the wilds and had learned some of their magic. He told us how they would take the first lamb born in the year, bind it in wicker and bury it in a pasture to ensure that the other lambs would be born healthy and strong.

'We still do that,' said Issa.

'Because your ancestors learned from the Old People,' Merlin said.

'In Benoic,' Galahad said, 'we used to take the skin of the first lamb and nail it to a tree.'

'That works too.' Merlin's voice echoed in the cool, dark passage.

'Poor lambs,' Ceinwyn said, and everyone laughed.

The fog lifted, but deep in the mound we had little sense of night or day except when we unblocked the entrance so that some of us could creep out. We had to do that from time to time if we were not to live in our own dung, and if it was daylight when we pulled down the stones then we would hide between the mound's earth horns and watch the dark riders searching the fields, caves, moors, rocks, cabins and small woods of wind-bent trees. They searched for five long days, and in that time we ate the last scraps of our food and drank the water that seeped down through the mound, but at last Diwrnach decided that our magic was superior to his and abandoned his search. We waited two more days to make sure he was not trying to entice us out of our hiding place, and then, at last, we left. We added gold to the treasures of the dead as payment of rent, we blocked the entrance behind us, then walked eastwards under a wintry sun. Once at the coast we used our swords to commandeer two fishing boats and so sailed away from the sacred isle. We went east, and as long as I live I shall remember the sun glinting from the Cauldron's golden ornaments and thick silver belly as the ragged sails dragged us to safety. We made a song as we sailed, the Song of the Cauldron, and even to this day it is sometimes sung, though it is a poor thing compared with the songs of the bards. We landed in Cornovia and from there walked south across Elmet into friendly Powys. 'And that, my Lady,' I concluded, 'is why all the tales say that Merlin vanished.'

Igraine frowned. 'Didn't the dark riders search the mound?'

'Twice,' I said, 'but they didn't know the entrance could be unblocked, or else they feared the spirits of the dead inside. And Merlin, of course, had woven us a charm of concealment.'

'I wish you had flown away,' she grumbled. 'It would make a much better tale.' She sighed for that lost dream. 'But the story of the Cauldron does not end there, does it?'

'Alas, no.'

'So . . .'

'So I will tell it in its proper place,' I interrupted her.

She pouted. Today she is wearing her cloak of grey wool edged with otter fur that makes her look so pretty. She is still not pregnant, which makes me think that either she is not destined to have children or else her husband, King Brochvael, is spending too much time with his mistress, Nwylle. It is cold today, and the wind gusts at my window and tugs at the small flames in the hearth that is big enough to hold a fire ten times the size of the one Bishop Sansum allows me. I can hear the saint scolding Brother Arun, who is our monastery's cook. The gruel was too hot this morning and scalded St Tudwal's tongue. Tudwal is a child in our monastery, the Bishop's close companion in Christ Jesus, and last year the Bishop declared Tudwal to be a saint. The devil sets many snares in the path of true faith.

'So it was you and Ceinwyn,' Igraine accuses me.

'Was what?' I asked.

'You were her lover,' Igraine said.

'For life, Lady,' I confessed.

'And you never married?'

'Never. She took her oath, remember?'

'But nor did she split in two with a baby,' Igraine said.

'The third child almost killed her,' I said, 'but the others were much easier.'

Igraine was crouching by the fire, holding her pale hands to its pathetic flames. 'You are lucky, Derfel.'

'I am?'

'To have known a love like that.' She looked wistful. The Queen is no older than Ceinwyn when I first knew her, and, like Ceinwyn, Igraine is beautiful and deserves a love fit for a bard's song.

'I was lucky,' I admitted. Outside my window Brother

Maelgwyn is finishing the monastery's log pile, splitting the trunks with a maul and hammer and singing as he goes about his business. His song tells the love story of Rhydderch and Morag, which means he will be reprimanded as soon as St Sansum has finished humiliating Arun. We are brothers in Christ, the saint tells us, united in love.

'Wasn't Cuneglas angry with his sister for running away with you?' Igraine asks me. 'Not even a bit?'

'Not in the least,' I said. 'He wanted us to move back to Caer Sws, but we both liked it in Cwm Isaf. And Ceinwyn never really liked her sister-in-law. Helledd was a grumbler, you see, and she had two aunts who were very tart. They all disapproved of Ceinwyn, and they were the ones who started all the stories of scandal, but we were never scandalous.' I paused, remembering those early days. 'Most people were very kind, in fact,' I went on. 'In Powys, you see, there was still some resentment about Lugg Vale. Too many people had lost fathers, brothers and husbands, and Ceinwyn's defiance was a kind of recompense to them. They enjoyed seeing Arthur and Lancelot embarrassed, so other than Helledd and her ghastly aunts, no one was unkind to us.'

'And Lancelot didn't fight you for her?' asked Igraine, shocked.

'I wish he had,' I said drily. 'I would have enjoyed that.'

'And Ceinwyn just made up her own mind?' Igraine asked, astonished at the very thought of a woman daring to do such a thing. She stood and walked to the window where she listened for a while as Maelgwyn sang. 'Poor Gwenhwyvach,' she said suddenly. 'You make her sound very plain and plump and dull.'

'She was all of those things, alas.'

'Not everyone can be beautiful,' she said, with the assurance of one who was.

'No,' I agreed, 'but you do not want tales of the commonplace. You want Arthur's Britain to be livid with passion and I could feel no passion for Gwenhwyvach. You cannot command love, Lady, only beauty or lust does that. Do you want the world to be fair? Then just imagine a world with no kings, no queens, no lords, no passion and no magic. You would want to live in such a dull world?'

'That has nothing to do with beauty,' Igraine protested.

'It has everything to do with beauty. What is your rank but the accident of your birth? And what is your beauty but another accident? If the Gods,' I paused and corrected myself, 'if God wanted us to be equal then he would have made us equal, and if we were all the same, where would your romance be?'

She abandoned the argument. 'Do you believe in magic, Brother Derfel?' she challenged me instead.

I thought about it. 'Yes,' I said. 'And even as Christians, we can believe in it. What else are the miracles, but magic?'

'And Merlin could really make a fog?'

I frowned. 'Everything Merlin did, my Lady, had another explanation. Fogs do come from the sea, and lost things are found every day.'

'And the dead come to life?'

'Lazarus did,' I said, 'and so did our Saviour.' I crossed myself.

Igraine dutifully made the sign of the cross. 'But did Merlin rise from the dead?' she demanded.

'I don't know that he was dead,' I said carefully.

'But Ceinwyn was certain?'

'Till her dying day, Lady.'

Igraine twisted her gown's braided belt in her fingers. 'But wasn't that the Cauldron's magic? That it could restore life?'

'So we are told.'

'And surely Ceinwyn's discovery of the Cauldron was magic,' Igraine said.

'Perhaps,' I said, 'but maybe it was just common sense. Merlin had spent months discovering every stray memory about Ynys Mon. He knew where the Druids had their sacred centre, and that was beside Llyn Cerrig Bach, and Ceinwyn merely led us to the nearest place where the Cauldron could be safely hidden. She did have her dream, though.'

'And so did you,' Igraine said, 'on Dolforwyn. What was it that Merlin gave you to drink?'

'The same thing Nimue gave Ceinwyn at Llyn Cerrig Bach,' I said, 'and that was probably an infusion of the red cap.'

'The mushroom!' Igraine sounded appalled.

I nodded. 'That was why I was twitching and couldn't stand.'

'But you could have died!' she protested.

I shook my head. 'Not many die from red caps, and besides, Nimue was skilled in such things.' I decided not to tell her that the best way to make the red cap safe was for the wizard himself to eat the mushroom, then give the dreamer a cup of his urine to drink. 'Or maybe she used rye-blight?' I said instead, 'but I think it was red cap.'

Igraine frowned as St Sansum ordered Brother Maelgwyn to stop singing his pagan song. The saint is in a testier mood than usual these days. He suffers pain when passing urine, maybe because of a stone. We pray for him.

'So what happens now?' Igraine asked, ignoring Sansum's ranting.

'We went home,' I said. 'Back to Powys.'

'And to Arthur?' she asked eagerly.

'To Arthur too,' I said, for this is his tale; the tale of our dear warlord, our law-giver, our Arthur.

That spring was so glorious in Cwm Isaf, or perhaps when you are in love everything appears fuller and brighter, but it seemed to me as though the world had never been so crammed with cowslips and dog mercury, with bluebells and violets, with lilies and great banks of cow parsley. Blue butterflies haunted the meadow where we ripped out tangled bundles of couch grass from beneath the apple trees that blossomed pink. Wrynecks sang in the blossom, there were sandpipers by the stream and a wagtail made its nest under Cwm Isaf's thatch. We had five calves, all healthy and greedy and soft-eyed, and Ceinwyn was pregnant.

I had made us both lovers' rings when we returned from Ynys Mon. They were rings incised with a cross, though not the Christian cross, and girls often wore them after they had passed from being maids to women. Most girls took a twist of straw from their lovers and wore it as a badge, and spearmen's women usually wore a warrior ring on which the cross had been scratched, while women of the highest rank rarely wore the rings at all, despising them as vulgar symbols. Some men wore them, too, and it had been just such a crossed lover's ring that Valerin, the chieftain of Powys, had worn when he died at Lugg Vale. Valerin had been Guinevere's betrothed before she met Arthur.

Our rings were both warrior rings made from a Saxon axehead, but before I left Merlin, who was continuing his journey southwards to Ynys Wydryn, I secretly broke off a fragment of the Cauldron's decoration; it was a miniature golden spear carried by a warrior and it came off easily. I hid the gold in a pouch and, once back at Cwm Isaf, I took the scrap of gold and the two warrior rings to a metalworker there and watched as he melted and fashioned the gold into two crosses that he burned onto the iron. I stood over him to make sure he did not substitute some other gold, and then I carried one of the rings to Ceinwyn and wore the other myself. Ceinwyn laughed when she saw the ring. 'A piece of straw would have done just as well, Derfel,' she said.

'Gold from the Cauldron will serve better,' I answered. We wore the rings always, much to Queen Helledd's disgust.

Arthur came to us in that lovely spring. He found me stripped to the waist and pulling couch grass, a job as unending as spinning wool. He hailed me from the stream, then strode uphill to greet me. He was dressed in a grey linen shirt and long dark leggings, and he carried no sword. 'I like to see a man working,' he teased me.

'Pulling couch is harder work than fighting,' I grumbled and pressed my hands into the small of my back. 'You've come to help?'

'I've come to see Cuneglas,' he said, then took a seat on a boulder near one of the apple trees that dotted the pasture.

'War?' I asked, as though Arthur might have any other business in Powys.

He nodded. 'Time to gather the spears, Derfel. Especially,' he smiled, 'the Warriors of the Cauldron.' Then he insisted on hearing the whole story, even though he must already have heard it a dozen times, and when it was told he had the grace to apologize for having doubted the Cauldron's existence. I am sure Arthur still thought it was all a nonsense, and even a dangerous nonsense, for the success of our quest had angered Dumnonia's Christians who, as Galahad had said, believed we performed the devil's work. Merlin had carried the precious Cauldron back to Ynys Wydryn where it was being stored in his tower. In time, Merlin said, he would summon its vast powers, but even now, just by being in Dumnonia, and despite the hostility of the Christians, the Cauldron was giving the land a new confidence. 'Though I confess,' Arthur told me, 'that I take more confidence from seeing spearmen gathered. Cuneglas tells me he will march next week, Lancelot's Silurians are gathering at Isca, and Tewdric's men are ready to march. And it will be a dry year, Derfel, a good year for fighting.'

I agreed. The ash trees had turned green before the oaks, and that signified a dry summer to come, and dry summers meant firm ground for shield-walls. 'So where do you want my men?' I asked.

'With me, of course,' he said, then paused before offering me a sly smile. 'I thought you would have congratulated me, Derfel.'

'You, Lord?' I asked, pretending ignorance so he could tell me the news himself.

His smile grew broader. 'Guinevere gave birth a month ago. A boy, a fine boy!'

'Lord!' I exclaimed, pretending he had surprised me with the news, though a report of the birth had reached us a week before.

'He's healthy and hungry! A good omen.' He was plainly

delighted, but he was always inordinately pleased with the commonplace things of life. He yearned for a sturdy family within a well-built house surrounded by properly tended crops. 'We call him Gwydre,' he said, and repeated the name fondly, 'Gwydre.'

'A good name, Lord,' I said, then told him of Ceinwyn's pregnancy and Arthur immediately decreed that her child must be a daughter and, of course, would marry his Gwydre when the time came. He put an arm round my shoulder and walked me up to the house where we found Ceinwyn skimming cream from a dish of milk. Arthur embraced her warmly then insisted she leave the cream-making to her servants and come into the sunlight to talk.

We sat on a bench Issa had made under the apple tree that grew beside the house door. Ceinwyn asked him about Guinevere. 'Was it an easy birth?' she asked.

'It was.' He touched an iron amulet that hung at his neck. 'It was indeed, and she's well!' He grimaced. 'She worries a little that having a child will make her look old, but that's nonsense. My mother never looked old. And having a child will be good for Guinevere.' He smiled, imagining that Guinevere would love a son as much as he would himself. Gwydre, of course, was not his first child. His Irish mistress, Ailleann, had given him twin boys, Amhar and Loholt, who were now old enough to take their places in the shield-wall, but Arthur was not looking forward to their company. 'They are not fond of me,' he admitted when I asked about the twins, 'but they do like our old friend Lancelot.' He offered us both a ruefully apologetic glance at the mention of that name. 'And they will fight with his men,' he added.

'Fight?' Ceinwyn asked warily.

Arthur gave her a gentle smile. 'I come to take Derfel away from you, my Lady.'

'Bring him back to me, Lord,' was all she said.

'With riches enough for a kingdom,' Arthur promised, but then he turned and looked at Cwm Isaf's low walls and the bulging heap of thatch that kept us warm and the steaming dungheap that lay beyond the gable's end. It was not as big as most farmhouses in Dumnonia, but it was still the kind of croft a prosperous freeman in Powys might own and we were fond of it. I thought Arthur was about to make some comment comparing my present humble state with my future wealth and I was ready to defend Cwm Isaf against such a comparison, but instead he looked rueful. 'I do envy you this, Derfel.'

'It's yours for the taking, Lord,' I said, hearing the yearning in his voice.

'I am doomed to marble pillars and soaring pediments.' He laughed the moment away. 'I leave tomorrow,' he said. 'Cuneglas will follow within ten days. Would you come with him? Or earlier if you can. And bring as much food as you can carry.'

'To where?' I asked.

'Corinium,' he replied, then stood and gazed up the cwm before smiling down at me. 'One last word?' he requested.

'I must be sure Scarach isn't scalding the milk,' Ceinwyn said, taking his broad hint. 'I wish you victory, Lord,' she said to Arthur, then stood to give him a parting embrace.

Arthur and I walked up the cwm where he admired the newly-pleached hedges, the trimmed apple trees and the small fish pool we had dammed into the stream. 'Don't become too rooted in this soil, Derfel,' he told me. 'I want you back in Dumnonia.'

'Nothing would give me more pleasure, Lord,' I said, knowing it was not Arthur who kept me from my homeland, but his wife and her ally Lancelot.

Arthur smiled, but said nothing more of my return. 'Ceinwyn,' he said instead, 'seems very happy.'

'She is. We are.'

He hesitated a second. 'You might discover,' he said with the authority of a new father, 'that pregnancy will make her turbulent.'

'Not so far, Lord,' I said, 'though these are early weeks.'

'You are fortunate in her,' he said softly, and looking back I think that was the very first time I ever heard him utter the faintest criticism of Guinevere. 'Childbirth is a stressful time,' he added in hasty explanation, 'and these preparations for war don't help. Alas, I can't be at home as much as I'd like.' He stopped beside an ancient oak that had been riven by lightning so that its fire-blackened trunk was split in two, though even now the old tree was struggling to put out new green shoots. 'I have a favour to ask of you,' he said softly.

'Anything, Lord.'

'Don't be hasty, Derfel, you don't know the favour yet.' He paused, and I sensed the request would be hard for he was embarrassed to be making it. For a moment or two he could not make the request at all, but instead stared towards the woods on the southern side of the cwm and muttered something about deer and bluebells.

'Bluebells?' I asked, thinking I must have misheard him.

'I was just wondering why deer never eat bluebells,' he said evasively. 'They eat everything else.'

'I don't know, Lord.'

He hesitated a heartbeat, then looked into my eyes. 'I have asked for a gathering of Mithras at Corinium,' he finally admitted.

I understood what was coming then and hardened my heart to it. War had given me many rewards, but none so precious as the fellowship of Mithras. He had been the Roman God of war and He had stayed in Britain when the Romans left; the only men admitted to His mysteries were those elected by his initiates. Those initiates came from every kingdom, and they fought against each other as often as they fought for each other, but when they met in Mithras's hall they met in peace and they would only elect the bravest of the brave to be their fellows. To be an initiate of Mithras was to receive the praise of Britain's finest warriors and it was an honour that I would not give lightly to any man. No women, of course, were permitted to worship Mithras. Indeed, if a woman even saw the mysteries she would be killed.

'I have called the gathering,' Arthur said, 'because I want us to admit Lancelot to the mysteries.' I had known that was the reason. Guinevere had made the same request of me the year before, and in the months that followed I had hoped her idea would fade away, but here, on the eve of war, it had returned.

I gave a politic answer. 'Would it not be better, Lord,' I asked, 'if King Lancelot were to wait until the Saxons are defeated? Then, surely, we will have seen him fight.' None of us had yet seen Lancelot in the shield-wall and, to be truthful, I would be astonished to see him fight in this coming summer, but I hoped the suggestion would delay the terrible moment of choice for a few further months.

Arthur offered a vague gesture as though my suggestion was somehow irrelevant. 'There is pressure,' he said vaguely, 'to elect him now.'

'What pressure?' I asked.

'His mother is unwell.'

I laughed. 'Hardly a reason to elect a man to Mithras, Lord.'

Arthur scowled, knowing his arguments were feeble. 'He is a King, Derfel,' he said, 'and he leads a King's army to our wars. He doesn't like Siluria, and I can't blame him. He yearns for the poets and harpists and halls of Ynys Trebes, but he lost that kingdom because I could not fulfil my oath and bring my army to his father's aid. We owe him, Derfel.'

'Not me, Lord.'

'We owe him,' Arthur insisted.

'He should still wait for Mithras,' I said firmly. 'If you propose his name now, Lord, then I dare say it will be rejected.'

He had feared I would say that, but still he did not abandon his arguments. 'You are my friend,' he said, and waved away any comment I might make, 'and it would please me, Derfel, if my friend were as honoured in Dumnonia as he is in Powys.' He had been staring down at the bole of the storm-blasted oak, but now he looked up at me. 'I want you at Lindinis, friend, and if you, above all others, support Lancelot's name in Mithras's hall, then his election is assured.'

There was far more there than Arthur's bare words had said.

He was subtly confirming to me that it was Guinevere who was pressing Lancelot's candidacy, and that my offences in Guinevere's eyes would be forgiven if I granted her this one wish. Elect Lancelot to Mithras, he was saying, and I could take Ceinwyn to Dumnonia and assume the honour of being Mordred's champion with all the wealth, land and rank which accompanied that high position.

I watched a group of my spearmen come down from the high northern hill. One of them was cradling a lamb, and I guessed it was an orphan that would need to be hand-fed by Ceinwyn. It was a laborious business, for the lamb would have to be nurtured on a cloth teat soaked in milk and as often as not the little things died, but Ceinwyn insisted on trying to save their lives. She had utterly forbidden any of her lambs to be buried in wicker or have their pelts nailed to a tree and the flock did not seem to have suffered as a result of that neglect. I sighed. 'So at Corinium,' I said, 'you will propose Lancelot?'

'Not I, no. Bors will propose him. Bors has seen him fight.'

'Then let us hope, Lord, that Bors is given a tongue of gold.'

Arthur smiled. 'You can give me no answer now?'

'None that you would want to hear, Lord.'

He shrugged, took my arm and walked me back. 'I do hate these secret guilds,' he said mildly, and I believed him for I had never yet seen Arthur at a meeting of Mithras even though I knew he had been initiated many years before. 'Cults like Mithras,' he said, 'are supposed to bind men together, but they only serve to drive them apart. They rouse envy. But sometimes, Derfel, you have to fight one evil with another and I am thinking of starting a new guild of warriors. Those men who bear arms against the Saxons will belong, all of them, and I shall make it the most honoured band in all Britain.'

'The largest too, I hope,' I said.

'Not the levies,' he added, thus restricting his honoured band to those men who carried a spear by oath-duty rather than by land obligation. 'Men will rather belong to my guild than to any secret mystery.'

'What will you call it?' I asked.

'I don't know. Warriors of Britain? The Comrades? The Spears of Cadarn?' He spoke lightly, but I could tell he was serious.

'And you think that if Lancelot belongs to these Warriors of Britain,' I said, snatching one of his suggested titles, 'then he won't mind being barred from Mithras?'

'It might help,' he admitted, 'but it isn't my prime reason. I shall impose an obligation on these warriors. To join they will have to take a blood-oath never to fight each other again.' He gave a swift smile. 'If the Kings of Britain squabble then I shall make it impossible for their warriors to fight each other.'

'Hardly impossible,' I said tartly. 'A royal oath supersedes all others, even your blood-oath.'

'Then I shall make it difficult,' he insisted, 'because I shall have peace, Derfel, I shall have peace. And you, my friend, will share it with me in Dumnonia.'

'I hope so, Lord.'

He embraced me. 'I shall meet you in Corinium,' he said. He raised a hand in greeting to my spearmen, then looked back to me. 'Think about Lancelot, Derfel. And consider the truth that sometimes we must yield a little pride in return for a great peace.'

And with those words he strode away and I went to warn my men that the time for farming was over. We had spears to sharpen, swords to hone and shields to repaint, revarnish and bind hard. We were back at war.

We left two days before Cuneglas, who was waiting for his western chieftains to arrive with their rough-pelted warriors from Powys's mountain fastnesses. He told me to promise Arthur that the men of Powys would be in Corinium within a week, then he embraced me and swore on his life that Ceinwyn would be safe. She was moving back to Caer Sws where a small band of men would guard Cuneglas's family while he was at war. Ceinwyn had been reluctant to leave Cwm Isaf and rejoin the women's hall where Helledd and her aunts ruled, but I remembered

Merlin's tale of a dog being killed and its skin draped on a crippled bitch in Guinevere's temple of Isis, and so I pleaded with Ceinwyn to take refuge for my sake, and at last she relented.

I added six of my men to Cuneglas's palace guard, and the rest, all Warriors of the Cauldron, marched south. All of us bore Ceinwyn's five-pointed star on our shields, we carried two spears each, our swords, and had huge bundles of twice-baked bread, salted meat, hard cheese and dried fish strapped to our backs. It was good to be marching again, even though our route did take us through Lugg Vale where the dead had been unearthed by wild pigs so that the fields of the vale looked like a boneyard. I worried that the sight of the bones would remind Cuneglas's men of their defeat, and so insisted that we spend a half day re-burying the corpses that had all had one foot chopped off before they were first buried. Not every dead man could be burned as we would have liked, so most of our dead we buried, but we took away one foot to stop the soul walking. Now we re-buried the one-footed dead, but even after that half day's work there was still no disguising the butchery of the place. I paused in the work to visit the Roman shrine where my sword had killed the Druid Tanaburs and where Nimue had extinguished Gundleus's soul, and there, on a floor still stained by their blood, I lay flat between the piles of cobwebbed skulls and prayed that I would return unwounded to my Ceinwyn.

We spent the next night at Magnis, a town that was a whole world away from fog-shrouded cauldrons and night-time tales of the Treasures of Britain. This was Gwent, Christian territory, and everything here was grim business. The blacksmiths were forging spearheads, the tanners were making shield covers, scabbards, belts and boots, while the town's women were baking the hard, thin loaves that could keep for weeks on a campaign. King Tewdric's men were in their Roman uniforms of bronze breastplates, leather skirts and long cloaks. A hundred such men had already marched to Corinium, another two hundred would follow, though not under the command of their King, for

Tewdric was sick. His son Meurig, the Edling of Gwent, would be their titular leader, though in truth Agricola would command them. Agricola was an old man now, but his back was straight and his scarred arm could still wield a sword. He was said to be more Roman than the Romans and I had always been a little scared of his severe frown, but on that spring day outside Magnis he greeted me as an equal. His close-cropped grey head ducked under the lintel of his tent, then, dressed in his Roman uniform, he strode towards me and, to my astonishment, greeted me with an embrace.

He inspected my thirty-four spearmen. They looked shaggy and unkempt beside his clean-shaven men, but he approved of their weapons and approved even more of the amount of food we carried. 'I've spent years,' he growled, 'teaching that it's no use sending a spearman to war without a pack full of food, but what does Lancelot of Siluria do? Sends me a hundred spearmen without a peck of bread between them.' He had invited me into his tent where he served me a sour, pale wine. 'I owe you an apology, Lord Derfel,' he said.

'I doubt that, Lord,' I said. I felt embarrassed to be in such intimacy with a famous warrior who was old enough to be my grandfather.

He waved away my modesty. 'We should have been at Lugg Vale.'

'It seemed a hopeless fight, Lord,' I said, 'and we were desperate. You were not.'

'But you won, didn't you?' he growled. He turned as a lick of wind tried to dislodge a wood shaving from his table that was covered with scores of other such shavings, each bearing lists of men and rations. He weighted the wisp of wood with an inkhorn, then looked back to me. 'I hear we are to meet with the bull.'

'At Corinium,' I confirmed. Agricola, unlike his master Tewdric, was a pagan, though Agricola had no time for the British Gods, only for Mithras.

'To elect Lancelot,' Agricola said sourly. He listened as a man shouted orders in his camp lines, heard nothing that would spring him out of the tent and so looked back to me. 'What do you know of Lancelot?' he asked.

'Enough,' I said, 'to speak against him.'

'You'd offend Arthur?' He sounded surprised.

'I either offend Arthur,' I said bitterly, 'or Mithras.' I made the sign against evil. 'And Mithras is a God.'

'Arthur spoke to me on his way back from Powys,' Agricola said, 'and told me that electing Lancelot would bind Britain's union.' He paused, looking morose. 'He hinted that I owed him a vote to make up for our absence at Lugg Vale.'

Arthur, it seemed, was buying votes however he could. 'Then vote for him, Lord,' I said, 'for his exclusion only needs one vote, and mine will suffice.'

'I don't tell lies to Mithras,' Agricola snapped, 'and nor do I like King Lancelot. He was here two months ago, buying mirrors.'

'Mirrors!' I had to laugh. Lancelot had always collected mirrors, and in his father's high, airy sea-palace at Ynys Trebes he had kept the walls of a whole room covered with Roman mirrors. They must all have melted in the fire when the Franks swarmed over the palace walls and now, it seemed, Lancelot was rebuilding his collection.

'Tewdric sold him a fine electrum mirror,' Agricola told me. 'Big as a shield and quite extraordinary. It was so clear that it was like looking into a black pool on a fine day. And he paid well for it.' He would have had to, I thought, for mirrors of electrum, an amalgam of silver and gold, were rare indeed. 'Mirrors,' Agricola said scathingly. 'He should be attending to his duties in Siluria, not buying mirrors.' He snatched up his sword and helmet as a horn sounded from the town. It called twice, a signal Agricola recognized. 'The Edling,' he growled, and led me out into the sunlight to see that Meurig was indeed riding out from Magnis's Roman ramparts. 'I camp out here,' Agricola told me as he watched his honour guard form into two ranks, 'to stay away from their priests.'

Prince Meurig came attended by four Christian priests who ran to keep up with the Edling's horse. The Prince was a young man, indeed I had first seen him when he was a child and that had not been so very long before, but he disguised his youth with a querulous and irritable manner. He was short, pale and thin, with a wispy brown beard. He was notorious as a creature of pettifogging detail who loved the quibbles of the lawcourts and the squabbles of the church. His scholarship was famous; he was, we were assured, an expert at refuting the Pelagian heresy that so harassed the Christian church in Britain, he knew by heart the eighteen chapters of tribal British law, and he could name the genealogies of ten British kingdoms going back twenty generations as well as the lineage of all their septs and tribes; and that, we were informed by his admirers, was only the beginning of Meurig's knowledge. To his admirers he seemed a youthful paragon of learning and the finest rhetorician of Britain, but to me it seemed that the Prince had inherited all of his father's intelligence and none of his wisdom. It was Meurig, more than any other man, who had persuaded Gwent to abandon Arthur before Lugg Vale and for that reason alone I had no love for Meurig, but I obediently went down on one knee as the Prince dismounted.

'Derfel,' he said in his curiously high-pitched voice, 'I remember you.' He did not tell me to rise, but just pushed past me into the tent.

Agricola beckoned me inside, thus sparing me the company of the four panting priests who had no business here except to stay close to their Prince who, dressed in a toga and with a heavy wooden cross hanging on a silver chain about his neck, seemed irritated by my presence. He scowled at me, then went on with a querulous complaint to Agricola, but as they spoke in Latin I had no idea what they talked about. Meurig was buttressing his argument with a sheet of parchment that he waved in front of Agricola who endured the harangue patiently.

Meurig at last abandoned his argument, rolled up the parchment and thrust it into his toga. He turned to me. 'You will not,' he said, speaking British again, 'be expecting us to feed your men?'

'We carry our own food, Lord Prince,' I said, then inquired after his father's health.

'The King suffers from fistula in the groin,' Meurig explained in his squeaking voice. 'We have used poultices and the physicians are bleeding father regularly, but alas, God has not seen fit to requite the condition.'

'Send for Merlin, Lord Prince,' I suggested.

Meurig blinked at me. He was very short-sighted, and it was those weak eyes, perhaps, that gave his face its permanent expression of ill-temper. He uttered a short snaffle of mocking laughter. 'You, of course, if you will forgive the remark,' he said snidely, 'are famous as one of the fools who risked Diwrnach to bring a bowl back to Dumnonia. A mixing bowl, yes?'

'A cauldron, Lord Prince.'

Meurig's thin lips flickered in a quick smile. 'You did not think, Lord Derfel, that our smiths could have hammered you a dozen cauldrons in as many days?'

'I shall know where to come for my cooking pots next time, Lord Prince,' I said. Meurig stiffened at the insult, but Agricola smiled.

'Did you understand any of that?' Agricola asked me when Meurig had left.

'I have no Latin, Lord.'

'He was complaining because a chieftain hasn't paid his taxes. The poor man owes us thirty smoked salmon and twenty cart-loads of cut timber, and we've had no salmon from him and only five carts of wood. But what Meurig won't grasp is that poor Cyllig's people have been struck by the plague this last winter, the river Wye's been poached empty, and Cyllig is still bringing me two dozen spearmen.' Agricola spat in disgust. 'Ten times a day!' he said, 'ten times a day the Prince will come out here with a problem that any half-witted treasury clerk could solve in twenty heartbeats. I just wish his father would just strap up his groin and get back on the throne.'

'How sick is Tewdric?'

Agricola shrugged. 'He's tired, not sick. He wants to give up his throne. He says he'll have his head tonsured and become a priest.' He spat onto the tent floor again. 'But I'll manage our Edling. I'll make sure his ladies come to war.'

'Ladies?' I asked, made curious by the ironic twist Agricola had put on the word.

'He might be blind as a worm, Lord Derfel, but he can still spot a girl like a hawk seeing a shrew. He likes his ladies, Meurig does, and plenty of them. And why not? That's the way of princes, isn't it?' He unstrapped his sword belt and hung it on a nail driven into one of the tent poles. 'You march tomorrow?'

'Yes, Lord.'

'Dine with me tonight,' he said, then ushered me out of the tent and squinted up at the sky. 'It will be a dry summer, Lord Derfel. A summer for killing Saxons.'

'A summer to breed great songs,' I said enthusiastically.

'I often think that the trouble with us Britons,' Agricola said gloomily, 'is that we spend too much time singing and not enough killing Saxons.'

'Not this year,' I said, 'not this year,' for this was Arthur's year, the year to slaughter the Sais. The year, I prayed, of total victory.

Once out of Magnis we marched on the straight Roman roads that tied Britain's heartland together. We made good time, reaching Corinium in just two days, and we were all glad to be back in Dumnonia. The five-pointed star on my shield might have been a strange device, but the moment the country folks heard my name they knelt for a blessing for I was Derfel Cadarn, the holder of Lugg Vale and a Warrior of the Cauldron, and my repute, it seemed, soared high in my homeland. At least among the pagans it did. In the towns and larger villages, where the Christians were more numerous, we were more likely to be met by preaching. We were told that we were marching to do God's will by fighting the Saxons, but that if we died in battle our souls would go to hell if we were still worshippers of the older Gods.

I feared the Saxons more than the Christian hell. The Sais were a dreadful enemy; poor, desperate and numerous. Once at Corinium, we heard ominous tales of new ships grounding almost daily on Britain's eastern shores, and how each ship brought its cargo of feral warriors and hungry families. The invaders wanted our land, and to take it they could muster hundreds of spears, swords and double-edged axes, yet still we had confidence. Fools that we were, we marched almost blithely to that war. I suppose, after the horrors of Lugg Vale, we believed we could never be beaten. We were young, we were strong, we were loved by the Gods and we had Arthur.

I met Galahad in Corinium. Since the day we had parted in Powys he had helped Merlin carry the Cauldron back to Ynys Wydryn, then he had spent the spring at Caer Ambra from which rebuilt fortress he had raided deep into Lloegyr with Sagramor's troops. The Saxons, he warned me, were ready for our coming and had set beacons on every hill to give warning of our approach. Galahad had come to Corinium for the great Council of War that Arthur had summoned, and he brought with him Cavan and those of my men who had refused to march north into Lleyn. Cavan went on one knee and begged that he and his men might renew their old oaths to me. 'We have made no other oaths,' he promised me, 'except to Arthur, and he says we should serve you if you'll have us.'

'I thought you'd be rich by now,' I told Cavan, 'and gone home to Ireland.'

He smiled. 'I still have the throwboard, Lord.'

I welcomed him back to my service. He kissed Hywelbane's blade, then asked if he and his men could paint the white star on their shields.

'You may paint it,' I said, 'but with only four points.'

'Four, Lord?' Cavan glanced at my shield. 'Yours has five.'

'The fifth point,' I told Cavan, 'is for the Warriors of the Cauldron.' He looked unhappy, but agreed. Nor would Arthur have approved, for he would have seen, rightly enough, that the fifth point was a divisive mark which implied that one group of men was superior to another, but warriors like such distinctions and the men who had braved the Dark Road deserved it.

I went to greet the men who accompanied Cavan and found them camped beside the River Churn that flowed to the east of Corinium. At least a hundred men were bivouacked beside that small river, for there was not nearly enough space inside the town for all the warriors who had assembled about the Roman walls. The army itself was gathering close to Caer Ambra, but every leader who had come for the Council of War had brought some retainers, and those men alone were sufficient to give the appearance of a small army in the Churn's water meadows. Their stacked shields showed the success of Arthur's strategy, for at a glance I could see the black bull of Gwent, the red dragon of Dumnonia, the fox of Siluria, Arthur's bear, and the shields of men, like me, who had the honour of carrying their own device: stars, hawks, eagles, boars, Sagramor's dread skull and Galahad's lone Christian cross.

Culhwch, Arthur's cousin, was camped with his own spearmen, but now hurried to greet me. It was good to see him again. I had fought at his side in Benoic and had come to love him like a brother. He was vulgar, funny, cheerful, bigoted, ignorant and coarse, and there was no better man to have alongside in a fight. 'I hear you've put a loaf in the Princess's oven,' he said when he had embraced me. 'You're a lucky dog. Did you have Merlin cast you a spell?'

'A thousand.'

He laughed. 'I can't complain. I've three women now, all clawing each other's eyes out and all of them pregnant.' He grinned, then scratched at his groin. 'Lice,' he said. 'Can't get rid of them. But at least they've infested that little bastard Mordred.'

'Our Lord King?' I teased him.

'Little bastard,' he said vengefully. 'I tell you, Derfel, I've beaten him bloody and he still won't learn. Sneaky little toad.' He spat. 'So tomorrow you speak against Lancelot?'

'How do you know?' I had told no one but Agricola of that firm decision, but somehow news of it had preceded me to Corinium, or else my antipathy to the Silurian King was too well known for men to believe I could do anything else.

'Everyone knows,' Culhwch said, 'and everyone supports you.' He looked past me and spat suddenly. 'Crows,' he growled.

I turned to see a procession of Christian priests walking alongside the Churn's far bank. There were a dozen of them, all black gowned, all bearded, and all chanting one of the dirges of their religion. A score of spearmen followed the priests and their shields, I saw with surprise, bore either Siluria's fox or Lancelot's sea-eagle. 'I thought the rites were in two days' time,' I said to Galahad, who had stayed with me.

'They are,' he said. The rites were the preamble to war and would ask the blessing of the Gods on our men, and that blessing would be sought from both the Christian God and the pagan deities. 'This looks more like a baptism,' Galahad added.

'What in Bel's name is a baptism?' Culhwch asked.

Galahad sighed. 'It is an outward sign, my dear Culhwch, of a man's sins being washed away by God's grace.'

That explanation made Culhwch bay with laughter, prompting a frown from one of the priests who had tucked his gown into his belt and was now wading into the shallow river. He was using a pole to discover a spot deep enough for the baptismal rite and his clumsy probing attracted a crowd of bored spearmen on the rushy bank opposite the Christians.

For a while nothing much happened. The Silurian spearmen made an embarrassed guard while the tonsured priests wailed their song and the lone paddler poked about in the river with the butt end of his long pole that was surmounted by a silver cross. 'You'll never catch a trout with that,' Culhwch shouted, 'try a fish spear!' The watching spearmen laughed, and the priests scowled as they sang drearily on. Some women from the town had come to the river and joined in the singing. 'It's a woman's religion,' Culhwch spat.

'It is my religion, dear Culhwch,' Galahad murmured. He and Culhwch had argued thus throughout the whole long war in Benoic and their argument, like their friendship, had no end.

The priest found a deep enough spot, so deep, indeed, that the water came right up to his waist, and there he tried to fix the pole in the river's bed, but the force of the water kept bearing the cross down and each failure prompted a chorus of jeers from the spearmen. A few of the spectators were Christians themselves, but they made no attempt to stop the mockery.

The priest at last managed to plant the cross, albeit precariously, and climbed back out of the river. The spearmen whistled and hooted at the sight of his skinny white legs and he hurriedly dropped the sopping skirts of his robe to hide them.

Then a second procession appeared and the sight of it was sufficient to cause a silence to drop on our bank of the river. The silence was one of respect, for a dozen spearmen were escorting an ox-cart that was hung with white linens and in which sat two women and one priest. One of the women was Guinevere and the other was Queen Elaine, Lancelot's mother, but most astonishing of all was the identity of the priest. It was Bishop Sansum. He was in his full bishop's regalia, a mound of gaudy copes and embroidered shawls, and had a heavy red-gold cross hanging about his neck. The shaven tonsure at the front of his head was burned pink by the sun, and above it his black hair stood up like mouse ears. Lughtigern, Nimue always called him, the mouse-lord. 'I thought Guinevere couldn't stand him,' I said, for Guinevere and Sansum had always been the bitterest of enemies, yet here the mouse-lord was, riding to the river in Guinevere's cart. 'And isn't he in disgrace?' I added.

'Shit sometimes floats,' Culhwch growled.

'And Guinevere isn't even a Christian,' I protested.

'And look at the other shit who's with her,' Culhwch said, and pointed to a group of six horsemen who followed the lumbering cart. Lancelot led them. He was mounted on a black horse and wore nothing but a simple pair of trews and a white shirt. Arthur's twin sons, Amhar and Loholt, flanked him, and they were dressed in full war gear with plumed helmets, mail coats and long boots. Behind them rode three other horsemen, one in armour and the other two in the long white robes of Druids.

'Druids?' I said. 'At a baptism?'

Galahad shrugged, no more able to find an explanation than I. The two Druids were both muscular young men with dark handsome faces, thick black beards and long, carefully brushed black hair that grew back from their narrow tonsures. They carried black staffs tipped with mistletoe and, unusually for Druids, had swords scabbarded at their sides. The warrior who rode with them, I saw, was no man, but a woman; a tall, straight-backed, red-haired woman whose extravagantly long tresses cascaded from beneath her silver helmet to touch the spine of her horse. 'Ade, she's called,' Culhwch told me.

'Who is she?' I asked.

'Who do you think? His kitchen-maid? She keeps his bed warm.' Culhwch grinned. 'Does she remind you of anyone?'

She reminded me of Ladwys, Gundleus's mistress. Was it the fate of Silurian Kings, I wondered, always to have a mistress who rode a horse and wore a sword like a man? Ade had a longsword at her hip, a spear in her hand and the sea-eagle shield on her arm. 'Gundleus's mistress,' I told Culhwch.

'With that red hair?' Culhwch said dismissively.

'Guinevere,' I said, and there was a distinct resemblance between Ade and the haughty Guinevere who sat next to Queen Elaine in the cart. Elaine was pale, but otherwise I could see no evidence of the sickness that was rumoured to be killing her. Guinevere looked as handsome as ever, and betrayed no sign of the ordeal of childbirth. She had not brought her child with her, but nor would I have expected her to. Gwydre was doubtless in Lindinis, safe in a wet nurse's arms and far enough away so that his cries could not disturb Guinevere's sleep.

Arthur's twins dismounted behind Lancelot. They were still very young, only just old enough, indeed, to carry a spear to war.

I had met them many times and did not like them for they had none of Arthur's pragmatic sense. They had been spoiled since childhood, and the result was a pair of tempestuous, selfish, greedy youths who resented their father, despised their mother Ailleann and took revenge for their bastardy on people who dared not fight back against Arthur's progeny. They were despicable. The two Druids slid off their horses' backs and stood beside the ox-cart.

It was Culhwch who first understood what Lancelot was doing. 'If he's baptized,' he growled to me, 'then he can't join Mithras, can he?'

'Bedwin did,' I pointed out, 'and Bedwin was a bishop.'

'Dear Bedwin,' Culhwch explained to me, 'played both sides of the throwboard. When he died we found an image of Bel in his house, and his wife told us he'd been sacrificing to it. No, you see if I'm not right. This is how Lancelot evades being rejected from Mithras.'

'Maybe he has been touched by God,' Galahad protested.

'Then your God must have filthy hands by now,' Culhwch responded, 'begging your pardon, seeing as he's your brother.'

'Half-brother,' Galahad said, not wanting to be too closely associated with Lancelot.

The cart had stopped very close to the river bank. Sansum now clambered down from its bed and, without bothering to tuck up his splendid robes, pushed through the rushes and waded into the river. Lancelot dismounted and waited on the bank as the Bishop reached and grasped the cross. He is a small man, Sansum, and the water came right up to the heavy cross on his narrow chest. He faced us, his unwitting congregation, and raised his strong voice. 'This week,' he shouted, 'you will carry your spears against the enemy and God will bless you. God will help you! And today, here in this river, you will see a sign of our God's power.' The Christians in the meadow crossed themselves while some pagans, like Culhwch and I, spat to avert evil.

'You see here King Lancelot!' Sansum bellowed, throwing a hand towards Lancelot as though none of us would have recognized him. 'He is the hero of Benoic, the King of Siluria and the Lord of Eagles!'

'The Lord of what?' Culhwch asked.

'And this week,' Sansum went on, 'this very week, he was to be received into the foul company of Mithras, that false God of blood and anger.'

'He was not,' Culhwch growled amidst the other murmurs of protest from the men in the field who were Mithraists.

'But yesterday,' Sansum's voice beat down the protest, 'this noble King received a vision. A vision! Not some belly-given nightmare spawned by a drunken wizard, but a pure and lovely dream sent on golden wings from heaven. A saintly vision!'

'Ade lifted her skirts,' Culhwch muttered.

'The holy and blessed mother of God came to King Lancelot,' Sansum shouted. 'It was the Virgin Mary herself, that lady of sorrows, from whose immaculate and perfect loins was born the Christ-child, the Saviour of all mankind. And yesterday, in a burst of light, in a cloud of golden stars, she came to King Lancelot and touched her lovely hand to Tanlladwyr!' He gestured behind him again, and Ade solemnly drew out Lancelot's sword that was called Tanlladwyr, which meant 'Bright Killer', and held it aloft. The sun slashed its reflection off the steel, blinding me for an instant.

'With this sword,' Sansum shouted, 'our blessed Lady promised the King that he would bring Britain victory. This sword, our Lady said, has been touched by the nail-scarred hand of the Son and blessed by the caress of His mother. From this day on, our Lady decreed, this sword shall be known as the Christ-blade, for it is holy.'

Lancelot, to give him credit, looked exquisitely embarrassed at this sermon; indeed the whole ceremony must have embarrassed him for he was a man of vast pride and fragile dignity, but even so it must have seemed better to him to be dunked in a river than publicly humiliated by losing election to Mithras. The certainty of his rejection must have prompted him to this public repudiation of all the pagan Gods. Guinevere, I saw, pointedly stared away from the river, gazing instead towards the war banners that had been hoisted on Corinium's earth and wooden ramparts. She was a pagan, a worshipper of Isis; indeed her hatred of Christianity was famous, yet that hatred had clearly been overcome by the need to support this public ceremony that spared Lancelot from Mithras's humiliation. The two Druids talked softly with her, sometimes making her laugh.

Sansum turned and faced Lancelot. 'Lord King,' he called loudly enough for those of us on the other bank to hear, 'come now! Come now to the waters of life, come now as a little child to receive your baptism into the blessed church of the one true God.'

Guinevere slowly turned to watch as Lancelot walked into the river. Galahad crossed himself. The Christian priests on the far bank had their arms spread wide in an attitude of prayer, while the town's women had fallen to their knees as they gazed ecstatically at the handsome, tall King who waded out to Bishop Sansum's side. The sun glittered on the water and slashed gold from Sansum's cross. Lancelot kept his eyes lowered, as though he did not want to see who witnessed this humiliating rite.

Sansum reached up and put his hand on the crown of Lancelot's head. 'Do you,' he shouted so we could all hear, 'embrace the one true faith, the only faith, the faith of Christ who died for our sins?'

Lancelot must have said 'Yes', though none of us could hear his response.

'And do you,' Sansum bellowed even louder, 'hereby renounce all other Gods and all other faiths and all the other foul spirits and demons and idols and devil-spawn whose filthy acts deceive this world?'

Lancelot nodded and mumbled his assent.

'And do you,' Sansum went on with relish, 'denounce and deride the practices of Mithras, and declare them to be, as indeed they are, the excrement of Satan and the horror of our Lord Jesus Christ?'

'I do.' That answer of Lancelot's came clear enough to us all.

'Then in the name of the Father,' Sansum shouted, 'and of the Son, and of the Holy Ghost, I pronounce you Christian,' and with that he gave a great heave that pushed down on Lancelot's oiled hair, and so forced the King under the Churn's cold water. Sansum held Lancelot there for so long that I thought the bastard would drown, but at last Sansum let him up. 'And,' Sansum finished as Lancelot sputtered and spat out water, 'I now proclaim you blessed, name you a Christian, and enrol you in the holy army of Christ's warriors.' Guinevere, uncertain how to respond, clapped politely. The women and priests burst into a new song that, for Christian music, was surprisingly spritely.

'What in the holy name of a holy harlot,' Culhwch asked Galahad, 'is a holy ghost?'

But Galahad did not wait to answer. In a rush of happiness caused by his brother's baptism he had plunged into the river and now waded across so that he emerged from the water at the same time as his blushing half-brother. Lancelot had not expected to see him and for a second he stiffened, doubtless thinking of Galahad's friendship for me, but then he suddenly remembered the duty of Christian love that had just been imposed upon him and so he submitted to Galahad's enthusiastic embrace.

'Shall we kiss the bastard too?' Culhwch asked me with a grin.

'Let him be,' I said. Lancelot had not seen me, and I did not feel any need to be seen, but just then Sansum, who had emerged from the river and was trying to wring the water from his heavy robes, spotted me. The mouse-lord never could resist provoking an enemy, nor did he now.

'Lord Derfel!' the Bishop called.

I ignored him. Guinevere, on hearing my name, looked up sharply. She had been talking to Lancelot and his half-brother, but now she snapped an order to the ox driver who stabbed his goad at his beasts' flanks and so lurched the cart forward. Lancelot hastily clambered onto the moving vehicle, abandoning his followers beside the river. Ade followed, leading his horse by its bridle.

'Lord Derfel!' Sansum called again.

I turned reluctantly to face him. 'Bishop?' I answered.

'Might I prevail on you to follow King Lancelot into the river of healing?'

'I bathed at the last full moon, Bishop,' I called back, provoking some laughter from the warriors on our bank.

Sansum made the sign of the cross. 'You should be washed in the holy blood of the Lamb of God,' he called, 'to wipe away the stain of Mithras! You are an evil thing, Derfel, a sinner, an idolater, an imp of the devil, a spawn of Saxons, a whore-master!'

That last insult tripped my rage. The other insults were mere words, but Sansum, though clever, was never a prudent man in public confrontations and he could not resist that final insult to Ceinwyn and his provocation sent me charging forward to the cheers of the warriors on the Churn's eastern bank, cheers that swelled as Sansum turned in panic and fled. He had a good start on me, and he was a lithe, swift man, but the sopping layers of his weighty robes tangled his feet and I caught him within a few paces of the Churn's far bank. I used my spear to knock his feet out from under him and so sent him sprawling among the daisies and cowslips.

Then I drew Hywelbane and put her blade to his throat. 'I did not quite hear, Bishop,' I said, 'the last name you called me.'

He said nothing, only glanced towards Lancelot's four companions who now gathered close. Amhar and Loholt had their swords drawn, but the two Druids left their swords scabbarded and just watched me with unreadable expressions. By now Culhwch had crossed the river and was standing beside me, as was Galahad, while Lancelot's worried spearmen watched us from a distance.

'What word did you use, Bishop?' I asked, tickling his throat with Hywelbane.

'The whore of Babylon!' he gabbled desperately, 'all pagans worship her. The scarlet woman, Lord Derfel, the beast! The anti-Christ!'

I smiled. 'And I thought you were insulting the Princess Ceinwyn.'

'No, Lord, no! No!' He clasped his hands. 'Never!'

'You promise me now?' I asked him.

'I swear it, Lord! By the Holy Ghost, I swear it.'

'I don't know who the Holy Ghost is, Bishop,' I said, giving his adam's apple a small blow with Hywelbane's tip. 'Swear your promise on my sword,' I said, 'kiss that, and I will believe you.'

He loathed me then. He had disliked me before, but now he hated me, yet still he put his lips to Hywelbane's blade and kissed the steel. 'I meant the Princess no insult,' he said, 'I swear it.'

I left Hywelbane at his lips for a heartbeat, then drew the sword back and let him stand. 'I thought, Bishop,' I said, 'that you had a Holy Thorn to guard in Ynys Wydryn?'

He brushed grass off his wet robes. 'God calls me to higher things,' he snapped.

'Tell me of them.'

He looked up at me, hate in his eyes, but his fear overcame his hate. 'God called me to King Lancelot's side, Lord Derfel,' he said, 'and His grace served to soften the Princess Guinevere's heart. I have hopes that she may yet see His everlasting light.'

I laughed at that. 'She has the light of Isis, Bishop, and you know it. And she hates you, you foul thing, so what did you bring her to change her mind?'

'Bring her, Lord?' he asked disingenuously. 'What have I to bring a Princess? I have nothing, I am made poor in God's service, I am but a humble priest.'

'You are a toad, Sansum,' I said, sheathing Hywelbane. 'You are dirt beneath my boots.' I spat to avert his evil. I guessed, from his words, that it had been his idea to propose baptism to Lancelot, and that idea had served well enough to spare the Silurian King his embarrassment with Mithras, but I did not believe the suggestion would have been sufficient to reconcile Guinevere to Sansum and his religion. He must have given her something, or promised her something, but I knew he would never confess it to me. I spat again, and Sansum, taking the spittle as his dismissal, scuttled off towards the town.

'A pretty display,' one of the two Druids said caustically.

'And the Lord Derfel Cadarn,' the other said, 'does not have a reputation for prettiness.' He nodded when I glared at him. 'Dinas,' he said, introducing himself.

'And I am Lavaine,' said his companion. They were both tall young men, both built like warriors and both with hard, confident faces. Their robes were dazzling white and their long black hair was carefully combed, betraying a fastidiousness that was made somehow chilling by their stillness. It was the same stillness that men like Sagramor possessed. Arthur did not. He was too restless, but Sagramor, like some other great warriors, had a stillness that was chilling in battle. I never fear the noisy men in a fight, but I take care when an enemy is calm for those are the most dangerous men, and these two Druids had that same calm confidence. They also looked very alike, and I supposed them to be brothers.

'We are twins,' Dinas said, perhaps reading my thoughts.

'Like Amhar and Loholt,' Lavaine added, gesturing towards Arthur's sons who still had their swords drawn. 'But you can tell us apart. I have a scar here,' Lavaine said, touching his right cheek where a white scar buried itself in his bristling beard.

'Which he took at Lugg Vale,' Dinas said. Like his brother he had an extraordinarily deep voice, a grating voice that did not match his youth.

'I saw Tanaburs at Lugg Vale,' I said, 'and I remember Iorweth, but I recall no other Druids in Gorfyddyd's army.'

Dinas smiled. 'At Lugg Vale,' he said, 'we fought as warriors.'

'And killed our share of Dumnonians,' Lavaine added.

'And only shaved our tonsures after the battle,' Dinas explained. He had an unblinking and unsettling gaze. 'And now,' he added softly, 'we serve King Lancelot.'

'His oaths are our oaths,' Lavaine said. There was a threat in his words, but it was a distant threat, not challenging.

'How can Druids serve a Christian?' I challenged them.

'By bringing an older magic to work alongside their magic, of course,' Lavaine answered.

'And we do work magic, Lord Derfel,' Dinas added, and he held out his empty hand, closed it into a fist, turned it, opened his fingers and there, on his palm, lay a thrush's egg. He tossed the egg carelessly away. 'We serve King Lancelot by choice,' he said, 'and his friends are our friends.'

'And his enemies our enemies,' Lavaine finished for him.

'And you,' Arthur's son Loholt could not resist joining in the provocation, 'are an enemy of our King.'

I looked at the younger pair of twins; callow, clumsy youths who suffered an excess of pride and a shortfall of wisdom. They both had their father's long bony face, but on them it was over-laid by petulance and resentment. 'How am I an enemy of your King, Loholt?' I asked him.

He did not know what to say, and none of the others answered for him. Dinas and Lavaine were too wise to start a fight here, not even with all Lancelot's spearmen so close, for Culhwch and Galahad were with me and scores of my supporters were just yards away across the slow-flowing Churn. Loholt reddened, but said nothing.

I knocked his sword aside with Hywelbane, then stepped close to him. 'Let me give you some advice, Loholt,' I said softly. 'Choose your enemies more wisely than you choose your friends. I have no quarrel with you, nor do I wish one, but if you desire such a quarrel, then I promise you that my love for your father and my friendship with your mother will not stop me from sinking Hywelbane in your guts and burying your soul in a dungheap.' I sheathed my sword. 'Now go.'

He blinked at me, but he had no belly for a fight. He went to fetch his horse and Amhar went with him. Dinas and Lavaine laughed, and Dinas even bowed to me. 'A victory!' he applauded me.

'We are routed,' Lavaine said, 'but what else could we expect from a Warrior of the Cauldron?' he pronounced that title mockingly.

'And a killer of Druids,' Dinas added, not at all mockingly.

'Our grandfather, Tanaburs,' Lavaine said, and I remembered how Galahad had warned me on the Dark Road about the enmity of these two Druids.

'It is reckoned unwise,' Lavaine said in his grating voice, 'to kill a Druid.'

'Especially our grandfather,' Dinas added, 'who was like a father to us.'

'As our own father died,' Lavaine said.

'When we were young.'

'Of a foul disease,' Lavaine explained.

'He was a Druid too,' Dinas said, 'and he taught us spells. We can blight crops.'

'We can make women moan,' Lavaine said.

'We can sour milk.'

'While it's still in the breast,' Lavaine added, then he turned abruptly away and, with an impressive agility, vaulted into his saddle.

His brother leapt onto his own horse and collected his reins. 'But we can do more than turn milk,' Dinas said, looking balefully down at me from his horse and then, as he had before, he held out his empty hand, made it into a fist, turned it over and opened it again, and there on his palm was a parchment star with five points. He smiled, then tore the parchment into scraps that he scattered on the grass. 'We can make the stars vanish,' he said as a farewell, then kicked his heels back.

The two galloped away. I spat. Culhwch retrieved my fallen spear and handed it to me. 'Who in all the world are they?' he asked.

'Tanaburs's grandsons.' I spat a second time to avert evil. 'The whelps of a bad Druid.'

'And they can make the stars disappear?' He sounded dubious.

'One star.' I gazed after the two horsemen. Ceinwyn, I knew, was safe in her brother's hall, but I also knew I would have to kill the Silurian twins if she was to remain safe. Tanaburs's curse was on me and the curse was called Dinas and Lavaine. I spat a third time, then touched Hywelbane's sword hilt for luck.

'We should have killed your brother in Benoic,' Culhwch growled to Galahad.

'God forgive me,' Galahad said, 'but you're right.'

Two days later Cuneglas arrived and that night there was a Council of War, and after the Council, under the waning moon and by the light of flaming torches, we pledged our spears to the war against the Saxons. We warriors of Mithras dipped our blades in bull's blood, but we held no meeting to elect new initiates. There was no need; Lancelot, by his baptism, had escaped the humiliation of rejection, though how any Christian could be served by Druids was a mystery that no one could explain to me.

Merlin came that day and it was he who presided over the pagan rites. Iorweth of Powys helped him, but there was no sign of Dinas or Lavaine. We sang the Battle Song of Beli Mawr, we washed our spears in blood, we vowed ourselves to the death of every Saxon and next day we marched.

THERE WERE TWO important Saxon leaders in Lloegyr. Like us the Saxons had chiefs and lesser kings, indeed they had tribes and some of the tribes did not even call themselves Saxons but claimed to be Angles or Jutes, but we called them all Saxons and knew they only possessed two important Kings and those two leaders were called Aelle and Cerdic. They hated each other.

Aelle, of course, was then the famous one. He called himself the *Bretwalda*, which in the Saxon tongue meant the 'ruler of Britain', and his lands stretched from south of the Thames to the border of distant Elmet. His rival was Cerdic, whose territory lay on Britain's southern coast and whose only borders were with Aelle's lands and Dumnonia. Of the two kings Aelle was older, richer in land and stronger in warriors, and that made Aelle our chief enemy; defeat Aelle, we believed, and Cerdic would inevitably fall afterwards.

Prince Meurig of Gwent, arrayed in his toga and with a ludicrous bronze wreath perched atop his thin, pale brown hair, had proposed a different strategy at the Council of War. With his usual diffidence and mock humility he had suggested we make an alliance with Cerdic. 'Let him fight for us!' Meurig said. 'Let him attack Aelle from the south while we strike from the west. I am, I know, no strategist,' he paused to simper, inviting one of us to contradict him, but we all bit our tongues, 'but it seems clear, even surely to the meanest of intelligences, that to fight one enemy is better than two.'

'But we have two enemies,' Arthur said plainly.

'Indeed we do, I have made myself master of that point, Lord

165

Arthur. But my point, if you can seize it in turn, is to make one of those enemies our friend.' He clasped his hands together and blinked at Arthur. 'An ally,' Meurig added, in case Arthur had still not understood him.

'Cerdic,' Sagramor growled in his atrocious British, 'has no honour. He will break an oath as easily as a magpie breaks a sparrow's egg. I will make no peace with him.'

'You fail to understand,' Meurig protested.

'I will make no peace with him,' Sagramor interrupted the Prince, speaking the words very slowly as though he spoke to a child. Meurig reddened and went silent. The Edling of Gwent was scared half to death of the tall Numidian warrior, and no wonder, for Sagramor's reputation was as fearsome as his looks. The Lord of the Stones was a tall man, very thin and quick as a whip. His hair and face were as black as pitch and that long face, cross-hatched from a lifetime of war, bore a perpetual scowl that hid a droll and even generous character. Sagramor, despite his imperfect grasp of our language, could keep a campfire enthralled for hours with his tales of far-off lands, but most men only knew him as the fiercest of all Arthur's warriors; the implacable Sagramor who was terrible in battle and sombre out of it, while the Saxons believed he was a black fiend sent from their underworld. I knew him well enough and liked him, indeed it had been Sagramor who had initiated me into Mithras's service, and Sagramor who had fought at my side all that long day in Lugg Vale. 'He's got himself a big Saxon girl now,' Culhwch had whispered to me at the council, 'tall as a tree and with hair like a haystack. No wonder he's so thin.'

'Your three wives keep you solid enough,' I said, poking him in his substantial ribs.

'I pick them for the way they cook, Derfel, not the way they look.'

'You have something to contribute, Lord Culhwch?' Arthur asked.

'Nothing, cousin!' Culhwch responded cheerfully.

'Then we shall continue,' Arthur said. He asked Sagramor

what chance there was of Cerdic's men fighting for Aelle, and the Numidian, who had guarded the Saxon frontier all winter, shrugged and said that anything was possible with Cerdic. He had heard, he said, that the two Saxons had met and exchanged gifts, but no one had reported that an actual alliance had been made. Sagramor's best guess was that Cerdic would be content to let Aelle be weakened, and that while the Dumnonian army was about that business he would attack along the coast in an effort to capture Durnovaria.

'If we were at peace with him . . .' Meurig tried again.

'We won't be,' King Cuneglas said curtly, and Meurig, outranked by the only King at the Council, went quiet again.

'There is one last thing,' Sagramor warned us. 'The Sais have dogs now. Big dogs.' He spread his hands to show the huge size of the Saxon war dogs. We had all heard of these beasts, and we feared them. It was said that the Saxons released the dogs just seconds before the shield-walls clashed, and that the beasts were capable of tearing huge holes in the wall into which the enemy spearmen poured.

'I will deal with the dogs,' Merlin said. It was the only contribution he made to the council, but the calm, confident statement relieved some worried men. Merlin's unexpected presence with the army was contribution enough, for his possession of the Cauldron made him, even for many of the Christians, a figure of more awesome power than ever. Not that many understood the purpose of the Cauldron, but they were pleased that the Druid had declared his willingness to accompany the army. With Arthur at our head, and Merlin on our side, how could we lose?

Arthur made his dispositions. King Lancelot, he said, with the spearmen of Siluria and a detachment of men from Dumnonia, would guard the southern frontier against Cerdic. The rest of us would assemble at Caer Ambra and march due east along the valley of the Thames. Lancelot made a show of being reluctant to be thus separated from the main army that would have to fight Aelle, but Culhwch, hearing the orders, shook his head in wonder. 'He's skipping out of battle again, Derfel!' he whispered to me.

'Not if Cerdic attacks him,' I said.

Culhwch glanced across at Lancelot who was flanked by the twins Dinas and Lavaine. 'And he's staying near his protectress, isn't he?' Culhwch said. 'Mustn't stray too far from Guinevere, else he has to stand up by himself.'

I did not care. I was only relieved that Lancelot and his men were not in the main army; it was enough to face the Saxons without worrying about Tanaburs's grandsons or a Silurian knife in my back.

And so we marched. It was a ragged army of contingents from three British kingdoms while some of our more distant allies had still not arrived. There were men promised to us from Elmet and even from Kernow, but they would follow us along the Roman road that ran south-east from Corinium and then east towards London.

London. The Romans had called it Londinium, and before that it had been plain Londo, which Merlin once told me meant 'a wild place', and now it was our goal, the once-great city that had been the largest in all Rome's Britain and which now lay decaying amidst Aelle's stolen lands. Sagramor had once led a famous raid into the old city and he had found its British inhabitants cowed by their new masters, but now, we hoped, we would take them back. That hope spread like wildfire through the army, though Arthur consistently denied it. Our task, he said, was to bring the Saxons to battle and not be lured by the ruins of a dead city, but in this Arthur was opposed by Merlin. 'I'm not coming to see a handful of dead Saxons,' he told me scornfully. 'What use am I in killing Saxons?'

'Every use, Lord,' I told him. 'Your magic frightens the enemy.'

'Don't be absurd, Derfel. Any fool can hop about in front of an army making faces and hurling curses. Frightening Saxons isn't skilled work. Even those ludicrous Druids of Lancelot's could just about manage that! Not that they're real Druids.'

'They're not?'

'Of course they're not! To be a real Druid you have to study. You have to be examined. You have to satisfy other Druids that you know your business, and I never heard of any Druid examining Dinas and Lavaine. Unless Tanaburs did, and what kind of Druid was he? Not a very good one, plainly, else he'd never have let you live. I do deplore inefficiency.'

'They can make magic, Lord,' I said.

'Make magic!' He hooted at that. 'One of the wretches produces a thrush's egg and you think that's magic? Thrushes do it all the time. Now if he'd made a sheep's egg, I'd take some notice.'

'He produced a star too, Lord.'

'Derfel! What an absurdly credulous man you are!' he exclaimed. 'A star made of scissors and parchment? Don't worry, I heard about that star and your precious Ceinwyn isn't in any danger. Nimue and I made sure of that by burying three skulls. You don't need to know the details, but you can rest assured that if those frauds go anywhere near Ceinwyn they'll be changed into grass-snakes. Then they can lay eggs for ever.' I thanked him for that, then asked him just why he was accompanying the army if not to help us against Aelle. 'Because of the scroll, of course,' he told me and patted a pocket of his dirty black robe to show me the scroll was safe.

'Caleddin's scroll?' I asked.

'Is there another?' he countered.

Caleddin's scroll was the treasure Merlin had brought from Ynys Trebes, and in his eyes it was as valuable as all the Treasures of Britain, and no wonder, for the secret of those Treasures was described in the ancient document. Druids were forbidden to write anything down because they believed that to record a spell was to destroy the writer's power to work the magic, and thus all their lore and rites and knowledge were handed down by voice alone. Yet the Romans, before they attacked Ynys Môn, had so feared the British religion that they had suborned a Druid named Caleddin and had persuaded him to dictate all he

169

knew to a Roman scribe, and Caleddin's traitorous scroll had thus preserved all the ancient knowledge of Britain. Much of it, Merlin once told me, had been forgotten in the passing centuries, for the Romans had persecuted the Druids cruelly and much of the old knowledge had vanished into time, but now, with the scroll, he could recreate that lost power. 'And the scroll,' I ventured, 'mentions London?'

'My, my, how curious you are,' Merlin mocked me, but then, perhaps because it was a fine day and he was in a sunny mood, he relented. 'The last Treasure of Britain is in London,' he said. 'Or it was,' he added hastily. 'It's buried there. I thought of giving you a spade and letting you dig the thing up, but you were bound to make a mess of it. Just look at what you did on Ynys Mon! Outnumbered and surrounded, indeed. Unforgivable. So I decided to do it myself. I have to find where it's buried first, of course, and that could be difficult.'

'And is that, Lord,' I asked, 'why you brought the dogs?' For Merlin and Nimue had collected a mangy pack of snapping mongrels that now accompanied the army.

Merlin sighed. 'Allow me, Derfel,' he said, 'to give you some advice. You do not buy a dog and bark yourself. I know the purpose of the dogs, Nimue knows their purpose, and you do not. That is how the Gods intended it to be. Do you have any more questions? Or may I now enjoy this morning's walk?' He lengthened his stride, thumping his big black staff into the turf with each emphatic step.

The smoke of great beacons welcomed us once we had passed Calleva. Those fires were the enemy's signals that we were in sight, and whenever a Saxon saw such a plume of smoke he was under orders to waste the land. The grain stores were emptied, the houses were burned and the livestock driven away. And always Aelle withdrew, staying ever a day's march ahead of us and thus tempting us forward into that wasted land. Wherever the road passed through woodland it would be blocked by trees, and sometimes, as our men laboured to pull the felled trunks out of the way, an arrow or spear would crash through the leaves to snatch a life, or else one of the big Saxon war dogs would come leaping and slavering out of the undergrowth, but they were the only attacks Aelle made and we never once saw his shield-wall. Back he went, and forward we marched, and each day the enemy spears or dogs would snatch a life or two.

Much more damage was done to us by disease. We had found the same thing before Lugg Vale, that whenever a large army gathered, so the Gods plagued it with sickness. The sick slowed us terribly, for if they could not march they had to be laid in a safe place and guarded by spearmen to keep them from the Saxon war-bands that prowled all about our flanks. We would see those enemy bands by day as distant ragged figures, while every night their fires flickered on our horizon. Yet it was not the sick that slowed us the most, but rather the sheer ponderousness of moving so many men. It was a mystery to me why thirty spearmen could cover an easy twenty miles on a relaxed day, but an army of twenty times that number, even trying hard, was lucky to cover eight or nine. Our markers were the Roman stones planted on the verge that recorded the number of miles to London, and after a while I refused to look at them for fear of their depressing message.

The ox-wagons also slowed us. We were equipped with forty capacious farm wagons that carried our food and spare weapons, and those wagons lumbered at a snail's pace in the army's rear. Prince Meurig had been given command of that rearguard and he fussed over the wagons, counted them obsessively, and forever complained that the spearmen ahead were marching too fast.

Arthur's famed horsemen led the army. There were fifty of them now, all mounted on the big shaggy horses that were bred deep inside Dumnonia. Other horsemen, who did not wear the mail armour of Arthur's band, ranged ahead as our scouts and sometimes those men failed to return, though we would always find their severed heads waiting for us on the road as we advanced.

The main body of the army was composed of five hundred

spearmen. Arthur had decided to take no levies with him, for such farmers rarely carried adequate weapons; so we were all oath-sworn warriors and all carried spears and shields and most possessed swords too. Not every man could afford a sword, but Arthur had sent orders throughout Dumnonia that every household possessing a sword which was not already sworn to the army's service should surrender the weapon, and the eighty blades so collected had been distributed among his army. Some men – a few – carried captured Saxon war axes, though others, like myself, disliked the weapon's clumsiness.

And to pay for all this? To pay for the swords and new spears and new shields and wagons and oxen and flour and boots and banners and bridles and cooking pots and helmets and cloaks and knives and horseshoes and salted meat? Arthur laughed when I asked him. 'You must thank the Christians, Derfel,' he said.

'They yielded more?' I asked. 'I thought that udder was dry.'

'It is now,' he said grimly, 'but it's astonishing how much their shrines yielded when we offered their guardians martyrdom, and it's even more astonishing how much we've promised to repay them.'

'Did we ever repay Bishop Sansum?' I asked. His monastery at Ynys Wydryn had provided the fortune that had purchased Aelle's peace during the autumn campaign that had ended at Lugg Vale.

Arthur shook his head. 'And he keeps reminding me of that.'

'The Bishop,' I said carefully, 'seems to have made new friends.'

Arthur laughed at my attempt at tact. 'He's Lancelot's chaplain. Our dear Bishop, it seems, cannot be kept down. Like an apple in a water barrel, he just bobs up again.'

'And he has made his peace with your wife,' I observed.

'I like to see folk resolve their arguments,' he said mildly, 'but Bishop Sansum does have strange allies these days. Guinevere tolerates him, Lancelot lifts him and Morgan defends him. How about that? Morgan!' He was fond of his sister, and it pained him that she was so estranged from Merlin. She ruled Ynys Wydryn with a fierce efficiency, almost as if to demonstrate to Merlin that she was a more suitable partner for him than Nimue, but Morgan had long lost the battle to be Merlin's chief priestess. She was valued by Merlin, Arthur said, but she wanted to be loved, and who, Arthur asked me sadly, could ever love a woman so scarred and shrivelled and disfigured by fire? 'Merlin was never her lover,' Arthur told me, 'though she pretended he was, and he never minded the pretence for the more folk think him odd the happier he is, but in truth he can't stand the sight of Morgan without her mask. She's lonely, Derfel.' So it was no wonder that Arthur was glad for his maimed sister's friendship with Bishop Sansum, though it puzzled me how the fiercest proponent of Christianity in Dumnonia could be such friends with Morgan who was a pagan priestess of famous power. The mouse-lord, I thought, was like a spider making a very strange web. His last web had tried to catch Arthur and it had failed, so who was Sansum busy weaving for now?

We heard no news from Dumnonia after the last of our allies joined us. We were cut off now, surrounded by Saxons, though the last news from home had been reassuring. Cerdic had made no move against Lancelot's troops, nor, it was thought, had he moved east to support Aelle. The last allied troops to join us were a war-band from Kernow led by an old friend who came galloping up the column to find me, then slid off his horse to trip and fall at my feet. It was Tristan, Prince and Edling of Kernow, who picked himself up, beat the dust off his cloak, then embraced me. 'You can relax, Derfel,' he said, 'the warriors of Kernow have arrived. All will be well.'

I laughed. 'You look well, Lord Prince.' He did too.

'I am free of my father,' he explained. 'He has let me out of the cage. He probably hopes a Saxon will bury an axe in my skull.' He made a grotesque face in imitation of a dying man and I spat to avert evil.

Tristan was a handsome, well-made man with black hair, a

forked beard and long moustaches. He had a sallow skin and a face that often looked sad, but which today was filled with happiness. He had disobeyed his father by bringing a small band of men to Lugg Vale, for which act, we had heard, he had been confined to a remote fortress on Kernow's northern coast all winter, but King Mark had now relented and released his son for this campaign. 'We're family now,' Tristan explained.

'Family?'

'My dear father,' he said ironically, 'has taken a new bride. Ialle of Broceliande.' Broceliande was the remaining British kingdom in Armorica and it was ruled by Budic ap Camran, who was married to Arthur's sister Anna, which meant that Ialle was Arthur's niece.

'What's this,' I asked, 'your sixth stepmother?'

'Seventh,' Tristan said, 'and she's only fifteen summers old and father must be fifty at least. I'm already thirty!' he added gloomily.

'And not married?'

'Not yet. But my father marries enough for both of us. Poor Ialle. Give her four years, Derfel, and she'll be dead like the rest. But he's happy enough for now. He's wearing her out like he wears them all out.' He put an arm round my shoulders. 'And I hear you're married?'

'Not married, but well harnessed.'

'To the legendary Ceinwyn!' He laughed. 'Well done, my friend, well done. One day I'll find my own Ceinwyn.'

'May it be soon, Lord Prince.'

'It'll have to be! I'm getting old! Ancient! I saw a white hair the other day, here in my beard.' He poked at his chin. 'See it?' he asked anxiously.

'It?' I mocked him. 'You look like a badger.' There might have been three or four grey strands among the black, but that was all.

Tristan laughed, then glanced at a slave who was running beside the road with a dozen leashed dogs. 'Emergency rations?' he asked me.

'Merlin's magic, and he won't tell me what they're for.' The Druid's dogs were a nuisance; they needed food we could not spare, kept us awake at night with their howling and fought like fiends against the other dogs that accompanied our men.

On the day after Tristan joined us we reached Pontes where the road crosses the Thames on a wondrous stone bridge made by the Romans. We had expected to find the bridge broken, but our scouts reported it whole and, to our astonishment, it was still whole when our spearmen reached it.

That was the hottest day of the march. Arthur forbade anyone to cross the bridge until the wagons had closed up on the main body of the army, and so our men sprawled by the river as they waited. The bridge had eleven arches, two on either bank where they lifted the roadway onto the seven-arch span that crossed the river itself. Tree trunks and other floating debris had piled against the upstream side of the bridge so that the river to the west was wider and deeper than to the east, and the make-shift dam made the water race and foam between the stone pilings. There was a Roman settlement on the far bank; a group of stone buildings surrounded by the remnants of an earth embankment, while at our end of the bridge a great tower guarded the road that passed beneath its crumbling arch on which a Roman inscription still existed. Arthur translated it for me, telling me that the Emperor Adrian had ordered the bridge to be built. '*Imperator*,' I said, peering up at the stone plaque. 'Does that mean Emperor?'

'It does.'

'And an Emperor is above a King?' I asked.

'An Emperor is a Lord of Kings,' Arthur said. The bridge had made him gloomy. He clambered about its landward arches, then walked to the tower and laid a hand on its stones as he peered up at the inscription. 'Suppose you and I wanted to build a bridge like this,' he said to me, 'how would we do it?'

I shrugged. 'Make it from timber, Lord. Good elm pilings, the rest from split oak.'

He grimaced. 'And would it still be standing when our great-great-grandchildren live?'

'They can build their own bridges,' I suggested.

He stroked the tower. 'We have no one who can dress stone like this. No one who knows how to sink a stone pier into a river bed. No one who even remembers how. We're like men with a treasure hoard, Derfel, and day by day it shrinks and we don't know how to stop it or how to make more.' He glanced back and saw the first of Meurig's wagons appearing in the distance. Our scouts had probed deep into the woods that grew either side of the road and they had reported neither sight nor smell of any Saxons, but Arthur was still suspicious. 'If I was them I'd let our army cross, then attack the wagons,' he said, so instead he had decided to throw an advance guard over the bridge, cross the wagons into what remained of the settlement's decaying earth wall, and only then bring the main part of his army over the river.

My men formed the advance guard. The land beyond the river was less thickly wooded and though some of the remaining trees grew close enough to hide a small army, no one appeared to challenge us. The only sign of the Saxons was a severed horse's head waiting at the bridge's centre. None of my men would pass it until Nimue came forward to dispel its evil. She merely spat at the head. Saxon magic, she said, was feeble stuff, and once its evil had been dissipated, Issa and I heaved the thing over the parapet.

My men guarded the earth wall as the wagons and their escort crossed. Galahad had come with me and the two of us poked about the buildings inside the wall. Saxons, for some reason, were loath to use Roman settlements, preferring their own timber and thatched halls, though some folk had been living here till recently, for the hearths contained ashes and some of the floors were swept clean. 'Could be our people,' Galahad said, for plenty of Britons lived among the Saxons, many of them as slaves, but some as free people who had accepted the foreign rule.

The buildings appeared to have been barracks once, but there were also two houses and what I took to be a huge granary which, when we pushed open its broken door, proved to be a beast house where cattle were sheltered overnight to protect them from wolves. The floor was a deep mire of straw and dung that smelt so rank that I would have left the building there and then, but Galahad saw something in the shadows at its far end and so I followed him across the wet, viscous floor.

The building's far end was not a straight gabled wall, but was broken by a curved apse. High on the apse's stained plaster, and barely visible through the dust and dirt of the years, was a painted symbol that looked like a big X on which was super-imposed a P. Galahad stared up at the symbol and made the sign of the cross. 'It used to be a church, Derfel,' he said in wonder.

'It stinks,' I said.

He gazed reverently at the symbol. 'There were Christians here.'

'Not any longer.' I shuddered at the overwhelming stench and batted helplessly at the flies that buzzed around my head.

Galahad did not care about the smell. He thrust his spear-butt into the compacted mass of cow dung and rotting straw, and finally succeeded in uncovering a small patch of the floor. What he found only made him work harder until he had revealed the upper part of a man depicted in small mosaic tiles. The man wore robes like a bishop, had a sun-halo round his head and in one uplifted hand was carrying a small beast with a skinny body and a great shaggy head. 'St Mark and his lion,' Galahad told me.

'I thought lions were huge beasts,' I said, disappointed. 'Sagramor says they're bigger than horses and fiercer than bears.' I peered at the dung-smeared beast. 'That's just a kitten.'

'It's a symbolic lion,' he reproved me. He tried to clear more of the floor, but the filth was too old, thick-packed and glutin-ous. 'One day,' he said, 'I shall build a great church like this. A huge church. A place where a whole people can gather before their God.'

'And when you're dead,' I pulled him back towards the door, 'some bastard will winter ten herds of cattle in it and be thankful to you.'

He insisted on staying one minute more and, while I held his shield and spear, he spread his arms wide and offered a new prayer in an old place. 'It's a sign from God,' he said excitedly as he at last followed me back into the sunshine. 'We shall restore Christianity to Lloegyr, Derfel. It's a sign of victory!'

It might have been a sign of victory to Galahad, but that old church was almost the cause of our defeat. The next day, as we advanced east towards London that was now so tantalizingly close, Prince Meurig stayed at Pontes. He sent the wagons on with most of their escort, but kept fifty men back to clear the church of its cloying filth. Meurig, like Galahad, was much moved by the existence of that ancient church and decided to re-dedicate the shrine to its God, and so he had his spearmen lay aside their war gear and clear the building of its dung and straw so that the priests who accompanied him could say whatever prayers were needed to restore the building's sanctity.

And while the rearguard forked dung, the Saxons who had been following us came over the bridge.

Meurig escaped. He had a horse, but most of the dung-sweepers died and so did two of the priests, and then the Saxons stormed up the road and caught the wagons. The remnant of the rearguard put up a fight, but they were outnumbered and the Saxons outflanked them, overran them, and began slaughtering the plodding oxen so that, one by one, the wagons were stopped and fell into the enemy's hands.

By now we had heard the commotion. The army stopped as Arthur's horsemen galloped back towards the sound of the killing. None of those horsemen was properly equipped for battle, for it was simply too hot for a man to ride in armour all day, yet their sudden appearance was enough to stampede the Saxons, but the damage had already been done. Eighteen of the forty wagons had been immobilized and, without oxen, they would have to be abandoned. Most of the eighteen had been plundered and barrels of our precious flour had been spilt onto the road. We salvaged what flour we could and wrapped it in cloaks, but the bread it would bake would be poor stuff and riddled with dust and twigs. Even before the raid we had been cutting down on rations, reckoning we had enough for two more weeks, but now, because most of the food had been in the rearward vehicles, we faced the prospect of abandoning the march in just one week and even then there would be barely enough food remaining to see us safe back to Calleva or Caer Ambra.

'There are fish in the river,' Meurig pointed out.

'Gods, not fish again,' Culhwch grumbled, recalling the privations of the last days of Ynys Trebes.

'There are not fish enough to feed an army,' Arthur answered angrily. He would have liked to have shouted at Meurig, to have stripped his stupidity bare, but Meurig was a Prince and Arthur's sense of what was proper would never let him humiliate a Prince. If it had been Culhwch or I who had divided the rearguard and exposed the wagons Arthur would have lost his temper, but Meurig's birth protected him.

We were at a Council of War north of the road which here ran straight across a dull, grassy plain that was studded with clumps of trees and with straggling banks of gorse and hawthorn. All the commanders were present, and dozens of lesser men crowded close to hear our discussions. Meurig, of course, denied all responsibility. If he had been given more men, he said, the disaster would never have happened. 'Besides,' he said, 'and you will forgive me for pointing this out, though I would have thought it an obvious point that should hardly need my explication, no success can attend an army that ignores God.'

'So why did God ignore us?' Sagramor asked.

Arthur hushed the Numidian. 'What is done is done,' he said. 'What happens next is our business here.'

But what happened next was up to Aelle rather than to us. He had won the first victory, though it was possible he did not know the extent of that triumph. We were miles inside his territory and we faced starvation unless we could trap his army, destroy it, and so break out into land that had not been stripped of supplies. Our scouts brought us deer, and once in a while they came across some cattle or sheep, but such delicacies were rare and not nearly sufficient to make up for the lost flour and dried meat.

'He has to defend London, surely?' Cuneglas suggested.

Sagramor shook his head. 'London is populated by Britons,' he said. 'The Saxons don't like it there. He'll let us have London.'

'There'll be food in London,' Cuneglas said.

'But how long will it last, Lord King?' Arthur asked. 'And if we take it with us, what do we do? Wander for ever, hoping Aelle will attack?' He stared at the ground, his long face hardened by thought. Aelle's tactics were clear enough now, the Saxon would let us march and march, and his men would always be ahead of us to sweep our path clean of food, and once we were weakened and dispirited, the Saxon horde would swarm around us. 'What we must do,' Arthur said, 'is draw him onto us.'

Meurig blinked rapidly. 'How?' he inquired, in a tone suggesting Arthur was being ridiculous.

The Druids who accompanied us, Merlin, Iorweth and two others from Powys, were all sitting in a group to one side of the Council and Merlin, who had commandeered a convenient ant hill as his seat, now commanded attention by raising his staff. 'What do you do,' he asked mildly, 'when you want something valuable?'

'Take it,' Agravain growled. Agravain commanded Arthur's heavy horsemen, leaving Arthur free to lead the whole army.

'When you want something valuable from the Gods,' Merlin amended his question, 'what do you do then?'

Agravain shrugged, and none of the rest of us could supply an answer.

Merlin stood so that his height dominated the Council. 'If you wish something,' he said very simply as though he was our teacher and we his pupils, 'you must give something. You must make an offering, a sacrifice. The thing I wanted above all things in this world was the Cauldron, so I offered my life to its search and I received my wish, but if I had not offered my soul for it, the gift would not have come. We must sacrifice something.'

Meurig's Christianity was offended and he could not resist taunting the Druid. 'Your life, perhaps, Lord Merlin? It worked last time.' He laughed and looked to his surviving priests to join the laughter.

The laughter died as Merlin pointed his black staff at the Prince. He kept the staff very still, its butt just inches from Meurig's face, and he held it there long after the laughter had stopped. And still Merlin held the staff, stretching the silence unbearably. Agricola, feeling he must support his Prince, cleared his throat, but a twitch of the black staff stilled whatever protest Agricola might have made. Meurig wriggled uncomfortably, but seemed struck dumb. He reddened, blinked and squirmed. Arthur frowned, but said nothing. Nimue smiled in anticipation of the Prince's fate, while the rest of us watched in silence and some of us shuddered in fear, and still Merlin did not move until, at last, Meurig could take the suspense no longer. 'I was jesting!' he almost shouted in desperation. 'I meant no offence.'

'Did you say something, Lord Prince?' Merlin inquired anxiously, pretending Meurig's panicked words had jolted him out of reverie. He lowered the staff. 'I must have been daydreaming. Where was I? Oh yes, a sacrifice. What do we have, Arthur, that is most precious?'

Arthur thought for a few seconds. 'We have gold,' he said, 'silver, my armour.'

'Baubles,' Merlin answered dismissively.

There was silence for a while, then men outside the Council offered their answers. Some took torques from about their necks and waved them in the air. Others suggested offering weapons, one man even called out the name of Arthur's sword, Excalibur. The Christians made no suggestions, because this was a pagan procedure and they would offer nothing but their prayers, but one man of Powys suggested we sacrifice a Christian and that idea prompted loud cheers. Meurig blushed again.

'I sometimes think,' Merlin said when no more suggestions were offered, 'that I am doomed to live among idiots. Is all the world mad but me? Cannot one poor blinkered fool among you see what is plainly the most precious thing we possess? Not one?'

'Food,' I said.

'Ah!' Merlin cried, delighted. 'Well done, you poor blinkered fool! Food, you idiots.' He spat the insult at the Council. 'Aelle's plans are predicated upon the belief that we lack food, so we must demonstrate the opposite. We must waste food like Christians waste prayer, we must scatter it to the empty heavens, we must squander it, we must throw it away, we must,' he paused to put stress on the next word, 'sacrifice it.' He waited for a voice to be raised in opposition, but no one spoke. 'Find a place near here,' Merlin ordered Arthur, 'where you will be content to offer Aelle battle. Do not make it too strong, for you don't want him to refuse combat. You're tempting him, remember, and you must make him believe he can defeat you. How long will it take him to ready his forces for battle?'

'Three days,' Arthur said. He suspected that Aelle's men were widely scattered in their loose ring that escorted us and it would take the Saxon at least two days to shrink that ring into a compact army, and another full day to shove it into battle order.

'I shall need two days,' Merlin said, 'so bake enough hard bread to keep us barely alive for five days,' he ordered. 'Not a generous ration, Arthur, for our sacrifice has to be real. Then find your battleground and wait. Leave the rest to me, but I want Derfel and a dozen of his men to do some labouring work. And do we have any men here,' he raised his voice so that all the men crowding about the Council could hear, 'who have skills in carving wood?'

He chose six men. Two were from Powys, one bore the hawk of Kernow on his shield, and the others were from Dumnonia. They were given axes and knives, but nothing to carve until Arthur had discovered his battleground.

He found it on a wide heath that rose to a gentle summit

182

crowned by a scattered grove of yew and whitebeam. The slope was nowhere steep, but we would still have the high ground and there Arthur planted his banners, and round the banners there grew an encampment of thatched shelters made from branches cut from the grove. Our spearmen would make a ring about the banners and there, we hoped, face Aelle. The bread that would keep us alive as we waited for the Saxons was baked in turf ovens.

Merlin chose his spot to the north of the heath. There was a meadow there, a place of stunted alders and rank grass edging a stream that curled south towards the distant Thames. My men were ordered to fell three oaks, then strip the trunks of their branches and bark, and afterwards dig three pits into which the oaks could be set up as columns, though first he ordered his six carvers to make the oak trunks into three ghoulish idols. Iorweth helped Nimue and Merlin, and the three loved that work for it allowed them to devise the most ghastly, fearsome things that bore small resemblance to any God I had ever known, but Merlin did not care. The idols, he said, were not for us, but for the Saxons, and so he and his woodcarvers made three things of horror with animal faces, female breasts and male genitalia, and when the columns were finished my men stopped their other work and hoisted the three figures into their pits while Merlin and the woodcarvers tamped their bases with earth so that at last the columns stood upright. 'The father,' Merlin capered in front of the idols, 'the son and the holy ghost!' he laughed.

My men, meanwhile, had been making a great stack of wood in front of the pits, and onto that wood we now piled what remained of our food. We killed the remaining oxen and heaved their heavy corpses onto the pile so that their fresh blood trickled down through the layers of timber, and onto the oxen we heaped everything they had hauled; dried meat, dried fish, cheese, apples, grain and beans, and on top of those precious supplies we put the carcasses of two newly caught deer and a freshly slaughtered ram. The ram's head, with its twin horns, was cut off and nailed to the central pillar.

The Saxons watched us work. They were on the stream's far bank and once or twice, on the first day, their spears had hurtled over the water, but after those first futile efforts to interfere with us they had been content to just watch and see exactly what strange things we did. I sensed that their numbers grew. On the first day we had glimpsed only a dozen men among the far trees, but by the second evening there were at least a score of fires smoking behind the leaf screen.

'Now,' Merlin said that evening, 'we give them something to watch.'

We carried fire in cooking pots down from the heath's low summit to the great pile of wood and thrust it deep into the tangle of branches. The wood was green, but we had stacked heaps of dry grass and broken twigs into the centre, and by nightfall the fire was raging fiercely. The flames lit our crude idols with a lurid glare, the smoke boiled in a great plume that drifted towards London and the smell of roasting meat wafted tantalizingly towards our hungry encampment. The fire crackled and collapsed, exploding streams of sparks into the air, and in its fierce heat the dead beasts twitched and twisted as the flames shrank their sinews and exploded their skulls. Melting fat hissed in the blaze, then flared up white and bright to cast black shadows on the three hideous idols. All night that fire seethed, burning our last hopes of leaving Lloegyr without victory, and in the dawn we watched as the Saxons crept out to investigate its smoking remnants.

Then we waited. We were not entirely passive. Our horsemen rode east to scout the London road, and came back to report bands of marching Saxons. Others of us cut timber and used it to begin constructing a hall beside the shrinking grove on the heath's summit. We had no need of such a hall, but Arthur wanted to give the impression that we were establishing a base deep in Lloegyr from which we would harass Aelle's lands. That belief, if it convinced Aelle, would surely provoke him to battle. We made the beginnings of an earthen rampart, but lacking the proper tools we made a poor showing of the wall, though it must have helped the deception.

We were busy enough, but that did not stop a rancorous division showing in the army. Some, like Meurig, believed we had adopted the wrong strategy from the start. It would have been better, Meurig now said, if we had sent three or more smaller armies to take the Saxon fortresses on the frontier. We should have harassed and provoked, but instead we were growing ever hungrier in a self-made trap deep in Lloegyr.

'And maybe he's right,' Arthur confessed to me on the third morning.

'No, Lord,' I insisted, and to prove my point I gestured north towards the wide smear of smoke that betrayed where a growing horde of Saxons was gathering beyond the stream.

Arthur shook his head. 'Aelle's army is there, right enough,' he said, 'but that doesn't mean he'll attack. They'll watch us, but if he has any sense, he'll let us rot here.'

'We could attack him,' I suggested.

He shook his head. 'Leading an army through trees and across a stream is a recipe for disaster. That's our last resort, Derfel. Just pray he comes today.'

But he did not come, and that was the end of the fifth day since the Saxons had destroyed our supplies. Tomorrow we would eat crumbs and in two days more we would be ravenous. In three we would gaze defeat in its horrid eyes. Arthur displayed no concern, whatever doom the grumblers in the army suggested, and that evening, as the sun drifted down over distant Dumnonia, Arthur beckoned for me to climb and join him on the growing wall of our crudely constructed hall. I clambered up the logs and pulled myself onto the top of the wall. 'Look,' he said, pointing east, and far off on the horizon I could see another smear of grey smoke and beneath the smoke, its buildings lit by the slanting sun, was a great town bigger than any I had ever seen before. Bigger then Glevum or Corinium, bigger even than Aquae Sulis. 'London,' Arthur said in a tone of wonder. 'Did you ever think to see it?'

'Yes, Lord.'

He smiled. 'My confident Derfel Cadarn.' He was perched on

the wall's top, holding onto an untrimmed pillar and staring fixedly at the city. Behind us, in the rectangle of the hall's timbers, the army's horses were stabled. Those poor horses were already hungry, for there was little grass on the dry heathland and we had brought no forage for them. 'It's odd, isn't it,' Arthur said, still gazing at London, 'that by now Lancelot and Cerdic could have done battle and we'll know nothing about it.'

'Pray Lancelot won,' I said.

'I do, Derfel, I do.' He kicked his heels against the half built wall. 'What a chance Aelle has!' he said suddenly. 'He could cut down the best warriors of Britain here. By year's end, Derfel, his men could hold our halls. They could stroll to the Severn Sea. All gone. All Britain! Gone.' He seemed to find the thought amusing, then he twisted about and looked down at the horses. 'We could always eat them,' he said. 'Their meat will keep us alive for a week or two.'

'Lord!' I protested at his pessimism.

'Don't worry, Derfel,' he laughed, 'I've sent our old friend Aelle a message.'

'You have?'

'Sagramor's woman. Malla, her name is. What odd names these Saxons have. You know her?'

'I've seen her, Lord.' Malla was a tall girl with long muscular legs and shoulders broad as a barrel. Sagramor had taken her captive in one of his raids late in the previous year and she had evidently accepted her fate with a passivity that was reflected in her flat, almost vacant face that was surrounded by a mass of gold-coloured hair. Other than that hair there was no one feature of Malla's that was particularly attractive, but somehow she was still oddly alluring; a great, strong, slow, robust creature with a calm grace and a demeanour as taciturn as her Numidian lover.

'She's pretending to have escaped us,' Arthur explained, 'and even now she should be telling Aelle that we plan to stay here through the coming winter. She says Lancelot's coming to join us with another three hundred spears, and that we need him here because a lot of our men are weak with sickness, despite our pits being filled with good food.' He smiled. 'She's spinning endless nonsense to him, or I hope she is.'

'Or maybe she's telling him the truth,' I suggested gloomily.

'Maybe.' He sounded unworried. He watched a line of men bringing skins of water from a spring that bubbled at the foot of the southern slope. 'But Sagramor trusts her,' he added, 'and I long ago learned to trust Sagramor.'

I made the sign against evil. 'I wouldn't let my woman go to an enemy camp.'

'She volunteered,' Arthur said. 'She says the Saxons won't harm her. It seems her father is one of their chiefs.'

'Pray she loves him less than she loves Sagramor.'

Arthur shrugged. The risk was taken now and discussing it would not lessen its dangers. He changed the subject. 'I want you in Dumnonia when all this is done.'

'Willingly, Lord, if you promise me Ceinwyn will be safe,' I answered and, when he tried to dismiss my fears with a wave of his hand, I persevered. 'I hear tales of a dog being killed and its bloody pelt draped on a bitch.'

Arthur twisted about, swung his legs over the wall and dropped down into the makeshift stables. He shoved a horse aside and beckoned for me to join him where no man could see us or hear us. He was angry. 'Tell me again what you hear,' he commanded me.

'That a dog was killed,' I said when I had jumped down, 'and its bloody pelt was draped on a crippled bitch.'

'And who did that?' he demanded.

'A friend of Lancelot's,' I answered, unwilling to name his wife.

He struck a hand against the crude timber wall, startling the closest horses. 'My wife,' he said, 'is a friend to King Lancelot.' I said nothing. 'As am I,' he challenged me, and still I said nothing. 'He's a proud man, Derfel, and he lost his father's kingdom because I failed in my oath. I owe him.' He said the last three words coldly.

I matched his coldness with my own. 'I hear,' I said, 'that the crippled bitch was given the name Ceinwyn.'

'Enough!' He slapped the wall again. 'Stories! Just stories! No one denies there's resentment for what you and Ceinwyn did, Derfel. I am not a fool, but I will not hear this nonsense from you! Guinevere attracts these rumours. People resent her. Any woman who is beautiful, who is clever, and who has hard opinions and isn't afraid to speak them attracts resentment, but are you saying she would work some filthy spell against Ceinwyn? That she'd slaughter a dog and skin it? Do you believe that?'

'I would like not to,' I said.

'Guinevere is my wife.' He had lowered his voice, but the tone was still bitter. 'I don't have other wives, I don't take slaves to my bed, I am hers and she is mine, Derfel, and I will not hear anything said against her. Nothing!' He shouted that last word and I wondered if he was remembering the filthy insults hurled by Gorfyddyd at Lugg Vale. Gorfyddyd had claimed to have bedded Guinevere, and claimed further that a whole legion of other men had bedded her as well. I remembered Valerin's lover's ring, cut by the cross and decorated with Guinevere's symbol, but I thrust the memories aside.

'Lord,' I said quietly, 'I never mentioned your wife's name.'

He stared at me, and for a second I thought he was going to strike me, then he shook his head. 'She can be difficult, Derfel. There are times when I wish she was not so ready to show scorn, but I cannot imagine living without her advice.' He paused and gave me a rueful smile. 'I cannot imagine living without her. She has killed no dogs, Derfel, she has killed no dogs. Trust me. That Goddess of hers, Isis, doesn't demand sacrifices, at least not of living things. Of gold, yes.' He grinned, his good mood suddenly restored. 'Isis swallows gold.'

'I believe you, Lord,' I said, 'but that doesn't make Ceinwyn safe. Dinas and Lavaine have threatened her.'

He shook his head. 'You hurt Lancelot, Derfel. I don't blame you, for I know what drove you, but can you blame him for resenting you? And Dinas and Lavaine serve Lancelot, and it's only right that men should share their master's grudges.' He paused. 'When this war is done, Derfel,' he went on, 'we shall make a reconciliation. All of us! When I make my band of warriors into brothers, we shall make peace between us all. You, Lancelot and everyone. And until that happens, Derfel, I swear Ceinwyn's protection. On my life if you insist. You can impose the oath, Derfel. You can demand whatever price you want, my life, my son's life even, because I need you. Dumnonia needs you. Culhwch is a good man, but he can't manage Mordred.'

'Can I?' I asked.

'Mordred is wilful,' Arthur ignored my question, 'but what do we expect? He's Uther's grandson, he has the blood of Kings and we don't want him to be a milksop, but he does need discipline. He needs guidance. Culhwch thinks it's enough to hit him, but that just makes him more stubborn. I want you and Ceinwyn to raise him.'

I shuddered. 'You make coming home ever more attractive, Lord.'

He scowled at my levity. 'Never forget, Derfel, that our oath is to give Mordred his throne. That is why I came back to Britain. That is my first duty in Britain, and all who are sworn to me are sworn to that oath. No one said it would be easy, but it will be done. Nine years from now we shall acclaim Mordred on Caer Cadarn. On that day, Derfel, we are all released from the oath and I pray to every God who will listen to me that on that day I will be able to hang up Excalibur and never fight again. But till that good day comes, whatever the difficulties, we shall cleave to our oath. Do you understand that?'

'Yes, Lord,' I said humbly.

'Good.' Arthur pushed a horse aside. 'Aelle will come tomorrow,' he said confidently as he walked away, 'so sleep well.'

The sun sank over Dumnonia, drowning it in red fire. To the north our enemy chanted war songs, and about our campfires we sang of home. Our sentinels gazed into the darkness, the horses whinnied, Merlin's dogs howled and some of us slept.

*

At dawn we saw that Merlin's three pillars had been thrown down during the night. A Saxon wizard, his hair dunged into spikes and his naked body barely hidden by the tattered scraps of wolfskin hanging from a band at his neck, whirled in a dance where the pillars had stood. The sight of that wizard convinced Arthur that Aelle was planning his assault.

We deliberately made no show of readiness. Our sentinels stood guard; other spearmen just lazed on the forward slope as if they expected another uneventful day, but behind them, in the shadows of the shelters and under the remains of the whitebeam and yew, and inside the walls of the half-built hall, the mass of our men made ready.

We tightened shield straps, honed swords and blades that were already ground to a wicked edge, then we hammered spearheads tight onto their staffs. We touched our amulets, we embraced each other, we ate what little bread we had left and prayed to whatever Gods we believed would help us this day. Merlin, Iorweth and Nimue wandered among the shelters touching blades and distributing sprigs of dried vervain to offer us protection.

I donned my battle gear. I had heavy knee-length boots with strips of iron sewn to protect my calves from the spear stroke that comes under the shield's edge. I wore the woollen shirt made from Ceinwyn's crudely spun wool and over it a leather coat on which I had pinned Ceinwyn's little golden brooch that had been my protective talisman all these long years. Over the leather I hauled a coat of chain mail, a luxury I had taken from a dead Powysian chief at Lugg Vale. It was an ancient coat of Roman make and had been forged with a skill that no man now possesses, and I often wondered what other spearmen had worn that knee-length coat of linked iron rings. The Powysian warrior had died in it, cut down through the skull by Hywelbane, but I suspected at least one other of the coat's wearers had been killed wearing the mail for its rings had a deep rent over the left breast. The shattered mail had been crudely repaired with links of iron chain.

I wore warrior rings on my left hand, for in battle they served to protect the fingers, but I put none on my right for the iron rings made gripping a sword or spear more difficult. I strapped leather greaves on my forearms. My helmet was of iron, a simple bowl shape lined with cloth-padded leather, but at the back of it there was a thick flap of hog leather to protect my neck, and earlier in the spring I had paid a smith at Caer Sws to rivet two cheek pieces onto its flanks. The helmet was surmounted by an iron knob from which hung a wolf-tail taken in the deep woods of Benoic. I belted Hywelbane at my waist, pushed my left hand through the leather loops of my shield and hefted my war spear. The spear was taller than a man, its shaft thick as Ceinwyn's wrist, and at its head was a long, heavy, leaf-shaped blade. The blade was razor sharp, and the steel's butt ends were rounded smooth so that the blade could not be trapped in an enemy's belly or armour. I wore no cloak for the day was too hot.

Cavan, dressed in his armour, came to me and knelt. 'If I fight well, Lord,' he asked, 'can I paint a fifth point on my shield?'

'I expect men to fight well,' I said, 'so why should I reward them for doing what is expected of them?'

'Then if I bring you a trophy, Lord?' he suggested. 'A chief-tain's axe? Gold?'

'Bring me a Saxon chief, Cavan,' I said, 'and you can paint a hundred points on your star.'

'Five will suffice, Lord,' he said.

The morning passed slowly. Those of us in metal armour sweated heavily in the heat. From beyond the northern stream, where the Saxons were shrouded by trees, it must have looked as if our encampment was asleep, or else peopled by sick, unmoving men, but that illusion did not serve to bring the Saxons through the trees. The sun climbed higher. Our scouts, the lightly armed horsemen who rode with only a sheaf of throwing spears as weapons, trotted out of the camp. They would have no place in a battle between shield-walls and so they took their nervous horses south towards the Thames. They could come back quickly enough, though if disaster struck they were under orders to ride westwards and take a warning of our defeat to distant Dumnonia. Arthur's own horsemen donned their heavy armour of leather and iron, and then, with straps that they draped about their horses' withers, they hung the clumsy leather shields that protected their horses' breasts.

Arthur, hidden with his horsemen inside the half-built hall, was wearing his famous scale armour that was a Roman suit made of thousands of small iron plates sewn onto a leather jerkin so that the scales overlapped like fish scales. There were silver plates among the iron so that the suit seemed to shimmer as he moved. He wore a white cloak and Excalibur, in its magical cross-hatched scabbard that protected its wearer from harm, hung at his left hip, while his servant Hygwydd held his long spear, his silver-grey helmet with its plume of goose feathers and his round shield with its mirror-like coating of silver. In peace Arthur liked to dress modestly, but in war he was flamboyant. He liked to think his reputation was made by honest government, but the dazzling armour and polished shield betrayed that he knew the real source of his fame.

Culhwch had once ridden with Arthur's heavy horsemen, but now, like me, he led a band of spearmen and at midday he sought me out and dropped beside me in the small shade of my turf shelter. He wore an iron breastplate, a leather jerkin and had greaves of Roman bronze on his bare calves. 'Bastard isn't coming,' he grumbled.

'Tomorrow, maybe?' I suggested.

He sniffed disgustedly, then offered me an earnest look. 'I know what you're going to say, Derfel, but I'll ask you just the same, though before you answer I want you to consider something. Who was it who fought beside you in Benoic? Who stood shield to shield with you at Ynys Trebes? Who shared his ale with you and even let you seduce that fisher-girl? Who held your hand at Lugg Vale? It was I. Remember that when you answer me. So what food have you got hidden?'

I smiled. 'None.'

'You're a big Saxon bag of useless guts,' he said, 'that's what you are.' He looked at Galahad who was resting with my men. 'Have you got food, Lord Prince?' he asked.

'I gave my last crust to Tristan,' Galahad answered.

'A Christian act, I suppose?' Culhwch asked scornfully.

'I should like to think so,' Galahad said.

'No wonder I'm a pagan,' Culhwch said. 'I need food. Can't kill Saxons on an empty belly.' He scowled about my men, but no one offered him anything, for they had nothing to offer. 'So you're going to take that bastard Mordred off my hands?' he asked me when he had abandoned hope of a morsel.

'That's what Arthur wants.'

'It's what I want,' he said vigorously. 'If I had food here, Derfel, I'd give you every last bite in return for that favour. You're welcome to the snivelling little bastard. Let him make your life a misery instead of mine, but I warn you, you'll wear your belt out on his rotten skin.'

'It might not be wise,' I said cautiously, 'to whip my future King.'

'It might not be wise, but it's pleasurable. Ugly little toad.' He twisted to look past the shelter. 'What's the matter with these Saxons? Don't they want a battle?'

His answer came almost immediately. Suddenly a horn sounded its deep, mournful call, then we heard the thump of one of the big drums that the Saxons carried to war and we all stirred in time to see Aelle's army come from the trees beyond the stream. One moment it was an empty landscape of leaves and spring sunshine, and then the enemy was there.

There were hundreds of them. Hundreds of fur-clad, iron-bound men with axes, dogs, spears and shields. Their banners were bull skulls lofted on poles and hung with rags, while their vanguard was a troop of wizards with dung-spiked hair who pranced ahead of the shield-wall and hurled their curses at us.

Merlin and the other Druids went down the slope to meet the wizards. They did not walk, but, like all Druids before battle, they hopped on one leg and kept their balance with their staffs while holding their free hands in the air. They stopped a hundred paces from the nearest wizards and returned their curses while the army's Christian priests stood at the top of the slope and spread their hands and gazed into the sky as they called for their God's aid.

The rest of us were scrambling into line. Agricola was on the left with his Roman-uniformed troops, the rest of us made up the centre, and Arthur's horsemen who, for the moment, remained hidden in the crude hall would eventually form our right wing. Arthur pulled on his helmet, struggled onto Llamrei's back, draped his white cloak over the horse's rump, then took his heavy spear and shining shield from Hygwydd.

Sagramor, Cuneglas and Agricola led the footmen. For the moment, and only until Arthur's horsemen appeared, my men had the right-hand end of the line and I saw we were likely to be outflanked as the Saxon line was much wider than ours. They outnumbered us. The bards will tell you there were thousands of the vermin at that battle, but I suspect Aelle had no more than six hundred men. The Saxon King, of course, possessed far more spearmen than those we saw in front of us, though he, like us, had been forced to leave strong garrisons in his border fortresses, but even six hundred spearmen was a large army. And there were just as many followers behind the shield-wall; mostly women and children who would take no part in the battle but who doubtless hoped to pick our corpses clean when the fighting was done.

Our Druids laboriously hopped back up the slope. Sweat poured down Merlin's face into the strapped plaits of his long beard. 'No magic,' he told us, 'their wizards don't know real magic. You're safe.' He pushed between our shields, going to seek Nimue. The Saxons marched slowly towards us. Their wizards spat and screamed, men shouted at their followers to keep the line straight while others shouted insults at us.

Our war horns had begun to blare their challenge and our men now began to sing. At our end of the shield-wall we were singing the great Battle Song of Beli Mawr that is a triumphant howl of slaughter that puts fire into a man's belly. Two of my men were dancing in front of the shield-wall, stepping and leaping over their swords and spears that were laid crosswise on the ground. I called them back into the wall because I thought the Saxons would keep marching straight up the shallow hill and thus precipitate a quick bloody clash, but instead they stopped a hundred paces away from us and realigned their shields to make the continuous wall of leather-strengthened timber. They fell silent as their wizards pissed towards us. Their huge dogs barked and jerked at their leashes, the war drums pounded on, and every now and then a horn would make its sad wail, but otherwise the Saxons remained silent except to beat their spear butts against their shields in time to the drums' heavy beat.

'First Saxons I've seen.' Tristan had come to my side and was staring at the Saxon army with its thick fur armour, double-bladed axes, dogs and spears.

'They die easily enough,' I told him.

'I don't like the axes,' he confessed, touching the iron-sheathed rim of his shield for luck.

'They're clumsy things,' I tried to reassure him. 'One swing and they're useless. Catch it plumb on your shield and thrust low with your sword. It always works.' Or almost always.

The Saxon drums suddenly ceased, the enemy line parted in its centre and Aelle himself appeared. He stood and stared at us for a few seconds, spat, then ostentatiously threw down his spear and shield to show that he wanted to talk. He strode towards us, a huge, tall, dark-haired man in a thick black bearskin robe. Two wizards accompanied him and a thin, balding man whom I presumed was his interpreter.

Cuneglas, Meurig, Agricola, Merlin and Sagramor went to meet him. Arthur had decided to stay with his horsemen and, because Cuneglas was the only King on our side of the field, it was right that Cuneglas should speak for us, but he invited the others to accompany him and beckoned me forward as his interpreter. It was thus that I met Aelle for the second time. He was a tall, broad-chested man with a flat, hard face and dark eyes. His beard was full and black, his cheeks were scarred, his nose broken and there were two fingers missing from his right hand.

He was dressed in a suit of mail and boots of leather, and he wore an iron helmet on which two bull's horns had been mounted. There was British gold at his throat and on his wrists. The bearskin robe that covered his armour must have been swelteringly uncomfortable on that hot day, but such a rich pelt could stop a sword blow as well as any iron armour. He glared at me. 'I remember you, worm,' he said. 'A Saxon turncoat.'

I bowed my head briefly. 'Greetings, Lord King.'

He spat. 'You think, because you are polite, that your death will be easy?'

'My death has nothing to do with you, Lord King,' I said. 'But I expect to tell my grandchildren of yours.'

He laughed, then cast a mocking glance at the five leaders. 'Five of you! And only one of me! And where's Arthur? Voiding his bowels in terror?'

I named our leaders to Aelle, then Cuneglas took up the dialogue that I translated for him. He began, as was customary, by demanding Aelle's immediate surrender. We would be merciful, Cuneglas said. We would demand Aelle's life and all his treasury and all his weapons and all his women and all his slaves, but his spearmen could go free, minus their right hands.

Aelle, as was customary, sneered at the demand, revealing a mouth of rotting, discoloured teeth. 'Does Arthur think,' he demanded, 'that because he stays hidden we do not know he is here with his horses? Tell him, worm, that I shall pillow my head on his corpse this night. Tell him his wife will be my whore, and that when I've exhausted her she shall be the pleasure of my slaves. And tell that moustached fool,' he gestured towards Cuneglas, 'that by nightfall this place will be known as the Grave of Britons. Tell him,' he went on, 'that I shall snip off his whiskers and make them a plaything for my daughter's cats. Tell him I shall carve a drinking cup from his skull and feed his belly to my dogs. And tell that demon,' he jerked his beard at Sagramor, 'that today his black soul will go to the terrors of Thor and that it will squirm in the circle of serpents for ever.

And as for him,' he looked at Agricola, 'I have long wanted his death and the memory of it will amuse me in the long nights to come. And tell that limpid thing,' he spat towards Meurig, 'that I shall slice off his balls and make him into my cup-bearer. Tell them all that, worm.'

'He says no,' I told Cuneglas.

'Surely he said more than that?' Meurig, who was only present because of his rank, insisted pedantically.

'You don't want to know,' Sagramor said tiredly.

'All knowledge is relevant,' Meurig protested.

'What are they saying, worm?' Aelle demanded of me, ignoring his own interpreter.

'They are arguing which of them should have the pleasure of killing you, Lord King,' I said.

Aelle spat. 'Tell Merlin,' the Saxon King glanced at the Druid, 'that I offered him no insult.'

'He knows already, Lord King,' I said, 'for he speaks your language.' The Saxons feared Merlin, and even now did not want to antagonize him. The two Saxon wizards were hissing curses at him, but that was their job and Merlin took no offence. Nor did he appear to take any interest in the conference, but just stared loftily into the distance, though he did bestow a smile on Aelle after the King's compliment.

Aelle stared at me for a few heartbeats. Finally he asked me, 'What is your tribe?'

'Dumnonia, Lord King.'

'Before that, fool! Your birth!'

'Your people, Lord,' I said. 'Aelle's folk.'

'Your father?' he demanded.

'I never knew him, Lord. My mother was captured by Uther when I was in her belly.'

'And her name?'

I had to think for a second or two. 'Erce, Lord King.' I remembered her name at last.

Aelle smiled at the name. 'A good Saxon name! Erce, the Goddess of the earth and mother of us all. How is your Erce?'

'I have not seen her, Lord, since I was a child, but I am told she lives.'

He stared broodingly at me. Meurig was squeaking impatiently as he demanded to know what was being said, but he quietened when everyone else ignored him. 'It is not good,' Aelle said at last, 'for a man to ignore his mother. What is your name?'

'Derfel, Lord King.'

He spat on my mail coat. 'Then shame on you, Derfel, for ignoring your mother. Would you fight for us today? For your mother's folk?'

I smiled. 'No, Lord King, but you do me honour.'

'May your death be easy, Derfel. But tell this filth,' he jerked his head at the four armed leaders, 'that I come to eat their hearts.' He spat a last time, turned and strode back towards his men.

'So what did he say?' Meurig demanded.

'He spoke to me, Lord Prince,' I said, 'of my mother. And he reminded me of my sins.' God help me, but on that day I liked Aelle.

We won the battle.

Igraine will want me to say more. She wants great heroics, and they were there, but there were also cowards present, and other men who fouled their breeches in their terror yet still kept to the shield-wall. There were men who killed no one, but just defended desperately, and there were men who gave the poets new challenges to find words to express their deeds. It was, in short, a battle. Friends died, Cavan was one, friends were wounded, Culhwch was such, and other friends lived untouched, like Galahad, Tristan and Arthur. I took an axe blow to my left shoulder, and though my mail coat took most of the blade's force, the wound still took weeks to heal and to this day there is a ragged red scar that aches in cold weather.

What was important was not the battle, but what happened after; but first, because my dear Queen Igraine will insist on my writing of the heroics of her husband's grandfather, King Cuneglas, I shall tell the tale briefly.

The Saxons attacked us. It took Aelle over an hour to persuade his men to assault our shield-wall and for all that time the dung-spiked wizards screamed at us, the drums beat and skins of ale were passed around the Saxon ranks. Many of our men were drinking mead, for though we might have exhausted our food, no British army ever seemed to run out of mead. At least half the men in that battle were fuddled by drink, but so men were at every battle for little else serves to give warriors the nerve to attempt that most terrifying of manoeuvres, the straightforward assault on a waiting shield-wall. I stayed sober because I always did, but the temptation to drink was strong. Some Saxons tried to provoke us into an ill-timed charge by coming close to our line and flaunting themselves without shields or helmets, but all they received for their trouble were some ill-aimed spears. A few spears were hurled back at us, but most thudded harmlessly into our shields. Two naked men, turned blood-mad by drink or magic, attacked us, and Culhwch cut down the first and Tristan the second. We cheered both victories. The Saxons, their tongues loosened by ale, shouted insults back.

Aelle's attack, when it came, went horribly wrong. The Saxons were relying on their war dogs to break our line, but Merlin and Nimue were ready with their own dogs, only ours were not dogs, but bitches, and enough of them were on heat to drive the Saxon beasts wild. Instead of attacking us the big war dogs headed straight for the bitches and there was a flurry of growls, fights, barks and howls, and suddenly there were fornicating dogs everywhere, with other dogs fighting to dislodge the luckier ones, but not one dog bit a Briton and the Saxons, who had been ready to launch their killing charge, were thrown off balance by the failure of their dogs. They hesitated and Aelle, fearing we would charge, roared them forward and so they came at us. But they came raggedly instead of in a disciplined line.

Coupling dogs howled as they were trampled underfoot, then the shields clashed with that terrible dull sound that echoes down the long years. It is the sound of battle, the sound of war-horns, men shouting, and then the splintering dull crash of shield on shield, and after the crash the screams began as spear-blades found the gaps between the shields and axes came hurtling down, but it was the Saxons who suffered most that day. The dogs between the shield-walls had broken their careful alignment and wherever that had happened to their advancing shield-wall our spearmen found gaps and pushed into them, while the ranks behind funnelled into the gaps to make shield-armoured wedges that drove ever deeper into the Saxon mass. Cuneglas led one of those wedges and very nearly reached Aelle himself. I did not see Cuneglas in the fight, though the bards sang of his part afterwards and he modestly assured me they did not exaggerate much.

I was wounded early. My shield deflected the axe blow and took most of its force, but the blade still struck my shoulder and numbed my left arm, though the wound did not stop my spear from slicing the throat of the axeman. Then, when the press of men was too great for the spear to be of more use, I drew Hywelbane and stabbed and hacked her blade into the grunting, swaying, shoving mass of men. It became a pushing match, but so do all battles until one side breaks. Just a sweaty, hot, filthy pushing match.

This one was made more difficult because the Saxon line, that was everywhere about five men deep, outflanked our shield-wall. To guard against envelopment we had bent our line back at its ends to present two smaller shield-walls to the attackers, and for a time those two Saxon flanks hesitated, perhaps hoping that the men in the centre would break through us first. Then a Saxon chieftain came to my end of the line and shamed his men into an assault. He ran forward on his own, swept aside two spears with his shield, and hurled himself at the centre of our flank's short line. Cavan died there, pierced by a lunge of the Saxon chief's sword, and the sight of that brave man single-handedly opening up our flank wall brought his men roaring forward in a wild, elated rush.

It was then that Arthur charged out of the unfinished hall. I did not see the charge, but I heard it. The bards say his horses' hooves shook the world, and indeed the ground did seem to quiver, though perhaps that was only the noise of those great beasts that were shod with flat iron plates strapped tight to their hooves. The big horses hit the exposed end of the Saxon line and the battle really ended with that terrible impact. Aelle had supposed that his men would break us with dogs, and that his rearward ranks would hold off our horsemen with their shields and spears, for he knew well enough that no horse would ever charge home into a well-defended spear-wall and I did not doubt that he had heard how Gorfyddyd's spearmen had thus kept Arthur at bay in Lugg Vale. But the exposed Saxon flank had become disordered as it charged and Arthur timed his intervention perfectly. He did not wait for his horsemen to form up, he just spurred out of the shadows, shouted at his men to follow and drove Llamrei hard into the open end of the Saxon ranks.

I was spitting at a bearded toothless Saxon who was cursing over the rim of our two shields when Arthur struck. His white cloak streamed behind, his white plumes soared above, and his bright shield threw down the Saxon chief's banner that was a blood-painted bull's skull as his spear lanced forward. He abandoned the spear in a Saxon's belly and ripped Excalibur free, carving it right and left as he drove deep into the enemy's ranks. Agravain came next, his horse scattering terrified Saxons, then Lanval and the others crashed into the breaking enemy line with swords and spears.

Aelle's men broke like eggs under a hammer. They just ran. I doubt that battle took more than ten minutes from the dogs beginning it to the horses ending it, though it took an hour or more for our horsemen to exhaust their slaughter. Our light horsemen raced screaming across the heath as they carried their spears towards the fleeing enemy and Arthur's heavier horses drove among the scattered men, killing and killing, while the spearmen ran after, eager for every scrap of plunder.

The Saxons ran like deer. They threw away cloaks, armour and weapons in their eagerness to escape. Aelle tried to check them for a moment, then saw the task was hopeless and so cast off his bearskin cloak and ran with his men. He escaped into the trees just a bare moment before our light horsemen plunged after him.

I stayed among the wounded and the dead. Injured dogs howled in pain. Culhwch was staggering with a bleeding thigh, but he would live and so I ignored him and crouched by Cavan. I had never seen him weep before, but his pain was terrible for the Saxon chief's sword had gone right through his belly. I held his hand, wiped his tears and told him that he had killed his enemy with his counter-thrust. Whether that was true I did not know nor care, I only wanted Cavan to believe it and so I promised him he would cross the bridge of swords with a fifth point on his shield. 'You will be the first of us to reach the Otherworld,' I told him, 'so you will make a place for us.'

'I will, Lord.'

'And we shall come to you.'

He gritted his teeth and arched his back, trying to suppress a scream, and I put my right hand round his neck and held my cheek against his. I was weeping. 'Tell them in the Otherworld,' I said in his ear, 'that Derfel Cadarn salutes you as a brave man.'

'The Cauldron,' he said. 'I should have . . .'

'No,' I interrupted him, 'no.' And then, with a mewing sound, he died.

I sat beside his body, rocking back and forth because of the pain in my shoulder and the grief in my soul. Tears ran down my cheeks. Issa stood beside me, not knowing what to say, so saying nothing. 'He always wanted to go home to die,' I said, 'to Ireland.' And after this battle, I thought, he could have done that with so much honour and wealth.

'Lord,' Issa said to me.

I thought he was trying to comfort me, but I did not want

comfort. The death of a brave man deserves tears and so I ignored Issa and held Cavan's corpse instead while his soul began its last journey to the bridge of swords that lies beyond Cruachan's Cave.

'Lord!' Issa said again, and something in his voice made me look up.

I saw he was pointing east towards London, but when I turned in that direction I could see nothing because the tears were blurring my view. I cuffed them angrily away.

And then I saw that another army had come to the field. Another fur-swathed army beneath banners of skulls and bull-horns. Another army with dogs and axes. Another Saxon horde.

For Cerdic had come.

I REALIZED LATER THAT all the ruses we had devised to make Aelle attack us and all that good food we had burned to entice his assault had been so much wasted effort, for the *Bretwalda* must have known that Cerdic was coming and that he was not coming to attack us, but to attack his fellow Saxon. Cerdic, indeed, was proposing to join us, and Aelle had decided that his best chance of surviving the combined armies was to beat Arthur first and deal with Cerdic afterwards.

Aelle lost that gamble. Arthur's horsemen broke him and Cerdic arrived too late to join the fight, though surely, for a few moments at least, the treacherous Cerdic must have been tempted to attack Arthur. One swift attack would have broken us and a week's campaigning would certainly have finished off Aelle's shattered army, and Cerdic would then have been the ruler of all southern Britain. Cerdic must have been tempted, but he hesitated. He had fewer than three hundred men, plenty enough to have overwhelmed what Britons remained on the heath's low summit, but Arthur's silver horn sounded again and again, and the horn-call summoned enough of the heavily armoured cavalry from the trees to make a brave show on Cerdic's northern flank. Cerdic had never faced those big horses in battle and the sight of them gave him pause long enough for Sagramor, Agricola and Cuneglas to assemble a shield-wall on the heath's summit. It was a perilously small wall, for most of our men were still too busy pursuing Aelle's warriors or sacking his encampment in search of food.

Those of us on the low hilltop readied ourselves for battle and it promised to be a grim business because our hurriedly assembled shield-wall was much smaller than Cerdic's line. At that time, of course, we still did not know it was Cerdic's army; at first we assumed these new Saxons were Aelle's own reinforcements come late to the battle, and the banner they were displaying, a wolf's skull painted red and hung with the tanned skin of a dead man, meant nothing to us. Cerdic's usual banner was a pair of horse-tails attached to a thigh bone mounted crosswise on a pole, but his wizards had devised this new symbol and it momentarily confused us. More men straggled back from their pursuit of Aelle's defeated remnant to thicken our wall as Arthur led his horsemen back to our hilltop. He trotted Llamrei down our ranks and I remember that his white cloak was spotted and streaked with blood. 'They'll die like the rest!' he encouraged us as he trotted past, the bloodstained Excalibur in his hand. 'They'll die like the rest.'

Then, just as Aelle's army had parted to let Aelle emerge from the ranks, so this new Saxon force divided and their leaders came towards us. Three of them walked, but six came on horseback, curbing their mounts to keep pace with the three men on foot. One of the men on foot carried the gruesome wolf's skull banner, then one of the horsemen raised a second banner and a gasp of astonishment ran down our army. The gasp made Arthur wheel his horse and stare aghast at the approaching men.

For the new banner showed a sea-eagle with a fish in its claws. It was Lancelot's flag, and now I could see that Lancelot himself was one of the six horsemen. He was splendidly arrayed in his white enamelled armour and his swan-winged helmet, and he was flanked by Arthur's twin sons, Amhar and Loholt. Dinas and Lavaine in their Druids' robes rode behind, while Ade, Lancelot's red-haired mistress, carried the Silurian King's banner.

Sagramor had come to stand beside me and he glanced at me to make certain that I was seeing what he was seeing, and then he spat onto the heath. 'Is Malla safe?' I asked him.

'Safe and unharmed,' he said, pleased I had asked. He looked back at the approaching Lancelot. 'Do you understand what's happening?'

'No.' None of us did.

Arthur sheathed Excalibur and turned to me. 'Derfel!' he called, wanting me as a translator, then he beckoned to his other leaders just as Lancelot broke away from the approaching delegation and spurred excitedly up the gently sloping hill towards us.

'Allies!' I heard Lancelot shout. He waved back at the Saxons. 'Allies!' he shouted again as his horse drew near to Arthur.

Arthur said nothing. He just stood his horse as Lancelot struggled to quieten his big black stallion. 'Allies,' Lancelot said a third time. 'It's Cerdic,' he added excitedly, gesturing towards the Saxon King who was walking slowly towards us.

Arthur asked quietly, 'What have you done?'

'I've brought you allies!' Lancelot said happily, then glanced at me. 'Cerdic has his own translator,' he said dismissively.

'Derfel stays!' Arthur snapped with a sudden and terrifying anger in his voice. Then he remembered that Lancelot was a King and sighed. 'What have you done, Lord King?' he asked again.

Dinas, who had spurred ahead with the other riders, was foolish enough to answer for Lancelot. 'We've made peace, Lord!' he said in his dark voice.

'Go!' Arthur roared, shocking and astonishing the Druid pair with his anger. They had only ever seen the calm, patient, peace-making Arthur and did not even suspect that he contained such fury. This anger was nothing to the rage that had consumed him at Lugg Vale when the dying Gorfyddyd had called Guinevere a whore, but it was a terrifying anger all the same. 'Go!' he shouted at Tanaburs's grandsons. 'This meeting is for Lords. And you too,' he pointed at his sons, 'go!' He waited until all Lancelot's followers had withdrawn, then looked back at the Silurian King. 'What have you done?' he asked a third time in a bitter voice.

Lancelot's affronted dignity made him stiff. 'I made peace,' he said acidly. 'I kept Cerdic from attacking you. I did what I could to help you.'

'What you did,' Arthur said in an angry voice, but so low that no man in Cerdic's approaching entourage could hear him, 'is fight Cerdic's battle. We've just half destroyed Aelle, so what does that make Cerdic? It makes him twice as powerful as before. That's what it does! The Gods help us!' With that he tossed his reins to Lancelot, a subtle insult, then slid off his horse's back, twitched his bloody cloak straight and stared imperiously at the Saxons.

That was the first time I met Cerdic, and though all the bards make him sound like a fiend with cloven hooves and a serpent's bite, in truth he was a short, slightly built man with thin fair hair that he combed straight back from his forehead and tied in a knot at the nape of his neck. He was very pale-skinned and had a broad forehead and a narrow, clean-shaven chin. His mouth was thin-lipped, his nose sharp-boned, and his eyes as pale as dawn-misted water. Aelle wore his emotions on his face, but even at a first glance I doubted whether Cerdic's self-control would ever allow his expression to betray his thoughts. He wore a Roman breastplate, woollen trews and a cloak of fox fur. He looked neat and precise; indeed, if it had not been for the gold at his throat and wrists, I might have mistaken him for a scribe. Except that his eyes were not those of a clerk; those pale eyes missed nothing and gave nothing away. 'I am Cerdic,' he announced himself in a soft voice.

Arthur stepped aside so that Cuneglas could name himself, then Meurig insisted on being a part of the conference. Cerdic glanced at both men, dismissed them as unimportant, then looked back to Arthur. 'I bring you a gift,' he said, and held a hand towards the chieftain who accompanied him. The man produced a gold-hilted knife that Cerdic presented to Arthur.

'The gift,' I translated Arthur's words, 'should go to our Lord King Cuneglas.'

Cerdic put the naked blade onto his left palm and closed his fingers about it. His eyes never left Arthur's, and when he opened his hand there was blood on the blade. 'The gift is for Arthur,' he insisted.

Arthur took it. He was uncharacteristically nervous, maybe fearing some magic in the bloody steel or else fearing that acceptance of the gift made him complicit in Cerdic's ambitions. 'Tell the King,' he told me, 'that I have no gift for him.'

Cerdic smiled. It was a wintry smile and I thought of how a wolf must appear to a stray lamb. 'Tell Lord Arthur that he has given me the gift of peace,' he told me.

'But suppose I choose war?' Arthur asked defiantly. 'Here and now!' He gestured to the hilltop where still more of our spearmen had rallied so that our numbers were now at least equal to Cerdic's.

'Tell him,' Cerdic ordered me, 'that these are not all my men,' he gestured at his shield-wall that watched us, 'and tell him, too, that King Lancelot gave me peace in Arthur's name.'

I told that to Arthur and I saw a muscle flicker in his cheek, but he kept his anger curbed. 'In two days,' Arthur said, and it was not a suggestion, but an order, 'we shall meet in London. There we shall discuss our peace.' He pushed the bloody knife into his belt and, when I had finished translating his words, he summoned me. He did not wait to hear Cerdic's response, but just led me up the hill until we were out of earshot of both delegations. He noticed my shoulder for the first time. 'How bad is your wound?'

'It'll heal,' I said.

He stopped, closed his eyes and took a deep breath. 'What Cerdic wants,' he told me when he opened his eyes, 'is to rule all Lloegyr. But if we let him do that then we have one terrible enemy instead of two weaker ones.' He walked in silence for a few paces, stepping among the dead left from Aelle's charge. 'Before this war,' he continued bitterly, 'Aelle was powerful and Cerdic was a nuisance, but with Aelle destroyed we could have turned on Cerdic. Now it's the other way round. Aelle is weakened, but Cerdic is powerful.'

'So fight him now,' I said.

He looked at me with weary brown eyes. 'Be honest, Derfel,' he said in a low voice, 'not boastful. Will we win if we fight?'

I looked at Cerdic's army. It was tightly arrayed and ready for battle, while our men were weary and hungry, but Cerdic's men had never faced Arthur's horsemen. 'I think we would win, Lord,' I said honestly.

'So do I,' Arthur said, 'but it will be hard fighting, Derfel, and at the end of it we'll have at least a hundred wounded men we'll need to carry back home with us and the Saxons will summon every garrison in Lloegyr to face us. We might beat Cerdic here, but we'll never reach home alive. We're too deep in Lloegyr.' He grimaced at the thought. 'And if we weaken ourselves fighting against Cerdic do you think Aelle won't be waiting to ambush us on the way home?' He shuddered with a sudden surge of anger. 'What was Lancelot thinking of? I can't have Cerdic as an ally! He'll gain half Britain, turn on us and we'll have a Saxon enemy twice as terrible as before.' He uttered one of his rare curses, then rubbed his bony face with a gloved hand. 'Well, the broth's spoilt,' he went on bitterly, 'but we still have to eat it. The only answer is to leave Aelle strong enough to frighten Cerdic still, so take six of my horsemen and find him. Find him, Derfel, and give him this wretched thing as a gift.' He thrust Cerdic's knife at me. 'Clean it first,' he said irritably, 'and you can take his bearskin cloak as well. Agravain found it. Give that to him as a second gift and tell him to come to London. Tell him I oath-swear his safety, and tell him it is his only chance to keep some land. You have two days, Derfel, so find him.'

I hesitated, not because I disagreed, but because I did not understand why Aelle needed to be in London. 'Because,' Arthur answered wearily, 'I cannot stay in London with Aelle loose in Lloegyr. He might have lost his army here, but he has garrisons enough to make another, and while we disentangle ourselves from Cerdic he could lay half Dumnonia waste.' He turned and stared balefully at Lancelot and Cerdic. I thought he was going to curse again, but he just sighed wearily. 'I'm going to make a peace, Derfel. The Gods know it isn't the peace I wanted, but we might as well make it properly. Now go, my friend, go.'

I stayed long enough to make certain that Issa would take proper care of the burning of Cavan's body and that he would find a lake and throw the dead Irishman's sword into the water, and then I rode north in the wake of a beaten army.

While Arthur, his dream skewed by a fool, marched to London.

I had long dreamed of seeing London, but even in my wildest fancies I had not imagined its reality. I had thought it would be like Glevum, a little larger perhaps, but still a place where a group of tall buildings would be clustered about a central open space with small streets huddled behind and an earth wall ringing it all, but in London there were six such open spaces, all with their pillared halls, arcaded temples and brick-built palaces. The ordinary houses, that in Glevum or Durnovaria were low and thatched, were here built two or three storeys high. Many of the houses had collapsed over the years, but plenty still had their tiled roofs and folk still climbed their steep timber stairs. Most of our men had never seen a flight of stairs inside a building and on their first day in London they had raced like excited children to see the view from the topmost floors. Finally one of the buildings had collapsed under their weight and Arthur then forbade any more stair-climbing.

The fortress of London was bigger then Caer Sws, and that fortress was merely the north-west bastion of the city's wall. There were a dozen barracks inside the fortress, each bigger than a feasting hall, and each made of small red bricks. Beside the fortress was an amphitheatre, a temple, and one of the city's ten bath-houses. Other towns had such things, of course, but everything here was taller and wider. Durnovaria's amphitheatre was a thing of grassy earth and I had always thought it impressive enough until I saw the London arena that could have swallowed five amphitheatres like Durnovaria's. The wall about the city was built of stone instead of earth, and though Aelle had allowed its ramparts to crumble, it was still a formidable barrier that was now crowned with Cerdic's triumphant men. Cerdic had occupied the city and the presence of his skull banners on the walls showed that he intended to keep it.

The river bank also possessed a stone wall that had first been built against the Saxon pirates. Gaps in that wall led to quays, and one gap opened into a canal that ran into the heart of a great garden about which a palace was built. There were still busts and statues in the palace, and long tiled corridors and a great pillared hall where I assumed our Roman rulers had once met in government. Rainwater now trickled down the painted walls, the floor tiles were broken and the garden was a mass of weeds, but the glory was still there, even if it was only a shadow. The whole city was a shadow of its old glory. None of the city's bath-houses still functioned. Their pools were cracked and empty, their furnaces were cold and their mosaic floors had heaved and cracked under the assault of frost and weeds. The stone streets had decayed into muddy strips, but despite the decay the city was still massive and magnificent. It made me wonder what Rome must be like. Galahad told me that London was a mere village in comparison, and that Rome's amphitheatre was big enough to swallow twenty arenas like London's, but I could not believe him. I could scarcely believe in London even when I was staring at it. It looked like the work of giants.

Aelle had never liked the city and would not live there, so its only inhabitants were a handful of Saxons and those Britons who had accepted Aelle's rule. Some of those Britons still prospered. Most were merchants who traded with Gaul, and their large houses were built beside the river and their storehouses were guarded by their own walls and spearmen, but much of the rest of the city was deserted. It was a dying place, a city given to rats, a city that once had borne the title Augusta. It had been known as London the Magnificent and its river had once been thick with the masts of galleys; now it was a place of ghosts.

Aelle came to London with me. I had found him a half day's

march north of the city. He had taken refuge in a Roman fort where he was trying to reassemble an army. At first he was suspicious of my message. He had shouted at me, accusing us of using witchcraft to defeat him, then he had threatened to kill me and my escort, but I had the sense to wait his anger out patiently and, after a while, he calmed down. He had hurled Cerdic's knife angrily away, but was pleased to have his thick bearskin cloak returned. I do not think I was ever in real danger, for I sensed that he liked me, and indeed, when his anger had fled, he threw a heavy arm round my shoulder and walked me up and down the ramparts. 'What does Arthur want?' he had asked me.

'Peace, Lord King.' The weight of his arm was hurting my wounded shoulder, but I dared not protest.

'Peace!' He had spat the word out like a scrap of tainted meat, but with none of the scorn he had used to reject Arthur's offer of peace before Lugg Vale. Then Aelle had been stronger and could afford to ask a higher price. Now he was humbled, and he knew it. 'We Saxons,' he said, 'are not meant to be at peace. We feed ourselves on our enemy's grain, we clothe ourselves with their wool, we pleasure ourselves on their women. What does peace offer us?'

'A chance to rebuild your strength, Lord King, or else Cerdic will be feeding on your grain and dressing in your wool.'

Aelle had grinned. 'He'd like the women too.' He had taken his arm from my shoulder and stared northwards across the fields. 'I'll have to yield land,' he grumbled.

'But if you choose war, Lord King,' I said, 'the price will be higher. You'll face Arthur and Cerdic, and might finish with no land at all except the grass above your grave.'

He had turned and given me a shrewd look. 'Arthur only wants peace so that I can fight Cerdic for him.'

'Of course, Lord King,' I answered.

He laughed at my honesty. 'And if I do not come to London,' he said, 'you will hunt me down like a dog.'

'Like a great boar, Lord King, whose tusks are still sharp.'

'You talk like you fight, Derfel. Well.' He had ordered his

wizards to make a poultice from moss and spiders' webs that they put on my wounded shoulder while he consulted his council. The consultation did not last long, for Aelle knew he had little choice. So, next morning, I marched with him down the Roman road that led back to the city. He insisted on taking an escort of sixty spearmen. 'You may trust Cerdic,' he told me, 'but there isn't a promise he's made that he hasn't broken. Tell that to Arthur.'

'You tell him, Lord King.'

Aelle and Arthur met secretly on the night before they were due to negotiate with Cerdic, and that night they wrangled their own separate peace. Aelle gave up much. He gave up great swathes of land on his western frontier, and agreed to repay Arthur all the gold that Arthur had given him the year before and more gold besides. In return Arthur promised four whole years of peace and his support for Aelle if Cerdic would not agree to terms the next day. They embraced when the peace was made and afterwards, as we walked back to our encampment outside the city's western wall, Arthur shook his head sadly. 'You should never meet an enemy face to face,' he said to me, 'not if you know that one day you'll have to destroy him. Either that or the Saxons must submit to our government and they won't. They won't.'

'Maybe they will.'

He shook his head. 'Saxon and Briton, Derfel, they don't mix.'

'I mix, Lord,' I said.

He laughed. 'But if your mother had never been captured, Derfel, you'd have been raised a Saxon and you'd probably have been in Aelle's army by now. You'd be an enemy. You'd worship his Gods, you'd dream his dreams, and you'd want our land. They need a lot of space, these Saxons.'

But we had at least penned Aelle in, and next day, in the great palace by the river, we met Cerdic. The sun shone that day, sparkling on the canal where the Governor of Britain had once moored his river barge. The sparkling sun-motes hid the scum and mud and dirt that now clogged the canal, but nothing could hide the stench of its sewage.

Cerdic held a council meeting first and while it debated we Britons met in a room that stood above the river wall and over-looked the water so that the ceiling, which was painted with curious beings that were half women and half fish, was dappled by shimmers of rippling light. Our spearmen guarded every door and window to make certain we could not be overheard.

Lancelot was there, and had been allowed to bring Dinas and Lavaine. The three men still insisted that their peace with Cerdic had been wise, but Meurig was their only supporter and the rest of us were angry in the face of their sullen defiance. Arthur listened to our protests for a while, then interrupted to say that nothing would be solved by arguing about the past. 'What's done is done,' he said, 'but I do need one assurance.' He looked at Lancelot. 'Promise me,' he said, 'that you made no promises to Cerdic.'

'I gave him peace,' Lancelot insisted, 'and suggested he help you fight Aelle. That is all.'

Merlin was seated in the window above the river. He had adopted one of the palace's stray cats and now petted the animal on his lap. 'What did Cerdic want?' he asked mildly.

'Aelle's defeat.'

'Just that?' Merlin asked, not bothering to hide his disbelief.

'Just that,' Lancelot insisted, 'nothing more.' We all watched him. Arthur, Merlin, Cuneglas, Meurig, Agricola, Sagramor, Galahad, Culhwch and myself. None of us spoke, but just watched him. 'He wanted nothing more!' Lancelot insisted and to me he looked like a small child telling plain lies.

'How remarkable in a king,' Merlin said placidly, 'to want so little.' He began teasing the cat by flicking one of the braided strands of his beard at its paws. 'And what did you want?' he asked, still mildly.

'Arthur's victory,' Lancelot declared.

'Because you did not think Arthur could win it by himself?' Merlin suggested, still playing with the cat.

'I wanted to make it certain,' Lancelot said. 'I was trying to help!' He looked round the room, seeking allies, and finding none but the youthful Meurig. 'If you don't want peace with Cerdic,' he said petulantly, 'then why don't you fight him now?'

'Because, Lord King, you used my name to secure his truce,' Arthur said patiently, 'and because our army is now many marches from home and his men lie in our path. If you had not made peace,' he explained, still speaking courteously, 'then half his army would be on the frontier watching your men and I would have been free to march south and attack the other half. As it is?' He shrugged. 'What will Cerdic demand of us today?'

'Land,' Agricola said firmly. 'It's all the Saxons ever want. Land, land, and more land. They won't be happy till they have every scrap of land in the world, and then they'll start looking for other worlds to put under their ploughs.'

'He must be satisfied,' Arthur said, 'with the land he's taken from Aelle. He'll get none from us.'

'We should take some from him,' I spoke for the first time. 'That land he stole last year.' It was a fine stretch of river-land on our southern frontier, a fertile and rich tract that ran from the high moors down to the sea. The land had belonged to Melwas, the client King of the Belgae whom Arthur had sent in punishment to Isca, and it was land we sorely missed for its loss brought Cerdic very close to the rich estates about Durnovaria and also meant that his ships were just minutes away from Ynys Wit, the great island that the Romans had called Vectis and which lay just off our coast. For a year now Cerdic's Saxons had raided Ynys Wit ruthlessly and its people were forever calling on Arthur for more spearmen to protect their holdings.

'We should have that land back,' Sagramor supported me. He had thanked Mithras for returning his Saxon girl unharmed by placing a captured sword in the God's London temple.

'I doubt,' Meurig intervened, 'that Cerdic made peace in order to yield land.'

'Nor did we march to war to cede land,' Arthur answered angrily.

'I thought, forgive me,' Meurig insisted, and a kind of quiet groan went through the room as he persisted with his argument, 'but you said, did you not, that you could not prosecute war? Being so far from home? Yet now, for a stretch of land, you would risk all our lives? I hope I am not being foolish,' he chuckled to show that he had made a joke, 'but I fail to understand why we risk the one thing we cannot afford to endure.'

'Lord Prince,' Arthur said softly, 'we may be weak here, but if we show our weakness, then we will be dead here. We do not go to Cerdic this morning ready to yield one furrow, we go making demands.'

'And if he refuses?' Meurig demanded indignantly.

'Then we shall have a difficult withdrawal,' Arthur admitted calmly. He glanced out of a window that looked down into the courtyard. 'It seems our enemies are ready for us. Shall we go to them?'

Merlin pushed the cat off his lap and used his staff to stand up. 'You won't mind if I don't come?' he asked. 'I'm too old to endure a day of negotiations. All that bluster and anger.' He brushed cat hairs off his robe, then turned suddenly on Dinas and Lavaine. 'Since when,' he asked disapprovingly, 'have Druids worn swords or served Christian Kings?'

'Since we decided to do both,' Dinas said. The twins, who were almost as tall as Merlin and much burlier, challenged him with their unblinking gaze.

'Who made you Druids?' Merlin demanded.

'The same power that made you a Druid,' said Lavaine.

'And what power was that?' Merlin asked, and when the twins did not answer, he sneered at them. 'At least you know how to lay thrushes' eggs. I suppose that kind of trick impresses Christians. Do you also turn their wine to blood and their bread to flesh?'

'We use our magic,' Dinas said, 'and theirs too. It's not the old Britain now, but a new Britain and it has new Gods. We blend their magic with the old. You could learn from us, Lord Merlin.'

Merlin spat to show his opinion of that advice, then, without another word, stalked from the room. Dinas and Lavaine were unmoved by his hostility. They possessed an extraordinary self-confidence.

We followed Arthur down to the great pillared hall where, as Merlin had foretold, we blustered and postured, shouted and cajoled. At first it was Aelle and Cerdic who made most of the noise and Arthur, as often as not, was the mediator between them, but even Arthur could not prevent Cerdic becoming land rich at Aelle's expense. He kept possession of London and gained the valley of the Thames and great stretches of fertile land north of the Thames. Aelle's kingdom shrank by a quarter, but he still possessed a kingdom and for that he owed Arthur thanks. He offered none, but just stalked from the room when the talking was done and left London that same day like a great wounded boar crawling back to his den.

It was mid afternoon when Aelle left and Arthur, using me as an interpreter, now raised the matter of the Belgic land Cerdic had captured the year before, and he went on demanding the return of that land long after the rest of us would have given up the effort. He made no threats, he just repeated his demand over and over until Culhwch was sleeping, Agricola yawning, and I was tired of taking the sting from Cerdic's reiterated rejections. And still Arthur persisted. He sensed that Cerdic needed time to consolidate the new lands he had taken from Aelle, and his threat was that he would give Cerdic no peace unless the river-lands were returned. Cerdic countered by threatening to fight us in London, but Arthur finally revealed that he would seek Aelle's help in such a fight and Cerdic knew he could not beat both our armies.

It was almost dark when Cerdic at last yielded. He did not yield outright, but grudgingly said he would discuss the matter with his private council. So we woke Culhwch and walked out to the courtyard, then through a small gate in the river wall to stand on a quay where we watched the Thames slide darkly by. Most of us said little, though Meurig irritably lectured Arthur about wasting time making impossible demands, but when

Arthur refused to argue the Prince gradually fell silent. Sagramor sat with his back against the wall, incessantly stroking a whetstone down his sword blade. Lancelot and the Silurian Druids stood apart from us; three tall, handsome men who were stiff with pride. Dinas stared at the darkening trees across the river while his brother gave me long speculative looks.

We waited an hour and then, at last, Cerdic came to the river bank. 'Tell Arthur this,' he told me without any preamble, 'that I trust none of you, like none of you and want nothing more than to kill all of you. But I will yield him the Belgic land on one condition. That Lancelot is made King of that land. Not a client King,' he added, 'but King, with all the powers of independent kingship.'

I stared into the Saxon's grey-blue eyes. I was so astonished by his condition that I said nothing, not even to acknowledge his words. It was all so clear suddenly. Lancelot had made this bargain with the Saxon, and Cerdic had hidden their secret agreement behind an afternoon of scornful rejections. I had no proof of that, but I knew it had to be true, and when I looked away from Cerdic I saw that Lancelot was staring expectantly at me. He spoke no Saxon, but he knew exactly what Cerdic had just said.

'Tell him!' Cerdic ordered me.

I translated for Arthur. Agricola and Sagramor spat in disgust and Culhwch gave a brief, sour bellow of a laugh, but Arthur just gazed into my eyes for a few grave seconds before nodding wearily. 'Agreed,' he said.

'You will leave this place at dawn,' Cerdic said abruptly.

'We will leave in two days,' I responded, without bothering to consult Arthur.

'Agreed,' Cerdic said, and turned away.

And thus we had our peace with the Sais.

It was not the peace Arthur wanted. He had believed we could so weaken the Saxons that their ships would stop arriving from beyond the German Sea, and that in another year or two we might have driven the rest out of Britain altogether. But it was peace.

'Fate is inexorable,' Merlin said to me next morning. I found him in the centre of the Roman amphitheatre where he slowly turned to gaze on the banked stone seats that rose in a full circle about the arena. He had commandeered four of my spearmen who sat at the arena's edge and watched him, though they were as ignorant as I was about their duties. 'Are you still looking for the last Treasure?' I asked him.

'I do like this place,' he said, ignoring my question as he turned around to give the whole arena another long inspection. 'I do like it.'

'I thought you hated the Romans.'

'Me? Hate the Romans?' he asked in pretended outrage. 'How I do pray, Derfel, that my teachings will not be passed to posterity through the mangled sieve you choose to call a brain. I love all mankind!' he declared magniloquently, 'and even the Romans are perfectly acceptable if they stay in Rome. I told you I was in Rome once, didn't I? Full of priests and catamites. Sansum would feel quite at home there. No, Derfel, the fault of the Romans was coming to Britain and spoiling everything, but not everything they did here was bad.'

'They did give us this,' I said, gesturing at the twelve tiers of seats and the lofted balcony where the Roman lords had watched the arena.

'Oh, do spare me Arthur's tedious lecture about roads and lawcourts and bridges and structure.' He spat the last word out. 'Structure! What is the structure of law and roads and forts but a harness? The Romans tamed us, Derfel. They made us into taxpayers and they were so clever at it that we actually believe they did us a favour! We once walked with the Gods, we were a free people, and then we put our stupid heads into the Roman yoke and became taxpayers.'

'So what,' I asked patiently, 'did the Romans do that was so good?'

He smiled wolfishly. 'They once crammed this arena full of

Christians, Derfel, then set the dogs on them. In Rome, mind you, they did it properly; they used lions. But in the long term, alas, the lions lost.'

'I saw a picture of a lion,' I said proudly.

'Oh, I am fascinated,' Merlin said, not bothering to hide a yawn. 'Why don't you tell me all about it?' Having silenced me thus, he smiled. 'I saw a real lion once. It was a very unimpressive threadbare sort of thing. I suspected it was receiving the wrong diet. Maybe they were feeding it Mithraists instead of Christians? That was in Rome, of course. I gave it a poke with my staff and it just yawned and scratched at a flea. I saw a crocodile there too, only it was dead.'

'What's a crocodile?'

'A thing like Lancelot.'

'King of the Belgae,' I added acidly.

Merlin laughed. 'He has been clever, hasn't he? He hated Siluria, and who can blame him? All those drab people in their dull valleys, not Lancelot's sort of place at all, but he'll like the Belgic land. The sun shines there, it's full of Roman estates and, best of all, it's not far from his dear friend Guinevere.'

'Is that important?'

'Don't be so disingenuous, Derfel.'

'I don't know what that means.'

'It means, my ignorant warrior, that Lancelot behaves as he likes with Arthur. He takes what he wants and does what he wants, and he can do it because Arthur has that ridiculous quality called guilt. He's very Christian in that. Can you understand a religion that makes you feel guilty? What an absurd idea, but Arthur would make a very good Christian. He believes he was oath-sworn to save Benoic, and when he failed he felt he had let Lancelot down, and so long as that guilt rankles Arthur, so long will Lancelot behave as he wishes.'

'With Guinevere too?' I asked, curious at his earlier mention of Lancelot and Guinevere's friendship, a mention that had possessed more than a hint of salacious rumour.

'I never explain what I cannot know,' Merlin said loftily. 'But

I surmise Guinevere is bored by Arthur, and why not? She's a clever creature and she enjoys other clever people, and Arthur, much as we love him, is not complicated. The things he desires are so pathetically simple; law, justice, order, cleanliness. He really wants everyone to be happy, and that's quite impossible. Guinevere isn't nearly so simple. You are, of course.'

I ignored the insult. 'So what does Guinevere want?'

'For Arthur to be King of Dumnonia, of course, and for herself to be the real ruler of Britain by ruling him, but till that happens, Derfel, she will amuse herself as best she can.' He looked mischievous as an idea occurred to him. 'If Lancelot becomes the Belgic King,' he said happily, 'then just you watch Guinevere decide that she doesn't want her new palace in Lindinis after all. She'll find somewhere much closer to Venta. You see if I'm not right.' He chuckled at that thought. 'They were both so very clever,' he added admiringly.

'Guinevere and Lancelot?'

'Don't be so obtuse, Derfel! Who on earth was talking about Guinevere? Really, your appetite for gossip is quite indecent. I mean Cerdic and Lancelot, of course. That was a very subtle piece of diplomacy. Arthur does all the fighting, Aelle gives up most of the land, Lancelot snatches himself a much more suitable kingdom, and Cerdic doubles his own power and gets Lancelot instead of Arthur as his neighbour on the coast. Very neatly done. How the wicked do prosper! I like to see that.' He smiled, then turned as Nimue appeared from one of the two tunnels that led under the seats into the arena. She hurried over the weed-strewn turf with a look of excitement on her face. Her gold eye, that so frightened the Saxons, gleamed in the morning sun.

'Derfel!' she exclaimed. 'What do you do with the bull's blood?'

'Don't confuse him,' Merlin said, 'he's being more than usually stupid this morning.'

'In Mithras,' she said excitedly. 'What do you do with the blood?'

'Nothing,' I said.

'They mix it with oats and fat,' Merlin said, 'and make puddings.'

'Tell me!' Nimue insisted.

'It's secret,' I said, embarrassed.

Merlin hooted at that. 'Secret? Secret! "Oh, great Mithras!"' he boomed in a voice that echoed from the tiered seats, '"whose sword is sharpened on the mountain peaks and whose spearhead was forged in the ocean deeps and whose shield doth shadow the brightest stars, hear us." Shall I go on, dear boy?' he asked me. He had been reciting the invocation with which we began our meetings, and which was supposed to be a part of our secret rituals. He turned from me in scorn. 'They have a pit, dear Nimue,' he explained, 'covered with an iron grille, and the poor beast gushes its life away into the pit and then they all dip their spears into the blood, get drunk and think they've done something significant.'

'I thought so,' Nimue said, then smiled. 'There's no pit.'

'Oh, dear girl!' Merlin said admiringly. 'Dear girl! To work.' He hurried away.

'Where are you going?' I called after him, but he just waved and walked on, beckoning to my lounging spearmen. I followed anyway and he made no attempt to stop me. We went through the tunnel and so out into one of the strange streets of tall buildings, then west towards the great fortress that formed the north-west bastion of the city's walls, and just beside the fort, built against the city wall, was a temple.

I followed Merlin inside.

It was a lovely building; long, dark, narrow and tall with a high painted ceiling supported by twin rows of seven pillars. The shrine was evidently used as a storehouse now, for bales of wool and stacks of leather hides were piled high in one side aisle, yet some folk must still have worshipped in the building for a statue of Mithras wearing his odd floppy hat stood at one end and smaller statues were arrayed in front of the fluted pillars. I supposed that those who worshipped here were the descendants of the Roman settlers who had chosen to stay in Britain when the Legions left, and it seemed they had abandoned most of their ancestors' deities, including Mithras, because the small offerings of flowers, food and guttered rush lights were clustered in front of just three images. Two of the three were elegantly carved Roman Gods, but the third idol was British: a smooth phallic stump of stone with a brutal, wide-eyed face carved into its tip and that statue alone was drenched in old dried blood, while the only offering beside Mithras's statue was the Saxon sword that Sagramor had left in thanks for Malla's return. It was a sunny day, but the only light inside the temple came through a patch of broken roof where the tiles had vanished. The temple was supposed to be dark, for Mithras had been born in a cave and we worshipped him in a cave's darkness.

Merlin rapped the floor's flagstones with his staff, finally settling on a spot at the end of the nave just beneath Mithras's statue. 'Is this where you'd dip your spears, Derfel?' he asked me.

I stepped into the side aisle where the hides and wool bales were stacked. 'Here,' I said, pointing to a shallow pit half hidden by one of the piles.

'Don't be absurd!' Merlin snapped. 'Someone made that later! You really think you're hiding the secrets of your pathetic religion?' He tapped the floor beside the statue again, then tried another spot a few feet away and evidently decided that the two places yielded different sounds, so tapped a third time at the statue's feet. 'Dig here,' he ordered my spearmen.

I shuddered for the sacrilege. 'She shouldn't be here, Lord,' I said, gesturing at Nimue.

'One more word from you, Derfel, and I'll turn you into a spavined hedgehog. Lift the stones!' he snapped at my men. 'Use your spears as levers, idiots. Come on! Work!'

I sat beside the British idol, closed my eyes, and prayed to Mithras that he would forgive me the sacrilege. Then I prayed that Ceinwyn was safe and that the babe in her belly was still alive, and I was still praying for my unborn child when the temple door scraped open and boots sounded loud on the stones. I opened my eyes, turned my head, and saw that Cerdic had come to the temple.

He had come with twenty spearmen, his interpreter, and, more surprisingly, with Dinas and Lavaine.

I scrambled to my feet and touched the bones in Hywelbane's handle for luck as the Saxon King walked slowly up the nave. 'This is my city,' Cerdic announced softly, 'and everything within its walls is mine.' He stared for a moment at Merlin and Nimue, then looked at me. 'Tell them to explain themselves,' he ordered.

'Tell the fool to go and douse his head in a bucket,' Merlin snapped at me. He spoke Saxon well enough, but it suited him to pretend otherwise.

'That is his interpreter, Lord,' I warned Merlin, gesturing to the man beside Cerdic.

'Then he can tell his King to douse his head,' said Merlin.

The interpreter duly did, and Cerdic's face flickered in a dangerous smile.

'Lord King,' I said, trying to undo Merlin's damage, 'my Lord Merlin seeks to restore the temple to its old condition.'

Cerdic considered that answer as he inspected what was being done. My four spearmen had levered up the flagstones to reveal a compact mass of sand and gravel, and they were now scooping out that heavy mass that lay above a lower platform of pitch-soaked timbers. The King stared into the pit, then gestured for my four spearmen to go on with their work. 'But if you find gold,' he said to me, 'it is mine.' I began to translate to Merlin, but Cerdic interrupted me with a wave of his hand. 'He speaks our tongue,' he said, looking at Merlin. 'They told me,' he jerked his head toward Dinas and Lavaine.

I looked at the baleful twins, then back to Cerdic. 'You keep strange company, Lord King,' I said.

'No stranger than you,' he answered, glancing at Nimue's gold eye. She levered it out with a finger and gave him the full horrid effect of the shrivelled bare socket, but Cerdic seemed quite unmoved by the threat, asking me instead to tell him what I knew about the temple's different Gods. I answered him as best I could, but it was plain he was not really interested. He interrupted me to look at Merlin again. 'Where's your Cauldron, Merlin?' he asked.

Merlin gave the Silurian twins a murderous look, then spat on the floor. 'Hidden,' he snapped.

Cerdic seemed unsurprised by that answer. He strolled past the deepening pit and picked up the Saxon sword Sagramor had donated to Mithras. He gave the blade a speculative cut in the air and seemed to approve of its balance. 'This Cauldron,' he asked Merlin, 'has great powers?'

Merlin refused to answer, so I spoke for him. 'So it is said, Lord King.'

'Powers,' Cerdic stared at me with his pale eyes, 'that will rid Britain of us Saxons?'

'That is what we pray for, Lord King,' I answered.

He smiled at that, then turned back to Merlin. 'What is your price for the Cauldron, old man?'

Merlin glared at him. 'Your liver, Cerdic.'

Cerdic stepped close to Merlin and stared up into the wizard's eyes. I saw no fear in Cerdic, none. Merlin's Gods were not his. Aelle might have feared Merlin, but Cerdic had never suffered from the Druid's magic and, so far as Cerdic was concerned, Merlin was merely an old British priest with an inflated reputation. He suddenly reached out and took hold of one of the black-wrapped plaits of Merlin's beard. 'I offer you a price of much gold, old man,' he said.

'I have named my price,' Merlin answered. He tried to step away from Cerdic, but the King tightened his grip on the plait of the Druid's beard.

'I will pay you your own weight in gold,' Cerdic offered.

'Your liver,' Merlin countered the offer.

Cerdic raised the Saxon blade and sawed fast with its edge and so severed the beard plait. He stepped away. 'Play with your

Cauldron, Merlin of Avalon,' he said, tossing the sword aside, 'but one day I will cook your liver in it and serve it to my dogs.'

Nimue stared white-faced at the King. Merlin was too shocked to move, let alone speak, while my four spearmen simply gaped. 'Get on with it, fools,' I snarled at them. 'Work!' I was mortified. I had never seen Merlin humiliated and never wanted to either. I had not thought it was even possible.

Merlin rubbed his violated beard. 'One day, Lord King,' he said quietly, 'I shall have my revenge.'

Cerdic shrugged away that feeble threat and walked back to his men. He gave the severed beard plait to Dinas, who bowed his thanks. I spat, for I knew the Silurian pair could now work a great evil. Few things are so powerful in the making of spells as the discarded hair or nail-clippings of an enemy, which is why, to prevent such things falling into malevolent hands, we all take such good care to burn them. Even a child can make mischief with a hank of hair. 'You want me to take the plait back, Lord?' I asked Merlin.

'Don't be absurd, Derfel,' he said wearily, gesturing at Cerdic's twenty spearmen. 'You think you could kill them all?' He shook his head, then smiled at Nimue. 'You see how far we are here from our Gods?' he said, trying to explain his helplessness.

'Dig,' Nimue snarled to my men, though now the digging was over and they were trying to lever up the first of the great baulks of timber. Cerdic, who had plainly come to the temple because Dinas and Lavaine had told him that Merlin was looking for treasure, ordered three of his own spearmen to help. The three leapt into the pit and rammed their spears under the timber's lip and slowly, slowly forced it up until my men could seize it and drag it free.

The pit was the blood pit, the place where the dying bull's life drained into mother earth, but at some time the pit had been cunningly disguised with the timbers, sand, gravel and stone. 'It was done,' Merlin told me out of earshot of all Cerdic's people, 'when the Romans left.' He rubbed his beard again.

'Lord,' I said awkwardly, saddened by his humiliation.

'Don't worry, Derfel.' He touched my shoulder in reassurance. 'You think I should command fire from the Gods? Make the earth gape and swallow him? Summon a serpent from the spirit world?'

'Yes, Lord,' I answered miserably.

He lowered his voice even more. 'You don't command magic, Derfel, you use it, and there's none here to use. That's why we need the Treasures. At Samain, Derfel, I shall collect the Treasures and unveil the Cauldron. We shall light fires and then work a spell that will make the sky shriek and the earth groan. That I promise you. I have lived my whole life for that moment and it will bring the magic back to Britain.' He leaned against the pillar and stroked the place where his beard had been cut. 'Our friends from Siluria,' he said, staring at the black-bearded twins, 'think to challenge me, but one lost strand of an old man's beard is nothing to the Cauldron's power. One strand of beard will hurt no one but me, but the Cauldron, Derfel, the Cauldron will make all Britain shudder and bring those two pretenders crawling on their knees for my mercy. But till then, Derfel, till then you must see our enemies prosper. The Gods go further and further away. They grow weak and we who love them grow weak too, but it will not last. We shall summon them back, and the magic that is now so weak in Britain will become as thick as that fog on Ynys Mon.' He touched my wounded shoulder again. 'I promise you that.'

Cerdic watched us. He could not hear us, but there was amusement on his wedge-shaped face. 'He will keep what's in the pit, Lord,' I murmured.

'I pray he will not know its value,' Merlin said softly.

'They will, Lord,' I said, looking at the two white-robed Druids.

'They are traitors and serpents,' Merlin hissed softly, staring at Dinas and Lavaine who had moved closer to the pit, 'but even if they keep what we find now, I will still possess eleven of the thirteen Treasures, Derfel, and I know where the twelfth is to be found, and no other man has gathered so much power in Britain in a thousand years.' He leaned on his staff. 'This King will suffer, I promise you.'

The last timber was brought out of the hole and thrown with a thump onto the flagstones. The sweating spearmen backed away as Cerdic and the Silurian Druids walked slowly forward and stared down into the pit. Cerdic gazed for a long time, then he began to laugh. His laughter echoed from the tall painted ceiling and it drew his spearmen to the pit's edge where they too began to laugh. 'I like an enemy,' Cerdic said, 'who puts such faith in rubbish.' He pushed his spearmen aside and beckoned to us. 'Come and see what you have discovered, Merlin of Avalon.'

I went with Merlin to the pit's edge and saw a tangle of old, dark and damp-ruined wood. It looked like nothing more than a heap of firewood, just scraps of timber; some of them rotted by the damp that had seeped into a corner of the brick-lined pit and the rest so old and fragile that they would have flared up and burned to ash in an instant. 'What is it?' I asked Merlin.

'It seems,' Merlin said in Saxon, 'that we have looked in the wrong place. Come,' he spoke British again as he touched my shoulder, 'I've wasted our time.'

'But not ours,' Dinas said harshly.

'I see a wheel,' Lavaine said.

Merlin turned slowly back, his face looking ravaged. He had tried to deceive Cerdic and the Silurian twins and the deception had failed utterly.

'Two wheels,' Dinas said.

'And a shaft,' Lavaine added, 'cut into three pieces.'

I stared again at the squalid tangle and again I saw nothing but wooden scraps, but then I saw that some of the pieces were curved and that if the curved fragments were joined together and braced with the many short rods, they would indeed make a pair of wheels. Mixed with the scraps of the wheels were some thin panels and one long shaft that was as thick as my wrist, but so long that it had been broken into three pieces so it would fit into the hole. There was also an axle boss visible, with a slit in its centre where a long knife blade could be fitted. The heap of wood was the remains of a small ancient chariot like those that had once carried the warriors of Britain into battle.

'The Chariot of Modron,' Dinas said reverently.

'Modron,' Lavaine said, 'the mother of the Gods.'

'Whose chariot,' Dinas said, 'connects earth to the heavens.'

'And Merlin doesn't want it,' Dinas said scornfully.

'So we shall take the chariot instead,' Lavaine announced.

Cerdic's interpreter had done his best to translate all this to the King, but it was plain that Cerdic remained unimpressed by the sorry collection of broken and decayed timber. He nevertheless ordered his spearmen to collect the fragments and lay them in a cloak that Lavaine picked up. Nimue hissed a curse at them, and Lavaine just laughed at her. 'Do you want to fight us for the chariot?' he demanded, gesturing at Cerdic's spearmen.

'You can't shelter behind Saxons for ever,' I said, 'and the time will come when you'll have to fight.'

Dinas spat into the empty pit. 'We are Druids, Derfel, and you cannot take our lives, not without consigning your soul, and every soul you love, to horror evermore.'

'I can kill you,' Nimue spat at them.

Dinas stared at her, then extended a fist towards her. Nimue spat at the fist to avert its evil, but Dinas just turned it over, opened his palm and showed her a thrush's egg. He tossed it to her. 'Something to fill your eye-socket, woman,' he said dismissively, then turned and followed his brother and Cerdic out of the temple.

'I'm sorry, Lord,' I said to Merlin when we had been left alone.

'For what, Derfel? You think you could have beaten twenty spearmen?' He sighed and rubbed at his violated beard. 'You see how the powers of the new Gods fight back? But so long as we possess the Cauldron we possess the greater power. Come.' He extended his arm to Nimue, not for comfort, but because he wanted her support. He suddenly looked old and tired as he walked slowly down the nave.

'What do we do, Lord?' one of my spearmen asked me.

'Make ready to go,' I answered. I was watching Merlin's stooped back. The cutting of his beard, I thought, was a greater tragedy than he dared admit, but I consoled myself that he still possessed the Cauldron of Clyddno Eiddyn. His power was still great, but there was something about that bent back and slow shuffle that was infinitely saddening. 'We make ready to go,' I said again.

We left next day. We were hungry still, but we were going home. And we did, after a fashion, have peace.

Just north of ruined Calleva, on land that had been Aelle's and was now ours again, we found the tribute waiting. Aelle had kept faith with us.

There were no guards there, just great piles of gold waiting unattended on the road. There were cups, crosses, chains, ingots, brooches and torques. We had no means of weighing the gold, and both Arthur and Cuneglas suspected that not all the agreed tribute had been paid, but it was enough. It was a hoard.

We bundled the gold in cloaks, hung the heavy bundles over the backs of the war horses, and went on. Arthur walked with us, his spirits brightening as we drew nearer and nearer to home, though regrets still lingered. 'You remember the oath I took near here?' he asked me shortly after we had collected Aelle's gold.

'I remember it, Lord.' The oath had been taken on the night after we had delivered much of this same gold to Aelle the previous year. The gold had been our bribe to turn Aelle away from our frontier and onto Ratae, the fortress of Powys, and Arthur had sworn that night that he would kill Aelle. 'Now I preserve him instead,' he commented ruefully.

'Cuneglas has Ratae back,' I said.

'But the oath is unfulfilled, Derfel. So many broken oaths.' He peered up at a sparrowhawk that slid in front of a great white heap of cloud. 'I suggested to Cuneglas and Meurig that they split Siluria in two, and Cuneglas suggested you might like to be the King of his portion. Would you?'

I was so astonished that I could hardly respond. 'If you wish it, Lord,' I finally said.

'Well, I don't. I want you as Mordred's guardian.'

I walked with that disappointment for a few paces. 'Siluria may not like being divided,' I said.

'Siluria will do as it's told,' Arthur said firmly, 'and you and Ceinwyn will live in Mordred's palace in Dumnonia.'

'If you say so, Lord.' I was suddenly reluctant to abandon Cwm Isaf's humbler pleasures.

'Cheer up, Derfel!' Arthur said. 'I'm not a King, why should you be one?'

'It was not the loss of a kingdom I regret, Lord, but the addition of a King to my household.'

'You'll manage him, Derfel, you manage everything.'

Next day we divided the army. Sagramor had already left the ranks, leading his spearmen to guard the new frontier with Cerdic's kingdom, and now the rest of us took two separate roads. Arthur, Merlin, Tristan and Lancelot went south, while Cuneglas and Meurig went west towards their lands. I embraced Arthur and Tristan, then knelt for Merlin's blessing, which he gave benignly. He had regained some of his old energy during our march from London, but he could not hide the fact that his humiliation in the temple of Mithras had hit him hard. He might still possess the Cauldron, but his enemies possessed a strand of his beard and he would need all his magic to ward off their spells. He embraced me, I kissed Nimue, then I watched them walk away before I followed Cuneglas westward. I was going to Powys to find my Ceinwyn and I was travelling with a share of Aelle's gold, but even so it did not seem like a triumph. We had beaten Aelle and secured peace, but Cerdic and Lancelot had been the real winners of the campaign, not us.

That night we all rested in Corinium, but at midnight a storm woke me. The tempest was far away to the south, but such was the violence of the distant thunder and so vivid were the flashes of lightning that flickered on the walls of the courtyard where I slept that it woke me. Ailleann, Arthur's old mistress and the mother of his twins, had offered me shelter and she now came from her bed-chamber with a worried face. I wrapped my cloak around me and went with her to the town walls, where I found half my men already watching the distant turmoil. Cuneglas and Agricola were also standing on the ramparts, but not Meurig, for he refused to find any portents in the weather.

We all knew better. Storms are messages from the Gods, and this storm was a tumultuous outburst. No rain fell on Corinium and no gale blew our cloaks, but far off to the south, somewhere in Dumnonia, the Gods flayed the land. Lightning tore the dark clean out of the sky and stabbed its crooked daggers at the earth. Thunder rolled incessantly, outburst after outburst, and with every echoing clap the lightning flickered and dazzled and split its ragged fire through the shuddering night.

Issa stood close beside me, his honest face lit by those distant spits of fire. 'Is someone dead?'

'We can't tell, Issa.'

'Are we cursed, Lord?' he asked.

'No,' I replied with a confidence I did not entirely feel.

'But I heard that Merlin had his beard cut?'

'A few hairs,' I said dismissively, 'nothing more. What of it?'

'If Merlin has no power, Lord, who does?'

'Merlin has power,' I tried to reassure him. And I had power, too, for soon I would be Mordred's champion and would live on a great estate. I would mould the child and Arthur would make the child's kingdom.

Yet still I worried about the thunder. And I would have worried more had I known what it meant. For disaster did come that night. We did not hear of it for three more days, but then at last we learned why the thunder had spoken and the lightning struck.

It had struck on the Tor, on Merlin's hall where the winds made moan about his hollow dream-tower. And there, in our hour of victory, the lightning had set the wooden tower alight and its flames had seared and leapt and howled into the night and in the morning, when the embers were being spattered and extinguished by the dying storm's rain, there were no Treasures left at Ynys Wydryn. There was no Cauldron in the ashes, only an emptiness at Dumnonia's fire-scarred heart.

The new Gods, it seemed, were fighting back. Or else the Silurian twins had worked a mighty charm on the cut braid of Merlin's beard, for the Cauldron was gone and the Treasures had vanished.

And I went north to Ceinwyn.

PART THREE

Camelot

'ALL THE TREASURES BURNED?' Igraine asked me.

'Everything,' I said, 'disappeared.'

'Poor Merlin,' Igraine said. She has taken her usual place on my window-sill, though she is well wrapped against this day's cold by a thick cloak of beaver fur. And she needs it, for it is bitterly cold today. There were flurries of snow this morning, and the sky to the west is ominous with leaden clouds. 'I cannot stay long,' she had announced when she arrived and settled down to skim through the finished parchments, 'in case it snows.'

'It will snow. The berries are thick in the hedgerows and that always means a hard winter.'

'Old men say that every year,' Igraine observed tartly.

'When you're old,' I said, 'every winter is hard.'

'How old was Merlin?'

'At the time he lost the Cauldron? Very close to eighty years. But he lived for a long while after that.'

'But he never rebuilt his dream-tower?' Igraine asked.

'No.'

She sighed and pulled the rich cloak about her. 'I should like a dream-tower. I would so like to have a dream-tower.'

'Then have one built,' I said. 'You're a Queen. Give orders, make a fuss. It's quite simple; nothing but a four-sided tower with no roof and a platform halfway up. Once it's built no one but you can go inside, and the trick of it is to sleep on the platform and wait for the Gods to send you messages. Merlin always said it was a horribly cold place to sleep in winter.'

'And the Cauldron,' Igraine guessed, 'had been hidden on the platform?'

'Yes.'

'But it wasn't burned, was it, Brother Derfel?' she insisted.

'The Cauldron's story goes on,' I admitted, 'but I won't tell it now.'

She stuck her tongue out at me. She is looking startlingly beautiful today. Perhaps it is the cold that has put the colour into her cheeks and the spark into her dark eyes, or maybe the beaver pelts suit her, but I suspect she is pregnant. I could always tell when Ceinwyn was with child, and Igraine shows that same surge of life. But Igraine has said nothing, so I will not ask her. She has prayed hard enough, God knows, for a child, and maybe our Christian God does hear prayers. We have nothing else to give us hope, for our own Gods are dead, or fled, or careless of us.

'The bards,' Igraine said, and I knew from her tone that another of my shortcomings as a storyteller was about to be aired, 'say that the battle near London was terrible. They say Arthur fought all day.'

'Ten minutes,' I said dismissively.

'And they all declare that Lancelot saved him, arriving at the last moment with a hundred spearmen.'

'They all say that,' I said, 'because Lancelot's poets wrote the songs.'

She shook her head sadly. 'If this,' she said, slapping the big leather bag in which she carries the finished parchments back to the Caer, 'is the only record of Lancelot, Derfel, then what will people think? That the poets lie?'

'Who cares what people think?' I answered testily. 'And poets always lie. It's what they're paid to do. But you asked me for the truth, I tell it, and then you complain.'

'"Lancelot's warriors,"' she quoted, '"spearmen so bold, Makers of widows and givers of gold. Slayers of Saxons, feared by the Sais . . ."'

'Do stop,' I interrupted her, 'please? I heard the song a week after it was written!'

'But if the songs lied,' she pleaded, 'why didn't Arthur protest?'

'Because he never cared about songs. Why should he? He was a warrior, not a bard, and so long as his men sang before battle he didn't care. And besides, he could never sing himself. He thought he had a voice, but Ceinwyn always said he sounded like a cow with wind.'

Igraine frowned. 'I still don't understand why Lancelot's making peace was so very bad.'

'It isn't difficult to understand,' I said. I slid off the stool and crossed to the hearth where I used a stick to pull some glowing embers from the small fire. I arranged six embers in a line on the floor, then split the row into two and four. 'The four embers,' I said, 'represent Aelle's forces. The two are Cerdic's. Now understand we could never have beaten the Saxons if all the embers had been together. We could not have defeated six, but we could beat four. Arthur planned to beat those four, then turn on the two, and that way we could have scoured Britain of the Sais. But by making peace, Lancelot increased Cerdic's power.' I added another ember to the two, so that four now faced a group of three, then shook the flame off the burning stick. 'We had weakened Aelle,' I explained, 'but we'd weakened ourselves too for we no longer had Lancelot's three hundred spearmen. They were pledged to peace. That increased Cerdic's power even more.' I pushed two of Aelle's embers into Cerdic's camp, dividing the line into five and two. 'So all we had done,' I said, 'was weaken Aelle and strengthen Cerdic. And that's what Lancelot's peacemaking achieved.'

'You are giving our Lady lessons in counting?' Sansum sidled into the room with a suspicious look on his face. 'And I thought you were composing a gospel,' he added slyly.

'The five loaves and two fishes,' Igraine said swiftly. 'Brother Derfel thought it might be five fishes and two loaves, but I'm sure I'm right, am I not, Lord Bishop?'

'My Lady is quite right,' Sansum said. 'And Brother Derfel is a poor Christian. How can such an ignorant man write a gospel for the Saxons?'

'Only with your loving support, Lord Bishop,' Igraine answered, 'and, of course, with my husband's support. Or shall I tell the King that you oppose him in this small thing?'

'You would be guilty of the grossest falsehood if you did,' Sansum lied to her, outmanoeuvred again by my clever Queen. 'I came to tell you, Lady, that your spearmen believe you should leave. The sky threatens more snow.'

She picked up the bag of parchments and gave me a smile. 'I shall see you when the snow has stopped, Brother Derfel.'

'I shall pray for that moment, Lady.'

She smiled again, then walked past the saint who half bowed as she went through the door, but once she had gone he straightened and stared at me. The tufts above his ears that made us call him the mouse-lord are white now, but age has not softened the saint. He can still bristle with vituperation and the pain that still afflicts him when he passes urine only serves to make his temper worse. 'There is a special place in hell, Brother Derfel,' he hissed at me, 'for the tellers of lies.'

'I shall pray for those poor souls, Lord,' I said, then turned from him and dipped this quill in ink to go on with my tale of Arthur, my warlord, my peace-maker and friend.

What followed were the glorious years. Igraine, who listens to the poets too much, calls them Camelot. We did not. They were the years of Arthur's best rule, the years when he shaped a country to his wishes and the years in which Dumnonia most closely matched his ideal of a nation at peace with itself and with its neighbours; but it is only by looking back that those years seem so much better than they were, and that is because the years that followed were so much worse. To hear the tales told at night-time hearths you would think we had made a whole new country in Britain, named it Camelot and peopled it with shining heroes, but the truth is that we simply ruled Dumnonia as best we could, we ruled it justly and we never called it Camelot. I did not even hear that name till two years ago. Camelot exists only in the poets' dreams, while in our Dumnonia, even in those good years, the harvests still failed, the plagues still ravaged us and wars were still fought.

Ceinwyn came to Dumnonia and it was in Lindinis that our first child was born. It was a girl and we called her Morwenna after Ceinwyn's mother. She was born with black hair, but after a while it turned pale gold like her mother's. Lovely Morwenna.

Merlin was proved right about Guinevere, for as soon as Lancelot had established his new government in Venta, she declared herself tired of the brand-new palace at Lindinis. It was too damp, she said, and much too exposed to the wet winds coming off the swamps about Ynys Wydryn, and too cold in winter, and suddenly nothing would do except to move back to Uther's old Winter Palace at Durnovaria. But Durnovaria was almost as far from Venta as Lindinis, so Guinevere then persuaded Arthur that they needed to prepare a house for the distant day when Mordred became King and, by a King's right, demanded the Winter Palace's return, so Arthur let Guinevere make the choice. Arthur himself dreamed of a stout hall with a palisade, beast house and granaries, but Guinevere found a Roman villa just south of the fort of Vindocladia that lay, just as Merlin had foretold, on the frontier between Dumnonia and Lancelot's new Belgic kingdom. The villa was built on a hill above a creek of the sea and Guinevere called it her Sea Palace. She had a swarm of builders renovate the villa and fill it with all the statues that had once graced Lindinis. She even commandeered the mosaic floor from Lindinis's entrance hall. For a time Arthur worried that the Sea Palace was dangerously close to Cerdic's land, but Guinevere insisted the peace negotiated at London would last and Arthur, realizing how she loved the place, relented. He never cared what place he called home, for he rarely was at home. He liked to be on the move, always visiting some corner of Mordred's kingdom.

Mordred himself moved into the ransacked palace at Lindinis, and Ceinwyn and I had his guardianship and so lived there too, and with us were sixty spearmen, ten horsemen to carry messages, sixteen kitchen girls and twenty-eight house slaves. We had a steward, a chamberlain, a bard, two huntsmen, a mead-brewer, a falconer, a physician, a doorkeeper, a candle-man and six cooks, and they all had slaves, and besides those house slaves there was a small army of other slaves who worked the land and pollarded the trees and kept the ditches drained. A small town grew around the palace, inhabited by potters and shoemakers and blacksmiths; the tradespeople who became rich off our business.

It all seemed a long way from Cwm Isaf. Now we slept in a tiled chamber with plaster-smooth walls and pillared door-ways. Our meals were taken in a feasting hall that could have seated a hundred, though as often as not we left it empty and ate in a small chamber that led directly from the kitchens for I never could abide food served cold when it was supposed to be hot. If it rained we could walk the covered arcade of the outer courtyard and thus stay dry, and in summer, when the sun beat hot on the tiles, there was a spring-fed pool in the inner courtyard where we could swim. None of it was ours, of course; this palace and its spacious lands were the honours due to a king and all of them belonged to the six-year-old Mordred.

Ceinwyn was accustomed to luxury, if not on this lavish scale, but the constant presence of slaves and servants never embar-rassed her as it did me, and she discharged her duties with an efficient lack of fuss that kept the palace calm and happy. It was Ceinwyn who commanded the servants and supervised the kit-chens and tallied the accounts, but I know she missed Cwm Isaf and still, of an evening, she would sometimes sit with her distaff and spin wool while we talked.

As often as not we talked of Mordred. Both of us had hoped that the tales of his mischief were exaggerations, but they were not, for if any child was wicked, it was Mordred. From the very first day when he came by ox-wagon from Culhwch's hall near Durnovaria and was lifted down into our courtyard, he misbehaved. I came to hate him, God help me. He was only a child and I hated him.

The King was always small for his age, but, apart from his clubbed left foot, he was solidly built with hard muscles and little fat. His face was very round, but was disfigured by a strangely bulbous nose that made the poor child ugly, while his dark-brown hair was naturally curly and grew in two great clumps that jutted out on either side of a centre parting and made the other children in Lindinis call him Brush-head, though never to his face. He had strangely old eyes, for even at six years old they were guarded and suspicious, and they became no kinder as his face hardened into manhood. He was a clever boy, though he obstinately refused to learn his letters. The bard of our household, an earnest young man named Pyrlig, was responsible for teaching Mordred to read, to count, to sing, to play the harp, to name the Gods and to learn the genealogy of his royal descent, but Mordred soon had Pyrlig's measure. 'He will do nothing, Lord!' Pyrlig complained to me. 'I give him parchment, he tears it, I give him a quill and he breaks it. I beat him and he bites me, look!' He held out a thin, flea-bitten wrist on which the marks of the royal teeth were red and sore.

I put Eachern, a tough little Irish spearman, into the schoolroom with orders to keep the King in order, and that worked well enough. One beating from Eachern persuaded the child he had met his match and so he sullenly submitted to the discipline, but still learned nothing. You could keep a child still, it seemed, but you could not make him learn. Mordred did try to frighten Eachern by telling him that when he became King he would take his revenge on the warrior for the frequent beatings, but Eachern just gave him another thrashing and promised that he would be back in Ireland by the time Mordred came of age. 'So if you want revenge, Lord King,' Eachern said, giving the boy another sharp blow, 'then bring your army to Ireland and we'll give you a proper grown-up whipping.'

Mordred was not simply a naughty boy – we could have coped with that – but positively wicked. His acts were designed to hurt, even to kill. Once, when he was ten, we found five adders in the dark cellar where we kept the vats of mead. No one but Mordred would have placed them there, and doubtless he did it in the hope that a slave or servant would be bitten. The cellar's cold had made the snakes sleepy and we killed them easily enough, but a month later a maidservant did die after eating mushrooms that we afterwards discovered were toad-stools. No one knew who had made the substitution, but every-one believed it was Mordred. It was as if, Ceinwyn said, there was a calculating adult mind inside that pugnacious little body. She, I think, disliked him as much as I did, but she tried hard to be kind to the boy and she hated the beatings we all gave him. 'They just make him worse,' she admonished me.

'I fear so,' I admitted.

'Then why do it?'

I shrugged. 'Because if you try kindness he just takes advantage of it.' At the beginning, when Mordred had first come to Lindinis, I had promised myself that I would never hit the boy, but that high ambition had faded within days and by the end of the first year I only had to see his ugly, sullen, bulbous-nosed, brush-headed face and I wanted to put him over my knee and beat him bloody.

And even Ceinwyn eventually struck him. She had not want-ed to, but one day I heard her scream. Mordred had found a needle and was idly pushing it at Morwenna's scalp. He had just decided to see what would happen if he pushed the needle into one of the baby's eyes when Ceinwyn came running to see why her daughter cried. She plucked Mordred into the air and gave him such a blow that he went spinning halfway across the room. After that our children were never left to sleep alone, a servant was always at their side and Mordred had added Ceinwyn's name to the list of his enemies.

'He's simply evil,' Merlin explained to me. 'Surely you remember the night he was born?'

'Distinctly,' I said, for I, unlike Merlin, had been there.

'They let the Christians tend the birth bed, didn't they?' he asked me. 'And only summoned Morgan when everything was going wrong. What precautions did the Christians take?'

I shrugged. 'Prayers. I remember a crucifix.' I had not been in the birth-chamber, of course, for no man ever went into a birth-chamber, but I had watched from Caer Cadarn's ramparts.

'No wonder it all went wrong,' Merlin said. 'Prayers! What use are prayers against an evil spirit? There has to be urine on the door sill, iron in the bed, mugwort on the fire.' He shook his head sadly. 'A spirit got into the boy before Morgan could help him and that's why his foot is so twisted. The spirit was probably clinging onto the foot when it sensed Morgan's arrival.'

'So how do we get the spirit out?' I asked.

'With a sword through the wretched child's heart,' he said, smiling and leaning back in his chair.

'Please, Lord,' I insisted, 'how?'

Merlin shrugged. 'Old Balise reckoned it could be done by putting the possessed person into a bed between two virgins. All of them naked, of course.' He chuckled. 'Poor old Balise. He was a good Druid, but the overwhelming majority of his spells involved taking young girls' clothes off. The idea was that the spirit would prefer to be in a virgin, you see, so you offered it two virgins so that it would be confused about which one to choose, and the knack of it was to get them all out of the bed at the exact moment that the spirit had come out of the mad person and was still trying to decide which virgin it preferred, and just at that moment you dragged all three off the bed and tossed a firebrand onto the bed-straw. It was supposed to burn the spirit to smoke, you see, but it never made much sense to me. I confess I did try the technique once. I tried to cure a poor old fool called Malldyn, and all I achieved was one idiot still mad as a cuckoo, two terrified slave girls, and all three of them slightly scorched.' He sighed. 'We sent Malldyn to the Isle of the Dead. Best place for him. You could send Mordred there?'

The Isle of the Dead is where we sent our terrible mad. Nimue had been there once, and I had fetched her out of its horror. 'Arthur would never allow it,' I said.

'I suppose not. I'll try a charm for you, but I can't say I'm very hopeful.' Merlin lived with us now. He was an old man dying slowly, or so it seemed to us, for the energy had been sucked out of him by the fire that had consumed the Tor, and with the energy had gone his dreams of assembling the Treasures of Britain. All that was left now was a dry husk growing ever older. He sat for hours in the sun and in winter he hunched over the fire. He kept his Druid's tonsure, though he no longer plaited his beard, but just let it grow wild and white. He ate little, but was always ready to talk, though never about Dinas and Lavaine, nor about the dreadful moment when Cerdic had sliced off the plait of his beard. It was that violation, I decided, as much as the lightning strike on the Tor, that had sucked the life from Merlin, yet he did retain one tiny flickering scrap of hope. He was convinced the Cauldron had not been burned, but had been stolen, and early in our stay at Lindinis he proved it to me in the garden. He built a mock tower of chopped firewood, placed a gold cup in its centre and a handful of tinder at its base, then ordered fire to be fetched from the kitchens.

Even Mordred behaved that afternoon. Fire always fascinated the King and he stared wide-eyed as the model tower blazed in the sunlight. The stacked logs collapsed into the centre, and still the flames leapt, and it was almost dark when Merlin fetched a gardener's rake and combed the ashes. He brought out the golden cup, no longer recognizable as a cup, misshapen and twisted as it was, but still gold. 'I reached the Tor the morning after the fire, Derfel,' he told me, 'and I searched and searched through the ashes. I had every scorched timber removed by hand, I sieved the cinders, I raked the remnants and I found no gold. Not one drop. The Cauldron was taken, and the tower was set on fire. I suspect the Treasures were stolen at the same time, for they were all stored there except for the chariot and the other one.'

'What other one?'

For a moment he looked as if he would not answer, then he shrugged as if none of it mattered now. 'The sword of Rhydderch. You know it as Caledfwlch.' He was speaking of Arthur's sword, Excalibur.

'You gave it to him even though it's one of the Treasures?' I asked in astonishment.

'Why not? He's sworn to return it to me when I need it. He doesn't know it's the sword of Rhydderch, Derfel, and you must promise me not to tell him. He'll only do something stupid if he finds out, like melt it down to prove he isn't frightened of the Gods. Arthur can be very obtuse at times, but he's the best ruler we have so I decided to give him a little extra secret power by letting him use Rhydderch's sword. He'd scoff if he knew, of course, but one day the blade will turn to flame and he won't scoff then.'

I wanted to know more about the sword, but he would not tell me. 'It doesn't matter now,' he said, 'it's all over. The Treasures are gone. Nimue will look for them, I suppose, but I'm too old, much too old.'

I hated to hear him say that. After all the effort that had gone into the collection of the Treasures he simply seemed to have abandoned them. Even the Cauldron, for which we had suffered the Dark Road, seemed not to matter any more. 'If the Treasures still exist, Lord,' I insisted, 'they can be found.'

He smiled indulgently. 'They will be found,' he said dismissively. 'Of course they'll be found.'

'Then why don't we look for them?'

He sighed as though my questions were a nuisance. 'Because they are hidden, Derfel, and their hiding place will be under a spell of concealment. I know that. I can sense it. So we have to wait until someone tries to use the Cauldron. When that happens, we'll know, for only I have the knowledge to use the Cauldron properly and if anyone else summons its powers they'll spill a horror across Britain.' He shrugged. 'We wait for the horror, Derfel, then we go to the heart of it and there we shall find the Cauldron.'

'So who do you think stole it?' I persisted.

He spread his hands to show ignorance. 'Lancelot's men? For Cerdic, probably. Or maybe for those two Silurian twins. I rather underestimated them, didn't I? Not that it matters now. Only time will tell who has it, Derfel, only time will tell. Wait for the horror to show, then we'll find it.' He seemed content to wait, and while he waited he told old tales and listened to news, though from time to time he would shuffle into his room that led off the outer courtyard and there he would work some charm, usually for Morwenna's sake. He still told fortunes, usually by spreading a layer of cold ashes on the courtyard's flagstones and letting a grass snake ripple its way through the dust so he could read its trail, but I noted that the fortunes were always bland and optimistic. He had no relish for the task. He did possess some power still, for when Morwenna caught a fever he made a charm of wool and beechnut shells, then gave her a concoction made from crushed woodlice that took the fever clean away, but when Mordred was sick he would always devise spells to make the sickness worse, though the King never did weaken and die. 'The demon protects him,' Merlin explained, 'and these days I'm too weak to take on young demons.' He would lean back in his cushions and entice one of the cats onto his lap. He had always liked cats, and we had plenty in Lindinis. Merlin was happy enough in the palace. He and I were friends, he was passionately fond of Ceinwyn and our growing family of daughters, and he was looked after by Gwlyddyn, Ralla and Caddwg, his old servants from the Tor. Gwlyddyn and Ralla's children grew up alongside ours and all of them were united against Mordred. By the time the King was twelve years old Ceinwyn had already given birth five times. All three of the girls lived, but both the boys died within a week of their births and Ceinwyn blamed

Mordred's evil spirit for their deaths. 'It doesn't want other boys in the palace,' she said sadly, 'only girls.'

'Mordred will go soon,' I promised her, for I was counting the days to his fifteenth birthday when he would be acclaimed King.

Arthur counted the days too, though with some dread for he feared that Mordred would undo all his achievements. Arthur came frequently to Lindinis in those years. We would hear hoofbeats in the outer courtyard, the door would be flung open and his voice would echo through the palace's big, half-empty rooms. 'Morwenna! Seren! Dian!' He would shout, and our three golden-haired daughters would run or toddle to be swept up in a huge embrace and then they would be spoiled with presents; honey on a comb, small brooches, or the delicate spiral-patterned shell of a snail. Then, draped by daughters, he would come to whatever room we occupied and give us his latest news: a bridge rebuilt, a lawcourt opened, an honest magistrate found, a highway robber executed; or else some tale of a natural wonder: a sea snake seen off the coast, a calf born with five legs or, once, tales of a juggler who ate fire. 'How is the King?' he would always ask when these wonders had been recounted.

'The King grows,' Ceinwyn would always reply blandly and Arthur would ask no more.

He would give us news of Guinevere, and it was always good, though both Ceinwyn and I suspected that his enthusiasm concealed a strange loneliness. He was never alone, but I think he never did discover the twin soul he wanted so much. Guinevere had once been as passionately interested in the business of government as Arthur, but she gradually turned her energies to the worship of Isis. Arthur, who was ever made uncomfortable by religious fervour, pretended to be interested in that woman's Goddess, but in truth I think he believed Guinevere was wasting her time searching for a power that did not exist, just as we had once wasted our time pursuing the Cauldron.

Guinevere gave him only the one son. Either, Ceinwyn said, they slept apart, or else Guinevere was using a woman's magic to prevent conception. Every village had a wise woman who knew what herbs would do that, just as they knew what substances could abort a child or cure a sickness. Arthur, I knew, would have liked more children for he adored them, and some of his happiest times were when he brought Gwydre to stay in our palace. Arthur and his son revelled in the wild pack of ragged, knot-haired children who raced carelessly about Lindinis, but who always avoided the sullen, brooding presence of Mordred. Gwydre played with our three, and Ralla's three, and with the two dozen slave or servant children who formed miniature armies for mock combat or else draped borrowed war-cloaks over the branch of a low-growing pear tree in the garden to turn it into a pretend house that imitated the passions and procedures of the larger palace. Mordred had his own companions, all boys, all slave sons, and they, being older, roamed more widely. We heard tales of a reaping hook stolen from a hut, of a thatch or a hayrick fired, of a sieve torn or a newly laid hedge broken, and, in later years, of a shepherd's girl or a farmer's daughter assaulted. Arthur would listen, shudder, then go and talk with the King, but it made no difference.

Guinevere rarely came to Lindinis, though my duties, that took me all across Dumnonia in Arthur's service, carried me to Durnovaria's Winter Palace frequently enough and it was there, as often as not, that I met Guinevere. She was civil to me, but then we were all civil in those days for Arthur had inaugurated his great band of warriors. He had first described his idea to me in Cwm Isaf, but now, in the years of peace that followed the battle outside London, he made his guild of spearmen into a reality.

Even to this day, if you mention the Round Table, some old men will remember and chuckle at that ancient attempt to tame rivalry, hostility and ambition. The Round Table, of course, was never its proper name, but rather a nickname. Arthur himself had decided to call it the Brotherhood of Britain, which sounded far more impressive, but no one ever called it that. They remembered it, if they remembered it at all, as the Round Table oath, and they probably forgot that it was supposed to bring us peace. Poor Arthur. He really did believe in brotherhood, and if kisses could bring peace then a thousand dead men would still be alive to this day. Arthur did try to change the world and his instrument was love.

The Brotherhood of Britain was supposed to have been inaugurated at the Winter Palace at Durnovaria in the summer after Guinevere's father, Leodegan the exiled King of Henis Wyren, had died of a plague. But that July, when we were all supposed to meet, the plague came to Durnovaria again and so, at the very last moment, Arthur diverted the great gathering to the Sea Palace that was now finished and shining on its hill above the creek. Lindinis would have been a better place for the inaugural rites because it was a much larger palace, but Guinevere must have decided that she wanted to show off her new home. Doubtless it pleased her to have Britain's crude, long-haired, rough-bearded warriors wandering through its civilized halls and shadowed arcades. This beauty, she seemed to be telling us, is what you live to protect, though she took good care to make sure that few of us actually slept inside the enlarged villa. We camped outside and, truth to tell, we were happier there.

Ceinwyn came with me. She was not well, for the ceremonies occurred not long after the birth of her third child, a boy, and it had been a difficult confinement that had ended with Ceinwyn desperately weak and the child dead, but Arthur pleaded for her to come. He wanted all the lords of Britain there, and though none came from Gwynedd, Elmet, or the other northern kingdoms, many others did make the long journey and virtually all Dumnonia's great men were present. Cuneglas of Powys came, Meurig of Gwent was there, Prince Tristan of Kernow attended, as, of course, did Lancelot, and all those Kings brought lords, Druids, bishops and chieftains so that the tents and shelters made a great swathe about the Sea Palace's hill. Mordred, who was then nine years old, came with us and he, to Guinevere's disgust, was given rooms with the other Kings inside the palace. Merlin refused to attend. He said he was too old for such nonsense. Galahad was named the Marshal of the Brotherhood and so he presided with Arthur and, like Arthur, believed devoutly in the whole idea.

I never confessed as much to Arthur, but I found the whole thing embarrassing. His notion was that we would all swear peace and friendship to one another, and thus heal our enmities and bind each other in oaths that would forbid any in the Brotherhood of Britain from ever raising a spear against another; but even the Gods seemed to mock that high ambition for the day of the ceremony dawned chill and gloomy, though it never did actually rain, which Arthur, who was ridiculously optimistic about the whole thing, declared to be a propitious sign.

No swords, spears or shields were carried to the ceremony, held in the Sea Palace's great pleasure garden which lay between two newly built arcades that stretched on grass embankments towards the creek. Banners hung from the arcades where two choirs sang solemn music to give the ceremonies a proper dignity. At the north end of the garden, close to a big arched door that led into the palace, a table had been set. It happened to be a round table, though there was nothing significant in that shape; it was simply the most convenient table to carry out into the garden. The table was not very large, maybe as far across as a man's outstretched hands could reach, but it was, I remember, very beautiful. It was Roman, of course, and made of a white translucent stone into which had been carved a remarkable horse with great spread wings. One of the wings had a grievous crack running through it, but the table was still an impressive object and the winged horse a wonder. Sagramor said he had never seen such a beast in all his travels, though he claimed that flying horses did exist in the mysterious countries that lay beyond the oceans of sand, wherever they were. Sagramor had married his sturdy Saxon Malla and was now the father of two boys.

The only swords allowed at the ceremony were those belonging to the Kings and Princes. Mordred's sword lay on the table, and criss-crossed above it were the blades of Lancelot, Meurig, Cuneglas, Galahad and Tristan. One by one we all stepped forward, Kings, Princes, chieftains and lords, and placed our hands where the six blades touched and swore Arthur's oath that pledged us to amity and peace. Ceinwyn had dressed the nine-year-old Mordred in new clothes, then trimmed and combed his hair in an attempt to stop its curly bristles jutting like twin brushes from his round skull, but he still looked an awkward figure as he limped on his clubbed left foot to mumble the oath. I admit that the moment when I put my hand on the six blades was solemn enough; like most men there, I had every intention of keeping the oath which was, of course, for men only, for Arthur did not consider this to be women's business, though plenty of women stood on the terrace above the arched door to witness the long ceremony. It was a long ceremony, too. Arthur had originally intended to restrict the membership of his Brotherhood to those oath-sworn warriors who had fought against the Saxons, but now he had widened it to include every great man he could lure to the palace, and when the oaths were finished he swore his own oath and afterwards stood on the terrace and told us that the vow we had just sworn was as sacred as any we had ever made, that we had promised Britain peace and that if any of us broke that peace then it was the sworn duty of every other member of the Brotherhood to punish the transgressor. Then he instructed us to embrace each other, and after that, of course, the drinking started.

The day's solemnity did not end as the drinking began. Arthur had watched carefully to see which men avoided other men's embraces, and then, group by group, those recalcitrant souls were summoned to the palace's great hall where Arthur insisted they should be reconciled. Arthur himself showed an example by first embracing Sansum, and afterwards Melwas, the dethroned Belgic King whom Arthur had exiled to Isca. Melwas submitted with a lumbering grace to the kiss of peace, but he died a month later after eating a breakfast of tainted oysters. Fate, as Merlin loved to tell us, is inexorable.

Those more intimate reconciliations inevitably delayed the serving of the feast which was to take place in the great hall where Arthur was bringing enemies together, and so more mead was carried out to the garden where the bored warriors waited and tried to guess which among them would be summoned to Arthur's peace-making next. I knew I would be summoned, for I had carefully avoided Lancelot during the whole ceremony, and sure enough Hygwydd, Arthur's servant, found me and insisted I go to the great hall where, as I feared, Lancelot and his courtiers waited for me. Arthur had persuaded Ceinwyn to attend and, to give her some added comfort, he had asked her brother Cuneglas to be present. The three of us stood on one side of the hall, Lancelot and his men on the other, while Arthur, Galahad and Guinevere presided from the dais where the high table stood ready for the great feast. Arthur beamed at us. 'I have in this room,' he declared, 'some of my dearest friends. King Cuneglas, the best ally any man could have in war or peace, King Lancelot, to whom I am sworn like a brother, Lord Derfel Cadarn, the bravest of all my brave men, and dear Princess Ceinwyn.' He smiled.

I stood as awkward as a pea-field scarecrow. Ceinwyn looked graceful, Cuneglas stared at the hall's painted ceiling, Lancelot scowled, Amhar and Loholt tried to look belligerent, while Dinas and Lavaine showed nothing but contempt on their hard faces. Guinevere watched us carefully and her striking face betrayed nothing, though I suspect she felt as scornful as Dinas and Lavaine of this invented ceremony that was so dear to her husband. Arthur fervently wanted peace, and only he and Galahad seemed unembarrassed by the occasion.

When none of us spoke Arthur spread his arms and stepped down from the dais. 'I demand,' he said, 'that the ill blood that exists between you be spilled now, spilled once and then forgotten.'

He waited again. I shuffled my feet and Cuneglas tugged at his long moustaches.

'Please,' Arthur said.

Ceinwyn gave a tiny shrug. 'I regret,' she said, 'the hurt I caused King Lancelot.'

Arthur, delighted that the ice was melting, smiled at the Belgic King. 'Lord King?' He invited a response from Lancelot. 'Will you forgive her?'

Lancelot, who that day was dressed all in white, glanced at her, then bowed.

'Is that forgiveness?' I growled.

Lancelot coloured, but managed to rise to Arthur's expectations. 'I have no quarrel with the Princess Ceinwyn,' he said stiffly.

'There!' Arthur was delighted with the grudging words and spread his arms again to invite them both forward. 'Embrace,' he said. 'I will have peace!'

They both walked forward, kissed each other on the cheek and stepped back. The gesture was about as warm as that star-bright night when we had waited about the Cauldron in the rocks by Llyn Cerrig Bach, but it pleased Arthur. 'Derfel,' he looked at me, 'will you not embrace the King?'

I steeled myself for conflict. 'I will embrace him, Lord,' I said, 'when his Druids retract the threats they made against the Princess Ceinwyn.'

There was silence. Guinevere sighed and tapped a foot on the mosaics of the dais, the same mosaics she had taken from Lindinis. She looked, as ever, superb. She wore a black robe, perhaps in recognition of the day's solemnity, and the robe was sewn with dozens of small silver crescent moons. Her red hair had been tamed into plaits that she had coiled about her skull and pinned into place with two gold clasps shaped as dragons. Around her neck she wore the barbaric Saxon gold necklace that Arthur had sent her after a long-ago battle against Aelle's Saxons. She had told me then that she disliked the necklace, but it looked magnificent on her. She might have despised this day's proceedings, but she still did her best to help her husband. 'What threats?' she asked me coldly.

'They know,' I said, staring at the twins.

'We have made no threats,' Lavaine protested flatly.

'But you can make the stars vanish,' I accused them.

Dinas allowed a slow smile to show on his brutal and handsome face. 'The little paper star, Lord Derfel?' he asked with mock surprise. 'Is that your insult?'

'It was your threat.'

'My Lord!' Dinas appealed to Arthur. 'It was a child's trick. It meant nothing.'

Arthur looked from me to the Druids. 'You swear that?' he demanded.

'On my brother's life,' Dinas said.

'And Merlin's beard?' I challenged them. 'You have it still?'

Guinevere sighed as if to suggest I was becoming tedious. Galahad frowned. Outside the palace the warriors' voices were becoming mead-loud and raucous.

Lavaine looked at Arthur. 'It is true, Lord,' he said courteously, 'that we possessed a strand of Merlin's beard, cut after he insulted King Cerdic. But on my life, Lord, we burned it.'

'We don't fight old men,' Dinas growled, then glanced at Ceinwyn. 'Or women.'

Arthur smiled happily. 'Come, Derfel,' he said, 'embrace. I will have peace between my dearest friends.'

I still hesitated, but Ceinwyn and her brother both urged me forward and so, for the second and last time in my life, I embraced Lancelot. This time, instead of whispering insults as we had at our first embrace, we said nothing. We just kissed and stepped apart.

'There will be peace between you,' Arthur insisted.

'I swear it, Lord,' I answered stiffly.

'I have no quarrel,' Lancelot answered just as coldly.

Arthur had to be content with our churlish reconciliation and he breathed a huge sigh of relief as though the most difficult part of his day was now done; then he embraced us both before insisting that Guinevere, Galahad, Ceinwyn and Cuneglas come and exchange kisses.

Our ordeal was over. Arthur's last victims were his own wife and Mordred, and that I did not want to see so I drew Ceinwyn out of the room. Her brother, at Arthur's request, stayed and so the two of us were alone. 'I'm sorry about that,' I told her.

Ceinwyn shrugged. 'It was an unavoidable ordeal.'

'I still don't trust the bastard,' I said vengefully.

She smiled. 'You, Derfel Cadarn, are a great warrior and he is Lancelot. Does the wolf fear the hare?'

'It fears the serpent,' I said gloomily. I did not feel like facing my friends and describing the reconciliation with Lancelot and so I led Ceinwyn through the Sea Palace's graceful rooms with their pillared walls, decorated floors and heavy bronze lamps that hung on long iron chains from ceilings painted with hunting scenes. Ceinwyn thought the palace immeasurably grand, but also cold. 'Just like the Romans,' she said.

'Just like Guinevere,' I retorted. We found a flight of stairs that led down to some busy kitchens and from there a door into the back gardens where fruit and herbs were growing in well-ordered beds. 'I can't think,' I said when we were in the open air, 'that this Brotherhood of Britain will achieve anything.'

'It will,' Ceinwyn said, 'if enough of you take the oath seriously.'

'Maybe.' I had suddenly stopped in embarrassment, for ahead of me, just straightening from bending over a bed of parsley, was Guinevere's younger sister Gwenhwyvach.

Ceinwyn greeted her happily. I had forgotten that they had been friends in the long years of Guinevere and Gwenhwyvach's exile in Powys, and when they had kissed Ceinwyn brought Gwenhwyvach to me. I thought she might resent my failure to marry her, but she seemed to bear no grudge. 'I have become my sister's gardener,' she told me.

'Surely not, Lady?' I said.

'The appointment is not official,' she said drily, 'nor are my high offices of chief steward or warden of the hounds, but someone has to do the work, and when father died he made Guinevere promise to look after me.'

'I was sorry about your father,' Ceinwyn said.

Gwenhwyvach shrugged. 'He just got thinner and thinner until one day he wasn't there any more.' Gwenhwyvach herself had grown no thinner, indeed she was obese now, a fat red-faced woman who, in her earth-stained dress and dirty white apron, looked more like a farmer's wife than a Princess. 'I live there,' she said, gesturing towards a substantial timber building that stood a hundred paces from the palace. 'My sister allows me to do my work each day, but come the evening bell I am expected to be safely out of sight. Nothing ill-favoured, you understand, can mar the Sea Palace.'

'Lady!' I protested at her self-deprecation.

Gwenhwyvach waved me to silence. 'I'm happy,' she said bleakly. 'I take the dogs for long walks and I talk to the bees.'

'Come to Lindinis,' Ceinwyn urged her.

'That would never be allowed!' Gwenhwyvach said with pretended shock.

'Why not?' Ceinwyn asked. 'We have rooms to spare. Please.'

Gwenhwyvach smiled slyly. 'I know too much, Ceinwyn, that's why. I know who comes and who stays and what they do here.' Neither of us wanted to probe those hints, so we both kept silent, but Gwenhwyvach needed to speak. She must have been lonely, and Ceinwyn was a friendly loving face from the past. Gwenhwyvach suddenly threw down the herbs she had just cut and hurried us back towards the palace. 'Let me show you,' she said.

'I'm sure we don't need to see,' Ceinwyn said, fearing whatever was about to be revealed.

'You can see,' Gwenhwyvach said to Ceinwyn, 'but Derfel can't. Or shouldn't. Men aren't supposed to enter the temple.'

She had led us to a door that stood at the bottom of some

brick steps and which, when she pushed it open, led into a great cellar that lay under the palace floor and was supported by huge arches of Roman brick. 'They keep wine here,' Gwenhwyvach said, explaining the jars and skins that stood racked on the shelves. She had left the door open so that some glimmers of daylight would penetrate the dark, dusty tangle of arches. 'This way,' she said, and disappeared between some pillars to our right.

We followed more slowly, groping our way ever more carefully as we went further and further from the daylight at the cellar door. We heard Gwenhwyvach lifting a door-bar, then a breath of cold air wafted by us as she pulled a huge door open. 'Is this a temple of Isis?' I asked her.

'You've heard about it?' Gwenhwyvach seemed disappointed.

'Guinevere showed me her temple in Durnovaria,' I said, 'years ago.'

'She wouldn't show you this one,' Gwenhwyvach said, and then she pulled aside the thick black curtains that hung a few feet inside the temple doors so that Ceinwyn and I could stare into Guinevere's private shrine. Gwenhwyvach, for fear of her sister's wrath, would not let me tread beyond the small lobby that lay between the door and the thick curtains, but she led Ceinwyn down two steps into the long room that had a floor made of polished black stone, walls and an arched ceiling painted with pitch, a black stone dais with a black stone throne, and behind the throne another black curtain. In front of the low dais was a shallow pit which, I knew, was filled with water during Isis's ceremonies. The temple, in truth, was almost exactly the same as the one Guinevere had shown me so many years before, and very like the deserted shrine we had discovered in Lindinis's palace. The only difference – other than that this cellar was larger and lower than both those previous temples – was that here daylight had been allowed to penetrate, for there was a wide hole in the arched ceiling directly above the shallow pit. 'There's a wall up there,' Gwenhwyvach whispered, pointing up the hole, 'higher than a man. That's so the moonlight can come down the shaft, but no one can see down it. Clever, isn't it?'

The existence of the moon-shaft suggested that the cellar had to run out under the side garden of the palace and Gwenhwyvach confirmed that. 'There used to be an entrance here,' she said, pointing to a jagged line in the pitch-covered brickwork halfway down the temple's length, 'so that supplies could be brought directly into the cellar, but Guinevere extended the arch, see? And covered it over with turf.'

There seemed nothing unduly sinister about the temple, other than its malevolent blackness, for there was no idol, no sacrificial fire and no altar. If anything, it was disappointing, for the arched cellar possessed none of the grandeur of the upstairs rooms. It seemed tawdry, even slightly soiled. The Romans, I thought, would have known how to make this room fit for the Goddess, but Guinevere's best efforts had simply turned a brick cellar into a black cave, though the low throne, which was made from a single block of black stone and was, I presumed, the same throne that I had seen in Durnovaria, was impressive enough. Gwenhwyvach walked past the throne and plucked aside the black curtain so that Ceinwyn could go beyond. They spent a long time behind the curtain, but when we left the cellars Ceinwyn told me there was not much to see there. 'It was just a small black room,' she told me, 'with a big bed and a lot of mouse droppings.'

'A bed?' I asked suspiciously.

'A dream-bed,' Ceinwyn said firmly, 'just like the one that used to be halfway up Merlin's tower.'

'Is that all it is?' I asked, still suspicious.

Ceinwyn shrugged. 'Gwenhwyvach tried to suggest it was used for other purposes,' she said disapprovingly, 'but she had no proof, and she did finally admit that her sister slept there to receive dreams.' She smiled sadly. 'I think poor Gwenhwyvach is touched in the head. She believes Lancelot will come for her one day.'

'She believes what?' I asked in astonishment.

'She's in love with him, poor woman,' Ceinwyn said. We had tried to persuade Gwenhwyvach to join us at the celebrations in the front garden, but she had refused. She would not, she had confided to us, be welcome and so she had hurried away, darting suspicious glances left and right. 'Poor Gwenhwyvach.' Ceinwyn said, then laughed. 'It's so typical of Guinevere, isn't it?'

'What is?'

'To adopt such an exotic religion! Why can't she worship the Gods of Britain like the rest of us? But no, she has to find something strange and difficult.' She sighed, then put an arm through mine. 'Do we really have to stay for the feast?'

She was feeling weak for she had still not fully recovered from the last birth. 'Arthur will understand if we don't go,' I said.

'But Guinevere won't,' she sighed, 'so I had better survive.'

We had been walking around the long western flank of the palace, past the high timber palisade of the temple's moon-shaft, and had now reached the end of the long arcade. I stopped her before we turned the corner and I put my hands on her shoulders. 'Ceinwyn of Powys,' I said, looking into her astonishing and lovely face, 'I do love you.'

'I know,' she said with a smile, then stood on tiptoe to kiss me before leading me a few paces on so that we could gaze up the length of the Sea Palace's pleasure garden. 'There,' Ceinwyn said with amusement, 'is Arthur's Brotherhood of Britain.'

The garden was reeling with drunken men. They had been kept too long from the feast so now they were offering each other elaborate embraces and flowery promises of eternal friendship. Some of the embraces had turned into wrestling matches that rolled fiercely over Guinevere's flower beds. The choirs had long abandoned their attempts to sing solemn music and some of the choirs' women were now drinking with the warriors. Not all the men were drunk, of course, but the sober guests had retreated to the terrace to protect the women, many of whom were Guinevere's attendants and among whom was Lunete, my first and long-ago love. Guinevere was also on the terrace, from where she was staring in horror at the wreckage being made of her garden, though it was her own fault for she had served mead brewed especially strong and now at least fifty men were roistering in the gardens; some had plucked flower stakes to use in mock sword fights and at least one man had a bloody face, while another was working free a loosened tooth and foully cursing the oath-sworn Brother of Britain who had struck him. Someone else had vomited onto the round table.

I helped Ceinwyn up to the safety of the arcade while beneath us the Brotherhood of Britain cursed and fought and drank itself insensible.

And that, although Igraine will never believe me, was how Arthur's Brotherhood of Britain, that the ignorant still call the Round Table, all began.

I would like to say that the new spirit of peace engendered by Arthur's Round Table oath spread happiness throughout the kingdom, but most common folk were quite unaware that the oath had even been taken. Most people neither knew nor cared what their lords did so long as their fields and families were left unmolested. Arthur, of course, set great store by the oath. As Ceinwyn often said, for a man who claimed to hate oaths he was uncommonly fond of making them.

But at least the oath was kept in those years and Britain prospered in that period of peace. Aelle and Cerdic fought each other for the mastery of Lloegyr, and their bitter conflict spared the rest of Britain from their Saxon spears. The Irish Kings in western Britain were forever testing their weapons against British shields, but those conflicts were small and scattered, and most of us enjoyed a long period of peace. Mordred's Council, of which I was now a member, could concern itself with laws, taxes and land disputes instead of worrying about enemies.

Arthur headed the Council, though he never took the chair at the table's head because that was the throne reserved for the King and it waited empty until Mordred came of age. Merlin was officially the King's chief councillor, but he never travelled to Durnovaria and said little on the few occasions that the Council met in Lindinis. Half a dozen of the councillors were warriors, though most of those never came. Agravain said the business bored him, while Sagramor preferred to keep the Saxon frontier peaceful. The other councillors were two bards who knew the laws and genealogies of Britain, two magistrates, a merchant, and two Christian bishops. One of the bishops was a grave, elderly man called Emrys, who had succeeded Bedwin as bishop in Durnovaria, and the other was Sansum.

Sansum had once conspired against Arthur and few men doubted that he should have lost his head when that conspiracy was revealed, but Sansum had somehow slithered free. He never learned to read or write, but he was a clever man and endlessly ambitious. He came from Gwent, where his father had been a tanner, and Sansum had risen to become one of Tewdric's priests, but he came to real prominence by marrying Arthur and Guinevere when they fled like fugitives from Caer Sws. He was rewarded for that service by being made a Dumnonian Bishop and Mordred's chaplain, though he lost the latter honour after he conspired with Nabur and Melwas. He was supposed to rot in obscurity after that as the guardian of the shrine of the Holy Thorn, but Sansum could not abide obscurity. He had saved Lancelot from the humiliation of Mithras's rejection, and in so doing he had earned Guinevere's wary gratitude, but neither his friendship with Lancelot nor his truce with Guinevere would have been sufficient to lift him onto Dumnonia's Council.

He had achieved that eminence by marriage, and the woman he married was Arthur's older sister, Morgan – Morgan, the priestess of Merlin, the adept of the mysteries, the pagan Morgan. With that marriage Sansum had sloughed off all traces of his old disgrace and had risen to the topmost heights of Dumnonian power. He had been placed on the Council, made Bishop of Lindinis and was reappointed as Mordred's chaplain, though luckily his distaste for the young King kept him away from Lindinis's palace. He assumed authority over all the churches in northern Dumnonia, just as Emrys held sway over all the southern churches. For Sansum it was a glittering marriage, and to the rest of us it was an astonishment.

The wedding itself took place in the church of the Holy Thorn at Ynys Wydryn. Arthur and Guinevere stayed at Lindinis, and we all rode to the shrine together on the great day. The ceremonies began with Morgan's baptism in the reed-edged waters of Issa's Mere. She had abandoned her old gold mask with its image of the horned God Cernunnos and had instead adopted a new mask that was decorated with a Christian cross and, to mark the day's joyousness, she had abandoned her usual black robe for a white gown. Arthur had cried with joy to see his sister limp into the mere where Sansum, with evident tenderness, supported her back as he lowered her into the water. A choir sang hallelujahs. We waited while Morgan dried herself and changed into a new white robe, then we watched as she limped to the altar where Bishop Emrys joined them as man and wife.

I think I could not have been more astonished had Merlin himself abandoned the old Gods to take up the cross. For Sansum, of course, it was a double triumph, for by marrying Arthur's sister he not only vaulted into the kingdom's royal Council, but by converting her to Christianity he struck a famous blow against the pagans. Some men sourly accused him of opportunism, but in all fairness I think he did love Morgan in his own calculating way and she undoubtedly adored him. They were two clever people united by resentments. Sansum ever believed that he should be higher than he was, while Morgan, who had once been beautiful, resented the fire that had twisted her body and turned her face into a horror. She resented Nimue too, for Morgan had once been Merlin's most trusted priestess and the younger Nimue had usurped that place and now, in revenge, Morgan became the most ardent of Christians. She was as strident in her protestations of Christ as she had ever been in her service of the older Gods and after her marriage all her formidable will was poured into Sansum's missionary campaign.

Merlin did not attend the marriage, but he did derive amusement from it. 'She's lonely,' he told me when he heard the news, 'and the mouse-lord is at least company. You don't think they rut together, do you? Dear Gods, Derfel, if poor Morgan undressed in front of Sansum he'd throw up! Besides, he doesn't know how to rut. Not with women, anyway.'

Marriage did not soften Morgan. In Sansum she found a man willing to be guided by her shrewd advice and whose ambitions she could support with all her fierce energy, but to the rest of the world she was still the shrewish, bitter woman behind the forbidding golden mask. She still lived in Ynys Wydryn, though instead of living on Merlin's Tor she now inhabited the Bishop's house in the shrine from where she could see the fire-scarred Tor where her enemy, Nimue, lived.

Nimue, bereft of Merlin now, was convinced that Morgan had stolen the Treasures of Britain. As far as I could see, that conviction was based solely on Nimue's hatred for Morgan whom Nimue considered the greatest traitor of Britain. Morgan, after all, was the pagan priestess who had abandoned the Gods to turn Christian, and Nimue, whenever she saw Morgan, spat and hurled curses that Morgan energetically flung back at her; pagan threat battling Christian doom. They would never be civil with each other, though once, at Nimue's urging, I did confront Morgan about the lost Cauldron. That was a year after the marriage and, though I was now a Lord and one of the wealthiest men in Dumnonia, I still felt nervous of Morgan. When I had been a child she had been a figure of awesome authority and terrifying appearance who had ruled the Tor with a brusque bad temper and an ever-ready staff with which we all were disciplined. Now, so many years later, I found her just as alarming.

I met her in one of Sansum's new buildings in Ynys Wydryn. The largest was the size of a royal feasting hall and was the school where dozens of priests were trained as missionaries. Those priests began their lessons at six years old, were proclaimed holy at sixteen and then sent on Britain's roads to gain converts. I often met those fervent men on my travels. They walked in pairs, carrying only a small bag and a staff, though sometimes they were accompanied by groups of women who seemed curiously drawn to the missionaries. They had no fear. Whenever I encountered them they would always challenge me and dare me to deny their God, and I would always courteously admit his existence then insist that my own Gods lived too, and at that they would hurl curses at me and their women would wail and howl insults. Once, when two such fanatics frightened my daughters, I used the butt of a spear on them and I admit I used it too hard, for at the end of the argument there was a broken skull and a shattered wrist, neither of them mine. Arthur insisted I stand trial as a demonstration that even the most privileged Dumnonians were not above the law, and thus I went to the Lindinis courthouse where a Christian magistrate charged me the bone-price of half my own weight in silver.

'You should have been whipped,' Morgan evidently remembered the incident and snapped her verdict at me when I was admitted to her presence. 'Whipped raw and bloody. In public!'

'I think even you would find that difficult now, Lady,' I said mildly.

'God would give me the needful strength,' she snarled from behind her new gold mask with its Christian cross. She sat at a table that was piled with parchment and ink-covered wood-shavings, for she not only ran Sansum's school, but tallied the treasuries of every church and monastery in northern Dumnonia, though the achievement of which she was most proud was her community of holy women who chanted and prayed in their

266

own hall where men were not allowed to set foot. I could hear their sweet voices singing now as Morgan looked me up and down. She evidently did not much like what she saw. 'If you've come for more money,' she snapped, 'you can't have it. Not till you repay the loans outstanding.'

'There are no outstanding loans that I know of,' I said mildly.

'Nonsense.' She snatched up one of the wood-shavings and read out a fictitious list of unpaid loans.

I let her have her say, then gently told her that the Council did not seek to borrow money from the church. 'And if it did,' I added, 'then I'm sure your husband would have told you.'

'And I'm sure,' she said, 'that you pagans on the Council are plotting things behind the saint's back.' She sniffed. 'How is my brother?'

'Busy, Lady.'

'Too busy to come and see me, plainly.'

'And you're too busy to visit him,' I said pleasantly.

'Me? Go to Durnovaria? And face that witch Guinevere?' She made the sign of the cross, then dipped her hand in a bowl of water and made the sign again. 'I would rather walk into hell and see Satan himself,' she said, 'than see that witch of Isis!' She was about to spit to avert evil, then remembered to make another sign of the cross instead. 'Do you know what rites Isis demands?' she asked me angrily.

'No, Lady,' I said.

'Filth, Derfel, filth! Isis is the scarlet woman! The whore of Babylon. It is the devil's faith, Derfel. They lie together, man and woman.' She shuddered at that horrid thought. 'Pure filth.'

'Men are not allowed in their temple, Lady,' I said, defending Guinevere, 'just as they are not allowed in your women's hall.'

'Not allowed!' Morgan cackled. 'They come by night, you fool, and worship their filthy Goddess naked. Men and women together, sweating like swine! You think I don't know? I, who was once such a sinner? You think you know better than I about pagan faiths? I tell you, Derfel, they lie together in their own sweat, naked woman and naked man. Isis and Osiris, woman and man, and the woman gives life to the man, and how do you think that's done, you fool? It's done by the filthy act of fornication, that's how!' She dipped her fingers in the water bowl and made the sign of the cross again, leaving a bead of the holy water on the forehead of her mask. 'You're an ignorant, credulous fool,' she snapped at me. I did not pursue the argument. The different faiths always insulted each other thus. Many pagans accused the Christians of similar behaviour at their so called 'love-feasts', and many country people believed that the Christians kidnapped, killed and ate children. 'Arthur's also a fool,' Morgan growled, 'for trusting Guinevere.' She gave me an unfriendly look with her one eye. 'So what do you want of me, Derfel, if it isn't money?'

'I want to know, Lady, what happened on the night the Cauldron disappeared.'

She laughed at that. It was an echo of her old laughter, the cruel cackling sound that had always presaged trouble on the Tor. 'You miserable little fool,' she said, 'wasting my time.' And with that she turned back to her work table. I waited while she made marks on her tally sticks or in the margins of parchment scrolls and pretended to ignore me. 'Still here, fool?' she asked after a while.

'Still here, Lady,' I said.

She turned on her stool. 'Why do you want to know? Is it that wicked little whore on the hill who sent you?' She waved through the window at the Tor.

'Merlin asked me, Lady,' I lied. 'He's curious about the past, but his memory wanders.'

'It'll wander into hell soon,' she said vengefully, then she pondered my question before, at last, offering a shrug. 'I will tell you what happened that night,' she said at last, 'and I will tell you only once, and when it is told you will never ask me of it again.'

'Once is enough, Lady.'

She stood and limped to the window from where she could stare up at the Tor. 'The Lord God Almighty,' she said, 'the one true God, the Father of us all, sent fire from heaven. I was there, so I know what happened. He sent the lightning and it struck the hall thatch and set it on fire. I was screaming, for I have good cause to fear fire. I know fire. I am a child of fire. Fire ruined my life, but this was a different fire. This was God's cleansing fire, the fire that burned away my sin. The fire spread from the thatch to the tower and it burned everything. I watched that fire and I would even have died in it if the blessed saint Sansum had not come to guide me to safety.' She made the sign of the cross, then turned back to me. 'That, fool,' she snapped, 'is what happened.'

So Sansum had been on the Tor that night? That was interesting, but I made no remark about it. Instead I said gently, 'The fire did not burn the Cauldron, Lady. Merlin came next day and he searched the ashes and found no gold.'

'Fool!' Morgan spat at me through the mouth-slit of her mask. 'You think God's fire burns like your feeble flames? The Cauldron was the pot of evil, the foulest blight on God's earth. It was the devil's pissing pot and the Lord God consumed it, Derfel, he consumed it to nothing! I saw it with this eye!' She tapped her mask beneath the one good eye. 'I saw it burn, and it was a bright, seething, hissing furnace glare in the innermost heart of the fire, it was a flame like the hottest flame of hell and I heard the demons screeching in their pain as their Cauldron turned to smoke. God burned it! He burned it and sent it back to hell where it belongs!' She paused and I sensed that her flame-mauled, ruined face was cracking into a smile behind the mask. 'It's gone, Derfel,' she said in a quieter voice, 'and now you can go, too.'

I left her, left the shrine and climbed to the Tor where I pushed back the half-broken water gate that hung crazily off one rope hinge. The blackened ashes of the hall and tower were being swallowed by the earth, and around them were the dozen dirty huts where Nimue and her people lived. Those people were the unwanted of our world; its cripples and beggars, its homeless folk and half-crazed creatures who all survived on the food Ceinwyn and I sent weekly from Lindinis. Nimue claimed her people spoke with the Gods, but all I ever heard from them was mad cackling or sad moaning. 'She denies everything,' I said to Nimue.

'Of course she does.'

'She says her God burned it to nothing.'

'Her God couldn't soft boil an egg,' Nimue said vengefully. She had decayed foully in the years since the Cauldron had disappeared and as Merlin had subsided into his gentle old age. Nimue was filthy these days, filthy and thin and almost as crazed as when I had rescued her from the Isle of the Dead. She shivered at times, or else her face grimaced in uncontrollable twitches. She had long ago sold or thrown away the golden eye, and now wore a leather patch over the empty socket instead. Whatever intriguing beauty she had once possessed was now hidden under dirt and sores, and lost beneath her matted mass of black hair that was so greasy with filth that even the country-folk who came to her for divination or healing would often recoil from her stench. Even I, who was oath-sworn to her and who had once loved her, could hardly bear to be near her.

'The Cauldron still lives,' Nimue told me that day.

'So Merlin says.'

'And Merlin lives too, Derfel.' She put a nail-bitten hand on my arm. 'He's waiting, that's all, saving his strength.'

Waiting for his balefire, I thought, but said nothing.

Nimue turned sunwise to stare all about the horizon. 'Somewhere out there, Derfel,' she said, 'the Cauldron is hidden. And someone is trying to work out how to use it.' She laughed softly. 'And when they do, Derfel, you will see the land turn red with blood.' She turned her one eye on me. 'Blood!' she hissed. 'The world will vomit blood that day, Derfel, and Merlin will ride again.'

Maybe, I thought; but it was a sunny day and Dumnonia was at peace. It was Arthur's peace, given by his sword and maintained by his lawcourts and enriched by his roads and sealed by his Brotherhood. It all seemed so distant from the world of the Cauldron and the missing Treasures, but Nimue still believed in their magic and for her sake I would not express disbelief, though on that bright day in Arthur's Dumnonia it seemed to me that Britain was forging its way from darkness into light, from chaos into order and from savagery into law. That was Arthur's achievement. That was his Camelot.

But Nimue was right. The Cauldron was not lost and she, like Merlin, was just waiting for its horror.

OUR CHIEF BUSINESS IN those years was to prepare Mordred for the throne. He was already our King for he had been acclaimed as a baby on Caer Cadarn's summit, but Arthur had decided to repeat the acclamation when Mordred came of age. I think Arthur hoped that some mystical power might invest Mordred with responsibility and wisdom at that second acclamation, for nothing else seemed capable of improving the boy. We tried, the Gods know we tried, but Mordred stayed the same sullen, resentful and loutish youth. Arthur disliked him but stayed wilfully blind to Mordred's grosser faults, for if Arthur held any religion truly sacred it was his belief in the divinity of kings. The time would come when Arthur would be forced to face the truth of Mordred, but in those years, whenever the subject of Mordred's suitability was raised in the royal Council, Arthur would always say the same thing. Mordred, he agreed, was an unattractive child, but we had all known such boys grow into proper men and the solemnity of acclamation and the responsibilities of kingship would surely temper the boy. 'I was hardly a model child myself,' he liked to say, 'but I don't think I've turned out ill. Have faith in the boy.' Besides, he would always add with a smile, Mordred would be guided by a wise and experienced Council. 'He'll appoint his own Council,' one of us would always object, but Arthur waved the matter aside. All, he blithely assured us, would turn out well.

Guinevere had no such illusions. Indeed, in the years following the Round Table oath she became obsessed with Mordred's fate. She did not attend the royal Council, for no woman could, but when she was in Durnovaria I suspect she listened from behind a curtained archway that opened into the council chamber. Much of what we discussed must have bored her; we spent hours discussing whether to place new stones in a ford or to spend money on a bridge, or whether a magistrate was taking bribes or to whom we should grant the guardianship of an orphaned heir or heiress. Those matters were the common coin of council meetings and I am sure she found them tedious, but how avidly she must have listened when we discussed Mordred.

Guinevere hardly knew Mordred, but she hated him. She hated him because he was King and Arthur was not, and one by one she tried to convert the royal councillors to her own view. She was even pleasant to me, for I suspect she saw into my soul and knew that I secretly agreed with her. After the first council meeting that followed the Round Table oath she took my arm and walked with me about Durnovaria's cloister which was misted from the smoke of herbs that were being burned in braziers to avert a return of the plague. Maybe it was the heady smoke that dizzied me, but more likely it was Guinevere's proximity. She wore a strong perfume, her red hair was full and wild, her body straight and slender, and her face so very finely boned and full of spirit. I told her I was sorry her father had died. 'Poor father,' she said. 'All he ever dreamed of was returning to Henis Wyren.' She paused, and I wondered whether she had reproved Arthur for not making more effort to dislodge Diwrnach. I doubt Guinevere ever wanted to see Henis Wyren's wild coast again, but her father had always wanted to return to his ancestors' lands. 'You never told me about your visit to Henis Wyren,' Guinevere said reproachfully. 'I hear you met Diwrnach?'

'And hope never to meet him again, Lady.'

She shrugged. 'Sometimes, in a king, a reputation for savagery can be useful.' She questioned me about Henis Wyren's condition, but I sensed she was not truly interested in my answers, any more than when she asked me how Ceinwyn was.

273

'Well, Lady,' I answered her, 'thank you.'

'Pregnant again?' she asked in mild amusement.

'We think so, Lady.'

'How busy the two of you do keep, Derfel,' she said in gentle mockery. Her annoyance at Ceinwyn had faded over the years, though they never did become friends. Guinevere snapped a leaf from a bay tree that grew in a Roman urn decorated with naked nymphs and rubbed the leaf between her fingers. 'And how is our Lord King?' she asked sourly.

'Troublesome, Lady.'

'Is he fit to be King?' That was typical of Guinevere; a straight question, brutal and honest.

'He was born to it, Lady,' I said defensively, 'and we are oath-sworn to it.'

She gave a derisive laugh. Her gold-laced sandals slapped the flagstones and a gold chain hung with pearls clinked about her neck. 'Many years ago, Derfel,' she said, 'you and I talked of this and you told me that of all the men in Dumnonia Arthur was fittest to be King.'

'I did,' I admitted.

'And you think Mordred is fitter?'

'No, Lady.'

'So?' She turned to look at me. Few women could look me straight in the eye, but Guinevere could. 'So?' she asked again.

'So I have sworn an oath, Lady, as has your husband.'

'Oaths!' she snarled, letting go of my arm. 'Arthur swore an oath to kill Aelle, and Aelle yet lives. He swore an oath to take back Henis Wyren, yet Diwrnach still rules there. Oaths! You men hide behind oaths like servants hide behind stupidity, but the moment an oath becomes inconvenient you forget it soon enough. You think your oath to Uther cannot be forgotten?'

'My oath is to the Prince Arthur,' I said, taking care, as ever, to call Arthur a Prince in front of Guinevere. 'You wish me to forget that oath?' I asked her.

'I want you, Derfel, to talk sense into him,' she said. 'He listens to you.'

'He listens to you, Lady.'

'Not on the subject of Mordred,' she said. 'On everything else, maybe, but not that.' She shuddered, perhaps remembering the embrace she had been forced to give Mordred at the Sea Palace, then she angrily crumpled the bay leaf and threw it onto the flagstones. Within minutes, I knew, a servant would silently sweep it away. Durnovaria's Winter Palace was always so tidy, while our palace at Lindinis was too littered with children ever to be neat and Mordred's wing was a midden. 'Arthur,' Guinevere now insisted tiredly, 'is the eldest living son of Uther. He should be King.'

And so he should, I thought, but we had all taken oaths to put Mordred on the throne and men had died at Lugg Vale to defend that oath. At times, the Gods forgive me, I just wished Mordred would die and so solve the problem for us, but despite his clubbed foot and the ill-omens of his birth, he seemed blessed with a rugged health. I looked into Guinevere's green eyes. 'I remember, Lady,' I said to her carefully, 'how years ago you took me through that doorway,' I pointed to a low archway that led off the cloister, 'and you showed me your temple of Isis.'

'I did. So?' She was defensive, maybe regretting that moment of intimacy. On that distant day she had been trying to make me an ally in the same cause that had prompted her to take my arm and bring me to this cloister. She wanted Mordred destroyed so that Arthur could rule.

'You showed me Isis's throne,' I said, careful not to reveal that I had seen that same black chair again at the Sea Palace, 'and you told me that Isis was the Goddess who determined which man should sit on a kingdom's throne. Am I right?'

'It's one of her powers, yes,' Guinevere said carelessly.

'Then you must pray to the Goddess, Lady,' I said.

'You think I don't, Derfel?' she demanded. 'You think I haven't worn out her ears with my prayers? I want Arthur as King, and Gwydre as King after him, but you can't force a man onto a throne. Arthur must want it before Isis will grant it.'

That seemed a feeble defence to me. If Isis could not alter Arthur's mind, how were we mere mortals expected to change it? We had tried often enough, but Arthur refused to discuss the matter, just as Guinevere gave up our conversation in the courtyard when she realized I could not be persuaded to join her campaign to replace Mordred with Arthur.

I wanted Arthur as King, but only once in all those years did I ever break through his bland assurances and talk seriously with him about his own claim to the kingship, and that conversation did not occur until five whole years after the Round Table oath. It was during the summer before the year in which Mordred was to be acclaimed King, and by then the whispers of hostility had become a deafening shout. Only the Christians supported Mordred's claim, and even they did it reluctantly, but it was known that his mother had been a Christian and that the child himself had been baptized and that was sufficient to persuade the Christians that Mordred might be sympathetic to their ambitions. Everyone else in Dumnonia looked to Arthur to save them from the boy, but Arthur serenely ignored them. That summer, as we have now learned to count the sun's turning, was four hundred and ninety-five years after the birth of Christ and it was a beautiful, sun-soaked season. Arthur was at the height of his powers, Merlin sunned himself in our garden with my three small daughters clamouring for stories, Ceinwyn was happy, Guinevere basked in her lovely new Sea Palace with its arcades and galleries and dark hidden temple, Lancelot seemed content in his kingdom by the sea, the Saxons fought each other, and Dumnonia was at peace. It was also, as I remember, a summer of utter misery.

For it was the summer of Tristan and Iseult.

Kernow is the wild kingdom that lies like a claw at Dumnonia's western tip. The Romans went there, but few settled in its wilderness and when the Romans left Britain the folk of Kernow went on with their lives as though the invaders had never existed.

They ploughed small fields, fished hard seas and mined precious tin. To travel in Kernow, I was told, was to see Britain as it had been before the Romans came, though I never went there, and nor did Arthur.

For as long as I could remember Kernow had been ruled by King Mark. He rarely troubled us, though once in a while – usually when Dumnonia was embroiled with some larger enemy to the east – he would decide that some of our western lands should belong to him and there would be a brief border war and savage raids on our coast by Kernow's fighting boats. We always won those wars, how could we not? Dumnonia was large and Kernow small, and when the wars were done Mark would send an envoy to say it had all been an accident. For a short time at the beginning of Arthur's rule, when Cadwy of Isca had rebelled against the rest of Dumnonia, Mark did capture some large portions of our land beyond his frontier, but Culhwch had ended that rebellion and when Arthur sent Cadwy's head as a gift to Mark, the spearmen of Kernow had quietly gone back to their old strongholds.

Such troubles were rare, for King Mark's most famous campaigns were fought in his bed. He was famous for the number of his wives, but where other such men might have kept several wives at one time, Mark married them in sequence. They died with appalling regularity, almost always, it seemed, just four years after the marriage ceremony was performed by Kernow's Druids, and though Mark always had an explanation for the deaths – a fever maybe, or an accident, or perhaps a difficult birth – most of us suspected it was the King's boredom that lay behind the balefires that burned the queenly corpses on Caer Dore, the King's stronghold. The seventh wife to die had been Arthur's niece, Ialle, and Mark had sent an envoy with a sad tale of mushrooms, toadstools and Ialle's ungovernable appetites. He had also sent a pack mule loaded with tin ingots and rare whalebones to avert any possibility of Arthur's wrath.

The deaths of the wives never seemed to prevent other princesses from daring the sea crossing to share Mark's bed. It was better, perhaps, to be a Queen in Kernow, even for a short time, than to wait in the women's hall for a suitor who might never come, and besides, the explanations for the deaths were always plausible. They were just accidents.

After Ialle's death there was no new marriage for a long time. Mark was getting old and men assumed he had abandoned the marriage game, but then, in that lovely summer of the year before Mordred assumed power in Dumnonia, the ageing King Mark did take a new wife. She was the daughter of our old ally, Oengus Mac Airem, the Irish King of Demetia who had delivered us victory at Lugg Vale, and for that deliverance Arthur forgave Oengus his myriad of trespasses that still harassed Cuneglas's land. Oengus's feared Blackshield warriors were forever raiding Powys and what had been Siluria, and through all those years Cuneglas was forced to keep expensive war-bands on his western frontier. Oengus always denied responsibility for the raids, saying that his chiefs were ungovernable and promising he would lop some heads, but the heads remained unlopped and at every harvest time the hungry Blackshields would return to Powys. Arthur sent some of our young spearmen to gain battle experience in those harvest wars that provided us with a chance to train unblooded warriors and keep the older men's instincts sharp. Cuneglas wanted to finish Demetia off once and for all, but Arthur liked Oengus and argued that his depredations were worth the experience he gave our spearmen and so the Blackshields survived.

The marriage of the ageing King Mark to his child-bride of Demetia was an alliance of two small kingdoms that troubled no one, and besides, no one believed Mark had married the Princess for any political advantage. He married her solely because he had an insatiable appetite for young royal flesh. He was then near sixty years old, his son Tristan was almost forty and Iseult, the new Queen, was just fifteen.

The misery began when Culhwch sent us a message saying that Tristan had arrived in Isca with his father's child-bride.

Culhwch, after Melwas had died of his surfeit of oysters, had been appointed the governor of Dumnonia's western province and his message reported that Tristan and Iseult were fugitives from King Mark. Culhwch himself was amused rather than troubled by their arrival for he, like me, had fought beside Tristan at Lugg Vale and outside London and he liked the Prince. 'At least this bride will live,' Culhwch's scribe had written to the Council, 'and deserves to. I have given them an old hall and a guard of spearmen.' The message went on to describe a raid by Irish pirates from across the sea and ended with Culhwch's usual request for a tax reduction and a warning, also quite usual, that the harvest looked thin. It was, in brief, a commonplace dispatch with nothing to alert the Council's apprehensions, for we all knew that the harvest looked fat and that Culhwch was positioning himself for his customary wrangle over taxes. As for Tristan and Iseult, their story was merely an amusement and none of us saw any danger there. Arthur's clerks filed the message away and the Council moved on to discuss Sansum's request that the Council should build a great church that would celebrate the five hundredth anniversary of Christ's birth. I argued against the proposal, Bishop Sansum snapped and barked and spat that the church was necessary if the world was not to be destroyed by the devil, and that happy wrangle kept the Council engaged till the midday meal was served in the palace courtyard.

That meeting was held in Durnovaria and, as usual, Guinevere had come from her Sea Palace to be in the town when the Council met and she joined us at the midday meal. She sat beside Arthur and, as ever, her proximity gave him a glowing happiness. He was so proud of her. The marriage might have yielded him disappointments, especially in the number of its children, but it was plain that he was still in love with her. Every look he gave her was a proclamation of his astonishment that such a woman would marry him, and it never occurred to Arthur that he was the prize, that he was the capable ruler and good man. He adored her, and that day, as we ate fruit, bread and cheese under a warm sunlight, it was easy to see why. She could be witty and cutting, amusing and wise, and her looks still commanded attention. The years did not seem to touch Guinevere. Her skin was as clear as skimmed milk and her eyes had none of the fine wrinkles that Ceinwyn's showed; it seemed, indeed, that she had not aged one moment since that far-off day when Arthur had first spied her across Gorfyddyd's crowded hall. And still, I think, every time Arthur returned home from some long dutiful journey across Mordred's realm he received the same shock of happiness at seeing Guinevere that he had received on that very first day he saw her. And Guinevere knew how to keep him fascinated by always staying one mysterious pace ahead of him and so drawing Arthur ever deeper into his passion. It was, I suppose, a recipe for love.

Mordred was with us that day. Arthur had insisted that the King begin to attend the Council before he was acclaimed with his full powers, and he always encouraged Mordred to take part in our discussions, but Mordred's only contribution was to sit scraping at the dirt under his fingernails or else yawning as the tedious business droned on. Arthur hoped he would learn responsibility by attending the Council, but I feared the King was merely learning to avoid the details of government. That day he sat, as was proper, at the centre of the meal table and made no pretence whatever to be interested in Bishop Emrys's story of a spring that had miraculously appeared when a priest blessed a hillside.

'That spring, Bishop,' Guinevere intervened, 'would it be in the hills north of Dunum?'

'Why yes, Lady!' Emrys said, pleased to have an audience other than the unresponsive Mordred. 'You have heard of the miracle?'

'Long before your priest arrived there,' Guinevere said. 'That spring comes and goes, Bishop, depending on the rainfall. And this year, you will remember, the late winter rains were unusually heavy.' She smiled triumphantly. Her opposition to the church still existed, but it was muted now.

'This is a new spring,' Emrys insisted. 'The countryfolk assure us it never existed before!' He turned back to Mordred. 'You should visit the spring, Lord King. It is truly a miracle.'

Mordred yawned and stared blankly at the pigeons on the far roof. His coat was stained with mead and his new curly beard filled with crumbs. 'Are we done with business?' he asked suddenly.

'Far from it, Lord King,' Emrys said enthusiastically. 'We have yet to receive a decision on the building of the church, and there are three names proposed as magistrates. I assume the men are here to be questioned?' he asked Arthur.

'They are, Bishop,' Arthur confirmed.

'A full day's work for us!' Emrys said, pleased.

'Not for me,' Mordred said. 'I'm going hunting.'

'But, Lord King . . .' Emrys protested mildly.

'Hunting,' Mordred interrupted the Bishop. He pushed his couch away from the low table and limped across the courtyard.

There was silence round the table. We all knew what the others were thinking, but none spoke aloud until I tried to be optimistic. 'He pays attention,' I said, 'to his weapons.'

'Because he likes to kill,' Guinevere said icily.

'I only wish the boy would talk sometimes!' Emrys complained. 'He just sits there, sullen! Picking at his nails.'

'At least it isn't his nose,' Guinevere said acidly, then looked up as a stranger was escorted into the courtyard. Hygwydd, Arthur's servant, announced the stranger as Cyllan, champion of Kernow, and he looked like a King's champion for he was a huge black-haired and rough-bearded brute who carried the blue tattoo of an axe on his forehead. He bowed to Guinevere, then drew a barbaric-looking longsword that he laid on the flagstones with its blade pointing at Arthur. That gesture was a sign that trouble existed between our countries.

'Sit, Lord Cyllan.' Arthur waved to Mordred's vacated couch. 'There's cheese, some wine. The bread is new baked.'

Cyllan tugged off his iron helmet that was crested with the

snarling mask of a wildcat. 'Lord,' he said in a rumbling voice, 'I come with a complaint . . .'

'You come with an empty belly too, I've no doubt,' Arthur interrupted him. 'Sit, man! Your escort will be fed in the kitchens. And do pick up the sword.'

Cyllan surrendered to Arthur's informality. He broke a loaf in half and sliced off a big wedge of cheese. 'Tristan,' he explained curtly when Arthur asked the nature of the complaint. Cyllan spoke with his mouth half full of food, making Guinevere shudder with horror. 'The Edling has fled to this land, Lord,' Kernow's champion went on, 'and brought the Queen with him.' He reached for the wine and drank a hornful. 'King Mark wants them back.'

Arthur said nothing, but just drummed on the table's edge with his fingers.

Cyllan swallowed more bread and cheese, then poured himself more wine. 'It's bad enough,' he went on after a prodigious belch, 'that the Edling is,' he paused, glanced at Guinevere, then amended his sentence, 'is with his stepmother.'

Guinevere interrupted to provide the word that Cyllan had not dared pronounce in her presence. He nodded, blushed and went on. 'Not right, Lady. Not to couple with his own stepmother. But he's also stolen half his father's treasury. He's broken two oaths, Lord. The oath to his royal father and the oath to his Queen, and now we hear he has been granted refuge near Isca.'

'I heard that the Prince is in Dumnonia,' Arthur said blandly.

'And my King wants him back. Wants both of them back.' Cyllan, his message delivered, attacked the cheese again.

The Council reassembled, leaving Cyllan to kick his heels in the sunlight. The three candidates for magistrate were told to wait and the vexed problem of Sansum's great church was set aside while we debated Arthur's answer to King Mark.

'Tristan,' I said, 'has ever been a friend to this country. When no one else would fight for us, he did. He brought men to Lugg Vale. He was with us in London. He deserves our help.'

'He has broken oaths made to a King,' Arthur said worriedly.

'Pagan oaths,' Sansum put in, as if that lessened Tristan's offence.

'But he has stolen money,' Bishop Emrys pointed out.

'Which he hopes will soon be his by right,' I answered, trying to defend my old battle comrade.

'And that is precisely what worries King Mark,' Arthur said. 'Put yourself in his place, Derfel, and what do you fear most?'

'A dearth of princesses?' I ventured.

Arthur scowled at my levity. 'He fears that Tristan will lead spearmen back to Kernow. He fears civil war. He fears that his son is tired of waiting for his death and he's right to fear it.'

I shook my head. 'Tristan was never calculating, Lord,' I said. 'He acts on impulse. He's stupidly fallen in love with his father's bride. He's not thinking of a throne.'

'Not yet,' Arthur said ominously, 'but he will.'

'If we give Tristan refuge, what will King Mark do?' Sansum asked shrewdly.

'Raids,' Arthur said. 'Some farms burned, cattle stolen. Or else he'll send his spears to take Tristan alive. His boatmen could manage that.' Alone among the British kingdoms the men of Kernow were confident sailors and the Saxons, in their early raids, had learned to fear the longboats of Mark's spearmen. 'It will mean constant, niggling trouble,' Arthur conceded. 'A dozen dead farmers and their wives every month. We'll have to keep a hundred spearmen on the border till it's all settled.'

'Expensive,' Sansum commented.

'Too expensive,' Arthur said grimly.

'King Mark's money must certainly be returned,' Emrys insisted.

'And the Queen, probably,' Cythryn, one of the magistrates who sat on the Council, put in. 'I cannot imagine that King Mark's pride will allow him to leave that insult unavenged.'

'What happens to the girl if she's returned?' Emrys asked.

'That,' Arthur said firmly, 'is a matter for King Mark to decide. Not us.' He rubbed his long bony face with his two hands. 'I suppose,' he said wearily, 'that we had better mediate the affair.' He smiled. 'It's been a long time since I was in that part of the world. Maybe it's time to go there again. Will you come, Derfel? You're a friend of Tristan. Maybe he'll listen to you.'

'With pleasure, Lord,' I agreed.

The Council agreed to let Arthur mediate the matter, sent Cyllan back to Kernow with a message describing what Arthur was doing and then, with a dozen of my spearmen in attendance, we rode south and west to find the errant lovers.

It began as a happy enough journey, despite the awkward problem that lay at its end. Nine years of peace had swollen the land's goodness and if the summer's warm weather lasted, and despite Culhwch's gloomy predictions, it looked set to be a fine harvest that year. Arthur took a real joy from seeing the well-tended fields and new granaries. He was greeted in every town and village and the greeting was always warm. Children's choirs sang for him and gifts were laid at his feet: corn dollies, baskets of fruit or a fox pelt. He returned gold for the gifts, discussed whatever problems afflicted the village, talked with the local magistrate and then we would ride on. The only sour note was struck by Christian hostility, for in nearly every village there was a small group of Christians who would shriek curses at Arthur until their neighbours hushed them up or pushed them away. New churches stood everywhere, usually built where pagans had once worshipped at a sacred well or spring. The churches were the products of Bishop Sansum's busy missionaries and I wondered why we pagans did not employ similar men to travel the roads and preach to the peasants. The Christians' new churches were, admittedly, small things, mere huts of wattle and thatch with a cross nailed to one gable, but they multiplied and the more rancorous of their priests cursed Arthur for being a pagan and detested Guinevere for her adherence to Isis. Guinevere never cared that she was hated, but Arthur disliked all religious rancour. On that journey to Isca he often stopped to talk to the Christians who spat at him, but his words had no effect. The Christians did not care that he had given the land peace, nor that they had become prosperous, only that Arthur was a pagan. 'They're like the Saxons,' he told me gloomily as we left another hostile group behind, 'they won't be happy till they own everything.'

'Then we should do to them what we did to the Saxons, Lord,' I said. 'Set them against each other.'

'They already fight amongst themselves,' Arthur said. 'Do you understand this argument about Pelagianism?'

'I wouldn't even want to understand it,' I answered flippantly, though in truth the argument was growing ever more vicious with one set of Christians accusing the other of heresy, and both sides inflicting deaths on their opponents. 'Do you understand it?'

'I think so. Pelagius refused to believe mankind is inherently evil, while men like Sansum and Emrys say we are all born evil.' He paused. 'I suspect,' Arthur went on, 'that if I were a Christian, I'd be a Pelagian.' I thought of Mordred and decided that mankind might well be inherently evil, but I said nothing. 'I believe in mankind,' Arthur said, 'rather more than in any God.'

I spat at the road's verge to avert the evil his words might bring. 'I often wonder,' I said, 'how things would have changed if Merlin had kept his Cauldron.'

'That old pot?' Arthur laughed. 'I haven't thought of that for years!' He smiled at the memory of those old days. 'Nothing would have changed, Derfel,' he went on. 'I sometimes think Merlin's whole life lay in collecting the Treasures, and once he had them there was nothing left for him to do! He didn't dare try to work their magic, because he suspected nothing would happen.'

I glanced at the sword hanging at his hip, one of the thirteen Treasures, but I said nothing for I was keeping my promise to Merlin not to reveal Excalibur's true power to Arthur. 'You think Merlin burned down his own tower?' I asked instead.

'I've wondered,' he admitted.

'No,' I said firmly, 'he believed. And sometimes, I think, he dares to believe he'll live to find the Treasures again.'

'Then he'd better hurry,' Arthur said tartly, 'because he can't have much time left.'

We spent that night in the old Roman governor's palace in Isca where Culhwch now lived. He was in a gloomy mood, not because of Tristan, but because the city was a hotbed of Christian fanatics. Just a week before a band of Christian youths had invaded the city's pagan temples and pulled down the statues of the Gods and splashed excrement on the walls. Culhwch's spearmen had caught some of the desecrators and filled the jail with them, but Culhwch was worried about the future. 'If we don't break the bastards now,' he said, 'they'll go to war for their God.'

'Nonsense,' Arthur said dismissively.

Culhwch shook his head. 'They want a Christian King, Arthur.'

'They'll have Mordred next year,' Arthur said.

'Is he a Christian?' Culhwch asked.

'If he's anything,' I said.

'But he's not who they want,' Culhwch said darkly.

'Then who is?' Arthur asked, intrigued at last by his cousin's warnings.

Culhwch hesitated, then shrugged. 'Lancelot.'

'Lancelot!' Arthur sounded amused. 'Don't they know he keeps his pagan temples open?'

'They don't know anything about him,' Culhwch said, 'but they don't need to. They think of him in the same way that people thought about you in the last years of Uther's life. They think of him as their deliverer.'

'Deliverer from what?' I asked scornfully.

'Us pagans, of course,' Culhwch said. 'They insist Lancelot is the Christian King who'll lead them all to heaven. And do you know why? Because of that sea eagle on his shield. It's got a fish in its claws, remember? And the fish is a Christian symbol.' He spat his disgust. 'They don't know anything about him,' he said again, 'but they see that fish and think it's a sign from their God.'

'A fish?' Arthur plainly did not believe Culhwch.

'A fish,' Culhwch insisted. 'Maybe they pray to a trout? How would I know? They already worship a holy ghost, a virgin and a carpenter, so why not a fish as well? They're all mad.'

'They're not mad,' Arthur insisted, 'excited, maybe.'

'Excited! Have you been to one of their rites lately?' Culhwch challenged his cousin.

'Not since Morgan's wedding.'

'Then come and look for yourself,' Culhwch said. It was night-time and we had finished supper, but Culhwch insisted we don dark cloaks and follow him out through one of the palace's side doors. We went up a dark alley to the forum where the Christians had their shrine in an old Roman temple that had once been dedicated to Apollo, but which had now been scoured of paganism, limewashed and dedicated to Christianity. We went in through the west door and found a shadowed niche where, in imitation of the big throng of worshippers, we knelt.

Culhwch had told us that the Christians worshipped here every evening, and every evening, he said, the same frenzy followed the gifts of bread and wine that the priest distributed to the faithful. The bread and wine were magical, supposed to be their God's blood and flesh, and we watched as the worshippers thronged about the altar to receive their scraps. At least half of the worshippers were women and those women, once they had taken the bread from the priests, began to fall into ecstasy. I had often seen such strange fervour, for Merlin's old pagan rites had frequently ended with screaming women dancing about the Tor's fires, and these women behaved in much the same way. They danced with closed eyes and with their waving hands held up to the white roof where the smoke from the torches and from the bowls of burning incense made a thick mist. Some wailed strange words, others were in a trance and just gazed at a statue of their God's mother, a few writhed on the floor, but most of the women danced in step to the rhythmic chanting of three priests. The men in the church mostly watched, but some joined the dancers and it was they who first stripped themselves to their waists and snatched up knotted thongs with which they began to lash their own backs. That astonished me, for I had never seen anything like it before, but my astonishment turned to horror when some of the women joined the men and began to scream with ecstatic joy as the lashes drew blood from their bare breasts and backs.

Arthur hated it. 'It's madness,' he whispered, 'pure madness!'

'It's spreading,' Culhwch warned him darkly. One of the women was beating her naked back with a length of rusty chain and her frenzied wailing echoed in the big stone chamber as her blood spattered thick on the tiled floor. 'They'll go on like this all night,' Culhwch said.

The worshippers had gradually edged forward to surround the ecstatic dancers, leaving the three of us isolated in our shadowed niche. A priest saw us there and darted towards us. 'Have you eaten the body of Christ?' he demanded.

'We ate roast goose,' Arthur said politely, standing up.

The priest stared at the three of us and recognized Culhwch. He spat into Culhwch's face. 'Pagan!' he shrieked. 'Idolater! You dare defile God's temple!' He struck at Culhwch – a mistake, for Culhwch gave him a blow that span the priest hard back across the floor, but the altercation had attracted attention and a howl went up from the men who had been watching the flagellating dancers.

'Time to go,' Arthur said, and the three of us retreated smartly across the forum to where Culhwch's spearmen guarded the palace's arcade. The Christians spilt out of their church in pursuit, but the spearmen stolidly closed into a shield-wall and lowered their blades, and the Christians made no attempt to storm the palace.

'They might not attack tonight,' Culhwch said, 'but they get braver by the day.'

Arthur watched the howling Christians from a palace window. 'What do they want?' he asked in puzzlement. He liked his religion to be decorous. When he came to Lindinis he would always join Ceinwyn and me at our morning prayers when we knelt quietly before our household Gods, offering them a piece of bread and then praying that our daily duties would be done properly, and that was the kind of worship Arthur liked. He was simply bemused by the things he had seen in Isca's church.

'They believe,' Culhwch began to explain the fanaticism we had witnessed, 'that their God is coming back to earth in five years, and they believe they have a duty to prepare the earth for his coming. Their priests tell them that the pagans have to be wiped out before their God will come back and they preach that Dumnonia must have a Christian king.'

'They'll have Mordred,' Arthur said grimly.

'Then you'd better change his dragon shield into a fish,' Culhwch said, 'for I tell you, their fervour is getting worse. There's going to be trouble.'

'We'll placate them,' Arthur said. 'We'll let them know Mordred's a Christian and perhaps that'll calm them down. Maybe we'd better build that church Sansum wants,' he added to me.

'If it stops them rioting,' I said, 'why not?'

We left Isca next morning, escorted now by Culhwch and a dozen of his men, and we crossed the Exe by the Roman bridge and then turned south into the deep sea-lands that lay on Dumnonia's furthest coasts. Arthur said nothing more about the Christian frenzy he had witnessed, but he was oddly silent that day and I guessed the rites had upset him deeply. He hated any kind of frenzy for it stripped men and women of their sense, and he must have feared what such a madness might do to his careful peace.

But for now our problem was not Dumnonia's Christians, but

Tristan. Culhwch had sent word to the Prince, warning him of our approach, and Tristan came to greet us. He rode alone, his horse's hoofs leaving spurts of dust as he galloped towards us. He greeted us happily, but recoiled from Arthur's chill reserve. That reserve was not caused by any innate dislike Arthur had for Tristan – indeed he liked the Prince – but rather sprang out of Arthur's recognition that he had not just come to mediate this dispute, but to sit in judgment on an old friend. 'He has worries,' I explained vaguely, trying to reassure Tristan that Arthur's coldness held no foreboding.

I was leading my own horse, for I was always happier on foot, and Tristan, having greeted Culhwch, slid out of his saddle and walked beside me. I described the wild Christian ecstasies and attributed Arthur's coldness to his worries about their meaning, but Tristan did not want to hear any of it. He was in love and, like all lovers, he could talk of nothing but his beloved. 'A jewel, Derfel,' he said, 'that's what she is, an Irish jewel!' He paced long-legged beside me, one arm round my shoulder and with his long black hair chinking from the warrior rings he had woven into its plaits. His beard was more heavily streaked with white now, but he was still a handsome man with a bony nose and dark, quick eyes that were bright with passion. 'Her name,' he said dreamily, 'is Iseult.'

'We heard,' I said drily.

'A child from Demetia,' he said, 'a daughter of Oengus Mac Airem. A Princess, my friend, of the Uí Liatháin.' He spoke the name of Oengus Mac Airem's tribe as though its syllables were forged in purest gold. 'Iseult,' he said, 'of the Uí Liatháin. Fifteen summers old and as beautiful as the night.'

I thought of Arthur's ungovernable passion for Guinevere and of my own soul's longings for Ceinwyn and my heart hurt for my friend. He had been blinded by love, swept by it, made mad by it. Tristan was ever a passionate man, given to black deeps of despair or to soaring heights of happiness, but this was the first time I had ever seen him assaulted by the storm winds of love. 'Your father,' I warned him carefully, 'wants Iseult back.'

'My father's old,' he said, dismissing every obstacle, 'and when he dies I shall sail my Princess of the Uí Liatháin to Tintagel's iron gates and build her a castle of silver towers that shall scrape the stars.' He laughed at his own extravagance. 'You'll adore her, Derfel!'

I said nothing more, but just let him talk and talk. He had no appetite for our news, cared not a bit that I had three daughters or that the Saxons were on the defensive, he had room in his universe for nothing but Iseult. 'Wait till you see her, Derfel!' he said again and again, and the nearer we drew to their refuge the more excited he became until at last, unable to be apart from his Iseult for a moment longer, he leapt onto his horse and galloped away ahead of us. Arthur looked quizzically at me and I grimaced. 'He's in love,' I said, as if I needed to explain.

'With his father's taste for young girls,' Arthur added grimly.

'You and I know love, Lord,' I said, 'be kind to them.'

The refuge of Tristan and Iseult was a beautiful place, maybe the loveliest I ever saw. It was a place where small hills were cut by streams and heavy woods, where rich rivers ran fast to the sea and where great cliffs were loud with screaming birds. It was a wild place, but beautiful, a place fit for love's raw madness.

And there, in the small dark hall among the deep green woods, I met Iseult.

Small and dark and fey and fragile is how I remember Iseult. Little more than a child, really, though she had been forced to woman's state by her marriage to Mark, yet to me she appeared as a shy, small, thin girl, nothing but a delicate wisp of near-womanhood who kept her huge dark eyes fixed on Tristan until he insisted that she greeted us. She bowed to Arthur. 'You don't bow to me,' Arthur said, lifting her up, 'for you are a Queen,' and he dropped to one knee and kissed her small hand.

Her voice was whispery like a shadow's voice. Her hair was black and she had tried to make herself look older by binding it in a great coil on the crown of her head and by hanging herself with jewels, though she wore the jewels awkwardly, reminding me of Morwenna dressing up in her mother's clothes. She gazed at us fearfully. Iseult realized, I think, even before Tristan did, that this incursion of armed spearmen was not the coming of friends, but the arrival of her judges.

Culhwch had provided the lovers with their refuge. It was a hall of timber and rye thatch, not big, but well built, and it had belonged to a chieftain who had supported Cadwy's rebellion and thereby lost his head. The hall, with three huts and a storehouse, stood circled by a palisade in a wooded hollow of land where the sea winds could not chafe its thatch, and there, with six loyal spearmen and a mound of stolen treasure, Tristan and Iseult had thought to make their love into a great song.

Arthur tore their music into shreds. 'The treasure,' he told Tristan that night, 'must be returned to your father.'

'He can have it!' Tristan declared. 'I only brought it so I would not have to call on your charity, Lord.'

'So long as you are in this land, Lord Prince,' Arthur said heavily, 'you will be our guests.'

'And how long will that be, Lord?' Tristan asked.

Arthur frowned and looked up into the hall's dark rafters. 'Is that rain? It seems so long since it rained.'

Tristan asked the question again, and again Arthur refused to answer. Iseult reached for her Prince's hand and held it as Tristan reminded Arthur of Lugg Vale. 'When no one else would come to your help, Lord, I came,' Tristan said.

'You did, Lord Prince,' Arthur admitted.

'And when you fought Owain, Lord, I stood beside you.'

'You did,' Arthur said.

'And I brought my hawks' shields to London.'

'You did, Lord Prince, and they fought well there.'

'And I took your Round Table oath,' Tristan said. No one ever called it the Brotherhood of Britain any more.

'So you did, Lord,' Arthur said heavily.

'So, Lord,' Tristan begged, 'have I not deserved your help?'

'You have deserved much, Lord Prince,' Arthur said, 'and I am mindful of it.' It was an evasive answer, but the only one Tristan received that night.

We left the lovers in the hall and made our own straw beds in the small storehouses. The rain passed in the night and the next morning dawned warm and beautiful. I woke late to discover Tristan and Iseult had already left the hall. 'If they have a peck of sense,' Culhwch growled to me, 'they'll have run as far away as they can.'

'Will they?'

'They don't have sense, Derfel, they're lovers. They think the world exists for their convenience.' Culhwch walked with a slight limp now, the legacy of the wound he had taken in the battle against Aelle's army. 'They've gone to the sea,' he told me, 'to pray to Manawydan.'

Culhwch and I followed the lovers, climbing out of the wooded hollow to a windswept hill that ended in a great cliff where the seabirds wheeled and against which the vast ocean broke white in tattered bursts of spray. Culhwch and I stood on the clifftop and stared down into a small cove where Tristan and Iseult walked on the sand. The previous night, watching the timid Queen, I had not really understood what had driven Tristan into love's madness, but that windy morning I did understand.

I watched as she suddenly broke away from Tristan and ran ahead, skipping, turning and laughing at her lover who walked slowly behind. She wore a loose white dress and her black hair, no longer bound in a coil, streamed free in the salt wind. She looked like a spirit, like one of the water nymphs who had danced in Britain before the Romans came. And then, perhaps to tease Tristan, or else to take her pleas closer to Manawydan, the sea God, she ran headlong into the great tumbling surf. She plunged into the waves so that she disappeared altogether and Tristan could only stand distraught on the sand and watch the churning white mass of breaking seas. And then, sleek as an otter in a stream, her head appeared.

She waved, swam a little, then waded back to the beach with her white wet dress clinging to her pathetic thin body. I could not help but see that she had small high breasts and long slender legs, and then Tristan hid her from our view by wrapping her in the wings of his great black cloak and there, beside the sea, he held her tight and leaned his cheek against her salt-wet hair. Culhwch and I stepped out of view, leaving the lovers alone in the long sea wind that blew from fabled Lyonesse.

'He can't send them back,' Culhwch growled.

'He mustn't,' I agreed. We stared across the endlessly moving sea.

'Then why won't Arthur reassure them?' Culhwch demanded angrily.

'I don't know.'

'I should have sent them to Broceliande,' Culhwch said. The wind lifted his cloak as we walked west around the hills above the cove. Our path led to a high place from where we could see down into a great natural harbour where the ocean had flooded a river valley and formed a chain of wide, well-sheltered sea lakes. 'Halcwm,' Culhwch named the harbour, 'and the smoke is from the salt works.' He pointed to a shimmer of grey on the far side of the lakes.

'There must be seamen here who could take them to Broceliande,' I said, for the harbour had at least a dozen ships anchored in its shelter.

'Tristan wouldn't go,' Culhwch told me bleakly. 'I suggested it to him, but he believes Arthur is his friend. He trusts Arthur. He can't wait to be King for he says that then all Kernow's spears will be at Arthur's service.'

'Why didn't he just kill his father?' I asked bitterly.

'For the same reason that none of us kills that little bastard, Mordred,' Culhwch said. 'It's no small thing to kill a king.'

That night we dined in the hall again, and again Tristan pressed Arthur to say how long he and Iseult could stay in Dumnonia, and again Arthur avoided giving an answer.

'Tomorrow, Lord Prince,' he promised Tristan, 'tomorrow we shall decide all.'

But next morning two dark ships with tall masts hung with ragged sails and with high rearing prows carved into the shapes of hawks' heads sailed into Halcwm's sea lakes. The two ships' thwarts were crowded with men who, as the loom of the land cheated their sails of wind, unshipped their oars and drove the long dark ships towards the beach. Spear bundles were propped at the sterns where steersmen heaved on their great steering oars. Green branches were tied to each hawk's head prow, signifying that the ships came in peace.

I did not know who had come in the two ships, but I could guess. King Mark had come from Kernow.

King Mark was a huge man, reminding me of Uther in his dotage. He was so fat he could not climb Halcwm's hills unaided and so four spearmen carried him in a chair that was equipped with two stout poles. Forty other spearmen accompanied their King who was preceded by Cyllan, his champion. The clumsy chair swayed up the hill, then down into the wooded hollow where Tristan and Iseult believed they had found refuge.

Iseult screamed when she saw them, then, in a panic, she ran desperately to escape her husband, but the palisade had only one entrance and Mark's huge chair filled it, so she ran back into the hall where her lover was trapped. The hall doors were guarded by Culhwch's men and they refused to allow Cyllan or any of Mark's spearmen into the building. We could hear Iseult crying, Tristan shouting and Arthur pleading. King Mark ordered his chair set down opposite the hall's door and there he waited until Arthur, his face pale and tight, emerged and knelt before him.

The King of Kernow had a jowly face blotched by broken veins. His beard was thin and white, his shallow breath rasped in his fat throat and his small eyes seeped rheum. He waved Arthur to his feet, then struggled out of his chair and on thick, unsteady legs followed Arthur to the largest of the huts. It was a warm day, but Mark's thick body was still draped in a sealskin cloak as though he found it cold. He put a hand on Arthur's arm to help him walk into the hut where two chairs had been placed.

Culhwch, disgusted, planted his bulk in the hall's doorway and stood there with a drawn sword. I stood beside him while, behind us, black-haired Iseult wept.

Arthur stayed a full hour in the hut, then emerged and looked at Culhwch and me. He seemed to sigh, then walked past us into the hall. We did not hear what he said, but we heard Iseult scream.

Culhwch glared at Kernow's spearmen, begging just one of them to challenge him, but none moved. Cyllan, the champion, stood motionless beside the gate with a great war spear and his huge longsword.

Iseult screamed again, then Arthur suddenly emerged into the sunlight and plucked my arm. 'Come, Derfel.'

'What of me?' Culhwch asked defiantly.

'Guard them, Culhwch,' Arthur said. 'No one is to enter the hall.' He walked away and I walked with him.

He said nothing as we climbed the hill from the hall and nothing as we walked along the hill path, and still said nothing as we walked out onto the cliff's high peak. The headland's stone jutted into the sea beneath us where the water broke high and ragged to shatter its spume eastwards on the undying wind. The sun shone on us, but out to sea there was a great cloud and Arthur stared at the dark rain falling on the empty waves. The wind rippled his white cloak. 'Do you know the legend of Excalibur?' he suddenly asked me.

Better than he did, I thought, but I said nothing of the blade being one of the Treasures of Britain. 'I know, Lord,' I said, wondering why he had asked me such a question at such a moment, 'that Merlin won it in a dream contest in Ireland and that he gave it to you at the Stones.'

'And he told me that if I was ever in great need then all I had to do was draw the sword, plunge it into the earth and Gofannon would come from the Otherworld to aid me. Isn't that right?'

'Yes, Lord.'

'Then, Gofannon!' he shouted into the sea wind as he drew the great blade. 'Come!' And with that injunction he rammed the sword hard into the turf.

A gull cried in the wind, the sea sucked at the rocks as it slid back to the deeps and the salt wind gusted our cloaks, but no God came. 'The Gods help me,' Arthur said at last, staring at the swaying blade, 'but how I wanted to kill that fat monster.'

'So why didn't you?' I asked harshly.

He said nothing for a while and I saw there were tears running down his long hollow cheeks. 'I offered them death, Derfel,' he said. 'Swift and painless.' He cuffed at his cheeks, and then, in a sudden rage, he kicked the sword. 'Gods!' He spat at the quivering blade. 'What Gods?'

I pulled Excalibur from the turf and wiped the earth from its tip. He refused to take the sword back, so I laid it reverently on a grey boulder. 'What will happen to them, Lord?' I asked.

He sat on another stone. For a time he did not answer me, but just stared at the rain on the far sea while the tears trickled down his cheeks. 'I have lived my life, Derfel,' he said at last, 'according to oaths. I know no other way. I resent oaths, and so should all men, for oaths bind us, they hobble our freedom, and who among us doesn't want to be free? But if we abandon oaths then we abandon guidance. We fall into chaos. We just fall. We become no better than beasts.' He suddenly could not continue, but just wept.

I stared at the grey heave of the sea. Where, I wondered, do those great waves begin and where do they end? 'Suppose,' I asked, 'that the oath is a mistake?'

'A mistake?' He glanced at me, then looked back to the ocean. 'Sometimes,' he said bleakly, 'an oath cannot be kept. I could not save Ban's kingdom, though God knows I tried, but it could not be done. And so I broke that oath and I will pay for it, but I did not break it willingly. I have yet to kill Aelle, and that is an oath that must be kept, but I have not yet broken the oath, merely delayed it. I have promised to take Henis Wyren back from Diwrnach, and I will. And maybe that oath was a mistake, but I am sworn to it. So there is your answer. If an oath is a mistake then you are still obligated because you are sworn to it.' He wiped his cheek. 'So yes, one day I must take my spears against Diwrnach.'

'You have no oath to Mark,' I said bitterly.

'None,' he agreed, 'but Tristan does, and Iseult does.'

'Are their oaths our business?' I asked.

He stared at his sword. Its grey blade that was chased with intricate whorls and long-tongued dragon heads reflected the far slate-dark clouds. 'A sword and a stone,' he said softly, perhaps thinking of the moment when Mordred would become King. He stood suddenly, and turned his back on the sword to stare inland at the green hills. 'Suppose,' he said to me, 'that two oaths clash. Suppose I have sworn to fight for you and sworn to fight for your enemy, which oath do I keep?'

'The first given,' I said, knowing the law as well as he.

'And if they were both given at once?'

'Then you submit to the King's judgment.'

'Why the King?' He quizzed me as though I was a new spearman being taught the laws of Dumnonia.

'Because your oath to the King,' I said dutifully, 'is above all other oaths, and your duty is to him.'

'So the King,' he said forcefully, 'is the keeper of our oaths, and without a King there is nothing but a tangle of conflicting oaths. Without a King, there is chaos. All oaths lead to the King, Derfel, all our duty ends with the King and all our laws are in the King's keeping. If we defy our King, we defy order. We can fight other Kings, we can even kill them, but only because they threaten our King and his good order. The King, Derfel, is the nation, and we belong to the King. Whatever you or I do, we must support the King.'

I knew he was not talking about Tristan and Mark. He was thinking of Mordred and so I dared to speak the unspoken thought that had lain so heavily on Dumnonia for all those years.

'There are those, Lord,' I said, 'who say you should be the King.'

'No!' He shouted the word into the wind. 'No!' he repeated more quietly, looking at me.

I looked down at the sword on the stone. 'Why not?'

'Because I swore an oath to Uther.'

'Mordred,' I said, 'is not fit to be King. And you know it, Lord.'

He turned and looked at the sea again. 'Mordred is our King, Derfel, and that is all you or I need to know. He has our oaths. We cannot judge him, he will judge us, and if you or I decide another man should be King, where is order then? If one man takes the throne unjustly, then any man can take it. If I take it, why should another not take it from me? All order would be gone. There would just be chaos.'

'You think Mordred cares about order?' I asked bitterly.

'I think Mordred has not yet been properly acclaimed,' Arthur said. 'I think that when the high duties are put on him then he may change. I think it more likely that he will not change, but above all, Derfel, I believe he is our King and we must endure him because that is what we have to do whether we like it or not. In all this world, Derfel,' he said, suddenly sweeping up Excalibur and swinging her blade about the whole horizon, 'in all this world there is only one sure order, and that is the King's order. Not the Gods. They've gone from Britain. Merlin thought he could bring them back, but look at Merlin now. Sansum tells us that his God has power and so He might, but not for me. I see only kings, and in kings are concentrated our oaths and our duties. Without them we would be so many wild things scrambling for place.' He rammed Excalibur back into its scabbard. 'I must support kings, for without them there would be chaos and so I have told Tristan and Iseult that they must stand trial.'

'Trial!' I exclaimed, then spat on the turf.

Arthur glared angrily at me. 'They are accused,' he said, 'of theft. They are accused of breaking oaths. They are accused of fornication.' The last word twisted his mouth and he turned away from me to spit it across the sea.

'They're in love!' I protested, and when he said nothing I attacked him more directly. 'And did you stand trial, Arthur ap Uther, when you broke an oath? And not the oath to Ban, but the oath you swore when you betrothed yourself to Ceinwyn. You broke an oath, and no one put you in front of magistrates!'

He turned on me in a flaring rage and for a few heartbeats I thought he was about to drag Excalibur free again and attack me with the blade, but then he shuddered and went still. His eyes glistened with tears again. He said nothing for a long while, then he nodded. 'I broke that oath, true. Do you think I haven't regretted it?'

'And you will not let Tristan break one oath?'

'He's a thief!' Arthur snarled at me in fury. 'You think we should risk years of border raids for a thief who fornicates with his stepmother? You could talk to the families of the dead farmers on our frontier and justify their deaths in the name of Tristan's love? You think women and children should die because a prince is in love? Is that your justice?'

'I think Tristan is our friend,' I said, and when he did not answer, I spat at his feet. 'You sent for Mark, didn't you?' I accused him.

He nodded. 'Yes. I sent a messenger from Isca.'

'Tristan is our friend,' I shouted at him.

He closed his eyes. 'He has stolen from a King,' he said stubbornly. 'He has stolen gold, a wife and pride. He has broken oaths. His father seeks justice and I am sworn to justice.'

'He is your friend,' I insisted. 'And he is mine!'

He opened his eyes and stared at me. 'A King comes to me, Derfel, and asks for justice. Am I to deny Mark justice because he is old and gross and ugly? Do youth and beauty deserve perverted justice? What have I fought for all these years, if not to make certain that justice is even-handed?' He was pleading with me now. 'When we travelled here, through all those villages and towns, did people run away because they saw our swords? No!

And why? Because they know that in Mordred's kingdom there is justice. And now, because a man beds his father's wife, you would have me toss that justice away like an inconvenient burden?'

'Yes,' I said, 'because he is a friend, and because if you make them stand trial they will be found guilty. They have no chance at trial,' I protested bitterly, 'because Mark is a Tongued One.'

Arthur gave a sad smile as he acknowledged the memory I had deliberately provoked. That memory was of our very first meeting with Tristan, and that meeting too had been a legal matter, and in that case a great injustice was almost done because the accused was a Tongued One. In our law the evidence given by a Tongued One was incontrovertible. A thousand people could swear the opposite, but their evidence was nothing if it was contradicted by a Lord, a Druid, a priest, a father speaking of his children, a gift-giver speaking of his gift, a maid talking of her virginity, a herdsman speaking of his animals or a condemned man saying his final words. And Mark was a Lord, a King, and his word outweighed those of a Prince or a Queen. No court in Britain would acquit Tristan and Iseult, and Arthur knew it. But Arthur had sworn an oath to uphold the law.

But on that far day, when Owain had so nearly perverted justice by using the privilege of a Tongued One to tell a lie, Arthur had appealed to the court of swords. For Tristan's benefit Arthur himself had fought Owain and Arthur had won. 'Tristan,' I now said to Arthur, 'could appeal to the court of swords.'

'That is his privilege,' Arthur said.

'And I am his friend,' I said coldly, 'and I can fight for him.'

Arthur stared at me as though he was only just realizing the true depths of my hostility. 'You, Derfel?' he asked.

'I shall fight for Tristan,' I said coldly, 'because he is my friend. As you once were.'

He paused a few heartbeats. 'That is your privilege,' he finally said, 'but I have done my duty.' He walked away and I followed ten paces behind; when he slowed, I slowed, and when he turned to look at me, I looked away. I was going to fight for a friend.

Arthur curtly ordered Culhwch's spearmen to escort Tristan and Iseult to Isca. There, he decreed, their trial would be held. King Mark could provide one judge and we Dumnonians the other.

King Mark sat in his chair, saying nothing. He had argued for the trial to be held in Kernow, but he must have known it did not matter. Tristan would not stand trial for Tristan would never survive a trial. Tristan could only appeal to the sword.

The Prince came to the door of the hall and there he faced his father. Mark's face showed nothing, Tristan was pale and Arthur stood with head bowed so that he did not need to look at either man.

Tristan wore no armour and carried no shield. His black hair with its warrior rings was combed back and tied with a strip of white linen that he must have torn from Iseult's dress. He wore a shirt, trews and boots and had a sword at his side. He walked halfway to his father and there stopped. He drew his sword, stared into his father's implacable eyes, then rammed the blade hard into the turf. 'I will be tried by the court of swords,' he insisted.

Mark shrugged and made a lethargic gesture with his right hand, and that gesture brought Cyllan forward. It was plain that Tristan knew the champion's prowess for he looked nervous as the huge man, whose beard grew down to his waist, stripped off his cloak. Cyllan pushed his black hair away from the axe tattoo, then pulled his iron helmet onto his head. He spat on his hands, rubbed the spittle into his palms and walked slowly forward and knocked Tristan's sword flat. With that gesture he had accepted battle.

I drew Hywelbane. 'I shall fight for Tristan,' I heard myself saying. I was oddly nervous, and it was not just the nervousness that precedes battle. It was fear of the great gulf that was opening in my life, the gulf that separated me from Arthur.

'I shall fight for Tristan,' Culhwch insisted. He came and stood beside me. 'You've got daughters, fool,' he muttered.

'So have you.'

'But I'll beat this bearded toad quicker than you, you Saxon bag of guts,' Culhwch said fondly. Tristan stepped between us and protested that he would fight Cyllan alone, that this was his battle and no one else's, but Culhwch growled at him to get back into the hall. 'I've beaten men twice as big as that bearded lout,' he told Tristan.

Cyllan drew his longsword and gave it a slash through the empty air. 'One of you,' he said carelessly, 'I don't care which.'

'No!' Mark suddenly shouted. He summoned Cyllan and two others of his spearmen and the three men knelt beside Mark's chair and listened to their King's instructions.

Culhwch and I both presumed that Mark was ordering his three men to fight the three of us. 'I'll take the bastard with the big beard and the dirty forehead,' Culhwch decided, 'you take that red-haired piece of dogshit, Derfel, and my Lord Prince can skewer the bald one. Two minutes' work?'

Iseult crept from the hall. She seemed terrified to be in Mark's sight, but she came to embrace Culhwch and me. Culhwch swamped her in his arms, while I knelt and kissed her thin pale hand. 'Thank you,' she said in her little shadow voice. Her eyes were red with tears. She stood on tiptoe to kiss Tristan, and then, with one scared backward look at her husband, she fled back into the hall's shadows.

Mark raised his heavy head from the collar of his sealskin fur. 'The court of swords,' he said in a voice thick with phlegm, 'demands one man on one man. It has always been thus.'

'Then send your virgins one at a time, Lord King,' Culhwch shouted, 'and I'll kill them one at a time.'

Mark shook his head. 'One man, one sword,' he insisted, 'and my son asked for the privilege, so he will fight.'

'Lord King,' I said, 'custom decrees that a man can fight for his friend in the court of swords. I, Derfel Cadarn, insist on the privilege.'

'I know of no such custom,' Mark lied.

'Arthur does,' I said harshly. 'He fought for your son in a court of swords and I will fight for him today.'

Mark turned his bleary eyes towards Arthur, but Arthur shook his head as if to suggest he wanted nothing to do with the argument. Mark looked back at me. 'My son's offence is filthy,' he said, 'and no one but he should defend it.'

'I will defend it!' I said, then Culhwch stepped beside me and insisted that he would fight for Tristan. The King just looked at us, raised his right hand and gave a weary gesture.

The spearmen of Kernow, instructed by the red-haired man and the bald warrior, formed a shield-wall at the King's signal. It was a wall two men deep and the front rank held their shields in a locked row while the second rank held their shields to protect the heads of the front rank. Then, on a word of command, they tossed their spears to the ground.

'Bastards,' Culhwch said, for he understood what was about to happen. 'Shall we break them, Lord Derfel?' he asked me.

'Let us break them, Lord Culhwch,' I said vengefully.

There were forty men of Kernow, and three of us. The forty shuffled slowly forward in their locked shield-wall with their eyes watching us warily from beneath the rims of their helmets. They carried no spears and had drawn no swords. They did not come to kill us, but to immobilize us.

And Culhwch and I charged them. I had not needed to break a shield-wall in years, but the old madness whirled in me as I screamed Bel's name, then I shouted Ceinwyn's name as I rammed Hywelbane's point at a man's eyes and as he ducked aside I threw my shoulder at the junction of his and his neighbour's shields.

The wall broke and I screamed in triumph as I thumped Hywelbane's hilt on the back of one man's head, then stabbed it forward to widen the gap. In battle, by now, my men would be thrusting behind me, opening the gap and soaking the ground with enemy blood, but I had no men behind me, and no weapons opposing me, just shields and more shields, and though I whirled in a circle, making Hywelbane's blade hiss as she slashed around, those shields closed inexorably on me. I dared not kill any of the spearmen, for that would have been dishonourable after they had so deliberately cast aside their own weapons, and bereft of that opportunity I could only try and frighten them. But they knew I would not kill and so a ring of shields circled me, closed on me, and Hywelbane was at last stopped dead by an iron shield-boss and suddenly the shields of Kernow were pressing hard about me.

I heard Arthur shout a harsh command, and I guessed that some of Culhwch's and my spearmen had wanted to help their lords, but Arthur held them back. He did not want a bloody fight, Kernow against Dumnonia. He just wanted this grim business done and finished.

Culhwch had been trapped like me. He raged at his captors, called them infants, dogs and worms, but the men of Kernow had their orders. We were neither of us to be hurt, but just held tight by a press of men and by the clamp of their shields, and so, like Iseult, we could only watch as the champion of Kernow walked forward, his sword held low, and gave his Prince a bow.

Tristan knew he would die. He had taken the ribbon from his hair and tied it about his sword's blade, and now he kissed the linen strip. Then he held his sword out, touched the champion's blade, and sprang forward in a lunge.

Cyllan parried. The sound of the two swords echoed back from the palisade, then echoed again as Tristan attacked a second time, this time swinging the sword in a fast downward slash, but once again Cyllan parried. He did it easily, almost wearily. Twice more Tristan attacked, and then he kept his blows going, swinging and lunging as fast as he could, trying desperately to wear Cyllan's defence down, but he only wearied his own arm, and the moment he paused for breath and took a step back, the champion lunged.

That lunge was so well done. It was even beautifully done if you cared to see a sword used properly. It was even mercifully done for Cyllan took Tristan's soul in an eyeblink. The Prince did not even have the time to look back at his lover in the hall's shadowed door. He just stared at his killer, and the blood gushed from his cut throat to turn his white shirt red, then his sword dropped as he made the dying, bubbling, choking sound, and as his soul fled, he just dropped.

'Justice is done, Lord King,' Cyllan said bleakly as he pulled his blade free from Tristan's neck and walked away. The spearmen who surrounded me, none of whom had dared meet my eyes, drew back. I raised Hywelbane and the sight of its grey blade was misted by my tears. I heard Iseult scream as her husband's men killed the six spearmen who had accompanied Tristan and who now took hold of their Queen. I closed my eyes.

I would not look at Arthur. I would not speak with Arthur. I walked to the headland and there I prayed to my Gods and I begged them to come back to Britain, and while I prayed the men of Kernow took Queen Iseult down to the sea-lake where the two dark ships waited. But they did not carry her home to Kernow. Instead the Princess of the Uí Liatháin, that child of fifteen summers who had skipped barefoot into the waves and whose voice had been a shadowy wisp like the seamen's ghosts who ride the long sea winds, was tied to a post and heaped around with the driftwood that lay so thick on Halcwm's shore, and there, before her husband's unforgiving eyes, she was burned alive. Her lover's corpse was burned on the same pyre.

I would not leave with Arthur. I would not talk to him. I let him go, and I slept that night in the dark old hall where the lovers had slept. Then I travelled home to Lindinis and that was when I confessed to Ceinwyn about the old massacre on the moor when I had killed the innocent to keep an oath. I told her about Iseult burning. Burning and screaming while her husband watched.

Ceinwyn held me. 'Did you not know that hardness in Arthur?' she asked me softly.

'No.'

'He is all that stands between us and horror,' Ceinwyn said, 'how could he be anything but hard?'

Even now, with my eyes closed, I sometimes see that child coming from the sea, her face smiling, her thin body outlined against the white clinging dress and her hands reaching for her lover. I cannot hear a gull's cry without seeing her for she will haunt me till the day I die, and after death, wherever it is my soul goes, she will be there; a child killed for a King, by law, in Camelot.

I DID NOT SEE Lancelot for many years after the Round Table oath, nor did I see any of his henchmen. Amhar and Loholt, Arthur's twins, lived in Lancelot's capital of Venta where they led bands of spearmen, but the only fighting they seemed to do was in its taverns. Dinas and Lavaine were also in Venta where they presided over a temple dedicated to Mercury, a Roman God, and their ceremonies rivalled the ones held in Lancelot's palace church that had been consecrated by Bishop Sansum. Sansum was a frequent visitor to Venta and he reported that the Belgic people seemed happy enough with Lancelot, which we took to mean that they were not openly rebellious.

Lancelot and his companions also visited Dumnonia, most often going across their border to the Sea Palace, but sometimes travelling as far as Durnovaria to attend some high feast, but I simply stayed away from such festivals if I knew they were coming, and neither Arthur nor Guinevere ever demanded that I attend. Nor was I invited to the great funeral that followed the death of Lancelot's mother, Elaine.

Lancelot, in truth, was not a bad ruler. He was no Arthur, he cared nothing for the quality of justice or the fairness of taxes or the state of the roads, he simply ignored those things, but as they had been ignored before his rule no one noticed any great difference. Lancelot, like Guinevere, cared only for his comfort and, like her, he built a lavish palace that was filled with statues, bright with painted walls and hung, of course, with the extravagant collection of mirrors in which he could admire his own endless reflection. The money for these luxuries was exacted in taxes, and if those taxes were heavy then the compensation was the freedom of the Belgic lands from Saxon raids. Cerdic, astonishingly, had kept his faith with Lancelot and the dreaded Sais spearmen never raided Lancelot's rich farmlands.

But nor did they need to raid, for Lancelot had invited them to come and live in his kingdom. The land had been depopulated by the long years of war and huge stretches of fine fields were growing back to woodland, and so Lancelot invited settlers from Cerdic's people to till the fields. The Saxons swore oaths of loyalty to Lancelot, they cleared the land, they built new villages, they paid their taxes, and their spearmen even marched in his war-band. His palace guard, we heard, were all Saxons now. The Saxon Guard, he called them, and he chose them for their height and for the colour of their hair. I did not see them in those years, though eventually I met them, and they were all tall blond men who carried axes polished to a mirror brightness. Rumour had it that Lancelot paid tribute to Cerdic, but Arthur angrily denied it when our Council asked him if it was true. Arthur disapproved of Saxon settlers being invited onto British land, but the matter, he said, was Lancelot's to decide, not ours, and at least the land was at peace. Peace, it seemed, excused all.

Lancelot even boasted that he had converted his Saxon Guard to Christianity, for his baptism, it seems, had not just been for show, but was real enough, or so Galahad told me on one of his frequent visits to Lindinis. He described the church Sansum had built in the Venta palace and told me that every day a choir sang and a bevy of priests celebrated the Christian mysteries. 'It's all very beautiful,' Galahad said wistfully. That was before I had seen the ecstasies in Isca and I had no idea such frenzies took place, so did not ask him whether they happened in Venta, or whether his brother encouraged Dumnonia's Christians to see him as a deliverer.

'Has Christianity changed your brother?' Ceinwyn asked.

Galahad watched the flicker of her hands as she teased a thread from the distaff onto the spindle. 'No,' he admitted. 'He thinks it's enough to say prayers once a day and then he behaves as he likes thereafter. But many Christians are like that, alas.'

'And how does he behave?' Ceinwyn asked.

'Badly.'

'Do you want me to leave the room,' Ceinwyn asked sweetly, 'so you can tell Derfel without embarrassing me? And then he can tell me when we go to bed.'

Galahad laughed. 'He's bored, Lady, and he alleviates his boredom in the usual way. He hunts.'

'So does Derfel, so do I. Hunting's not bad.'

'He hunts girls,' Galahad said bleakly. 'He doesn't treat them badly, but they don't really have much choice. Some of them like it and they all become rich enough, but they also become his whores.'

'He sounds like most kings,' Ceinwyn said drily. 'Is that all he does?'

'He spends hours with those two wretched Druids,' Galahad said, 'and no one knows why a Christian King would do that, but he claims it's just friendship. He encourages his poets, he collects mirrors and he visits Guinevere's Sea Palace.'

'To do what?' I asked.

'To talk, he says.' Galahad shrugged. 'He says they talk about religion. Or rather they argue about it. She's become very devout.'

'To Isis,' Ceinwyn said disapprovingly. In the years after the Round Table oath we had all heard how Guinevere was retreating more and more into the practice of her religion so that now the Sea Palace was said to be one huge shrine to Isis, and Guinevere's attendants, who were all women chosen for their grace and looks, were the priestesses of Isis.

'The Supreme Goddess,' Galahad said disparagingly, then carefully crossed himself to keep the pagan evil at bay. 'Guinevere evidently believes the Goddess has enormous power that can be channelled into human affairs. I can't imagine Arthur likes it.'

'He's bored by it all,' Ceinwyn said, spinning the last of the thread off the distaff and laying it down. 'All he ever does now,' she went on, 'is complain that Guinevere won't talk to him about anything except her religion. It must be horribly tedious for him.' This conversation took place long before Tristan fled to Dumnonia with Iseult, and when Arthur was still a welcome guest at our house.

'My brother claims to be fascinated by her ideas,' Galahad said, 'and maybe he is. He claims she's the most intelligent woman in Britain and says he won't marry till he finds another just like her.'

Ceinwyn laughed. 'A good job he lost me, then. How old is he now?'

'Thirty-three, I think.'

'So ancient!' Ceinwyn said, smiling at me, for I was only a year younger. 'What happened to Ade?'

'She gave him a son, and died doing it.'

'No!' Ceinwyn said, upset as always at hearing of a death in childbirth. 'And you say he has a son?'

'A bastard,' Galahad said disapprovingly. 'Peredur, he's called. Four years old now, and not a bad little boy. In truth I rather like him.'

'Has there ever been a child you didn't like?' I asked him drily.

'Brush-head,' he said, and we all smiled at that old nickname.

'Imagine Lancelot having a son!' Ceinwyn said with that intonation of surprised import with which women greet such news. To me the existence of another royal bastard seemed entirely unremarkable, but men and women, I notice, respond to these things quite differently.

Galahad, like his brother, had never married. Nor did he have land, but he was happy and was kept busy serving as an envoy for Arthur. He tried to keep the Brotherhood of Britain alive, though I noticed how quickly those duties fell away, and he travelled through all the British kingdoms, carrying messages, settling disputes and using his royal rank to ease whatever problems Dumnonia might have with other states. It was usually

Galahad who travelled to Demetia to curb Oengus Mac Airem's raids on Powys and it was Galahad who, after Tristan's death, carried the news of Iseult's fate to her father. I did not see him after that, not for many months.

I tried not to see Arthur either. I was too angry with him, and I would neither answer his letters nor go to the Council. He came to Lindinis twice in the months after Tristan's death and both times I was coldly polite and both times I left him as soon as I could. He did talk for a long time with Ceinwyn and she tried to reconcile us, but I could not shake the thought of that burning child from my head.

But nor could I ignore Arthur altogether. Mordred's second acclamation was now just months away and the preparations had to be made. The ceremony would be held at Caer Cadarn, just a short walk east of Lindinis, and inevitably Ceinwyn and I were drawn into the planning. Mordred himself even took an interest, perhaps because he realized that the ceremony would at last free him of all discipline. 'You have to decide,' I told him one day, 'who will acclaim you.'

'Arthur will, won't he?' he asked sullenly.

'It's usually done by a Druid,' I said, 'but if you want a Christian ceremony then you must choose between Emrys or Sansum.'

He shrugged. 'Sansum, I suppose.'

'Then we should go and see him,' I said.

We went on a hard midwinter day. I had other business in Ynys Wydryn, but first went with Mordred to the Christian shrine where a priest told us that Bishop Sansum was busy saying mass and that we must wait. 'Does he know his King is here?' I demanded.

'I shall tell him, Lord,' the priest said, and scuttled away across the frozen ground.

Mordred had wandered off to stand beside his mother's grave where, even on that cold day, a dozen pilgrims knelt in worship. It was a very simple grave, nothing but a low mound of earth with a stone cross that was dwarfed by the lead urn Sansum had placed to receive the pilgrims' offerings. 'The Bishop will be with us soon,' I said. 'Shall we wait inside?'

He shook his head and frowned at the low grassy mound. 'She should have a better grave,' he said.

'I think that's true,' I said, surprised he had spoken at all. 'You can build it.'

'It would have been better,' he said snidely, 'if others had paid her that respect.'

'Lord King,' I said, 'we were so busy defending the life of her child that we had small time to worry about her bones. But you are right, and we were remiss.'

He kicked moodily at the urn, then peered inside to see the small treasures that had been left by the pilgrims. Those who were praying at the grave edged away, not for fear of Mordred whom I doubt they even recognized, but because the iron amulet I wore about my neck betrayed that I was a pagan. 'Why was she buried?' Mordred suddenly asked me. 'Why wasn't she burned?'

'Because she was a Christian,' I said, hiding my horror at his ignorance. I explained that Christians believed their bodies would be used again at the final coming of Christ, while we pagans took new shadowbodies in the Otherworld and thus had no need of our corpses which, if we could, we burned to prevent our spirits wandering the earth. If we could not afford a funeral pyre then we burned the dead person's hair and cut off one foot.

'I shall make her a vault,' he said when I had finished my theological explanation. He asked me how his mother had died and I told him the whole story of how Gundleus of Siluria had treacherously married Norwenna, then murdered her as she knelt to him. And I told him how Nimue had taken her revenge on Gundleus.

'That witch,' Mordred said. He feared Nimue, and no wonder, for she was becoming ever fiercer, ever gaunter and ever dirtier. She was a recluse now, grubbing a life in the remnants of Merlin's compound where she chanted her spells, lit fires to her Gods and received few visitors, though once in a while, unannounced, she would stride into Lindinis to consult with Merlin. I would try to feed her on those rare visits, the children would run from her, and she would walk away, muttering to herself with her one eye wild, her robe caked with mud and ashes, and her matted black hair tangled with filth. Beneath her refuge on the Tor she was forced to watch the Christian shrine grow larger, stronger and ever more organized. The old Gods, I thought, were losing Britain fast. Sansum, of course, was desperate for Merlin to die so he could take the Tor for himself and build a church on its fire-scarred summit, but what Sansum did not know was that all Merlin's land was willed to me.

Mordred, standing beside his mother's grave, wondered at the similarity of names between my eldest daughter and his dead mother and I told him that Ceinwyn was Norwenna's cousin. 'Morwenna and Norwenna are old names in Powys,' I explained.

'Did she love me?' Mordred asked, and the incongruity of that word in his mouth gave me pause. Maybe, I thought, Arthur was right. Maybe Mordred would grow into his responsibilities. Certainly, in all the years I had known him, I had never held such a courteous discussion before.

'She loved you very much,' I answered truthfully. 'The happiest I ever saw your mother,' I went on, 'was when you were with her. It was up there.' I pointed to the black scar where Merlin's hall and his dream-tower had stood on the Tor. It was there that Norwenna had been murdered and Mordred had been snatched away from her. He had been a baby then, even younger than I had been when I was snatched from my mother, Erce. Did Erce still live? I still had not travelled to Siluria to find her, and that omission made me feel guilty. I touched the iron amulet.

'When I die,' Mordred said, 'I want to be in the same grave as my mother. And I'll make the grave myself. A vault of stone,' he declared, 'with our bodies lifted on a pedestal.'

'You must talk to the Bishop,' I said, 'and I'm sure he'll be pleased to do whatever he can to help.' So long, I thought cynically, as he did not have to pay for the vaulted sepulchre.

I turned as Sansum hurried across the grass. He bowed to

Mordred, then welcomed me to the shrine. 'You come, I hope, in search of truth, Lord Derfel?'

'I come to visit that shrine,' I said, pointing to the Tor, 'but my Lord King has business of his own with you.' I left them there alone and led my horse up to the Tor, passing by the group of Christians who, day and night, prayed at the Tor's foot that its pagan inhabitants would be driven away. I endured their insults, then climbed the steep hill to discover that the water-gate had fallen from its last hinge. I tied my horse to a stake in what remained of the palisade, then carried the bundle of clothes and furs that Ceinwyn had packed so that the poor folk who shared Nimue's refuge would not freeze in the bitter weather. I gave Nimue the clothes and she dropped them care-lessly in the snow, then plucked at my sleeve and drew me into her new hut that she had built exactly where Merlin's dream-tower had once stood. The hut stank so foully that I almost gagged, but she was oblivious to its mephitic stench. It was a freezing day and an icy sleet was whipping out of the east on a damp wind, yet even so I would rather have stood in the freezing downpour than endure that reeking hut. 'Look,' she said proud-ly, and showed me a cauldron, not the Cauldron, but just a common, patched iron cauldron that hung from a roof beam and was filled with some dark liquid. Sprigs of mistletoe, a pair of bat wings, the sloughed skin of snakes, a broken antler and bunches of herbs also hung from the rafters that were so low that I had to bend double to get inside the hut, which was eye-stingingly full of smoke. A naked man lay on a pallet in the far shadows and complained about my presence.

'Quiet,' Nimue snarled at him, then she took a stick and poked it into the cauldron's dark liquid which steamed gently above a small fire that was generating far more smoke than heat. She stirred the cauldron about, found whatever she wanted and levered it up from the liquid. I saw it was a human skull. 'You remember Balise?' Nimue asked me.

'Of course,' I said. Balise had been a Druid, an old man when I was young, and now long dead.

'They burned his body,' Nimue told me, 'but not his head, and a Druid's head, Derfel, is a thing of awesome power. A man brought it to me last week. He had it in a barrel of beeswax. I bought it from him.'

Which meant I had purchased the head. Nimue was forever buying objects of cultic power: the caul of a dead child, the teeth of a dragon, a piece of the Christian's magical bread, elf bolts, and now a dead man's head. She used to come to the palace and demand the money for these tawdry things, but I now found it easier to leave her with a little gold, even if it did mean that she would waste the metal on whatever oddity was offered her. She once paid a whole gold ingot for the carcass of a lamb that had been born with two heads, and she had nailed the carcass to the palisade where it overlooked the Christian shrine and there let it rot. I did not like to ask what she had paid for a barrel of wax containing a dead man's head. 'I stripped the wax away,' she told me, 'and boiled the flesh off the head in the pot.' That in part explained the hut's overwhelming stench. 'There is no more powerful augury,' she told me, her one eye glinting in the dark hut, 'than a Druid's head seethed in a pot of urine with the ten brown herbs of Crom Dubh.' She let the skull go and it sank beneath the liquid's dark surface. 'Now wait,' she ordered me.

My head was reeling with the smoke and stench, but I obediently waited as the liquid's surface shivered, glinted and finally subsided until it was nothing but a dark sheen as smooth as a fine mirror with only a hint of steam drifting from its black surface. Nimue leaned close and held her breath, and I knew she was seeing portents in the liquid's surface. The man on the pallet coughed horribly, then feebly clawed at a threadbare blanket to half cover his nakedness. 'I'm hungry,' he whined. Nimue ignored him.

I waited. 'I'm disappointed in you, Derfel,' Nimue suddenly said, her breath just wrinkling the liquid's surface.

'Why?'

'I see a Queen was burned to death on a seashore. I would

have liked her ashes, Derfel,' she said reprovingly. 'I could have used a Queen's ashes,' she went on. 'You should have known that.' She fell silent and I said nothing. The liquid was still again, and when Nimue next spoke it was in a strange, deep voice that did not blur the black liquid's surface at all. 'Two Kings will come to Cadarn,' she said, 'but a man who is no King shall rule there. The dead will be taken in marriage, the lost will come to the light and a sword will lie on the neck of a child.' Then she screamed terribly, startling the naked man who scuttled frantically into the furthest corner of the hut where he crouched with his hands covering his head. 'Tell that to Merlin,' Nimue said to me in her normal voice. 'He'll know what it means.'

'I will tell him,' I promised her.

'And tell him,' she said with a desperate fervour, clutching my arm with a dirt-encrusted claw of a hand, 'that I have seen the Cauldron in the liquid. Tell him it will be used soon. Soon, Derfel! Tell him that.'

'I will,' I said, and then, unable to take the smell any more, I pulled away from her grip and backed out into the sleet.

She followed me out of the hut and plucked a wing of my cloak to cover herself from the sleet. She walked with me towards the broken water-gate and was oddly cheerful. 'Everyone thinks we're losing, Derfel,' she said, 'everyone thinks those filthy Christians are taking over the land. But they're not. The Cauldron will be revealed soon, Merlin will be back and the power will be loosed.'

I stopped in the gate and stared down at the group of Christians who were always gathered at the foot of the Tor to pray their extravagant prayers with their arms spread wide. Sansum and Morgan arranged for them to be there so that their constant prayers might serve to drive the pagans off the Tor's fire-scarred summit. Nimue stared scornfully down at the group. Some of the Christians recognized her and made the sign of the cross. 'You think Christianity is winning, Derfel?' she asked me.

'I fear it,' I said, listening to the howls of rage from the Tor's foot. I remembered the frenzied worshippers in Isca and wondered how long the horror of that fanaticism could be kept under control. 'I do fear it is,' I said sadly.

'Christianity isn't winning,' Nimue said scornfully. 'Watch.' She ducked out from under my cloak and lifted her dirty dress to expose her wretched nakedness to the Christians, and then she thrust her hips obscenely towards them and gave a wailing cry that died in the wind as she dropped the dress. Some of the Christians made the sign of the cross, but most, I noted, instinctively made the pagan sign against evil with their right hands and then spat on the ground. 'You see?' she said with a smile, 'they still believe in the old Gods. They still believe. And soon, Derfel, they will have proof. Tell that to Merlin.'

I did tell Merlin. I stood before him and reported that two Kings would come to Cadarn, but a man who was not a King would rule there, that the dead would be taken in marriage, the lost would come to the light and a sword be laid on the neck of a child.

'Say it again, Derfel,' he said, squinting up at me and stroking an old tabby cat that was stretched out on his lap.

I repeated it all solemnly, then added Nimue's promise that the Cauldron would soon be unveiled and that its horror was imminent. He laughed, shook his head, then laughed again. He soothed the cat on his lap. 'And did you say she had a Druid's head?' he asked.

'Balise's head, Lord.'

He tickled the cat under the chin. 'Balise's head was burned, Derfel, years ago. It was burned, then pounded into a powder. Pounded to nothing. I know, because I did it.' He closed his eyes and slept.

Next summer, on the eve of a full moon, when the trees that grew about the foot of Caer Cadarn were heavy with leaf, on a morning of brilliant sunshine that shone on hedgerows bright with bryony and bindweed and willowherb and old man's beard, we acclaimed Mordred our King on the ancient summit of the Caer.

Caer Cadarn's old fortress stood deserted for much of the year, but it was still our hill of kingship, the solemn place of ritual at Dumnonia's royal heart, and the fort's ramparts were kept strong, but the interior of the fort was a sad place of decaying huts that crouched around the big gaunt feasting hall that was a home to birds, bats and mice. That hall occupied the lower part of Caer Cadarn's wide summit, while on the higher part, to the west, stood a circle of lichen-covered stones surrounding the grey, slab-like boulder that was Dumnonia's ancient stone of kingship. Here the great God Bel had anointed his half-God, half-human child Beli Mawr as the first of our Kings and ever since, even in the years when the Romans had ruled, our Kings had come to this place to be acclaimed. Mordred had been born on this hill and here too he had been acclaimed as a baby, though that ceremony had merely been a sign of his kingly status and had placed no duties on him. But now he was at the dawn of his manhood and from this day on he would be King in more than name. This second acclamation discharged Arthur's oath and gave Mordred all of Uther's power.

The crowds gathered early. The feasting hall had been swept, then hung with banners and decorated with green boughs. Vats of mead and pots of ale were set on the grass, while smoke poured from the great fires where oxen, pigs and deer were being roasted for the feast. Tattooed tribesmen from Isca mingled with the elegant, toga-clad citizens from Durnovaria and Corinium, and both listened to the white-robed bards who sang specially composed songs praising Mordred's character and forecasting the glories of his reign. Bards never were to be trusted.

I was Mordred's champion and so, alone among the lords on the hill, I was dressed in my full war gear. It was no longer the shabby, ill-repaired stuff I had worn at that fight outside London, for now I possessed a new and expensive armour that reflected my high status. I had a coat of fine Roman mail that was trimmed with golden rings at its neck, hem and sleeves. I had knee-high boots that gleamed with bronze strips, elbow-length gloves lined with iron plates that protected my forearms and fingers, and a fine silver-chased helmet with a mail flap that protected the back of my neck. The helmet had cheek pieces that hinged across my face and a gold finial from which my freshly brushed wolf-tail hung. I had a green cloak, Hywelbane at my hip and a shield which, in honour of this day, bore Mordred's red dragon instead of my own white star.

Culhwch had come from Isca. He embraced me. 'This is a farce, Derfel,' he growled.

'A great and happy day, Lord Culhwch,' I said, straight-faced.

He did not smile, but instead looked sullenly about the expectant crowd. 'Christians,' he spat.

'There do seem a lot of them.'

'Is Merlin here?'

'He felt tired,' I said.

'You mean he's got more sense than to come,' Culhwch said. 'So who does the honours today?'

'Bishop Sansum.'

Culhwch spat. His beard had gone grey in the last few months and he moved stiffly, though he was still a great bear of a man. 'Are you talking to Arthur yet?' he demanded.

'We speak when we have to,' I answered evasively.

'He wants to be friends with you,' Culhwch told me.

'He deals very strangely with friends,' I said stiffly.

'He needs friends.'

'Then he's lucky to have you,' I retorted, and turned as a horn-call interrupted our conversation. Spearmen were making a passage in the crowd, using their shields and spear-staffs to press the people gently back, and in the spearmen's corridor a procession of lords, magistrates and priests walked slowly towards the ring of stones. I took my place in the procession alongside Ceinwyn and my daughters.

The gathering that day was a tribute to Arthur rather than to

Mordred, for all Arthur's allies were there. Cuneglas had come from Powys, bringing a dozen lords and his Edling, the Prince Perddel who was now a good-looking boy with his father's round and earnest face. Agricola, old and stiff-jointed now, accompanied King Meurig, both men in togas. Meurig's father Tewdric still lived, but the old King had given up his throne, shaved his head into the tonsure of a priest and retired to a monastery in the valley of the Wye where he patiently gathered a library of Christian texts and allowed his pedantic son to rule Gwent in his place. Byrthig, who had succeeded his father as King of Gwynedd, and who now possessed only two teeth, stood fidgeting as though the rituals were a necessary irritant that needed to be finished before he could get back to the waiting mead vats. Oengus Mac Airem, Iseult's father and the King of Demetia, had come with a party of his dreaded Blackshields, while Lancelot, King of the Belgae, was escorted by a dozen giant men of his Saxon Guard and by the baleful pairs of twins, Dinas and Lavaine and Amhar and Loholt.

Arthur, I noticed, embraced Oengus, who returned the gesture happily. No ill-will there, it seemed, despite Iseult's awful death. Arthur wore a brown cloak, perhaps not wanting one of his white cloaks to outshine the day's hero. Guinevere looked splendid in a russet dress that was trimmed with silver and embroidered with her symbol of the moon-crowned stag. Sagramor came in a black gown and had brought his pregnant Saxon wife, Malla, and their two sons. No one came from Kernow.

The banners of the Kings, chiefs and Lords were hung from the ramparts where a ring of spearmen, all equipped with newly painted dragon shields, stood guard. A horn sounded again, its noise mournful in the sunny air as twenty other spearmen escorted Mordred towards the stone ring where, fifteen years before, we had first acclaimed him. That first ceremony had been in wintertime and the baby Mordred had been wrapped in fur and carried about the stones in an upturned war shield. Morgan had supervised that first acclamation which had been marked by the sacrifice of a Saxon captive, but this time the ceremony would be an entirely Christian rite. The Christians, I thought grimly, whatever Nimue might think, had won. There were no Druids here except for Dinas and Lavaine and they had no role to play, Merlin was sleeping in Lindinis's garden, Nimue was on the Tor and no captive would be slaughtered to discover the auguries for the newly acclaimed King's reign. We had killed a Saxon prisoner at Mordred's first acclamation, spearing him high in the belly so that his death would be slow and agonizing, and Morgan had watched every painful stagger and every splatter of blood for signs of the future. Those auguries, I remembered, had not been good, though they had promised Mordred a long reign. I tried to remember that poor Saxon's name, but all I could remember was his terrified face and the fact that I had liked him, and then suddenly his name came winging back across the years. Wlenca! Poor shivering Wlenca. Morgan had insisted on his death, but now, with a crucifix dangling beneath her mask, she was only here as Sansum's wife and would play no part in the rites.

A muted cheer greeted Mordred's arrival. The Christians applauded, while we pagans just touched our hands dutifully together and then fell silent. The King was dressed entirely in black: black shirt, black trews, black cloak and a pair of black boots, one of which was monstrously fashioned to encase his clubbed left foot. A gold crucifix hung about his neck and it seemed to me that there was a smirk on his round, ugly face, or perhaps that grimace just betrayed his nervousness. He had kept his beard, but it was a thin thing that did little to improve his bulbous face with its jutting hedges of hair. He walked alone into the royal circle and took his place beside the royal stone.

Sansum, splendid in white and gold, hurried to stand beside the King. The Bishop raised his arms and, without any preamble, began to pray aloud. His voice, always strong, carried right across the huge crowd that pressed behind the Lords, right out to the motionless spearmen on the rampart's fighting platforms. 'Lord God!' he shouted, 'pour down Thy blessing on this

Thy son Mordred, on this blessed King, this light of Britain, this monarch who will lead Thy kingdom of Dumnonia into its new and blessed age.' I confess I paraphrase the prayer, for in truth I hardly took much notice as Sansum harangued his God. He was good at such harangues, but they were all much alike; always too long, always full of praise for Christianity and always replete with mockery of paganism, so instead of listening I watched the crowd to see who among it spread their arms and closed their eyes. Most did. Arthur, ever ready to show respect to any religion, just stood with head bowed. He held his son's hand while, on Gwydre's other side, Guinevere gazed into the sky with a secret smile on her handsome face. Amhar and Loholt, Arthur's sons by Ailleann, prayed with the Christians, while Dinas and Lavaine just stood, arms folded across their white robes, and stared at Ceinwyn who, just as on that day when she had run from her betrothal, wore neither gold nor silver. Her hair still shone so fine and pale, and she remained for me the loveliest creature that ever walked this earth. Her brother, King Cuneglas, stood on her other side, and catching my eye during one of Sansum's higher flights of fancy he offered me a wry smile. Mordred, his arms spread in prayer, watched us all with a crooked smile.

When the prayer was done Bishop Sansum took the King's arm and led him to Arthur who, as the guardian of the kingdom, would now present the new ruler to his people. Arthur smiled at Mordred, as though to give him courage, then led him round the outside of the stone circle and, as Mordred passed, those who were not kings dropped to their knees. I, as his champion, walked behind him with a drawn sword. We walked against the sun, the only time a circle was ever walked thus, to show that our new King was descended from Beli Mawr and could thus defy the natural order of all living things, though Bishop Sansum, of course, declared that the walk against the sun proved the death of pagan superstition. Culhwch, I saw, managed to hide himself during the circle walk so that he would not have to kneel.

When two full circles of the stones had been completed Arthur led Mordred to the royal stone and handed him up so that the King stood there alone. Dian, my youngest daughter, then toddled forward with cornflowers woven into her hair and laid a loaf of bread at Mordred's mismatched feet to symbolize his duty to feed his people. The women murmured at the sight of her, for Dian, like her sisters, had inherited her mother's careless beauty. She put the loaf down, then looked about her for a sign of what she was supposed to do next and, receiving none, she looked solemnly up into Mordred's face and immediately burst into tears. The women sighed happily as the child fled crying to her mother and as Ceinwyn scooped her up and dried her tears. Gwydre, Arthur's son, next carried a leather scourge that he laid at the King's feet as a symbol of Mordred's duty to offer the land justice, and then I carried the new royal sword, forged in Gwent and with a hilt of black leather wrapped with golden wire, and gave the sword into Mordred's right hand. 'Lord King,' I said, looking into his eyes, 'this is for your duty to protect your people.' Mordred's smirk had vanished and he stared at me with a cold dignity that made me hope Arthur was right and that the solemnity of this ritual would indeed give Mordred the power to be a good King.

Then, one by one, we presented our gifts. I gave him a fine helmet, trimmed with gold and with a red enamel dragon burned onto its skullpiece. Arthur gave him a scale coat, a spear, and a box of ivory filled with gold coins. Cuneglas offered him ingots of gold from the mines of Powys. Lancelot presented him with a massive cross of gold and a small, gold-framed electrum mirror. Oengus Mac Airem laid two thick bear pelts at his feet, while Sagramor placed a golden Saxon image of a bull's head on the pile. Sansum presented the King with a piece of the cross on which, he loudly proclaimed, Christ had been crucified. The scrap of dark timber was encased in a Roman glass flask that had been sealed with gold. Only Culhwch presented nothing. Indeed, when the gifts were given and the Lords made a line to kneel before the King and swear their oaths of loyalty, Culhwch was nowhere to be seen. I was the second man to give the oath, following Arthur to the royal stone where I knelt opposite the great heap of shining gold and put my lips to the tip of Mordred's new sword and swore on my life that I would serve him faithfully. It was a solemn moment, for that was the royal oath, the oath that ruled all others.

There was one new thing at that acclamation, a ritual Arthur had devised as a means of continuing the peace he had so carefully constructed and maintained throughout the years. The new ceremony was an extension of his Brotherhood of Britain, for he had persuaded the Kings of Britain – at least those present – to exchange kisses with Mordred and swear oaths never to fight against each other. Mordred, Meurig, Cuneglas, Byrthig, Oengus and Lancelot all embraced each other, touched their sword blades together and took the oath to keep each other's peace. Arthur beamed and Oengus Mac Airem, a rogue if ever there was one, gave me a broad wink. Come harvest time, I knew, his spearmen would be raiding Powys's granaries, whatever oaths he might have sworn.

When the royal oath had been made, I performed the final act of the acclamation. First I gave Mordred my gloved hand and helped him down from the stone and then, when I had conducted him to the northernmost stone of the outer circle, I took his royal sword and laid its bare blade flat on the royal stone. It lay there, glittering, a sword on a stone, the true sign of a King, and then I did the duty of the King's champion by striding about the circle and spitting at the onlookers and challenging all who listened to dare deny the right of Mordred ap Mordred ap Uther to be the King of this land. I winked at my daughters as I passed, made certain my spittle landed on Sansum's shining robes, and made equally sure it did not land on Guinevere's embroidered dress. 'I declare Mordred ap Mordred ap Uther to be the King!' I shouted again and again, 'and if any man denies it, let him fight me now.' I walked slowly with Hywelbane naked in my hand, and shouted my challenge loud. 'I declare Mordred ap Mordred ap Uther to be the King, and if any man denies it, let him fight me now.'

I had almost completed the circle when I heard the blade rasp from its scabbard. 'I deny it!' A voice shouted and the shout was followed by gasps of horror from the crowd. Ceinwyn blanched, and my daughters, who were already frightened to see me dressed in my unfamiliar iron and steel and leather and wolf-hair, hid their faces in her linen skirt.

I turned slowly and saw that Culhwch had come back to the circle and now faced me with his big battle sword drawn. 'No,' I called to him, 'please.'

Culhwch, grim-faced, strode to the circle's centre and plucked the King's gold-hilted sword from the stone. 'I deny Mordred ap Mordred ap Uther,' Culhwch said ceremoniously, then threw the royal blade down onto the grass.

'Kill him,' Mordred shouted from his place beside Arthur. 'Do your duty, Lord Derfel!'

'I deny his fitness to rule!' Culhwch shouted at the assembly. A wind lifted the banners on the walls and stirred Ceinwyn's golden hair.

'I order you to kill him!' Mordred shouted excitedly.

I walked into the circle to face Culhwch. My duty now was to fight him, and if he killed me then another King's champion would be selected and so the stupid business would go on until Culhwch, battered and bloody, lay twitching his life blood into Caer Cadarn's soil, or, more likely, till a full-scale battle erupted on the summit that would end with either Culhwch's or Mordred's party triumphant. I pulled the helmet off my head, shook the hair out of my eyes and hung the helmet over the throat of my scabbard. Then, with Hywelbane still in my hand, I embraced Culhwch. 'Don't do this,' I whispered in his ear. 'I can't kill you, my friend, so you will just have to kill me.'

'He's a bastard little toad, a worm, not a King,' he murmured.

'Please,' I said. 'I cannot kill you. You know that.'

He hugged me tight. 'Make peace with Arthur, my friend,' he

whispered, then he stepped away and rammed his sword back into its scabbard. He picked Mordred's sword out of the grass, gave the King a sour look, then laid the blade back on the stone. 'I yield the fight,' he called so that all on the summit could hear him, then he crossed to Cuneglas and knelt at his feet. 'Will you have my oath, Lord King?'

It was an embarrassing moment, for if the King of Powys accepted Culhwch's loyalty then Powys's first act of this new Dumnonian reign was to welcome an enemy of Mordred's, but Cuneglas did not hesitate. He pushed his sword hilt forward for Culhwch's kiss. 'Gladly, Lord Culhwch,' he said, 'gladly.'

Culhwch kissed Cuneglas's sword, then rose and walked to the west gate. His spearmen followed him and thus, with Culhwch's going, Mordred at last had the kingdom's power unchallenged. There was silence, then Sansum began to cheer and the Christians followed his lead and so acclaimed their new ruler. Men gathered about the King, calling their congratulations, and I saw that Arthur was left to one side, alone. He looked at me and smiled, but I turned away. I sheathed Hywelbane, then crouched by my still frightened daughters and told them there was nothing to be worried about. I gave Morwenna my helmet to hold, and showed her how the cheek pieces swung back and forward on their hinges. 'Don't break it!' I warned her.

'Poor wolf,' Seren said, stroking the wolf-tail.

'It killed a lot of lambs.'

'Is that why you killed the wolf?'

'Of course.'

'Lord Derfel!' Mordred's voice suddenly called, and I straightened and turned round to see that the King had shaken off his admirers and was limping across the royal circle towards me.

I walked to meet him, then bowed my head. 'Lord King.'

The Christians gathered behind Mordred. They were the masters now, and their victory was plain on their faces. 'You swore an oath, Lord Derfel,' Mordred said, 'to obey me.'

'I did, Lord King.'

'But Culhwch still lives,' he said in a puzzled voice. 'Does he not still live?'

'He lives, Lord King,' I said.

Mordred smiled. 'A broken oath, Lord Derfel, deserves punishment. Isn't that what you always taught me?'

'Yes, Lord King.'

'And the oath, Lord Derfel, was sworn on your life, was it not?'

'Yes, Lord King.'

He scratched at his thin beard. 'But your daughters are pretty, Derfel, so I would be sorry to lose you from Dumnonia. I forgive you that Culhwch still lives.'

'Thank you, Lord King,' I said, fighting back a temptation to hit him.

'But a broken oath still deserves punishment,' he said excitedly.

'Yes, Lord King,' I agreed. 'It does.'

He paused a heartbeat, then struck me hard across the face with the leather flail of justice. He laughed, and was so delighted with the surprised reaction on my face that he hit me with the flail a second time. 'Punishment given, Lord Derfel,' he said, then turned away. His supporters laughed and applauded.

We did not stay for the feast, nor for the wrestling matches and the mock bouts of swordplay and the displays of juggling, nor for the tame dancing bear and the competition of the bards. We walked, a family, back to Lindinis. We walked beside the stream where the willows grew and the purple loosestrife flowered. We walked home.

Cuneglas followed us within the hour. He planned to stay with us for one week, then he would go back to Powys. 'Come back with me,' he said.

'I'm sworn to Mordred, Lord King.'

'Oh, Derfel, Derfel!' He put his arm around my neck and walked up the outer courtyard with me. 'My dear Derfel, you're as bad as Arthur! You think Mordred cares if you keep your oath?'

'I hope he doesn't want me as an enemy.'

'Who knows what he wants?' Cuneglas asked. 'Girls, probably, and fast horses and running deer and strong mead. Come home, Derfel! Culhwch will be there.'

'I shall miss him, Lord,' I said. I had hoped that Culhwch would be waiting at Lindinis when we returned from Caer Cadarn, but he had plainly not dared waste a moment and was already racing north to escape the spearmen who would be sent to find him before he crossed the frontier.

Cuneglas abandoned his attempt to persuade me north. 'What was that rogue Oengus doing there?' he asked me peevishly. 'And making that promise to keep the peace too!'

'He knows, Lord King,' I said, 'that if he loses Arthur's friendship then your spears will invade his land.'

'He's right,' Cuneglas said grimly. 'Maybe I'll give that job to Culhwch. Will Arthur have any power now?'

'That depends on Mordred.'

'Let's assume Mordred isn't a complete fool. I can't comprehend Dumnonia without Arthur.' He turned as a shout from the gate announced more visitors. I half expected to see dragon shields and a party of Mordred's men searching for Culhwch, but instead it was Arthur and Oengus Mac Airem who had arrived with a score of spearmen. Arthur hesitated at the gate's threshold. 'Am I welcome?' he called to me.

'Of course, Lord,' I replied, though not warmly.

My daughters spied him from a window and a moment later they ran shrieking to welcome him. Cuneglas joined them, pointedly ignoring King Oengus Mac Airem who crossed to my side. I bowed, but Oengus pushed me upright and enfolded me in his arms. His fur collar stank of sweat and old grease. He grinned at me. 'Arthur tells me you haven't fought a decent war in ten years,' he said.

'It must be that long, Lord.'

'You'll be out of practice, Derfel. First proper fight and some slip of a boy will rip your belly out to feed his hounds. How are you?'

'Older than I was, Lord. But well. And you?'

'I'm still alive,' he said, then glanced back at Cuneglas. 'I assume the King of Powys doesn't want to greet me?'

'He feels, Lord King, that your spearmen are too busy on his frontier.'

Oengus laughed. 'Have to keep them busy, Derfel, you know that. Idle spearmen are trouble. And besides, I've got too many of the bastards these days. Ireland's going Christian!' he spat. 'Some interfering Briton called Padraig turned them into milk-sops. You never dared conquer us with your spears so you sent that piece of seal shit to weaken us, and any Irishman with proper guts is coming to the Irish kingdoms in Britain to escape his Christians. He preached to them with a clover leaf! Can you imagine that? Conquering Ireland with a clover leaf? No wonder all the decent warriors are coming to me, but what can I do with them?'

'Send them to kill Padraig?' I suggested.

'He's dead already, Derfel, but his followers are all too much alive.' Oengus had drawn me into a corner of the courtyard where he stopped and looked up into my face. 'I hear you tried to protect my daughter.'

'I did, Lord,' I said. I saw that Ceinwyn had come from the palace and was embracing Arthur. They held each other as they talked and as Ceinwyn glanced reprovingly towards me. I turned back to Oengus. 'I drew a sword for her, Lord King.'

'Good of you, Derfel,' he said carelessly, 'good of you, but it isn't important. I've several daughters. Not even sure I can remember which one Iseult was. Skinny little thing, yes?'

'A beautiful girl, Lord King.'

He laughed. 'Anything young with tits is beautiful when you're old. I do have one beauty in the brood. Argante, she's called, and she'll break a few hearts before her life's done. Your new King will be looking for a bride, won't he?'

'I suppose so.'

'Argante would do for him,' Oengus said. He was not being kind to Mordred by suggesting his beautiful daughter as Dumnonia's Queen, but rather making sure that Dumnonia would go on protecting Demetia from the men of Powys. 'Maybe I'll bring Argante on a visit here,' he said. Then he abandoned the subject of that possible marriage and shoved a scarred fist hard into my chest. 'Listen, my friend,' he said forcefully, 'it isn't worth falling out with Arthur over Iseult.'

'Is that why he brought you here, Lord?' I asked suspiciously.

'Of course it is, you fool!' Oengus said happily. 'And because I can't stand all those Christians on the Caer. Make your peace, Derfel. Britain isn't so big that decent men can start spitting at each other. I hear Merlin lives here?'

'You'll find him through there,' I said, pointing towards an arch that led to a garden where Ceinwyn's roses blossomed, 'what's left of him.'

'I'll go and kick some life into the bastard. Maybe he can tell me what's so special about a clover leaf. And I need a charm to help me make new daughters.' He laughed and walked away. 'Getting old, Derfel, getting old!'

Arthur gave my three daughters into the keeping of Ceinwyn and their Uncle Cuneglas, then walked towards me. I hesitated, then gestured through the outer gate and walked ahead of him into the meadows where I waited and stared at Caer Cadarn's banner-hung ramparts above the intervening trees.

He stopped behind me. 'It was at Mordred's first acclamation,' he said softly, 'that you and I first met Tristan. Do you remember?'

I did not turn round. 'Yes, Lord.'

'I am no longer your lord, Derfel,' he said. 'Our oath to Uther is done, it's finished. I am not your lord, but I would be your friend.' He hesitated. 'And for what happened,' he went on, 'I am sorry.'

I still did not turn round. Not out of pride, but because there were tears in my eyes. 'I am sorry too,' I said.

'Will you forgive me?' he asked humbly. 'Will we be friends?'

I stared at the Caer and thought of all the things I had done that needed forgiveness. I thought of the bodies on the moor. I had been a young spearman then, but youth was no excuse for slaughter. It was not up to me, I thought, to forgive Arthur for what he had done. He had to do that for himself. 'We shall be friends,' I said, 'till death.' And then I turned.

And we embraced. Our oath to Uther was done. And Mordred was King.

PART FOUR

The Mysteries of Isis

'WAS ISEULT BEAUTIFUL?' Igraine asks me.

     I thought about the question for a few heartbeats. 'She was young,' I said at last, 'and as her father said . . .'

'I read what her father said,' Igraine interrupted me curtly. When she comes to Dinnewrac Igraine always sits and reads through the finished skins before sitting on the window-sill and talking to me. Today that window is hung with a leather curtain to try and keep the cold out of the room, which is badly lit with rush lights on my writing-desk and filled with smoke because the wind is in the north and the smoke from the fire cannot find its way out of the roof-hole.

'It was a long time ago,' I said wearily, 'and I only saw her for a day and two nights. I remember her as beautiful, but I suppose we always make the dead beautiful if they are young.'

'The songs all say she was beautiful,' Igraine said wistfully.

'I paid the bards for those songs,' I said. Just as I had paid men to carry Tristan's ashes back to Kernow. It was right, I had thought, that Tristan should go to his own land in death, and I had mixed his bones and Iseult's bones, and his ashes and her ashes, and no doubt a fair amount of ordinary wood ash too, and sealed them all in a jar we found in the hall where they had shared their impossible dream of love. I had been wealthy then, a great lord, master of slaves and servants and spearmen, wealthy enough to buy a dozen songs about Tristan and Iseult that are sung to this day in all the feasting halls. I made sure, too, that the songs put the blame for their deaths on Arthur.

'But why did Arthur do it?' Igraine said.

I rubbed my face with my one hand. 'Arthur worshipped

order,' I explained. 'I don't think he ever really believed in the Gods. Oh, he believed they existed, he was no fool, but he didn't think they cared about us any more. I remember he once laughed and said it was so arrogant of us to think that the Gods had nothing better to do than to worry about us. Do we lose sleep over the mice in the thatch? he asked me. So why would the Gods care about us? So all that was left to him, if you took away the Gods, was order, and the only thing that kept order was the law, and the only thing that made the powerful obey the law was their oaths. It was really quite simple.' I shrugged. 'He was right, of course; he almost always was.'

'He should have let them live,' Igraine insisted.

'He obeyed the law,' I said bleakly. I have often regretted allowing the bards to blame Arthur, but he forgave me.

'And Iseult was burned alive?' Igraine shuddered. 'And Arthur just let it happen?'

'He could be very hard,' I said, 'and he had to be, for the rest of us, God knows, could be soft.'

'He should have spared them,' Igraine insisted.

'And there would have been no songs or stories if he had,' I answered. 'They would have grown old and fat and squabbled and died. Or else Tristan would have gone home to Kernow when his father died and taken other wives. Who knows?'

'How long did Mark live?' Igraine asked me.

'Just another year,' I said. 'He died of the strangury.'

'The what?'

I smiled. 'A foul disease, Lady. Women, I think, are not subject to it. A nephew became King then, and I can't even remember his name.'

Igraine grimaced. 'But you can remember Iseult running from the sea,' she said accusingly, 'because her dress was wet.'

I smiled. 'Like it was yesterday, Lady.'

'The Sea of Galilee,' Igraine said brightly, for St Tudwal had suddenly come into our room. Tudwal is now ten or eleven years old, a thin boy with black hair and a face that reminds me of Cerdic. A rat face. He shares both Sansum's cell and his authority. How lucky we are to have two saints in our small community.

'The saint wishes you to decipher these parchments,' Tudwal demanded, putting them on my table. He ignored Igraine. Saints, it seems, can be rude to queens.

'What are they?' I asked him.

'A merchant wants to sell them to us,' Tudwal said. 'He claims they're psalms, but the saint's eyes are too dim to read them.'

'Of course,' I said. The truth, of course, is that Sansum cannot read at all and Tudwal is much too lazy to learn, though we have all tried to teach him and we all now pretend that he can. I carefully uncurled the parchment that was old, cracking and feeble. The language was Latin, a tongue I can barely understand, but I did see the word *Christus*. 'They aren't psalms,' I said, 'but they are Christian. I suspect they're gospel fragments.'

'The merchant wants four pieces of gold.'

'Two pieces,' I said, though I did not really care whether we bought them or not. I let the parchments curl up. 'Did the man say where he got them?' I asked.

Tudwal shrugged. 'The Saxons.'

'We should certainly preserve them,' I said dutifully, handing them back. 'They should be in the treasure store.' Where, I thought, Hywelbane rested with all the other small treasures I had brought from my old life. All but for Ceinwyn's little golden brooch that I keep hidden from the older saint. I humbly thanked the younger saint for consulting me, and bowed my head as he left.

'Spotty little toad,' Igraine said when Tudwal had gone. She spat towards the fire. 'Are you a Christian, Derfel?'

'Of course I am, Lady!' I protested. 'What a question!'

She frowned quizzically at me. 'I ask it,' she said, 'because it seems to me that you are less of a Christian today than you were when you began writing this tale.'

That, I thought, was a clever observation. And a true one too, but I dared not confess it openly for Sansum would love to have an excuse to accuse me of heresy and burn me to death. He

337

wouldn't stint on that firewood, I thought, even if he did ration what we could burn in our hearths. I smiled. 'You make me remember the old things, Lady,' I said, 'that is all.' It was not all. The more I recall of the old years the more some of those old things come back to me. I touched an iron nail in my wooden writing-desk to avert the evil of Sansum's hatred. 'I long ago abandoned paganism,' I said.

'I wish I was a pagan,' Igraine said wistfully, drawing the beaver-pelt cloak tight about her shoulders. Her eyes are still bright and her face is so full of life that I am sure that she must be pregnant. 'Don't tell the saints I said that,' she added swiftly. 'And Mordred,' she asked, 'was he a Christian?'

'No. But he knew that was where his support in Dumnonia was, so he did enough to keep them happy. He let Sansum build his great church.'

'Where?'

'On Caer Cadarn.' I smiled, remembering it. 'It was never finished, but it was supposed to be a great big church in the form of a cross. He claimed the church would welcome the second coming of Christ in the year 500, and he pulled down most of the feasting hall and used its timbers to build the wall and the stone circle to make the church's foundations. He left the royal stone, of course. Then he took half the lands that belonged to Lindinis's palace and used their wealth to pay for the monks on Caer Cadarn.'

'Your land?'

I shook my head. 'It was never my land, always Mordred's. And, of course, Mordred wanted us evicted from Lindinis.'

'So he could live in the palace?'

'So Sansum could. Mordred moved into Uther's Winter Palace. He liked it there.'

'So where did you go?'

'We found a home,' I said. It was Ermid's old hall, south of Issa's Mere. The mere was not named for my Issa, of course, but for an old chieftain and Ermid had been another chief who had lived on its southern bank. When he died I had bought his lands, and after Sansum and Morgan took over Lindinis I moved there. The girls missed Lindinis's open corridors and echoing rooms, but I liked Ermid's Hall. It was old, thatched, shadowed by trees and full of spiders that made Morwenna scream and, for my oldest daughter's sake, I became Lord Derfel Cadarn, the slayer of spiders.

'Would you have killed Culhwch?' Igraine asks me.

'Of course not!'

'I hate Mordred,' she said.

'You are not alone in that, Lady.'

She stared at the fire for a few moments. 'Did he really have to become King?'

'So long as it was in Arthur's hands, yes. If it had been me? No, I would have killed him with Hywelbane, even if it did mean breaking my oath. He was a sad boy.'

'It all seems so sad,' Igraine said.

'There was plenty of happiness in those years,' I answered, 'and even afterwards, sometimes. We were happy enough back then.' I still remember the girls' shouts echoing in Lindinis, the rush of feet and their excitement at some new game or some strange discovery. Ceinwyn was always happy – she had a gift for it – and those around her caught the happiness and passed it on. And Dumnonia, I suppose, was happy. It prospered, certainly, and the hard workers made themselves wealthy. The Christians seethed with discontent, but even so those were the glory years, the time of peace, the time of Arthur.

Igraine shuffled the new sheets of parchment to find one particular passage. 'About the Round Table,' she began.

'Please,' I said, holding up my one hand to still what I knew would be a protest.

'Derfel!' she said sternly. 'Everyone knows that it was a serious thing! An important thing! All the best warriors of Britain, all sworn to Arthur, and all of them friends. Everyone knows it!'

'It was a cracked stone table that by the day's end was cracked even more and smeared with vomit. They all got very drunk.'

She sighed. 'I expect you've just forgotten the truth,' she said, dismissing the subject much too easily, which makes me think that Dafydd, the clerk who translates my words into the British tongue, will come up with something altogether more to Igraine's liking. I even heard one tale not so long ago which claimed that the table was a vast wooden circle around which the whole Brotherhood of Britain sat and looked solemn, but there never was such a table, nor could there have been unless we had cut down half the woods of Dumnonia to build it.

'The Brotherhood of Britain,' I said patiently, 'was an idea of Arthur's that never really worked. It couldn't! Men's royal oaths took preference over the Round Table oath, and besides, no one except Arthur and Galahad ever really believed in it. By the end, believe me, even he was embarrassed if anyone even mentioned it.'

'I'm sure you're right,' she said, meaning that she was utterly sure I was wrong. 'And I want to know,' she went on, 'what happened to Merlin.'

'I will tell you. I promise.'

'Now!' she insisted. 'Tell me now. Did he just fade away?'

'No,' I said. 'His time did come. Nimue was right, you see. At Lindinis he was just waiting. He always liked to pretend, remember, and in those years he pretended to be an old, dying man, but underneath, where none of us saw it, the power was always there. But he was old, and he did have to hoard his power. He was waiting, you see, for the time when the Cauldron would be unveiled. He knew he would need his power then, but till it was needed he was happy to let Nimue guard the flame.'

'So what happened?' Igraine demanded excitedly.

I wrapped the sleeve of my cowl about the stump of my wrist. 'If God lets me live, my Lady, I will tell you,' I said, and I would not tell her more then. I was close to tears, remembering that last savage instance of Merlin's power in Britain, but that moment lies a long, long way ahead in this story, long past the time when Nimue's prophecy about the Kings coming to Cadarn came true.

'If you won't tell me,' Igraine said, 'then I won't tell you my news.'

'You're pregnant,' I said, 'and I am so very happy for you.'

'You beast, Derfel,' she protested. 'I wanted to surprise you!'

'You have prayed for this, Lady, and I have prayed for you, and how could God not answer our prayers?'

She grimaced. 'God sent Nwylle the pox, that's what God did. She was all spots and sores and weeping pus, so the King sent her away.'

'I'm very glad.'

She touched her belly. 'I just hope he lives to rule, Derfel.'

'He?' I asked.

'He,' she said firmly.

'Then I will pray for that too,' I said piously, though whether I will pray to Sansum's God or to the wilder Gods of Britain I do not know. So many prayers have been said in my lifetime, so very many, and where did they bring me? To this damp refuge in the hills while our old enemies sing in our ancient halls. But that ending is also far ahead, and Arthur's story is far from done. It is hardly begun in some ways, for now, as he discarded his glory and gave his power to Mordred, the times of testing came, and they were to prove the trials of Arthur, my Lord of oaths, my hard Lord, but my friend till death.

At first, nothing happened. We held our breath, expected the worst, and nothing happened.

We made hay, then cut the flax and laid the fibrous stems in the retting ponds so that our villages stank for weeks. We reaped the fields of rye, barley and wheat, then listened to the slaves singing their songs around the threshing floor or the endlessly turning millstones. The harvest straw was used to repair the thatch so that, for a time, patches of roof-gold shone in the late summer sun. We picked the orchards clean, cut the winter firewood and harvested willow rods for the basket-makers. We ate blackberries and nuts, smoked the bees out of their hives and pressed their honey in sacks that we hung in front of the kitchen fires where we left food for the dead on Samain Eve.

The Saxons stayed in Lloegyr, justice was done in our courts, maids were given in marriage, children were born and children died. The waning year brought mists and frost. The cattle were slaughtered and the stink of the retting ponds gave way to the nauseous smell of the tanning pits. The newly woven linen was bucked in vats filled with wood-ash, rainwater and the urine we had collected all year, the winter taxes were paid, and at the solstice we Mithraists killed a bull at our annual festival that honoured the sun while on the same day the Christians celebrated their God's birth. At Imbolc, the great feast of the cold season, we fed two hundred souls in our hall, made sure three knives were laid on the table for the use of the invisible Gods and offered sacrifices for the new year's crops. New-born lambs were the first sign of that awakening year, then came the time for ploughing and sowing and of new green shoots on old bare trees. It was the first new year of Mordred's rule.

That rule had brought some changes. Mordred demanded to be given his grandfather's Winter Palace, and that surprised no one, but I was surprised when Sansum demanded Lindinis's palace for himself. He made the demand in Council, saying he needed the palace's space for his school and for Morgan's community of holy women, and because he wanted to be close to the church he was building on Caer Cadarn's summit. Mordred waved his assent, and so Ceinwyn and I were summarily evicted, but Ermid's Hall was empty and we moved to its mist-haunted compound beside the mere. Arthur argued against letting Sansum into Lindinis, just as he opposed Sansum's demand that the royal treasury pay for the repair of the damage done to the palace by, Sansum claimed, too many ill-disciplined children, but Mordred overruled Arthur. Those were Mordred's only decisions, for he was usually content to let Arthur manage the kingdom's affairs. Arthur, though he was no longer Mordred's protector, was now the senior councillor and the King rarely came to Council, preferring to hunt. It was not always deer or wolves that he hunted and Arthur and I became accustomed to taking gold to some peasant's hut to recompense the man for his daughter's virginity or his wife's shame. It was not a pleasant duty, but it was a rare and lucky kingdom where it was not necessary.

Dian, our youngest daughter, fell ill that summer. It was a fever that would not go away, or rather it came and went, but with such ferocity that three times we thought she was dead, and three times Merlin's concoctions revived her, though nothing the old man did seemed able to shake the affliction clean away. Dian promised to be the liveliest of our three daughters. Morwenna, the oldest, was a sensible child who loved to mother her younger sisters and was fascinated by the workings of the household; ever curious about the kitchens, or the retting ponds or the linen vats. Seren, the star, was our beauty, a child who had inherited all her mother's delicate looks, but had added to them a wistful and enchanting nature. She spent hours with the bards learning their songs and playing their harps, but Dian, Ceinwyn always said, was my daughter. Dian had no fear. She could shoot with a bow and arrow, loved to ride horses, and even at six years old could handle a coracle as well as any of the mere's fishermen. She was in her sixth year when the fever gripped her, and if it had not been for that fever we would probably all have travelled to Powys together, for it was a month short of the first anniversary of Mordred's acclamation when the King suddenly demanded that Arthur and I travel to Cuneglas's realm.

Mordred made the demand at one of his rare appearances at the royal Council. The suddenness of the demand surprised us, as did the need for the errand he proposed, but the King was determined. There was, of course, an ulterior motive, though neither Arthur nor I saw it at the time and nor did anyone else on the Council except Sansum who had proposed the idea, and it took us all a long time to smoke out the mouse-lord's reasons for the suggestion. Nor was there any obvious reason why we should be suspicious of the King's proposal for it seemed reasonable enough, though neither Arthur nor I understood why we should both be dispatched to Powys.

The matter sprang from an old, old story. Norwenna, Mordred's mother, had been murdered by Gundleus, the King of Siluria, and though Gundleus had received his punishment, the man who had betrayed Norwenna still lived. His name was Ligessac, and he had been the chief of Mordred's guard when the King was just a baby. But Ligessac had taken Gundleus's bribes and opened the gates of Merlin's Tor to the Silurian King's murderous intent. Mordred had been snatched to safety by Morgan, but his mother had died. Ligessac, whose treachery had caused Norwenna's death, had survived the war that followed the murder, just as he had survived the battle at Lugg Vale.

Mordred had heard the tale, of course, and it was only natural that he should take an interest in Ligessac's fate, but it was Bishop Sansum who fanned that interest into an obsession. Sansum somehow discovered that Ligessac had taken refuge with a band of Christian hermits in a remote and mountainous area of northern Siluria that was now under Cuneglas's rule. 'It hurts me to betray a fellow Christian,' the mouse-lord announced sanctimoniously in the Council meeting, 'but it hurts just as much that a Christian should have been guilty of so foul a treachery. Ligessac still lives, Lord King,' he said to Mordred, 'and should be brought to your justice.'

Arthur suggested that Cuneglas be asked to arrest the fugitive and send him back to Dumnonia, but Sansum shook his head at that proposal and said it was surely discourteous to ask another King to initiate a vengeance that touched so closely on Mordred's honour. 'This is Dumnonian business,' Sansum insisted, 'and Dumnonians, Lord King, should be the agents of its success.'

Mordred nodded agreement and then insisted that both Arthur and I go to capture the traitor. Arthur, surprised as always when Mordred asserted himself at Council, demurred.

Why, he wanted to know, should two lords go on an errand that could be safely left to a dozen spearmen? Mordred smirked at that question. 'You think, Lord Arthur, that Dumnonia will fall if you and Derfel are absent?'

'No, Lord King,' Arthur said, 'but Ligessac must be an old man now and it won't need two war-bands to capture him.'

The King thumped the table with his fist. 'After my mother's murder,' he accused Arthur, 'you let Ligessac escape. At Lugg Vale, Lord Arthur, you again let Ligessac escape. You owe me Ligessac's life.'

Arthur stiffened momentarily at this accusation, but then inclined his head to acknowledge the obligation. 'But Derfel,' he pointed out, 'was not responsible.'

Mordred glanced at me. He still disliked me for all the beatings he had taken as a child, but I hoped that the blows he had given me at his acclamation and his petty triumph in evicting us from Lindinis had slaked his thirst for revenge. 'Lord Derfel,' he said, as ever making the title sound mocking, 'knows the traitor. Who else would recognize him? I insist you both go. And you don't need to take two whole war-bands either,' he reverted to Arthur's earlier objection. 'Just a few men will do.' He must have been embarrassed at giving Arthur such military advice for his voice tailed weakly away and he looked shiftily at the other councillors before recovering what little poise he did possess. 'I want Ligessac here before Samain,' he insisted, 'and I want him here alive.'

When a King insists, men obey, so Arthur and I both rode north with thirty men apiece. Neither of us believed we would need so many, but it was an opportunity to give some under-employed men the exercise of a long march. My remaining thirty spearmen stayed behind to guard Ceinwyn, while Arthur's other men either stayed in Durnovaria or else went to reinforce Sagramor who still guarded the northern Saxon frontier. The usual Saxon war-bands were active on that frontier, not trying to invade us, but rather attempting to snatch cattle and slaves as they had through all the years of peace. We made similar raids, but both sides were careful not to let the raids turn into full-scale war. The makeshift peace we had forged at London had lasted remarkably well, though there had been little peace between Aelle and Cerdic. Those two had fought each other to a standstill and their squabbles had largely left us unmolested. We had, indeed, grown accustomed to peace.

My men walked north while Arthur's rode, or at least led their horses, on the good Roman roads that took us first to Meurig's kingdom of Gwent. The King gave us a grudging feast at which our men were outnumbered by priests, and after that we made a detour to the Wye Valley to see old Tewdric, whom we found living in a humble thatched hut that was half the size of the building where he kept his collection of Christian parchments. His wife, Queen Enid, grumbled at the fate that had driven her from Gwent's palaces to this mice-ridden life in the woods, but the old King was happy. He had taken Christian orders and blithely ignored Enid's scoldings. He gave us a meal of beans, bread and water and rejoiced at the news of Christianity's spread in Dumnonia. We asked him about the prophecies which foretold the return of Christ in four years' time and Tewdric said he prayed they were true, but suspected it was much more likely that Christ would wait a full thousand years before returning in glory. 'But who knows?' he asked. 'It's possible He will come in four years' time. What a glorious thought!'

'I just wish your fellow Christians would be content to wait in peace,' Arthur said.

'They have a duty to prepare the earth for His coming,' Tewdric said sternly. 'They must make converts, Lord Arthur, and cleanse the land of sin.'

'They'll make a war between themselves and the rest of us if they aren't careful,' Arthur grumbled. He told Tewdric how there had been riots in every Dumnonian town as Christians tried to pull down or defile pagan temples. The things we had seen in Isca had just been the beginnings of those troubles and the unrest was spreading fast, and one of the symptoms of that burgeoning trouble was the sign of the fish, a simple scrawl of two curving lines, that the Christians painted on pagan walls or carved into the trees of Druidic groves. Culhwch had been right: the fish was a Christian symbol.

'It's because the Greek word for fish is *ichthus*,' Tewdric told us, 'and the Greek letters spell Christ's name. *Iesous Christos, Theou Uios, Soter*. Jesus Christ, Son of God, Saviour. Very neat, very neat indeed.' He chuckled with pleasure at his explanation, and it was easy to see from where Meurig had inherited his annoying pedantry. 'Of course,' Tewdric went on, 'if I were still a ruler then I'd be concerned by all this turmoil, but as a Christian I must welcome it. The holy fathers tell us there will be many signs and portents of the last days, Lord Arthur, and civil disturbances are merely one of those signs. So maybe the end is near?'

Arthur crumbled a piece of bread into his dish. 'You truly welcome these riots?' he asked. 'You approve of attacks on pagans? Of shrines burned and defaced?'

Tewdric stared out of the open door at the green woods that pressed hard about his small monastery. 'I suppose they must be hard for others to understand,' he said, evading a direct answer to Arthur's question. 'You must see the riots as symptoms of excitement, Lord Arthur, not signs of our Lord's grace.' He made the sign of the cross and smiled at us. 'Our faith,' he said earnestly, 'is a faith of love. The Son of God humbled Himself to save us from our sins, and we are enjoined to imitate Him in all we do or think. We are encouraged to love our enemies and to do good to those who hate us, but those are hard commandments, too hard for most folk. And you must remember what it is that we pray for most fervently, and that is for the return to this earth of our Lord Jesus Christ.' He made the sign of the cross again. 'Folk pray and long for His second coming, and they fear that if the world is still ruled by pagans then He might not come and so they feel impelled to destroy heathenism.'

'Destroying paganism,' Arthur observed tartly, 'hardly seems proper to a religion that preaches love.'

'Destroying paganism is an act full of love,' Tewdric insisted. 'If you pagans refuse to accept Christ then you will surely go to hell. It will not matter that you have lived a virtuous life, for you will still burn for all eternity. We Christians have a duty to save you from that fate, and is that duty not an act of love?'

'Not if I don't want to be saved,' Arthur said.

'Then you must endure the enmity of those that love you,' Tewdric said, 'or at least you must endure it until the excitement dies down. And it will. These enthusiasms never last long, and if our Lord Jesus Christ does not return in four years then the excitement will surely wane until the millennium comes.' He stared again at the deep woods. 'How glorious it would be,' he said in a voice full of wonder, 'if I could live to see my Saviour's face in Britain.' He turned back to Arthur. 'And the portents of His return will be disturbing, I fear. Doubtless the Saxons will be a nuisance. Are they much trouble these days?'

'No,' Arthur said, 'but their numbers grow every year. I fear they won't be quiet for much longer.'

'I shall pray that Christ returns before they do,' Tewdric said. 'I don't think I could bear to lose land to the Saxons. Not that it's my business any longer, of course,' he added hastily, 'I leave all those things to Meurig now.' He stood as a horn sounded from the nearby chapel. 'Time for prayers!' he said happily. 'You'll join me, perhaps?'

We excused ourselves, and next morning climbed the hills away from the old King's monastery and crossed into Powys. Two nights later we were in Caer Sws where we were reunited with Culhwch who was prospering in his new kingdom. That night we all drank too much mead and next morning, when Cuneglas and I rode to Cwm Isaf, my head was sore. I found the King had kept our little house intact. 'I never know when you might need it again, Derfel,' he told me.

'Maybe soon,' I admitted glumly.

'Soon? I do hope so.'

I shrugged. 'We are not truly welcome in Dumnonia. Mordred resents me.'

'Then ask to be released from your oath.'

'I did ask,' I said, 'and he refused me.' I had asked him after the acclamation, when the shame of the two blows was still keen in me, and then I had asked him again six months later and still he had refused me. I think he was clever enough to know that the best way to punish me was to force me to serve him.

'Is it your spearmen he wants?' Cuneglas asked, sitting on the bench under the apple tree by the house door.

'Just my grovelling loyalty,' I said bitterly. 'He doesn't seem to want to fight any wars.'

'So he's not a complete fool,' Cuneglas said drily. Then we spoke of Ceinwyn and the girls and Cuneglas offered to send Malaine, his new chief Druid, to Dian's side. 'Malaine has a remarkable skill with herbs,' he said. 'Better than old Iorweth. Did you know he died?'

'I heard. And if you can spare Malaine, Lord King, I would be glad.'

'He'll leave tomorrow. I can't have my nieces sick. Doesn't your Nimue help?'

'No more and no less than Merlin,' I said, touching the tip of an old sickle blade that was embedded in the apple tree's bark. The touch of iron was to ward off the evil that threatened Dian. 'The old Gods,' I said bitterly, 'have abandoned Dumnonia.'

Cuneglas smiled. 'It never does, Derfel, to underestimate the Gods. They'll have their day in Dumnonia again.' He paused. 'The Christians like to call themselves sheep, don't they? Well, just you listen to them bleat when the wolves come.'

'What wolves?'

'The Saxons,' he said unhappily. 'They've given us ten years of peace, but their boats still land on the eastern shores and I can feel their power growing. If they start fighting us again then your Christians will be glad enough of pagan swords.' He stood and laid a hand on my shoulder. 'The Saxons are unfinished business, Derfel, unfinished business.'

That night he gave us a feast and next morning, with a guide given us by Cuneglas, we travelled south into the bleak hills that lay across the old frontier of Siluria.

We were going to a remote Christian community. Christians were still few in Powys, for Cuneglas ruthlessly ejected Sansum's missionaries from his kingdom whenever he discovered their presence, but some Christians lived in the kingdom and there were many in the old lands of Siluria. This one group in particular was famous among Britain's Christians for their sanctity, and they displayed that sanctity by living in extreme poverty in a wild, hard place. Ligessac had found his refuge among these Christian fanatics who, as Tewdric had told us, mortified their flesh, by which he meant that they competed with each other to see which could lead the most miserable lives. Some lived in caves, some refused shelter altogether, others ate only green things, some eschewed all clothes, others dressed in hair shirts with brambles woven into the fabric, some wore crowns made of thorns and others beat themselves bloody day after day like the flagellants we had seen in Isca. To me it seemed that the best punishment for Ligessac was to leave him in such a community, but we were ordered to fetch him out and take him home which meant we would have to defy the community's leader, a fierce bishop named Cadoc whose belligerence was famous.

That reputation persuaded us to don our armour as we approached Cadoc's squalid fastness in the high hills. We did not wear our best armour, at least those of us who had a choice did not, for that finery would have been wasted on a half-crazed pack of holy fanatics, but we were all helmeted and wore mail or leather and carried shields. If nothing else, we thought, the war gear might overawe Cadoc's disciples who, our guide assured us, did not number more than twenty souls. 'And all of them are mad,' our guide told us. 'One of them stood dead still for a whole year! Didn't move a muscle, they say. Just stood like a beanpole while they shovelled food into one end of him and dung away from the other. Funny sort of God who asks that of a man.'

350

The road to Cadoc's refuge had been beaten into the earth by pilgrims' feet, and it twisted up the flanks of wide, bare hills where the only living things we saw were sheep and goats. We saw no shepherds, but they undoubtedly saw us. 'If Ligessac has any sense,' Arthur said, 'he'll be long gone. They must have seen us by now.'

'And what will we tell Mordred?'

'The truth, of course,' Arthur said bleakly. His armour was a spearman's plain helmet and a leather breastcoat, yet even such humble things looked neat and clean on him. His vanity was never flamboyant like Lancelot's, but he did pride himself on cleanliness, and somehow this whole expedition into the raw uplands offended his sense of what was clean and proper. The weather did not help, for it was a bleak, raw summer's day, with rain whipping out of the west on a chill wind.

Arthur's spirits might have been low, but our spearmen were cheerful. They made jokes about assaulting the stronghold of mighty King Cadoc and boasted of the gold, warrior rings and slaves they would capture in the assault, and the joke's extravagant claims made them laugh when at last we breasted the final saddle in the hills and could look down into the valley where Ligessac had found his refuge. It was indeed a squalid place; a sea of mud in which a dozen round stone huts surrounded a small square stone church. There were some ragged vegetable gardens, a small dark lake, some stone pens for the community's goats, but no palisade.

The only defence the valley boasted was a great stone cross carved with intricate patterns and an image of the Christian God enthroned in glory. The cross, which was a marvellous piece of stonework, marked the saddle where Cadoc's land began and it was beside the cross, in plain sight of the tiny settlement that lay only a dozen spear throws away, that Arthur halted our war-band. 'We shan't trespass,' he told us mildly, 'till we've had a chance to talk with them.' He rested his spear-butt on the ground beside his horse's front hoofs and waited.

A dozen folk were visible in the compound and on seeing us

they fled to the church, from which, a moment later, a huge man appeared and strode up the road towards us. He was a giant of a man, as tall as Merlin and with a massive chest and big, capable hands. He was also filthy, with an unwashed face and a brown robe caked with mud and dirt, while his grey hair, as dirty as his robe, seemed never to have been cut. His beard grew wild to below his waist, while behind his tonsure his hair sprang in dirty tangles like a great grey freshly sheared fleece. His face was tanned dark and he had a wide mouth, a jutting forehead and angry eyes. It was an impressive face. He carried a staff in his right hand, while at his left hip, unscabbarded, there hung a huge rusty sword. He looked as if he had once been a useful spearman, and I did not doubt that he could still deal a hard blow or two. 'You are not welcome here,' he shouted as he drew nearer to us, 'unless you come to lay your miserable souls before God.'

'Our souls are already laid before our Gods,' Arthur answered pleasantly.

'Heathen!' the big man, whom I assumed had to be the famous Cadoc, spat at us. 'You come in iron and steel to a place where Christ's children play with the Lamb of God?'

'We come in peace,' Arthur insisted.

The bishop spat a great yellow gob of sputum towards Arthur's horse. 'You are Arthur ap Uther ap Satan,' he said, 'and your soul is a rag of filth.'

'And you, I assume, are Bishop Cadoc,' Arthur answered courteously.

The Bishop stood beside the cross and scratched a line in the road with the butt of his staff. 'Only the faithful and the penitent can cross this line,' he declared, 'for this is God's holy ground.'

Arthur gazed for a few heartbeats at the muddy squalor ahead, then smiled gravely at the defiant Cadoc. 'I have no wish to enter your God's ground, Bishop,' he said, 'but I do ask you, in peace, to bring us the man called Ligessac.'

'Ligessac,' Cadoc boomed at us as though he was addressing a congregation of thousands, 'is God's blessed and holy child. He has been given sanctuary here and neither you nor any other so-called lord can invade that sanctuary.'

Arthur smiled. 'A King rules here, Bishop, not your God. Only Cuneglas can offer sanctuary, and he has not.'

'My King, Arthur,' Cadoc said proudly, 'is the King of Kings, and He has commanded me to refuse you entrance.'

'You will resist me?' Arthur asked with polite surprise in his voice.

'To death!' Cadoc shouted.

Arthur shook his head sadly. 'I am no Christian, Bishop,' he said mildly, 'but do you not preach that your Otherworld is a place of utter delights?' Cadoc made no answer and Arthur shrugged. 'So I do you a favour, do I not, by hurrying you to that destination?' He asked the question, then drew Excalibur.

The Bishop used his staff to deepen the line he had scratched across the muddy track. 'I forbid you to cross this line,' he shouted. 'I forbid it in the name of the Father, and of the Son, and of the Holy Ghost!' Then he raised the staff and pointed it at Arthur. He held the staff still for a heartbeat, then swept its tip to encompass the rest of us, and I confess that I felt a chill at that moment. Cadoc was no Merlin, and his God, I thought, had no power like Merlin's Gods, but I still shuddered as that staff pointed my way and my fear made me touch my iron mail and spit onto the road. 'I am going to my prayers now, Arthur,' Cadoc said, 'and you, if you wish to live, will turn and go from this place, for if you pass by this holy cross then I swear to you, by the sweet blood of the Lord Jesus Christ, that your souls will burn in torment. You will know the fire everlasting. You will be cursed from the beginning of time till its ending and from the vaults of heaven to the bottom-most pits of hell.' And with that heavy curse delivered he spat one more time, then turned and walked away.

Arthur used the tail of his cloak to wipe the rain off Excalibur, then scabbarded the sword. 'It seems we're not welcome,' he said with some amusement, then he turned and beckoned to Balin who was the oldest cavalryman present. 'Take the horsemen,' Arthur ordered him, 'and get behind the village. Make sure no one can escape. Once you're in place I'll bring Derfel and his men to search the houses. And listen!' – he raised his voice so that all sixty men could hear him – 'these folk will resist. They'll taunt and fight us, but we have no quarrel with any of them. Only with Ligessac. You will not steal from them and you will not hurt any of them unnecessarily. You will remember that you are soldiers and they are not. You will treat them with respect and return their curses with silence.' He spoke sternly, and then, when he was sure that all our men had understood him, he smiled at Balin and gestured him forward.

The thirty armoured horsemen rode ahead, streaming off the road to gallop around the valley's edge to reach the far slope beyond the village. Cadoc, who was still walking towards his church, glanced at them, but showed no alarm.

'I wonder,' Arthur said, 'how he knew who I was?'

'You're famous, Lord,' I said. I still called him Lord and always would.

'My name is known, perhaps, but not my face. Not here.' He shrugged the mystery off. 'Was Ligessac always a Christian?'

'Since first I knew him. But never a good one.'

He smiled. 'The virtuous life becomes easier when you're older. At least I think it does.' He watched his horsemen gallop past the village, their horses' hoofs kicking up great spouts of water from the soaking grass, then he hefted his spear and looked back at my men. 'Remember now! No theft!' I wondered what there could possibly be to steal in such a drab place, but Arthur knew that all spearmen will usually find something as a keepsake. 'I don't want trouble,' Arthur told them. 'We just look for our man, then leave.' He touched Llamrei's flanks and the black mare started obediently forward. We foot-soldiers followed, our boots obliterating Cadoc's scratched line in the muddy road beside the intricately carved cross. No fire came from heaven.

The Bishop had reached his church now and he stopped at its entrance, turned, saw us coming and ducked inside. 'They knew we were coming,' Arthur said to me, 'so we'll not find Ligessac here. I fear it's a waste of our time, Derfel.' A lame sheep hobbled over the road and Arthur checked his horse to give it passage. I saw him shudder and I knew he was offended by the settlement's dirt that almost rivalled the squalor of Nimue's Tor.

Cadoc reappeared at the church door when we were just a hundred paces away. By now our horsemen were waiting behind the village, but Cadoc did not bother to look to see where they were. He just raised a big ram's horn to his lips and blew a call that echoed hollowly in the bare bowl of hills. He sounded the horn once, paused to take a deep breath, then sounded it again.

And suddenly we had a battle on our hands.

They had known we were coming right enough, and they had been ready for us. Every Christian in Powys and Siluria must have been summoned to Cadoc's defence and those men now appeared on the crests all around the valley while others ran to block the road behind us. Some carried spears, some had shields and some hefted nothing but reaping hooks or hay forks, but they looked confident enough. Many, I knew, would once have been spearmen who served in the war levy, but what gave these Christians real confidence, apart from their faith in their God, was that they numbered at least two hundred men. 'The fools!' Arthur said angrily. He hated unnecessary violence and he knew that some killing was now unavoidable. He knew, too, that we would win, for only fanatics who believed their God would fight for them would take on sixty of Dumnonia's finest warriors. 'Fools!' He spat again, then glanced at the village to see more armed men coming from the huts. 'You stay here, Derfel,' he said. 'Just hold them, and we'll see them off.' He kicked back his spurs and galloped alone about the village's edge towards his horsemen.

'Shield-ring,' I said quietly. We were only thirty men and our double-ranked ring made a circle so small that it must have looked like an easy target to those howling Christians who now ran down the hills or out of the village to annihilate us. The shield-ring is never a popular formation with soldiers because the splay of the spears out of the circle means that their points are spread far apart and the smaller the ring the wider those gaps between the spearheads, but my men were well trained. The front rank knelt, their shields touching and the butts of their long spears jammed into the ground behind them. We in the second rank laid our shields over the first rank's shields, propping them on the ground so that our attackers faced a double thick wall of leather-covered timber. Then each of us stood behind a kneeling man and levelled our spears over their heads. Our job was to protect the front rank and their job was to stay staunch. It would be hard, bloody work, but so long as the kneeling men held their shields high and kept their spears firm, and so long as we protected them, the shield-ring should be safe enough. I reminded the kneeling men of their training, told them they were there just as an obstacle and to leave the killing to the rest of us. 'Bel is with us,' I said.

'So is Arthur,' Issa added enthusiastically.

For it was Arthur who would do the day's real killing. We were the lure and he was the executioner, and Cadoc's men took that lure like a hungry salmon rising to a mayfly. Cadoc himself led the charge from the village, carrying his rusty sword and a big round shield that was painted with a black cross behind which I could just see the ghostly outline of Siluria's fox that betrayed his previous allegiance as a spearman in Gundleus's ranks.

That Christian horde did not come as a shield-wall. That might have brought them victory, but instead they attacked in the old manner that the Romans had beaten out of us. In the old days, when the Romans were new in Britain, the tribes would charge them in one glorious, howling, mead-fuelled rush. Such a charge was fearsome to see, but easy for disciplined men to defeat, and my spearmen were wonderfully disciplined.

They doubtless felt fear. I felt fear, for the howling charge is a terrible thing to see. Against ill-disciplined men it works because of the terror it provokes, and this was the first time I had ever seen that old way of Britain's battles. Cadoc's

Christians rushed fanatically at us, competing to see who could be first onto our spears. They shrieked and hurled curses, and it seemed as though each one of them wanted to be a martyr or else a hero. Their wild rush even included women who screamed as they swung wooden clubs or reaping knives. There were even children among that howling rabble.

'Bel!' I shouted as the first man tried to leap the kneeling men of the front rank and so died on my spear. I spitted him clean as a hare ready to be roasted, then threw him, spear and all, out of the circle so that his dying body would form an obstacle to his comrades. Hywelbane killed the next man and I could hear my spearmen keening their dreadful battle chant as they ripped and lunged and cut and stabbed. We were all so good, so fast, and so thoroughly trained. Hours of dull training had gone into that shield-ring and though it had been years since most of us had fought in a battle, we discovered that our old instincts were as quick as ever, and it was instinct and experience that kept us alive that day. The enemy was a shrieking, milling press of fanatics who crammed themselves about our ring and thrust their spears towards us, but our outer shield-ring stayed firm as a rock and the mound of dead and dying attackers that grew so swiftly in front of our shields hindered the other attackers. For the first minute or two, when the ground about our shield-ring was still free of obstacles and the bravest of the enemy could still get close, it was a frantic fight, but once the ring of dead and dying protected us then only the bravest attackers tried to reach us and we fifteen of the inner rank could then pick our targets and use them for spear or sword practice. We fought fast, we cheered each other and we killed without mercy.

Cadoc himself came early to the fight. He came swinging the huge rusty sword so vigorously that it whistled in the air. He knew his business well enough and he tried to batter down one of the kneeling men, for he knew that once that outer ring was broken then the rest of us would die quickly enough. I parried the great blow on Hywelbane, back-cut him with a quick swing that wasted itself in his filthy thatch of hair, then Eachern, the tough little Irish spearman who still served me despite Mordred's threats, rammed his spear-shaft at the Bishop's face. Eachern's spearhead had vanished, torn off by a sword blow, but he cracked the iron tip of the staff's butt onto Cadoc's forehead. The Bishop looked cross-eyed for a heartbeat, his mouth gaped rotten teeth, then he just sank to the mud.

The last attacker to try and breach the shield-ring was a straggle-haired woman who climbed over the ring of dead and shrieked a curse at me as she tried to jump over the kneeling men of the front rank. I seized her hair, let her reaping knife blunt itself on my mail coat, then dragged her inside the ring where Issa stamped hard on her head. It was just then that Arthur struck.

Thirty horsemen with long spears slashed into the Christian rabble. We, I suppose, had been defending ourselves for all of three minutes, but once Arthur arrived the fight was over in an eyeblink. His horsemen came with couched spears, galloping hard, and I saw a terrible misting spray of blood as one of the spears slammed home, and then our attackers were fleeing in panic and Arthur, his spear discarded and with Excalibur shining in his hand, was shouting at his men to stop the killing. 'Just drive them away!' he shouted. 'Drive them away!' His horsemen split into small groups that scattered the terrified survivors and chased them back up the road towards the guardian cross.

My men relaxed. Issa was still sitting on the straggle-haired woman and Eachern was searching for his lost spearhead. Two men in the shield-ring had taken nasty wounds, and one man of the second rank had a broken and bloodied jaw, but otherwise we were unhurt, while around us were twenty-three corpses and at least as many badly wounded men. Cadoc, groggy from Eachern's blow, still lived and we tied his hands and feet, and then, despite Arthur's instructions to show our enemy respect, we cut off his hair and beard to shame him. He spat and cursed at us, but we stuffed his mouth with cut hanks of his greasy beard, then walked him back to the village.

And it was there I discovered Ligessac. He had not fled after all, but had simply waited beside the little altar in the church. He was an old man now, thin and grey-haired, and he yielded himself meekly, even when we cut off his beard and wove a crude rope from its hair that we leashed around his neck to show that he was a condemned traitor. He even seemed quite pleased to meet me again after all the years. 'I told them they wouldn't beat you,' he said, 'not Derfel Cadarn.'

'They knew we were coming?' I asked him.

'We've known for a week now,' he said, quietly holding out his hands so that Issa could lash his wrists with rope. 'We even wanted you to come. We thought this was our chance to rid Britain of Arthur.'

'Why would you want to do that?' I asked him.

'Because Arthur's an enemy of the Christians, that's why,' Ligessac said.

'He is not,' I said scornfully.

'And what do you know, Derfel?' Ligessac asked me. 'We're readying Britain for Christ's return and we have to scour the heathen from the land!' He made that proclamation in a loud, defiant voice, then he shrugged and grinned. 'But I told them this was no way to kill Arthur and Derfel. I told Cadoc you were too good.' He stood and followed Issa out of the church, but then turned back to me in the doorway. 'I suppose I'm to die now?' he asked.

'In Dumnonia,' I said.

He shrugged. 'I shall see God face to face,' he said, 'so what is there to fear?'

I followed him out of the church. Arthur had unplugged the Bishop's mouth and Cadoc was now cursing us with a stream of filthy language. I tickled the Bishop's newly shaved chin with Hywelbane. 'He knew we were coming,' I told Arthur, 'and they planned to kill us here.'

'He failed,' Arthur said, jerking his head aside to avoid a gob of the Bishop's spittle. 'Put the sword away,' he ordered me.

'You don't want him dead?' I asked.

'His punishment is to live here,' Arthur decreed, 'instead of in heaven.'

We took Ligessac and walked away, and none of us really reflected on what Ligessac had revealed in the church. He had said they had known we were coming for a whole week, but a week before we had been in Dumnonia, not in Powys, and that meant someone in Dumnonia had sent the warning of our approach. But we never thought to connect anyone in Dumnonia with that muddy massacre in the squalid hills; we ascribed the slaughter to Christian fanaticism, not to treachery, but that ambush was plotted.

To this day, of course, there are Christians who tell a different story. They say that Arthur surprised Cadoc's refuge, raped the women, killed the men and stole all Cadoc's treasures, but I saw no rape, we killed only those who tried to kill us, and I found no treasure to steal – but even if there had been, Arthur would not have touched it. A time would come, and not far off either, when I did see Arthur kill wantonly, but those dead were all to be pagans; yet the Christians still insisted he was their enemy and the story of Cadoc's defeat only increased their hatred for him. Cadoc was elevated into a living saint and it was about that time that the Christians began to taunt Arthur as the Enemy of God. That angry title stuck to him for the rest of his days.

His crime, of course, was not the breaking of a few Christian heads in Cadoc's valley, but rather his toleration of paganism during the time he governed Dumnonia. It never occurred to the more rabid Christians that Arthur was himself a pagan and tolerated Christianity, they just condemned him because he had the power to obliterate heathenism and did not do it, and that sin made him the Enemy of God. They also remembered, of course, how he had rescinded Uther's exemption of the church from forced loans.

Not all Christians hated him. At least a score of the spearmen who fought alongside us in Cadoc's valley were themselves Christians. Galahad loved him, and there were many others, like

Bishop Emrys, who were his quiet supporters, but the church, in those unquiet days at the end of the first five hundred years of Christ's rule on earth, was not listening to the quiet, decent men, it was listening to the fanatics who said that the world must be cleansed of pagans if Christ were to come again. I know now, of course, that the faith of our Lord Jesus Christ is the only true faith, and that no other faith can exist in the glorious light of its truth, but it still seemed strange to me, and does to this day, that Arthur, the most just and lawful of rulers, was called the Enemy of God.

Whatever. We gave Cadoc a headache, tied Ligessac's throat with a leash made from his beard, and walked away.

Arthur and I parted company beside the stone cross at the head of Cadoc's valley. He would take Ligessac north and then go east to find the good roads that led back to Dumnonia, while I had decided to travel deeper into Siluria to find my mother. I took Issa and four other spearmen and let the rest march home with Arthur.

We six men circled Cadoc's valley where a woeful band of bruised and bloody Christians had gathered to chant prayers for their dead, and then we walked across the high bare hills and down into the steep green valleys that led to the Severn Sea. I did not know where Erce lived, but I suspected she would not be hard to find for Tanaburs, the Druid I had killed at Lugg Vale, had sought her out to work a dreadful spell on her and surely the Saxon slave woman so wickedly cursed by the Druid would be well enough known. And she was.

I found her living by the sea in a tiny village where the women made salt and the men caught fish. The villagers shrank away from my men's unfamiliar shields, but I ducked into one of the hovels where a child fearfully pointed me towards the Saxon woman's house that proved to be a cottage high up on a ragged bluff above the beach. It was not even a cottage, but rather a crude shelter made of driftwood and roofed with a ragged thatch of seaweed and straw. A fire burned on the small space outside the shelter and a dozen fish were smoking above its flames, while still more choking smoke drifted up from the coal fires that simmered the salt pans at the base of the low cliff. I left my spear and shield at the foot of the bluff and climbed the steep path. A cat bared its teeth and hissed at me as I crouched to look into the dark hut. 'Erce?' I called. 'Erce?'

Something heaved in the shadows. It was a monstrous dark shape that shed layers of skins and ragged cloth to peer back at me. 'Erce?' I said. 'Are you Erce?'

What did I expect that day? I had not seen my mother in over twenty-five years, not since the day I was torn from her arms by Gundleus's spearmen and given to Tanaburs for the sacrifice in the death-pit. Erce had screamed as I was snatched away from her, and then she had been taken away to her new slavery in Siluria and she must have supposed me dead until Tanaburs had revealed to her that I still lived. In my nervous mind, as I had walked south through Siluria's steep valleys, I had foreseen an embrace, tears, forgiveness and happiness.

But instead a huge woman, her blonde hair turned into a dirty grey, crawled out from the jumble of skins and blankets to blink at me suspiciously. She was a vast creature, a great heap of decaying flesh with a face as round as a shield and blotched by disease and scars, and with eyes that were small and hard and bloodshot. 'I was called Erce once,' she said in a hoarse voice.

I backed out of the hut, repelled by its stench of urine and rot. She followed me, crawling heavily on all fours to blink in the morning sunlight. She was dressed in rags. 'You are Erce?' I asked her.

'Once,' she said, and yawned to show a ravaged, toothless mouth. 'Long ago. Now they call me Enna.' She paused. 'Mad Enna,' she added sadly, then peered at my fine clothes and rich sword belt and tall boots. 'Who are you, Lord?'

'My name is Derfel Cadarn,' I said, 'a Lord of Dumnonia.' The name meant nothing to her. 'I am your son,' I added.

She showed no reaction to that, but just settled back against the driftwood wall of her hut that sagged dangerously under her weight. She thrust a hand deep inside the rags and scratched at her breast. 'All my sons are dead,' she said.

'Tanaburs took me,' I reminded her, 'and threw me into the death-pit.'

The story seemed to mean nothing to her. She lay slumped against the wall, her huge body heaving with the effort of each laboured breath. She toyed with the cat and stared out across the Severn Sea to where, dim in the distance, the Dumnonian coast was a dark line under a row of rainclouds. 'I did have a son once,' she said at last, 'who was given to the Gods in the death-pit. Wygga, his name was. Wygga. A fine boy.'

Wygga? Wygga! That name, so raw and ugly, stilled me for a few heartbeats. 'I am Wygga,' I finally said, hating the name. 'I was given a new name after I was rescued from the pit,' I explained to her. We spoke in Saxon, a language in which I was now more fluent than my mother, for it had been many years since she had spoken it.

'Oh, no,' she said, frowning. I could see a louse crawling along the edge of her hair. 'No,' she insisted again. 'Wygga was just a little boy. Just a little boy. My firstborn, he was, and they took him away.'

'I lived, mother,' I said. I was revolted by her, fascinated by her and regretting that I had ever come to find her. 'I survived the pit,' I told her, 'and I remember you.' And so I did, but in my memory she was as slim and lithe as Ceinwyn.

'Just a little boy,' Erce said dreamily. She closed her eyes and I thought she was sleeping, but it seemed she was passing urine for a trickle appeared at the edge of her clothes and dripped down the rock towards the struggling fire.

'Tell me about Wygga,' I said.

'I was heavy with him,' she said, 'when Uther captured me. A big man, Uther, with a great dragon on his shield.' She scratched at the louse, which disappeared into her hair. 'He gave me to Madog,' she went on, 'and it was at Madog's holding that Wygga was born. We were happy with Madog,' she said. 'He was a good Lord, kind to his slaves, but Gundleus came and they killed Wygga.'

'They didn't,' I insisted. 'Didn't Tanaburs tell you?'

At the mention of the Druid's name she shuddered and pulled her tattered shawl tighter about her mountainous shoulders. She said nothing, but after a while tears showed at the corners of her eyes.

A woman climbed the path towards us. She came slowly and suspiciously, glancing warily towards me as she sidled onto the rock platform. When at last she felt safe she scuttled past me and crouched beside Erce. 'My name,' I told the newcomer, 'is Derfel Cadarn, but I was once called Wygga.'

'My name is Linna,' the woman said in the British tongue. She was younger than me, but the hard life of this shore had put deep lines on her face, bowed her shoulders and stiffened her joints, while the hard business of tending the salt-pan fires had left her skin blackened by coal.

'You're Erce's daughter?' I guessed.

'Enna's daughter,' she corrected me.

'Then I am your half-brother,' I said.

I do not think she believed me, and why should she? No one came from a death-pit alive, yet I had, and thereby I had been touched by the Gods and given to Merlin, but what could that tale mean to these two tired and ragged women?

'Tanaburs!' Erce suddenly said, and raised both hands to ward off evil. 'He took away Wygga's father!' She wailed and rocked to and fro. 'He went inside me and took away Wygga's father. He cursed me and he cursed Wygga and he cursed my womb.' She was weeping now and Linna cradled her mother's head in her arms and looked at me reproachfully.

'Tanaburs,' I said, 'had no power over Wygga. Wygga killed him, because he had power over Tanaburs. Tanaburs could not take away Wygga's father.'

Maybe my mother heard me, but she did not believe me. She rocked in her daughter's arms and the tears ran down her pock-marked, dirty cheeks as she half remembered the

364

half-understood scraps of Tanaburs's curse. 'Wygga would kill his father,' she told me, 'that's what the curse said, that the son will kill the father.'

'So Wygga does live,' I insisted.

She stopped her rocking motion suddenly and peered at me. She shook her head. 'The dead come back to kill. Dead children! I see them, Lord, out there,' she spoke earnestly and pointed at the sea, 'all the little dead going to their revenge.' She rocked in her daughter's arms again. 'And Wygga will kill his father.' She was crying heavily now. 'And Wygga's father was such a fine man! Such a hero. So big and strong. And Tanaburs has cursed him.' She sniffed, then sighed a lullaby for a moment before talking more about my father, saying how his people had sailed across the sea to Britain and how he had used his sword to make himself a fine house. Erce, I gathered, had been a servant in that house and the Saxon Lord had taken her to his bed and so given me life, the same life that Tanaburs had failed to take at the death-pit. 'He was a lovely man,' Erce said of my father, 'such a lovely, handsome man. Everyone feared him, but he was good to me. We used to laugh together.'

'What was his name?' I asked, and I think I knew the answer even before she gave it.

'Aelle,' she said in a whisper, 'lovely, handsome Aelle.'

Aelle. The smoke whirled about my head, and my brains, for a moment, were as addled as my mother's wits. Aelle? I was Aelle's son?

'Aelle,' Erce said dreamily, 'lovely, handsome Aelle.'

I had no other questions and so I forced myself to kneel before my mother and give her an embrace. I kissed her on both cheeks, then held her tight as if I could give back to her some of the life she had given to me, and though she succumbed to the embrace, she still would not acknowledge that I was her son. I took lice from her.

I drew Linna down the steps and discovered she was married to one of the village fishermen and had six children living. I gave her gold, more gold, I think, than she had ever expected to see, and more gold, probably, than she even suspected existed. She stared at the little bars in disbelief.

'Is our mother still a slave?' I asked her.

'We all are,' she said, gesturing at the whole miserable village.

'That will buy your freedom,' I said, pointing to the gold, 'if you want it.'

She shrugged and I doubted that being free would make any difference to their lives. I could have found their Lord and bought their freedom myself, but doubtless he lived far away and the gold, if it was wisely spent, would ease their hard life whether they were slave or free. One day, I promised myself, I would come back and try to do more.

'Look after our mother,' I told Linna.

'I will, Lord,' she said dutifully, but I still did not think she believed me.

'You don't call your own brother Lord,' I told her, but she would not be persuaded.

I left her and walked down to the shore where my men waited with the baggage. 'We're going home,' I said. It was still morning and we had a long day's march ahead. A march towards home.

Home to Ceinwyn. Home to my daughters who were sprung from a line of British Kings and from their Saxon enemy's royal blood. For I was Aelle's son. I stood on a green hill above the sea and wondered at the extraordinary weave of life, but I could make no sense of it. I was Aelle's son, but what difference did that make? It explained nothing and it demanded nothing. Fate is inexorable. I would go home.

IT WAS ISSA WHO first saw the smoke. He always had eyes like a hawk and that day, as I stood on the hill trying to find some meaning in my mother's revelations, Issa spied smoke across the sea. 'Lord?' he said, and at first I did not respond for I was too dazed by what I had learned. I was to kill my father? And that father was Aelle? 'Lord!' Issa said more insistently, waking me from my thoughts. 'Look, Lord, smoke.'

He was pointing south towards Dumnonia and at first I thought the whiteness was merely a paler patch among the rain-clouds, but Issa was certain and two of the other spearmen asserted that what we saw was smoke and not cloud or rain. 'There's more, Lord,' one of them said, pointing further west where another small smear of whiteness showed against the grey.

One fire might have been an accident, perhaps a hall burning or a dry field blazing, but in that wet weather no field would have burned and in all my life I had never seen two halls ablaze unless an enemy had put them to the torch.

'Lord?' Issa prompted me, for he, like me, had a wife in Dumnonia.

'Back to the village,' I said. 'Now.'

Linna's husband agreed to take us over the sea. The voyage was not long, for the sea here was only eight or so miles wide and it offered us our swiftest route home, but like all spearmen we preferred a long dry journey to a short wet one, and that crossing was an ordeal of sodden cold misery. A brisk wind had sprung from the west to bring more clouds and rain, and with it came a short, rising sea that splashed over the boat's low gunwales. We bailed for our lives while the ragged sail bellied and slapped and dragged us southward. Our boatman, who was called Balig and was my brother-in-law, declared that there was no joy like a good boat in a brisk wind and he roared his thanks to Manawydan for sending us such weather, but Issa was sick as a dog, I was retching dry, and we were all glad when, in the middle of the afternoon, he ran us ashore on a Dumnonian beach no more than three or four hours from home.

I paid Balig, then we struck inland through a flat, damp country. There was a village not far from the beach, but the folk there had seen the smoke and were frightened and they mistook us for enemies and ran to their huts. The village possessed a small church, merely a thatched hut with a wooden cross nailed to a gable, but the Christians had all gone. One of the remaining pagan villagers told me that the Christians had all gone eastwards. 'They followed their priest, Lord,' he told me.

'Why?' I asked. 'Where?'

'We don't know, Lord.' He glanced at the distant smoke. 'Are the Saxons back?'

'No,' I reassured him, and hoped I was right. The thinning smoke looked to be no more than six or seven miles away and I doubted that either Aelle or Cerdic could have reached this far into Dumnonia. If they had then all Britain was lost.

We hurried on. At that moment all we wanted was to reach our families and, once we knew they were safe, the time would come to find out what was happening. We had a choice of two routes to Ermid's Hall. One, the longer, lay inland and would take us four or five hours, much of it in darkness, but the other lay across the great sea-marshes of Avalon; a treacherous swamp of creeks, willow-edged bogs and sedge-covered wastes where, when the tide was high and the wind from the west, the sea could sometimes seep and fill and flood the levels and drown unwary travellers. There were routes through that great swamp, and even wooden walkways that led to where the willow pollards grew and the eel and fish traps were set, but none of us knew the marsh paths. Yet still we chose those treacherous paths for they offered the swiftest way home.

As evening fell we found a guide. Like most of the marsh folk he was a pagan and, once he knew who I was, he gladly offered his services. In the middle of the marsh, rising black in the falling light, we could see the Tor. We would have to go there first, our guide said, and then find one of Ynys Wydryn's boatmen to take us in a reed punt across the shallow waters of Issa's Mere.

It was still raining as we left the marsh village, the drops pattering on the reeds and dappling the pools, but it lifted within the hour and gradually a wan, milky moon glowed dimly behind the thinning clouds that scudded from the west. Our path crossed black ditches on plank bridges, passed by the intricate woven wickerwork of willow eel traps, and snaked incomprehensibly across blank shining morasses where our guide would mutter incantations against the marsh spirits. Some nights, he said, strange blue lights glimmered in the wet wastes; the spirits, he thought, of the many folk who had died in this labyrinth of water, mud and sedge. Our footfalls startled screeching wildfowl up from their nests, their panicked wings dark against the cloud-racked sky. Our guide talked to me as we went, telling me of the dragons that slept under the marsh and the ghouls that slithered through its muddy creeks. He wore a necklace made from the spine of a drowned man, the only sure charm, he claimed, against those fearsome things that haunted our path.

It seemed to me that the Tor came no closer, but that was just our impatience and yard by yard, creek by creek, we did get nearer and, as the great hill loomed higher and higher in the ragged sky, we saw a bright smear of light show at its foot. It was a great flamelight, and at first we thought the shrine of the Holy Thorn must be burning, but as we drew still nearer the flames grew no brighter and I guessed the light came from bonfires, perhaps lit to illuminate some Christian rite that sought to keep the shrine from harm. We all made the sign against evil, then at last we reached an embankment that led straight from the wet land to Ynys Wydryn's higher ground.

Our guide left us there. He preferred the dangers of the marsh to the perils of firelit Ynys Wydryn, so he knelt to me and I rewarded him with the last of my gold, then raised him up and thanked him.

The six of us walked on through the small town of Ynys Wydryn, a place of fishermen and basket-makers. The houses were dark and the alleyways deserted except for dogs and rats. We were heading towards the wooden palisade that surrounded the shrine, and though we could see the glowing smoke of the fires churning above the fence we still could not see anything that happened inside; but our path took us past the shrine's main gate and, as we drew closer, I saw there were two spearmen standing guard at the entrance. The flamelight coming through the open gate illuminated one of their shields and on that shield was the last symbol I had ever expected to see in Ynys Wydryn. It was Lancelot's sea-eagle with the fish in its claws.

Our own shields were slung on our backs and so their white stars were invisible, and though we all wore the grey wolf-tail, the spearmen must have thought we were friends for they made no challenge as we approached. Instead, thinking that we want-ed to enter the shrine, they moved aside, and it was only when I was halfway through the gate, drawn there by my curiosity about Lancelot's part in this night's strange events, that the two men realized we were not their comrades. One tried to bar my way with a spear. 'Who are you?' he challenged me.

I pushed his spear aside and then, before he could shout a warning, I shoved him backwards out of the gate while Issa dragged his comrade away. A huge crowd was gathered inside the shrine, but they all had their backs to us and none saw the scuffle at the main gate. Nor could they hear anything, for the crowd was chanting and singing and their confused babble drowned the small noise we made. I dragged my captive into the shadows by the road where I knelt beside him. I had dropped my spear when I had pushed him out of the gateway, so now I pulled out the short knife I wore at my belt. 'You're Lancelot's man?' I asked him.

'Yes,' he hissed.

'Then what are you doing here?' I asked. 'This is Mordred's country.'

'King Mordred is dead,' he said, frightened of the knife blade that I was holding against his throat. I said nothing, for I was so astonished by his answer that I could find nothing to say. The man must have thought my silence presaged his death for he became desperate. 'They're all dead!' he exclaimed.

'Who?'

'Mordred, Arthur, all of them.'

For a few heartbeats it seemed as if my world lurched in its foundations. The man struggled briefly, but the pressure of my knife quietened him. 'How?' I hissed at him.

'I don't know.'

'How?' I demanded more loudly.

'We don't know!' he insisted. 'Mordred was killed before we came and they say Arthur died in Powys.'

I rocked back, gesturing at one of my men to keep the two captives quiet with his spear-blade. Then I counted the hours since I had seen Arthur. It was only days since we had parted at Cadoc's cross, and Arthur's route home was much longer than mine; if he had died, I thought, then the news of his death would surely not have reached Ynys Wydryn before me. 'Is your King here?' I asked the man.

'Yes.'

'Why?' I asked.

His answer was scarcely above a whisper. 'To take the kingdom, Lord.'

We cut strips of woollen cloth from the two men's cloaks, bound their arms and legs and rammed handfuls of wool into their mouths to keep them silent. We pushed them into a ditch, warned them to stay still and then I led my five men back to the gate of the shrine. I wanted to look inside for a few moments, learn what I could, and only then would I hurry home. 'Cloaks over your helmets,' I ordered my men, 'and shields reversed.'

We hoisted the cloaks up over our helmet crests so that their wolf-tails were hidden, then we held our shields with their faces low against our legs so that their stars would be obscured, and so disguised we filed quietly into the now unguarded shrine. We moved in the shadows, circling around the back of the excited crowd until we reached the stone foundations of the shrine Mordred had started to build for his dead mother. We climbed onto the unfinished sepulchre's highest course of stones and from there we could watch over the heads of the crowd and see what strange thing happened between the twin rows of fire that lit Ynys Wydryn's night.

At first I thought it was another Christian rite like the one I had witnessed in Isca, because the space between the rows of fire was filled with dancing women, swaying men and chanting priests. The noise they made was a cacophony of shrieks and screams and wails. Monks with leather flails were wandering among the ecstatics and lashing their naked backs, and each hard stroke only provoked more screams of joy. One woman was kneeling by the Holy Thorn. 'Come, Lord Jesus!' she shrieked. 'Come!' A monk beat her in a frenzy, beat her so hard that her naked back was a lurid sheet of blood, but every new blow only increased the fervour of her desperate prayer.

I was about to jump down from the sepulchre and go back to the gate when spearmen appeared from the shrine's buildings and pushed the worshippers roughly aside to clear a space between the fires that lit the Holy Thorn. They dragged the screaming woman away. More spearmen followed, two of them carrying a litter, and behind that litter Bishop Sansum led a group of brightly clothed priests. Lancelot and his attendants walked with the priests. Bors, Lancelot's champion, was there, and Amhar and Loholt were with the Belgic King, but I could not see the dread twins Lavaine and Dinas.

The crowd shrieked even louder when they saw Lancelot. They stretched their hands towards him and some even knelt as he passed. He was arrayed in his white-enamelled scale armour that he swore had been the war gear of the ancient hero Agamemnon, and he was wearing his black helmet with its crest of spread swan's wings. His long black hair that he oiled so it shone fell down his back beneath the helmet to lie smooth against a red cloak that hung from his shoulders. The Christ-blade was at his side and his legs were clad in tall red leather war-boots. His Saxon Guard came behind, all of them huge men in silver mail coats and carrying broad-bladed war axes that reflected the leaping flames. I could not see Morgan, but a choir of her white-clad holy women were vainly trying to make their song heard above the wails and shouts of the excited crowd.

One of the spearmen carried a stake that he placed in a hole that had been prepared beside the Holy Thorn. For a moment I feared we were about to see some poor pagan burned at that stake and I spat to avert evil. The victim was being carried on the litter, for the men carrying it brought their burden to the Holy Thorn and then busied themselves tying their prisoner to the stake, but when they stepped away and we could at last see properly, I realized that it was no prisoner, and no burning. Indeed, it was no pagan tied to that stake, but a Christian, and it was no death we were watching, but a marriage.

And I thought of Nimue's strange prophecy. The dead would be taken in marriage.

Lancelot was the groom and he now stood beside his bride who was roped to the stake. She was a Queen, the one-time Princess of Powys who had become a Princess of Dumnonia and then the Queen of Siluria. She was Norwenna, daughter-in-law of High King Uther, the mother of Mordred, and she had been dead these fourteen years. She had lain in her grave for all those years, but now she had been disinterred and her remains were lashed to the post beside the votive-hung Holy Thorn.

I stared in horror, then made the sign against evil and stroked the iron mail of my armour. Issa touched my arm as though to reassure himself that he was not in the throes of some unimaginable nightmare.

The dead Queen was little more than a skeleton. A white shawl had been draped on her shoulders, but the shawl could not hide the ghastly strips of yellowing skin and thick hanks of white fatty flesh that still clung to her bones. Her skull, that canted from one of the ropes pinioning her to the stake, was half covered with stretched skin, her jawbone had fallen away at one side and dangled from her skull, while her eyes were nothing but black shadows in the firelit death mask of her face. One of the guards had placed a wreath of poppies on the dome of her skull from which dank strands of hair fell ragged to the shawl.

'What's happening?' Issa asked me in a soft voice.

'Lancelot is claiming Dumnonia,' I whispered back, 'and by marrying Norwenna he marries into Dumnonia's royal family.' There could be no other explanation. Lancelot was stealing Dumnonia's throne, and this grisly ceremony among the great fires would give him a thin legal excuse. He was marrying the dead to make himself Uther's heir.

Sansum signalled for silence and the monks who carried the flails shouted at the excited crowd that slowly calmed down from their frenzy. Every now and then a woman would scream and the crowd would give a nervous shudder, but at last there was silence. The choir's voices tailed away and Sansum raised his arms and prayed that Almighty God would bless this union of a man and a woman, this King and his Queen, and then he instructed Lancelot to take the bride's hand. Lancelot reached down with his gloved right hand and lifted the yellow bones. The cheek pieces of his helmet were open and I could see he was grinning. The crowd shouted for joy and I remembered Tewdric's words about signs and portents, and I guessed that in this unholy marriage the Christians were seeing proof that their God's return was imminent.

'By the power invested in me by the Holy Father and by

the grace given to me by the Holy Ghost,' Sansum shouted, 'I pronounce you man and wife!'

'Where's our King?' Issa asked me.

'Who knows?' I whispered back. 'Dead probably.' Then I watched as Lancelot lifted the yellow bones of Norwenna's hand and pretended to give her fingers a kiss. One of the fingers dropped away as he let the hand go.

Sansum, never able to resist a chance to preach, began to harangue the crowd and it was then that Morgan accosted me. I had not seen her approach and the first I knew of her presence was when I felt a hand tugging at my cloak and I turned in alarm to see her gold mask glinting in the firelight. 'When they find the guards missing from the gate,' she hissed, 'they'll search this compound and you'll be dead men. Follow me, fools.'

We jumped guiltily down and followed her humped black figure as it scuttled behind the crowd into the shadows of the shrine's big church. She stopped there and stared up into my face. 'They said you were dead,' she told me. 'Killed with Arthur at Cadoc's shrine.'

'I live, Lady.'

'And Arthur?'

'He lived three days ago, Lady,' I answered. 'None of us died at Cadoc's shrine.'

'Thank God,' she breathed, 'thank God.' Then she gripped my cloak and hauled my face down close to her mask. 'Listen,' she said urgently, 'my husband had no choice in this thing.'

'If you say so, Lady,' I said, not believing her for one moment, but understanding that Morgan was doing her best to straddle both sides of this crisis that had come so suddenly to Dumnonia. Lancelot was taking the throne, and someone had conspired to make sure Arthur was out of the country when he did it. Worse, I thought, someone had sent Arthur and me to Cadoc's high valley and arranged for men to ambush us there. Someone wanted us dead, and it had been Sansum who had first revealed Ligessac's refuge to us and Sansum who had argued against allowing Cuneglas's men to make the arrest, and Sansum who now stood before Lancelot and a corpse in the light of this night's fires. I smelt the mouse-lord's paws all over this wicked business, though I doubted Morgan knew half of what her husband had done or planned. She was too old and wise to be infected by religious frenzy, and she at least was trying to pick a safe path through the cascading horrors.

'Promise me Arthur lives!' she appealed to me.

'He did not die in Cadoc's valley,' I said. 'That much I can promise you.'

She was silent for a while and I think she was crying beneath the mask. 'Tell Arthur we had no choice,' she said.

'I will,' I promised her. 'What can you tell me of Mordred?'

'He's dead,' she hissed. 'Killed while he was hunting.'

'But if they lied about Arthur,' I said, 'then why not about Mordred?'

'Who knows?' she crossed herself and plucked at my cloak. 'Come,' she said abruptly, and led us down the side of the church towards a small wooden hut. Someone was trapped inside the hut for I could hear fists beating on its door that was secured by the knotted loops of a leather leash. 'You should go to your woman, Derfel,' Morgan told me as she fumbled at the knot with her one good hand. 'Dinas and Lavaine rode south to your hall after nightfall. They took spearmen.'

Panic whipped inside me, making me use my spear-point to slash at the leather leash. The moment the binding was cut the door flew open and Nimue leapt out, hands hooked like claws, but then she recognized me and stumbled against my body for support. She spat at Morgan.

'Go, you fool,' Morgan snarled at her, 'and remember it was I who saved you from death today.'

I took Morgan's two hands, the burned and the good, and put them to my lips. 'For this night's deeds, Lady,' I said, 'I am in your debt.'

'Go, you fool,' she said, 'and hurry!' and we ran through the back parts of the shrine, past storehouses and slave huts and granaries, then out through a wicket gate to where the fishermen kept their reed punts. We took two of the small craft and used our long spear-shafts as quant poles, and I remembered that far-off day of Norwenna's death when Nimue and I had escaped from Ynys Wydryn in just this fashion. Then, as now, we had headed for Ermid's Hall and then, as now, we had been hunted fugitives in a land overrun by enemies.

Nimue knew little of what had happened to Dumnonia. Lancelot, she said, had come and declared himself King, but of Mordred she could only repeat what Morgan had said, that the King had been killed while hunting. She told us how spearmen had come to the Tor and taken her captive to the shrine where Morgan had imprisoned her. Afterwards, she heard, a mob of Christians had climbed the Tor, slaughtered whoever they found there, pulled down the huts and begun to build a church out of the salvaged timbers.

'So Morgan did save your life,' I said.

'She wants my knowledge,' Nimue said. 'How else will they know what to do with the Cauldron? That's why Dinas and Lavaine have gone to your hall, Derfel. To find Merlin.' She spat into the mere. 'It's as I told you,' she finished, 'they've unleashed the Cauldron and they don't know how to control its power. Two Kings have come to Cadarn. Mordred was one and Lancelot was the second. He went there this afternoon and stood upon the stone. And tonight the dead are being taken in marriage.'

'And you also said,' I reminded her bitterly, 'that a sword would be laid at a child's throat,' and I thrust my spear down into the shallow mere in my desperate hurry to reach Ermid's Hall. Where my children lay. Where Ceinwyn lay. And where the Silurian Druids and their spearmen had ridden not three hours before.

Flames lit our homeward path. Not the flames that illuminated Lancelot's marriage to the dead, but new flames that sprang red and high from Ermid's Hall. We were halfway across the mere when that fire flared up to shiver its long reflections on the black water.

I was praying to Gofannon, to Lleullaw, to Bel, to Cernunnos, to Taranis, to all the Gods, wherever they were, that just one of them would stoop from the realm of stars and save my family. The flames leapt higher, spewing sparks of burning thatch into the smoke that blew east across poor Dumnonia.

We travelled in silence once Nimue had finished her tale. Issa had tears in his eyes. He was worrying about Scarach, the Irish girl he had married, and he was wondering, as I was, what had happened to the spearmen we had left to guard the hall. There had been enough men, surely, to hold up Dinas and Lavaine's raiders? Yet the flames told another tale and we thrust the spear-shafts down to make the punts go even faster.

We heard the screams as we came closer. There were just six of us spearmen, but I did not hesitate, or try to make a circuitous approach, but simply drove the punts hard into the tree-shadowed creek that lay alongside the hall's palisade. There, next to Dian's little coracle that Gwlyddyn, Merlin's servant, had made for her, we leapt ashore.

Later I put together the tale of that night. Gwilym, the man who commanded the spearmen who had stayed behind while I marched north with Arthur, had seen the distant smoke to the east and surmised there was trouble brewing. He had placed all his men on guard, then debated with Ceinwyn whether they should take to the boats and hide in the marshes that lay beyond the mere. Ceinwyn said no. Malaine, her brother's Druid, had given Dian a concoction of leaves that had lifted the fever, but the child was still weak, and besides, no one knew what the smoke meant, nor had any messengers come with a warning; so instead Ceinwyn sent two of the spearmen east to find news and then waited behind the wooden palisade.

Nightfall brought no news, but it did bring a measure of relief for few spearmen marched at night and Ceinwyn felt safer than she had in daylight. From inside the palisade they saw the flames across the mere at Ynys Wydryn and wondered what they meant, but no one heard Dinas and Lavaine's horsemen come into the nearby woods. The horsemen dismounted a long way from the hall, tied their beasts' reins to trees and then, under the pale, cloud-misted moon, they had crept towards the palisade. It was not till Dinas and Lavaine's men attacked the gate that Gwilym even realized the hall was under attack. His two scouts had not returned, there were no guards in the woods and the enemy was already within feet of the palisade's gate when the alarm was first raised. It was not a formidable gate, no more than the height of a man, and the first rank of the enemy rushed it without armour, spears or shields and succeeded in climbing over before Gwilym's men could assemble. The gate guards fought and killed, but enough of those first attackers survived to lift the bar of the gate and so open it to the charge of Dinas and Lavaine's heavily armoured spearmen. Ten of those spearmen were Lancelot's Saxon Guards, while the rest were Belgic warriors sworn to their King's service.

Gwilym's men rallied as best they could, and the fiercest fight took place at the hall's door. It was there that Gwilym himself lay dead with another six of my men. Six more were lying in the courtyard where a storehouse had been set on fire and those were the flames that had lit our path across the lake and which now, as we reached the open gate, showed us the horror inside.

The battle was not over. Dinas and Lavaine had planned their treachery well, but their men had failed to get through the hall door and my surviving spearmen were still holding the big building. I could see their shields and spears blocking the door's arch, and I could see another spear showing from one of the high windows that let the smoke out from the gable end. Two of my huntsmen were in that window, and their arrows were preventing Dinas and Lavaine's men carrying the fire from the burning store house to the hall thatch. Ceinwyn, Morwenna and Seren were all inside the hall, together with Merlin, Malaine and most of the other women and children who lived inside the compound, but they were surrounded and outnumbered; and the enemy Druids had found Dian.

Dian had been sleeping in one of the huts. She often did,

liking to be in the company of her old wet-nurse who was married to my blacksmith, and maybe it was her golden hair that had given her away or maybe, being Dian, she had spat defiance at her captors and told them her father would take his revenge.

And now Lavaine, robed in black and with an empty scabbard hanging at his hip, held my Dian against his body. Her small grubby feet were sticking out from beneath the little white robe she wore and she was struggling as best she could, but Lavaine had his left arm tight about her waist and in his right hand he held a naked sword against her throat.

Issa clutched my arm to stop me charging madly at the line of armoured men who faced the beleaguered hall. There were twenty of them. I could not see Dinas, but he, I suspected, was with the other enemy spearmen at the rear of the hall, where they would be cutting off the escape of all the souls trapped inside.

'Ceinwyn!' Lavaine called in his deep voice. 'Come out! My King wants you!'

I laid the spear down and drew Hywelbane. Her blade hissed softly on the scabbard's throat.

'Come out!' Lavaine called again.

I touched the strips of pig bone on the sword hilt, then prayed to my Gods that they would make me terrible this night.

'You want your whelp dead?' Lavaine called, and Dian screamed as the sword blade tightened on her throat. 'Your man's dead!' Lavaine shouted. 'He died in Powys with Arthur, and he won't come to help you.' He pressed the sword harder and Dian screamed again.

Issa kept his hand on my arm. 'Not yet, Lord,' he whispered, 'not yet.'

The shields parted at the hall door and Ceinwyn stepped out. She was dressed in a dark cloak that was clasped at her throat. 'Put the child down,' she told Lavaine calmly.

'The child will be released when you come to me,' Lavaine said. 'My King demands your company.'

'Your King?' Ceinwyn asked. 'What King is that?' She knew well enough whose men had come here this night, for their shields alone told that tale, but she would make nothing easy for Lavaine.

'King Lancelot,' Lavaine said. 'King of the Belgae and King of Dumnonia.'

Ceinwyn pulled her dark cloak tighter about her shoulders. 'So what does King Lancelot want of me?' she asked. Behind her, in the space at the back of the hall and dimly lit by the burning storehouse, I could see more of Lancelot's spearmen. They had taken the horses from my stables and now they watched the confrontation between Ceinwyn and Lavaine.

'This night, Lady,' Lavaine explained, 'my King has taken a bride.'

Ceinwyn shrugged. 'Then he does not need me.'

'The bride, Lady, cannot give my King the privileges that a man demands on his wedding night. You, Lady, are to be his pleasure instead. It is an old debt of honour that you owe him. Besides,' Lavaine added, 'you are a widow now. You need another man.'

I tensed, but Issa again gripped my arm. One of the Saxon Guards close to Lavaine was restless and Issa was mutely suggesting we wait until the man relaxed again.

Ceinwyn dropped her head for a few seconds, then looked up again. 'And if I come with you,' she said in a bleak voice, 'you will let my daughter live?'

'She will live,' Lavaine promised.

'And all the others too?' she asked, gesturing to the hall.

'Those too,' said Lavaine.

'Then release my daughter,' Ceinwyn demanded.

'Come here first,' Lavaine retorted, 'and bring Merlin with you.' Dian kicked at him with her bare heels, but he tightened the sword again and she went still. The storehouse roof collapsed, exploding sparks and burning scraps of straw into the night. Some of the flames landed on the hall's thatch where they flickered feebly. The rainwater in the thatch was protecting the hall for the moment, but soon, I knew, the hall roof must catch the blaze.

I tensed, ready to charge, but then Merlin appeared behind Ceinwyn. His beard, I saw, was bound in plaits again, he carried his great staff and he stood straighter and grimmer than I had seen him stand in years. He placed his right arm about Ceinwyn's shoulders. 'Let the child go,' he ordered.

Lavaine shook his head. 'We made a spell with your beard, old man, and you have no power over us. But tonight we shall have the pleasure of your conversation while our King has the pleasure of the Princess Ceinwyn. Both of you,' he demanded, 'come here.'

Merlin lifted the staff and pointed it at Lavaine. 'At the next full moon,' he said, 'you will die beside the sea. You and your brother shall both die and your screams will journey the waves through all time. Let the child go.'

Nimue hissed softly behind me. She had plucked up my spear and lifted the leather patch from her ghastly empty eye-socket.

Lavaine was unmoved by Merlin's prophecy. 'At the next full moon,' he said, 'we shall boil your beard scraps in bull's blood and give your soul to the worm of Annwn,' he spat. 'Both of you,' he snapped, 'come here.'

'Release my daughter,' Ceinwyn demanded.

'When you reach me,' Lavaine said, 'she will be freed.'

There was a pause. Ceinwyn and Merlin spoke together softly. Morwenna cried out from inside the hall and Ceinwyn turned and spoke to her daughter, then she took Merlin's hand and began to walk towards Lavaine. 'Not like that, Lady,' Lavaine called to her. 'My Lord Lancelot demands that you come to him naked. My Lord will have you taken naked through the countryside and naked through the town and naked to his bed. You shamed him, Lady, and this night he will return his shame on you a hundredfold.'

Ceinwyn stopped and glared at him. But Lavaine simply pressed his sword blade against Dian's throat, the child gasped with the pain, and Ceinwyn instinctively tore at the brooch that clasped her cloak and let the garment drop to reveal a simple white dress.

'Take the gown off, Lady,' Lavaine ordered her harshly, 'take it off, or your daughter dies.'

I charged then. I screamed Bel's name and I charged like a mad thing. My men came with me, and more men came from the hall when they saw the white stars on our shields and the grey tails on our helms. Nimue charged with us, shrieking and wailing, and I saw the line of enemy spearmen turn with horror on their faces. I ran straight at Lavaine. He saw me, recognized me and froze in terror. He had disguised himself as a Christian priest by hanging a crucifix around his neck. This was no time for men to ride Dumnonia dressed as Druids, but it was time for Lavaine to die and I screamed my God's name as I charged at him.

Then a Saxon Guard ran in front of me, his bright axe glittering reflected flamelight as he swung its heavy blade at my skull. I parried it with the shield and the force of the blow jarred down my arm. Then I slid Hywelbane forward, twisted her blade in his belly and dragged it free in a rush of spilling Saxon guts. Issa had killed another Saxon and Scarach, his fiery Irish wife, had come from the hall to slash at a wounded Saxon with a boar spear, while Nimue was driving her spear into a man's belly. I parried another spear blow, put the spearman down with Hywelbane and looked desperately around for Lavaine. I saw him running with Dian in his arms. He was trying to reach his brother behind the hall when a rush of spearmen cut him off and he turned, saw me and fled towards the gate. He held Dian like a shield.

'I want him alive!' I roared and plunged towards him through the firelit chaos. Another Saxon came at me roaring the name of his God, and I cut the God's name out of his throat with a lunge of Hywelbane. Then Issa shouted a warning and I heard the hoofs and saw that the enemy who had been guarding the back of the hall were charging on horseback to their comrades' rescue. Dinas, who was dressed like his brother in the black robes of a Christian priest, led the charge with a drawn sword.

'Stop them!' I shouted. I could hear Dian screaming. The enemy was panicking. They outnumbered us, but the irruption of spearmen from the black night had torn their hearts to ribbons and one-eyed Nimue, shrieking and wild with her bloody spear, must have appeared to them as a ghastly night ghoul come for their souls. They fled in terror. Lavaine waited for his brother close to the burning storehouse and still held his sword at Dian's throat. Scarach, hissing like Nimue, stalked him with her spear, but she dared not risk my daughter's life. Others of the enemy scrambled over the palisade, some ran for the gate, some were cut down in the shadows between the huts and some escaped by running alongside the terrified horses that pounded past us into the night.

Dinas rode straight for me. I raised my shield, hefted Hywelbane and shouted a challenge, but at the very last moment he swerved his white-eyed horse aside and hurled the sword at my head. He rode towards his twin brother instead and as he neared Lavaine he leaned down from the saddle and extended his arm. Scarach flung herself out of the path of the charging horse just as Lavaine leapt up into Dinas's saving embrace. He dropped Dian and I saw her sprawl away from him as I ran after the horse. Lavaine was clinging desperately to his brother who clung just as desperately to the saddle-bar as the horse galloped away. I shouted at them to stay and fight, but the twins just galloped into the black trees where the enemy's other survivors had fled. I cursed their souls. I stood in the gate and called them vermin, cowards, creatures of evil.

'Derfel?' Ceinwyn called from behind me. 'Derfel?'

I abandoned my curses and turned to her. 'I live,' I said, 'I live.'

'Oh, Derfel!' she wailed, and it was then that I saw that Ceinwyn was holding Dian and that Ceinwyn's white dress was white no longer, but red.

I ran to their side. Dian was cradled tight in her mother's

arms, and I dropped my sword, tore the helmet from my head and fell to my knees beside them. 'Dian?' I whispered, 'my love?'

I saw the soul flicker in her eyes. She saw me – she did see me – and she saw her mother before she died. She looked at us for an instant and then her young soul flew away as soft as a wing in darkness and with as little fuss as a candle flame blown out by a wisp of wind. Her throat had been cut as Lavaine leapt for his brother's arm, and now her small heart just gave up the struggle. But she did see me first. I know she did. She saw me, then she died, and I put my arms around her and around her mother and I cried like a child.

For my little lovely Dian, I wept.

We had taken four unwounded prisoners. One was a Saxon Guard and three were Belgic spearmen. Merlin questioned them, and when he had finished I hacked all four to pieces. I slaughtered them. I killed in a rage, sobbing as I killed, blind to anything but Hywelbane's weight and the empty satisfaction of feeling her blade bite into their flesh. One by one, in front of my men, in front of Ceinwyn, in front of Morwenna and Seren, I butchered all four men and when it was done Hywelbane was wet and red from tip to hilt and still I hacked at their lifeless bodies. My arms were soaked in blood, my rage could have filled the whole world and still it would not bring little Dian back.

I wanted more men to kill, but the enemy's wounded had already had their throats cut and so, with no more revenge to take and bloody as I was, I walked to my terrified daughters and held them in my arms. I could not stop crying; nor could they. I held them as though my life depended on theirs, and then I carried them to where Ceinwyn still cradled Dian's corpse. I gently unfolded Ceinwyn's arms and placed them about her living children, then I took Dian's little body and carried it to the burning storehouse. Merlin came with me. He touched his staff on Dian's forehead, then nodded to me. It was time, he was saying, to let Dian's soul cross the bridge of swords, but first I kissed her, then I laid her body down and used my knife to cut away a thick strand of her golden hair that I placed carefully in my pouch. That done, I raised her up, kissed her one last time and threw her corpse into the flames. Her hair and her little white dress flared bright.

'Feed the fire!' Merlin snapped at my men. 'Feed it!'

They tore down a hut to make the fire into a furnace that would burn Dian's body into nothing. Her soul was already going to its shadowbody in the Otherworld, and now her balefire roared into the dark while I knelt in front of the flames with an empty ravaged soul.

Merlin lifted me up. 'We must go, Derfel.'

'I know.'

He embraced me, holding me in his long strong arms like a father. 'If I could have saved her,' he said softly.

'You tried,' I said, and cursed myself for lingering in Ynys Wydryn.

'Come,' Merlin said. 'We must be a long way off by dawn.'

We took what little we could carry. I discarded the bloody armour I was wearing and took my good coat of mail that was trimmed with gold. Seren took three kittens in a leather bag, Morwenna a distaff and a bundle of clothes, while Ceinwyn carried a bag of food. There were eighty of us altogether; spearmen, families, servants and slaves. All of them had thrown some small token into the balefire; a scrap of bread mostly, though Gwlyddyn, Merlin's servant, had tossed Dian's coracle into the flames so that she could paddle it through the lakes and creeks of the Otherworld.

Ceinwyn, walking with Merlin and Malaine, her brother's Druid, asked what happened to children in the Otherworld. 'They play,' Merlin said with all his ancient authority. 'They play beneath the apple trees and wait for you.'

'She will be happy,' Malaine reassured her. He was a tall, thin, stooped young man who carried Iorweth's old staff. He seemed shocked by the night's horror, and he was plainly nervous of Nimue in her filthy, blood-spattered robe. Her eye patch had disappeared, and her ghastly hair hung lank and draggled.

Ceinwyn, once she had satisfied herself of Dian's fate, came and walked beside me. I was still in agony, blaming myself for pausing to watch Lancelot's ceremony of marriage, but Ceinwyn was calmer now. 'It was her fate, Derfel,' she said, 'and she's happy now.' She took my arm. 'And you're alive. They told us you were dead. Both you and Arthur.'

'He lives,' I promised her. I walked in silence, following the white robes of the two Druids. 'One day,' I said after a while, 'I shall find Dinas and Lavaine and their deaths will be terrible.'

Ceinwyn squeezed my arm. 'We were all so happy,' she said. She had begun crying again and I tried to find words to console her, but there could be no explanation of why the Gods had snatched Dian away. Behind us, bright in the night sky, the flames and smoke of Ermid's Hall boiled towards the stars. The hall thatch had at last caught the fire and our old life was being burned to ashes.

We followed a twisting path beside the mere. The moon had slid from behind its clouds to cast a silver light on the rushes and willows and on the shallow, wind-rippled lake. We walked towards the sea, but I had scarcely thought what we should do when we reached the shore. Lancelot's men would search for us, that much was certain, and somehow we would need to find safety.

Merlin had questioned our prisoners before I killed them and he now told Ceinwyn and me what he had learned. Much of it we already knew. Mordred was said to have been killed while hunting, and one of the prisoners had claimed that the King had been murdered by the father of a girl he had raped. Arthur was rumoured to be dead and so Lancelot had declared himself the King of Dumnonia. The Christians had welcomed him in the belief that Lancelot was their new John the Baptist, a man who had presaged the first coming of Christ just as Lancelot now presaged the second.

'Arthur didn't die,' I said bitterly. 'He was meant to, and I was meant to die with him, but they failed. And how,' I asked, 'if I saw Arthur just thee days ago, did Lancelot hear of his death so soon?'

'He hasn't heard of it,' Merlin said calmly. 'He's just hoping for it.'

I spat. 'It's Sansum and Lancelot,' I said angrily. 'Lancelot probably arranged for Mordred's death and Sansum arranged ours. Now Sansum has his Christian King and Lancelot has Dumnonia.'

'Except that you live,' Ceinwyn said quietly.

'And Arthur lives,' I said, 'and if Mordred's dead, then the throne is Arthur's.'

'Only if he defeats Lancelot,' Merlin said drily.

'Of course he'll defeat Lancelot,' I said scornfully.

'Arthur's weakened,' Merlin warned me gently. 'Scores of his men have been killed. All Mordred's guards are dead and so are all the spearmen at Caer Cadarn. Cei and his men are dead in Isca, or if they're not dead, they're fugitives. The Christians have risen, Derfel. I hear they marked their houses with the sign of the fish, and any house that didn't carry the mark had its inhabitants slaughtered.' He paced in gloomy silence for a while. 'They're cleansing Britain for the coming of their God.'

'But Lancelot hasn't killed Sagramor,' I said, hoping that what I said was true, 'and Sagramor leads an army.'

'Sagramor lives,' Merlin assured me, and then delivered the worst news of that terrible night, 'but he's been attacked by Cerdic. It seems to me,' he went on, 'that Lancelot and Cerdic might well have agreed to divide Dumnonia between them. Cerdic will take the frontier lands and Lancelot will rule the rest.'

I could find nothing to say. It seemed incomprehensible. Cerdic was loose in Dumnonia? And the Christians had risen to make Lancelot their King? And it had all happened so swiftly, within days, and there had been no sign of it before I left Dumnonia.

'There were signs,' Merlin said, reading my mind. 'There were signs, it was just that none of us took them seriously. Who cared if a few Christians painted the fish on their house walls? Who took any notice of their frenzies? We became so used to their priests' ranting that we no longer listened to what they were saying. And which of us believes that their God will come to Britain in four years' time? There were signs all around us, Derfel, and we were blind to them. But that's not what caused this horror.'

'Sansum and Lancelot caused it,' I said.

'The Cauldron brought it,' Merlin said. 'Someone has used it, Derfel, and its power is loose in the land. I suspect Dinas and Lavaine have it, but they don't know how to control it and so they've spilt its horror.'

I walked on in silence. The Severn Sea was visible now, a crawling flood of silver black beneath a sinking moon. Ceinwyn was crying softly and I took her hand. 'I discovered,' I said to her, trying to distract her from her grief, 'who my father is. Just yesterday I found it out.'

'Your father is Aelle,' Merlin said placidly.

I gazed at him. 'How did you know?'

'It's in your face, Derfel, in your face. Tonight, when you came through the gate, you only needed a black bear cloak to be him.' He smiled at me. 'I remember you as an earnest little boy, all questions and frowns, then tonight you came like a warrior of the Gods, a terrifying thing of iron and steel and plume and shield.'

'Is it true?' Ceinwyn asked me.

'Yes,' I admitted, and feared what her reaction might be.

I need not have feared. 'Then Aelle must be a very great man,' she said firmly, and gave me a sad smile, 'Lord Prince.'

We reached the sea and turned north. We had nowhere else to go except towards Gwent and Powys where the madness had not spread, but our path ended at a place where the sand of the beach petered out into a spit where the incoming tide broke white on a rippled expanse of mud. To our left was the sea, to

389

our right were the marshes of Avalon, and it seemed to me that we were trapped there, but Merlin told us we should not worry. 'Rest,' he said, 'for help will come soon.' He looked east to see a glimmer of light showing above the hills beyond the marsh. 'Dawn,' he announced, 'and when the sun is full up, our help will come.' He sat and played with Seren and her kittens while the rest of us lay on the sand, our bundles beside us, as Pyrlig, our bard, sang the Love Song of Rhiannon that had always been Dian's favourite song. Ceinwyn, one arm around Morwenna, wept while I just stared at the fretting grey sea and dreamed of revenge.

The sun rose, promising another lovely summer's day in Dumnonia, only on this day the iron-clad horsemen would be spreading across the countryside to find us. The Cauldron had at last been used, the Christians had flocked to Lancelot's banner, horror was spilling across the land and all Arthur's work was under siege.

Lancelot's men were not the only ones who searched for us that morning. The marsh villages had heard the news of Ermid's Hall, just as they had heard that the ghoulish ceremony in Ynys Wydryn had been a Christian wedding, and any enemy of the Christians was a friend of the marsh folk, so their boatmen and trackers and hunters ranged wide across the swamps in search of us.

They found us two hours after sunrise and led us north through the marsh paths where no enemy would dare intrude. By nightfall, out of the marshes now, we were close to the town of Abona where ships sailed for the Silurian coast with cargoes of grain, pottery, tin and lead. A band of Lancelot's men guarded the Roman-built wharves that lined the river-port, but his army was thinly scattered and there were no more than twenty spearmen watching the ships, and most of those spearmen were half drunk from a looted cargo of mead. We killed them all. Death had already come to Abona, for the bodies of a dozen pagans lay on the mud above the river's tide line. The fanatical Christians who had slaughtered the pagans had already left, gone to join Lancelot's army, and the folk who remained in the town were fearful. They told us what had happened in the town, swore their own innocence in the killings, then barred their doors that all bore the mark of the fish. Next morning, on a rising tide, we sailed for Silurian Isca, the fort on the Usk where Lancelot had once made his palace when he had sulked on Siluria's inadequate throne.

Ceinwyn sat next to me in the boat's scuppers. 'It's strange,' she said, 'how wars come and go with kings.'

'How?' I asked.

She shrugged. 'Uther died and there was nothing but fighting till Arthur killed my father, then we had peace, and now Mordred comes to the throne and we have war again. It's like the seasons, Derfel. War comes and it goes.' She leaned her head on my shoulder. 'So what will happen now?' she asked.

'You and the girls will go north to Caer Sws,' I said, 'and I shall stay and fight.'

'Will Arthur fight?' she asked.

'If Guinevere's been killed,' I said, 'he'll fight till there isn't an enemy left alive.' We had heard nothing of Guinevere, but with Christians marauding throughout Dumnonia it seemed unlikely that she would have been left unmolested.

'Poor Guinevere,' Ceinwyn said, 'and poor Gwydre.' She was very fond of Arthur's son.

We landed in the River Usk, safe at last on territory ruled by Meurig, and from there we walked north to Gwent's capital, Burrium. Gwent was a Christian country, but it had not been infected by the madness that had swept Dumnonia. Gwent already had a Christian King, and maybe that circumstance had been sufficient to keep its people calm. Meurig blamed Arthur. 'He should have suppressed paganism,' he told us.

'Why, Lord King?' I asked. 'Arthur's a pagan himself.'

'Christ's truth is blindingly obvious, I should have thought,' Meurig said. 'If a man cannot read the tides of history, then he only has himself to blame. Christianity is the future, Lord Derfel, and paganism is its past.'

'Not much of a future,' I said scornfully, 'if history is to end in four years.'

'It doesn't end!' Meurig said. 'It begins! When Christ comes again, Lord Derfel, the days of glory arrive! We shall all be Kings, all be joyful and all be blessed.'

'Except us pagans.'

'Naturally, hell must be fed. But there is still time for you to accept the true faith.'

Both Ceinwyn and I declined his invitation of baptism and next morning she left for Powys with Morwenna, Seren and the other wives and children. We spearmen embraced our families, then watched them walk north. Meurig gave them an escort, and I sent six of my own men with orders to come back south as soon as the women were safe under Cuneglas's guard. Malaine, Powys's Druid, went with them, but Merlin and Nimue, whose quest for the Cauldron was suddenly burning as hot as ever it had on the Dark Road, stayed with us.

King Meurig travelled with us to Glevum. That town was Dumnonian, but right on the border of Gwent, and its earth and timber walls guarded Meurig's land, so, sensibly enough, he had already garrisoned it with his own spearmen to make sure that the tumults of Dumnonia did not spread north into Gwent. It took us a half day to reach Glevum and there, in the great Roman hall where Uther's last High Council had been held, I found the rest of my men, Arthur's men, and Arthur himself.

He saw me come into the hall and the look of relief on his face was so heartfelt that tears came to my eyes. My spearmen, those who had stayed with Arthur when I went south to find my mother, cheered, and the next few moments were a bluster of reunions and news. I told them of Ermid's Hall, told them the names of the men who had died, assured them that their women still lived, then looked at Arthur. 'But they killed Dian,' I said.

'Dian?' I think he did not believe me at first.

'Dian,' I said, and the wretched tears came again.

Arthur eased me out of the hall and walked with his right arm about my shoulders to Glevum's ramparts where Meurig's red-cloaked spearmen now manned every fighting platform. He made me tell him the whole tale again, right from the moment I had left him until the moment we took ship from Abona. 'Dinas and Lavaine.' He spoke the names bitterly, then he drew Excalibur and kissed the grey blade. 'Your vengeance is mine,' he said formally, then slid the sword back into her scabbard.

For a time we said nothing, but just leaned on the top of the wall and stared at the wide valley south of Glevum. It looked so peaceful. The hay crop was nearly ready for cutting and there were bright poppies in the growing corn. 'Do you have news of Guinevere?' Arthur broke the silence and I heard something close to desperation in his voice.

'No, Lord.'

He shuddered, then regained control of himself. 'The Christians hate her,' he said softly, and then, uncharacteristically, he touched the iron of Excalibur's hilt to avert evil.

'Lord,' I tried to reassure him, 'she has guards. And her palace is by the sea. She would have escaped if there was danger.'

'To where? Broceliande? But suppose Cerdic sent ships?' He closed his eyes for a few seconds, then shook his head. 'We can only wait for news.'

I asked him about Mordred, but he had heard nothing more than the rest of us. 'I suspect he is dead,' he said bleakly, 'for if he had escaped then he should have reached us here by now.'

He did have news of Sagramor, and that news was bad. 'Cerdic hurt him hard. Caer Ambra's fallen, Calleva's gone and Corinium is under siege. It should hold out a few days yet, for Sagramor managed to add two hundred spears to its garrison, but their food will be gone by the month's end. It seems we have war again.' He gave a short, harsh bark of laughter. 'You were right about

Lancelot, weren't you? and I was blind. I thought him a friend.' I said nothing, but just glanced at him and saw, to my surprise, that there were grey hairs at his temples. To me he still seemed young, but I supposed that if any man were to meet him now for the first time they would think him on the edge of his middle years. 'How could Lancelot have brought Cerdic into Dumnonia,' he asked angrily, 'or encouraged the Christians in their madness?'

'Because he wants to be King of Dumnonia,' I said, 'and he needs their spears. And Sansum wants to be his chief councillor, his royal treasurer and everything else too.'

Arthur shuddered. 'You think Sansum really planned our deaths at Cadoc's shrine?'

'Who else?' I asked. It was Sansum, I believed, who had first linked the fish on Lancelot's shield with the name of Christ, and Sansum who had whipped the excited Christian community into a fervour that would sweep Lancelot onto Dumnonia's throne. I doubted that Sansum put much faith in his Christ's imminent coming, but he did want to hold as much power as he could and Lancelot was Sansum's candidate for Dumnonia's kingship. If Lancelot succeeded in holding the throne, all the reins of power would lead back to the mouse-lord's paws. 'He's a dangerous little bastard,' I said vengefully. 'We should have killed him ten years ago.'

'Poor Morgan,' Arthur sighed. Then he grimaced. 'What did we do wrong?' he asked me.

'We?' I said indignantly. 'We did nothing wrong.'

'We never understood what the Christians wanted,' he said, 'but what could we have done if we had? They were never going to accept anything less than utter victory.'

'It's nothing we did,' I said, 'only what the calendar does to them. The year 500 has made them mad.'

'I had hoped,' he said softly, 'that we had weaned Dumnonia away from madness.'

'You gave them peace, Lord,' I said, 'and peace gave them the chance to breed their madness. If we'd been fighting the Saxons all those years their energies would have gone into battle and survival, but instead we gave them the chance to foment their idiocies.'

He shrugged. 'But what do we do now?'

'Now?' I said. 'We fight!'

'With what?' he asked bitterly. 'Sagramor has his hands full with Cerdic. Cuneglas will send us spears, I'm sure, but Meurig won't fight.'

'He won't?' I asked, alarmed. 'But he swore the Round Table oath!'

Arthur smiled sadly. 'These oaths, Derfel, how they haunt us. And these sad days, it seems, men take them so lightly. Lancelot swore the oath too, did he not? But Meurig says that with Mordred dead there is no *casus belli*.' He quoted the Latin bitterly, and I remembered Meurig using the same words before Lugg Vale, and how Culhwch had mocked the King's erudition by twisting the Latin into 'cow's belly'. 'Culhwch will come,' I said.

'To fight for Mordred's land?' Arthur asked. 'I doubt it.'

'To fight for you, Lord,' I said. 'For if Mordred is dead, you're King.'

He smiled bitterly at that statement. 'King of what? Of Glevum?' He laughed. 'I have you, I have Sagramor, I have whatever Cuneglas gives me, but Lancelot has Dumnonia and he has Cerdic.' He walked in silence for a short while, then gave me a crooked smile. 'We do have one other ally, though hardly a friend. Aelle has taken advantage of Cerdic's absence to retake London. Maybe Cerdic and he will kill each other?'

'Aelle,' I said, 'will be killed by his son, not by Cerdic.'

He gave me a quizzical glance. 'What son?'

'It's a curse,' I said, 'and I am Aelle's son.'

He stopped and gazed at me to see if I was jesting. 'You?' he asked.

'Me, Lord.'

'Truly?'

'Upon my honour, Lord, I am your enemy's son.'

He still stared at me, then began to laugh. The laughter was genuine and extravagant, ending in tears that he wiped away as he shook his head in amusement. 'Dear Derfel! If only Uther and Aelle knew!' Uther and Aelle, the great enemies, whose sons had become friends. Fate is inexorable.

'Maybe Aelle does know,' I said, remembering how gently he had reprimanded me for ignoring Erce.

'He's our ally now,' Arthur said, 'whether we want him or not. Unless we choose not to fight.'

'Not to fight?' I asked in horror.

'There are times,' Arthur said softly, 'when all I want is to have Guinevere and Gwydre back and a small house where we can live in peace. I'm even tempted to make an oath, Derfel, that if the Gods give me back my family then I'll never trouble them again. I'll go to a house like the one you had in Powys, remember?'

'Cwm Isaf,' I said, and wondered how Arthur could ever believe that Guinevere might be happy in such a place.

'Just like Cwm Isaf,' he said wistfully. 'A plough, some fields, a son to raise, a King to respect and songs by the evening hearth.' He turned and gazed south again. To the east of the valley great green hills rose steep, and Cerdic's men were not so very far away from those summits. 'I am tired of it all,' Arthur said. For a moment he looked close to tears. 'Think of all we achieved, Derfel, all the roads and lawcourts and bridges, and all the disputes we settled and all the prosperity we made, and all of it is turned to nothing by religion! Religion!' He spat across the ramparts. 'Is Dumnonia even worth fighting for?'

'Dian's soul is worth fighting for,' I said, 'and while Dinas and Lavaine live then I am not at peace. And I pray, Lord, that you won't have such deaths to revenge, but still you must fight. If Mordred's dead, then you're King, and if he lives, we have our oaths.'

'Our oaths,' he said resentfully, and I am sure he was thinking of the words we had spoken above the sea beside which Iseult was to die. 'Our oaths,' he said again.

But oaths were all we had now, for oaths were our guide in times of chaos and chaos was now thick across Dumnonia. For someone had spilt the Cauldron's power and its horror threatened to engulf us all.

DUMNONIA, IN THAT summer, was like a giant throwboard and Lancelot had thrown his pieces well, taking half the board with his opening throw. He had surrendered the valley of the Thames to the Saxons, but the rest of the country was now his, thanks to the Christians who had blindly fought for him because his shield displayed their mystical emblem of a fish. I doubted that Lancelot was any more of a Christian than Mordred had been, but Sansum's missionaries had spread their insidious message and, as far as Dumnonia's poor deceived Christians were concerned, Lancelot was the harbinger of Christ.

Lancelot had not won every point. His plot to kill Arthur had failed, and while Arthur lived Lancelot was in danger, but on the day after I arrived in Glevum he tried to sweep the throwboard clean. He tried to win it all.

He sent a horseman with an upturned shield and a sprig of mistletoe tied to his spear-point. The rider carried a message that summoned Arthur to Dun Ceinach, an ancient earth fortress that reared its summit just a few miles south of Glevum's ramparts. The message demanded that Arthur go to the ancient fort that very same day, it swore his safety and it allowed him to bring as many spearmen as he wished. The message's imperious tone almost invited refusal, but it finished by promising Arthur news of Guinevere, and Lancelot must have known that promise would bring Arthur out of Glevum.

He left an hour later. Twenty of us rode with him, all of us in full armour beneath a blazing sun. Great white clouds sailed above the hills that rose steep from the eastern side of Severn's wide valley. We could have followed the tracks that twisted up into those hills, but they led through too many places where an ambush might be set and so we took the road south along the valley, a Roman road that ran between fields where poppies blazed among the growing rye and barley. After an hour we turned east and cantered beside a hedge that was white with hawthorn blossom, then across a hay meadow almost ready for the sickle, and so we reached the steep grassy slope that was topped by the ancient fort. Sheep scattered as we climbed the slope, which was so precipitous that I preferred to slide off my horse's back and lead it by the reins. Bee orchids blossomed pink and brown among the grass.

We stopped a hundred paces below the summit and I climbed on alone to make sure that no ambush waited behind the fort's long grassy walls. I was panting and sweating by the time I gained the wall's summit, but no enemy crouched behind the bank. Indeed the old fort seemed deserted except for two hares that fled from my sudden appearance. The silence of the hilltop made me cautious, but then a single horseman appeared among some low trees that grew in the northern part of the fort. He carried a spear that he ostentatiously threw down, turned his shield upside down, then slid off his horse's back. A dozen men followed him out of the trees and they too threw down their spears as if to reassure me that their promise of a truce was genuine.

I waved Arthur up. His horses breasted the wall, then he and I walked forward. Arthur was in his finest armour. He did not appear here as a supplicant, but as a warrior in a white-plumed helmet and a silvered coat of scale armour.

Two men walked to meet us. I had expected to see Lancelot himself, but instead it was his cousin and champion, Bors, who approached us. Bors was a tall black-haired man, heavily bearded, broad-shouldered, and a capable warrior who thrust through life like a bull where his master slid like a snake. I had no dislike of Bors nor he of me, but our loyalties dictated that we should be enemies.

Bors nodded a curt greeting. He was in armour, but his companion was dressed in priest's robes. It was Bishop Sansum. That surprised me, for Sansum usually took good care to disguise his loyalties and I thought our little mouse-lord must be very confident of victory if he displayed his allegiance to Lancelot so openly. Arthur gave Sansum a dismissive glance, then looked at Bors. 'You have news of my wife,' he said curtly.

'She lives,' Bors said, 'and she is safe. So is your son.'

Arthur closed his eyes. He could not hide his relief, indeed for a moment he could not even speak. 'Where are they?' he asked when he had collected himself.

'At her Sea Palace,' Bors said, 'under guard.'

'You keep women prisoners?' I asked scornfully.

'They are under guard, Derfel,' Bors answered just as scornfully, 'because Dumnonia's Christians are slaughtering their enemies. And those Christians, Lord Arthur, have no love for your wife. My Lord King Lancelot has your wife and son under his protection.'

'Then your Lord King Lancelot,' Arthur said with just a trace of sarcasm, 'can have them brought north under escort.'

'No,' Bors said. He was bare-headed and the heat of the sun was making the sweat run down his broad, scarred face.

'No?' Arthur asked dangerously.

'I have a message for you, Lord,' Bors said defiantly, 'and the message is this. My Lord King grants you the right to live in Dumnonia with your wife. You will be treated with honour, but only if you swear an oath of loyalty to my King.' He paused and glanced up into the sky. It was one of those portentous days when the moon shared the sky with the sun and he gestured towards the moon that was swollen somewhere between the half and the full. 'You have,' he said, 'until the moon is full to present yourself to my Lord King at Caer Cadarn. You may come with no more than ten men, you will swear your oath, and you may then live under his dominion in peace.'

I spat to show my opinion of his promise, but Arthur held up a hand to still my anger. 'And if I do not come?' he asked.

Another man might have been ashamed to deliver the message, but Bors showed no qualms. 'If you do not come,' he said, 'then my Lord King will presume that you are at war with him, in which case he will need every spear he can collect. Even those who now guard your wife and child.'

'So his Christians,' Arthur jerked his chin towards Sansum, 'can kill them?'

'She can always be baptized!' Sansum put in. He clutched the cross that hung over his black robe. 'I will guarantee her safety if she is baptized.'

Arthur stared at him. Then, very deliberately, he spat full in Sansum's face. The Bishop jerked back. Bors, I noticed, was amused and I suspected little affection was lost between Lancelot's champion and his chaplain. Arthur looked again at Bors. 'Tell me of Mordred,' he demanded.

Bors looked surprised at the question. 'There's nothing to tell,' he said after a pause. 'He's dead.'

'You've seen his body?' Arthur asked.

Bors hesitated again, then shook his head. 'He was killed by a man whose daughter he had raped. Beyond that I know nothing. Except that my Lord King came into Dumnonia to quell the riots that followed the killing.' He paused as if he expected Arthur to say something more, but when nothing was said he just looked up at the moon. 'You have till the full,' he said and turned away.

'One minute!' I called, turning Bors back. 'What of me?' I asked.

Bors's hard eyes stared into mine. 'What of you?' he said scornfully.

'Does the killer of my daughter demand an oath of me?' I asked.

'My Lord King wants nothing of you,' Bors said.

'Then tell him,' I said, 'that I want something of him. Tell him I want the souls of Dinas and Lavaine, and if it is the last thing I do on this earth, I shall take them.'

Bors shrugged as though their deaths meant nothing to him,

then looked back to Arthur. 'We shall be waiting at Caer Cadarn, Lord,' he said, then walked away. Sansum stayed to shout at us, telling us that Christ was coming in his glory and that all pagans and sinners would be wiped clean from the earth before that happy day. I spat at him, then turned and followed Arthur. Sansum dogged us, shouting at our heels, but then suddenly called my name. I ignored him. 'Lord Derfel!' he called again, 'you whoremaster! You whore-lover!' He must have known those insults would draw me back to him in anger, and though he did not want my anger, he did want my attention. 'I meant nothing, Lord,' he said hastily as I hurried back towards him. 'I must talk with you. Quickly.' He glanced behind to make sure Bors was out of earshot, then gave another bellow demanding my repentance just to make certain that Bors thought he was harassing me. 'I thought you and Arthur were dead,' he said in a low voice.

'You arranged our deaths,' I accused him.

He blanched. 'On my soul, Derfel, no! No!' He made the sign of the cross. 'May the angels tear out my tongue and feed it to the devil if it lies to you. I swear by Almighty God, Derfel, that I knew nothing.' That lie told, he glanced round again, then looked back to me. 'Dinas and Lavaine,' he said softly, 'stand guard over Guinevere at the Sea Palace. Remember it was I, Lord, who told you that.'

I smiled. 'You don't want Bors to know you betrayed that knowledge to me, do you?'

'No, Lord, please!'

'Then this should convince him of your innocence,' I said, and gave the mouse-lord a box round his ears that must have had his head ringing like the great bell at his shrine. He spun down to the turf from where he shrieked curses at me as I walked away. I understood now why Sansum had come to this high fortress beneath the sky. The mouse-lord could see clearly enough that Arthur's survival threatened Lancelot's new throne and no man could blithely keep his faith in a master who was opposed by Arthur. Sansum, just like his wife, was making sure I owed him thanks.

'What was that about?' Arthur asked me when I caught up with him.

'He told me Dinas and Lavaine are at the Sea Palace. They guard Guinevere.'

Arthur grunted, then looked up at the sun-blanched moon hanging above us. 'How many nights till the full, Derfel?'

'Five?' I guessed. 'Six? Merlin will know.'

'Six days to decide,' he said, then stopped and stared at me. 'Will they dare kill her?'

'No, Lord,' I said, hoping I was right. 'They daren't make an enemy out of you. They want you to come to take their oath and then they'll kill you. After that they might kill her.'

'And if I don't come,' he said softly, 'they'll still hold her. And so long as they hold her, Derfel, I'm helpless.'

'You have a sword, Lord, and a spear and a shield. No man would call you helpless.'

Behind us Bors and his men clambered into their saddles and rode away. We stayed a few moments longer to gaze west from Dun Ceinach's ramparts. It was one of the most beautiful views in all Britain, a hawk's-eye view west across the Severn and deep into distant Siluria. We could see for miles and miles, and from this high place it looked so sunlit, green and beautiful. It was a place to fight for.

And we had six nights till the moon was full.

'Seven nights,' Merlin said.

'You're sure?' Arthur asked.

'Maybe six,' Merlin allowed. 'I do hope you don't expect me to make the computation? It's a very tedious business. I did it often enough for Uther and almost always got it wrong. Six or seven, near enough. Maybe eight.'

'Malaine will work it out,' Cuneglas said. We had returned from Dun Ceinach to find that Cuneglas had come from Powys. He had brought Malaine with him after meeting the Druid who had been accompanying Ceinwyn and the other women north-wards. The King of Powys had embraced me and sworn his own revenge on Dinas and Lavaine. He had brought sixty spearmen in his entourage and told us another hundred were already following him southwards. More would come, he said, for Cuneglas expected to fight and he was generously providing every warrior he commanded.

His sixty warriors now squatted with Arthur's men around the edges of Glevum's great hall as their lords talked in the hall's centre. Only Sagramor was not there, for he was with his remaining spearmen harrying Cerdic's army near Corinium. Meurig was present, and unable to hide his annoyance that Merlin had taken the large chair at the head of the table. Cuneglas and Arthur flanked Merlin, Meurig faced Merlin down the table's length and Culhwch and I had the other two places. Culhwch had come to Glevum with Cuneglas and his arrival had been like a gust of fresh clean air in a smoky hall. He could not wait to fight. He declared that with Mordred dead Arthur was King of Dumnonia and Culhwch was ready to wade through blood to protect his cousin's throne. Cuneglas and I shared that belligerence, Meurig squeaked about prudence, Arthur said nothing, while Merlin appeared to be asleep. I doubted he was sleeping for a small smile showed on his face, but his eyes were closed as he pretended to be blissfully unaware of all we said.

Culhwch scorned Bors's message. He insisted Lancelot would never kill Guinevere, and that all Arthur needed to do was ride south at the head of his men and the throne would fall into his hands. 'Tomorrow!' Culhwch told Arthur. 'We'll ride tomorrow. It'll all be over in two days.'

Cuneglas was slightly more cautious, advising Arthur that he should wait for the rest of his Powysian spearmen to arrive, but once those men had come he was sure we should declare war and go southwards. 'How big is Lancelot's army?' he asked.

Arthur shrugged. 'Not counting Cerdic's men? Maybe three hundred?'

'Nothing!' Culhwch roared. 'Have them dead before breakfast.'

'And a lot of fiery Christians,' Arthur warned him.

Culhwch offered an opinion of Christians that had the Christian Meurig spluttering with indignation. Arthur calmed the young King of Gwent. 'You're all forgetting something,' he said mildly. 'I never wanted to be King. I still don't.'

There was a momentary silence around the table, though some of the warriors at the hall's edge muttered a protest at Arthur's words. 'Whatever you might want,' Cuneglas broke our silence, 'does not matter any more. The Gods, it seems, have made that decision for you.'

'If the Gods wanted me to be King,' Arthur said, 'they would have arranged for my mother to have been married to Uther.'

'So what do you want?' Culhwch bellowed in despair.

'I want Guinevere and Gwydre back,' Arthur said softly. 'And Cerdic defeated,' he added before staring down at the table's scarred top for a moment. 'I want to live,' he went on, 'like an ordinary man. With a wife and a son and a house and a farm. I want peace,' and for once he was not talking of all Britain, but just of himself. 'I don't want to be tangled in oaths, I don't want to be forever dealing with men's ambitions and I don't want to be the arbiter of men's happiness any more. I just want to do what King Tewdric did. I want to find a green place and live there.'

'And rot away?' Merlin gave up his pretence of sleep.

Arthur smiled. 'There is so much to learn, Merlin. Why does a man make two swords from the same metal in the same fire and one blade will be true and the other will bend in its first battle? There is so much to find out.'

'He wants to be a blacksmith,' Merlin said to Culhwch.

'What I want is Guinevere and Gwydre back,' Arthur declared firmly.

'Then you must take Lancelot's oath,' Meurig said.

'If he goes to Caer Cadarn to take Lancelot's oath,' I said bitterly, 'he'll be met by a hundred armed men and cut down like a dog.'

'Not if I take Kings with me,' Arthur said gently.

We all stared at him and he seemed surprised that we had been nonplussed by his words. 'Kings?' Culhwch finally broke the silence.

Arthur smiled. 'If my Lord King Cuneglas and my Lord King Meurig were to ride with me to Caer Cadarn then I doubt that Lancelot would dare to kill me. If he's faced by the Kings of Britain he will have to talk, and if he talks we shall come to an agreement. He fears me, but if he discovers there is nothing to fear, he will let me live. And he will let my family live.'

There was another silence while we digested that, then Culhwch roared a protest. 'You'd let that bastard Lancelot be King?' Some of the spearmen at the hall's edge growled their agreement.

'Cousin, cousin!' Arthur soothed Culhwch. 'Lancelot is not an evil man. He's weak, I think, but not evil. He doesn't make plans, he has no dreams, but only a greedy eye and quick hands. He snatches things as they appear, then hoards them and waits for another thing to snatch. He wants me dead now, because he fears me, but when he discovers the price of my death is too high, then he'll accept what he can get.'

'He'll accept your death, you fool!' Culhwch hammered the table with his fist. 'He'll tell you a thousand lies, protest his friendship and slide a sword between your ribs the moment your Kings have gone home.'

'He'll lie to me,' Arthur agreed placidly. 'All kings lie. No kingdom could be ruled without lies, for lies are the things we use to build our reputations. We pay the bards to make our squalid victories into great triumphs and sometimes we even believe the lies they sing to us. Lancelot would love to believe all those songs, but the truth is that he's weak and he desperately craves strong friends. He fears me now, for he assumes my enmity, but when he discovers I am not an enemy then he will also find that he needs me. He will need every man he can find if he's to rid Dumnonia of Cerdic.'

'And who invited Cerdic into Dumnonia?' Culhwch protested. 'Lancelot did!'

'And he'll regret it soon,' Arthur said calmly. 'He used Cerdic to snatch his prize, and he'll find Cerdic is a dangerous ally.'

'You'd fight for Lancelot?' I asked, horrified.

'I will fight for Britain,' Arthur said firmly. 'I can't ask men to die to make me what I don't want to be, but I can ask them to fight for their homes and their wives and their children. And that's what I fight for. For Guinevere. And to defeat Cerdic, and once he is defeated, what does it matter if Lancelot rules Dumnonia? Someone has to and I dare say he'll make a better King that Mordred ever did.' Again there was silence. A hound whined at the edge of the hall and a spearman sneezed. Arthur looked at us and saw we were still bemused. 'If I fight Lancelot,' he told us, 'then we go back to the Britain we had before Lugg Vale. A Britain in which we fight each other instead of the Saxons. There is only one principle here, and that is Uther's old insistence that the Saxons must be kept from the Severn Sea. And now,' he said vigorously, 'the Saxons are closer to the Severn than they've ever been. If I fight for a throne I don't want I give Cerdic the chance to take Corinium and then this city, and if he does take Glevum then he has split us into two parts. If I fight Lancelot then the Saxons will win everything. They'll take Dumnonia and Gwent and after that they'll go north into Powys.'

'Exactly.' Meurig applauded Arthur.

'I won't fight for Lancelot,' I said angrily and Culhwch applauded me.

Arthur smiled at me. 'My dear friend Derfel, I would not expect you to fight for Lancelot, though I do want your men to fight Cerdic. And my price for helping Lancelot defeat Cerdic is that he gives you Dinas and Lavaine.'

I stared at him. I had not understood till that moment just how far ahead he had been thinking. The rest of us had seen nothing but Lancelot's treachery, but Arthur was thinking only of Britain and of the desperate need to keep the Saxons away from the Severn. He would brush Lancelot's hostility aside, force my revenge on him, then go on with the work of defeating Saxons.

'And the Christians?' Culhwch asked derisively. 'You think they'll let you back into Dumnonia? You think those bastards won't build a bonfire for you?'

Meurig squawked another protest that Arthur stilled. 'The Christian fervour will spend itself,' Arthur said. 'It's like a madness, and once it's exhausted they'll go home to pick up the pieces of their lives. And once Cerdic is defeated Lancelot can pacify Dumnonia. I shall just live with my family, which is all I want.'

Cuneglas had been leaning back in his chair to stare at the remaining patches of Roman paintings on the hall's ceiling. Now he straightened and looked at Arthur. 'Tell me again what you want,' he asked softly.

'I want the Britons at peace,' Arthur said patiently, 'and I want Cerdic pushed back, and I want my family.'

Cuneglas looked at Merlin. 'Well, Lord?' he invited the old man's judgment.

Merlin had been tying two of his beard braids into knots, but now he looked mildly startled and hastily untangled the strands. 'I doubt that the Gods want what Arthur wants,' he said. 'You are all forgetting the Cauldron.'

'This has nothing to do with the Cauldron,' Arthur said firmly.

'It has everything to do with it,' Merlin said with a sudden and surprising harshness, 'and the Cauldron brings chaos. You desire order, Arthur, and you think that Lancelot will listen to your reason and that Cerdic will submit to your sword, but your reasonable order will no more work in the future than it worked in the past. Do you really think men and women thanked you for bringing them peace? They just became bored with your peace and so brewed their own trouble to fill the boredom. Men don't want peace, Arthur, they want distraction from tedium, while you desire tedium like a thirsty man seeks mead. Your reason won't defeat the Gods, and the Gods will make sure of that. You think you can crawl away to a homestead and play at being a blacksmith? No.' Merlin gave an evil smile and picked up his long black staff. 'Even at this moment,' Merlin said, 'the Gods are making trouble for you.' He pointed the staff at the hall's front doors. 'Behold your trouble, Arthur ap Uther.'

We all turned to see Galahad standing in the doorway. He was clothed in mail armour, had a sword at his side and spatters of mud up to his waist. And with him was a miserable, club-footed, squashed-nosed, round-faced, skimpy-bearded brush-head.

For Mordred still lived.

There was an astonished silence. Mordred limped into the hall and his small eyes betrayed his resentment for the lack of welcome. Arthur just stared at his oath-lord and I knew he was undoing in his head all the careful plans he had just described to us. There could be no reasonable peace with Lancelot, for Arthur's oath-lord still lived. Dumnonia still possessed a King, and it was not Lancelot. It was Mordred and Mordred had Arthur's oath.

Then the silence broke as men gathered round the King to discover his news. Galahad stepped aside to embrace me. 'Thank God you live,' he said with heartfelt relief.

I smiled at my friend. 'Do you expect me to thank you for saving my King's life?' I asked him.

'Someone should, for he hasn't. He's an ungrateful little beast,' Galahad said. 'God knows why he lives and so many good men died. Llywarch, Bedwyr, Dagonet, Blaise. All gone.' He was naming those of Arthur's warriors who had been killed in Durnovaria. Some of the deaths I had already known, others were new to me, but Galahad did know more about the manner of their deaths. He had been in Durnovaria when the rumour of Mordred's death had sparked the Christians into riot, but Galahad swore there had been spearmen among the rioters. He believed Lancelot's men had infiltrated the town under the guise of pilgrims travelling to Ynys Wydryn and that those spearmen had led the massacre. 'Most of Arthur's men were in the taverns,' he said, 'and they stood little chance. A few survived, but God alone knows where they are now.' He made the sign of the cross. 'This isn't Christ's doing, Derfel, you do know that, don't you? It's the devil at work.' He gave me a pained, almost frightened look. 'Is it true about Dian?'

'True,' I said. Galahad embraced me wordlessly. He had never married and had no children, but he loved my daughters. He loved all children. 'Dinas and Lavaine killed her,' I told him, 'and they live still.'

'My sword is yours,' he said.

'I know it,' I said.

'And if this was Christ's doing,' Galahad said earnestly, 'then Dinas and Lavaine would not be serving Lancelot.'

'I don't blame your God,' I told him. 'I don't blame any God.' I turned to watch the commotion around Mordred. Arthur was shouting for silence and order, servants had been sent to bring food and clothes fit for a King and other men were trying to hear his news. 'Didn't Lancelot demand your oath?' I asked Galahad.

'He didn't know I was in Durnovaria. I was staying with Bishop Emrys and the Bishop gave me a monk's robe to wear over this,' he patted his mail coat, 'then I went north. Poor Emrys is distraught. He thinks his Christians have gone mad and I think they have too. I suppose I could have stayed and fought, but I didn't. I ran. I had heard that you and Arthur were dead, but I didn't believe it. I thought I'd find you, but I found our King instead.' He told me how Mordred had been hunting boar north of Durnovaria, and Lancelot, Galahad believed, had sent men to intercept the King as he returned to Durnovaria; but some village girl had taken Mordred's fancy and by the time he and his companions were done with her it was near dark, and so he had commandeered the village's largest house and ordered food. His assassins had waited at the city's northern gate while Mordred feasted a dozen miles away, and some time during that evening Lancelot's men must have decided to start the killing even though the Dumnonian King had somehow escaped their ambush. They had spread a rumour of his death and used that rumour to justify Lancelot's usurpation.

Mordred heard of the troubles when the first fugitives arrived from Durnovaria. Most of his companions had melted away, the villagers were summoning the courage to kill the King who had raped one of their girls and stolen much of their food, and Mordred had panicked. He and his last friends fled north in villagers' clothes. 'They were trying to reach Caer Cadarn,' Galahad told me, 'reckoning they'd find loyal spearmen there, but they found me instead. I was aiming to reach your house, but we heard your folk had fled, so I brought him north.'

'Did you see Saxons?'

He shook his head. 'They're in the Thames Valley. We avoided it.' He stared at the jostling crowd around Mordred. 'So what happens now?' he asked.

Mordred had firm ideas. He was robed in a borrowed cloak and sitting at the table where he crammed bread and salt beef into his mouth. He was demanding that Arthur march south immediately, and whenever Arthur tried to interrupt, the King would slap the table and repeat his demand. 'Are you denying your oath?' Mordred finally shouted at Arthur, spewing half chewed scraps of bread and beef.

'The Lord Arthur,' Cuneglas answered acidly, 'is trying to preserve his wife and child.'

Mordred looked blankly at the Powysian King. 'Above my kingdom?' he finally asked.

'If Arthur goes to war,' Cuneglas explained to Mordred, 'Guinevere and Gwydre die.'

'So we do nothing?' Mordred screamed. He was hysterical.

'We give the matter thought,' Arthur said bitterly.

'Thought?' Mordred shouted, then stood up. 'You'll just think while that bastard rules my land? Do you have an oath?' he demanded of Arthur. 'And what use are these men if you won't fight?' He waved at the spearmen who now stood in a ring about the table. 'You'll fight for me, that's what you'll do! That's what your oath demands. You'll fight!' He slapped the table again. 'You don't think! You fight!'

I had taken enough. Perhaps the dead soul of my daughter came to me at that moment, for almost without thinking I strode

411

forward and unbuckled my sword belt. I stripped Hywelbane off the belt, threw the sword down, then folded the leather strap in two. Mordred watched me and spluttered a feeble protest as I approached him, but no one moved to stop me.

I reached my King's side, paused, then struck him hard across the face with the doubled belt. 'That,' I said, 'is not in return for the blows you gave me, but for my daughter, and this' – I struck him again, much harder – 'is for your failure to keep the oath to guard your kingdom.'

Spearmen bellowed approval. Mordred's lower lip was trembling as it had when he had taken all those beatings as a child. His cheeks were reddened from the blows and a trickle of blood showed at a tiny cut under his eye. He touched a finger to that blood, then spat a gob of half-chewed beef and bread into my face. 'You'll die for that,' he promised me, and then, in a swelling rage, he tried to slap me. 'How could I defend the kingdom?' he shouted. 'You weren't there! Arthur wasn't there.' He tried to slap me a second time, but again I parried his blow with my arm, then lifted the belt to give him another beating.

Arthur, horrified at my behaviour, pushed down my arm and dragged me away. Mordred followed, flailing at me with his fists, but then a black staff struck his arm hard and he turned in fury to assault his new attacker.

But it was Merlin who now towered above the angry King. 'Hit me, Mordred,' the Druid said quietly, 'and I shall turn you into a toad and feed you to the serpents of Annwn.'

Mordred gazed at the Druid, but said nothing. He did try to push the staff away, but Merlin held it firm and used it to thrust the young King back towards his chair. 'Tell me, Mordred,' Merlin said as he pushed Mordred back down into the chair, 'why you sent Arthur and Derfel so far away?'

Mordred shook his head. He was frightened of this new, straight-backed, towering Merlin. He had only ever known the Druid as a frail old man sunning himself in Lindinis's garden and this reinvigorated Merlin with his wrapped and plaited beard terrified him.

Merlin raised his staff and slammed it down on the table. 'Why?' he asked gently when the echo of the staff's blow had died away.

'To arrest Ligessac,' Mordred whispered.

'You squirming little fool,' Merlin said. 'A child could have arrested Ligessac. Why did you send Arthur and Derfel?'

Mordred just shook his head.

Merlin sighed. 'It has been a long time, young Mordred, since I used the greater magic. I am sadly out of practice, but I think, with Nimue's help, I can turn your urine into the black pus that stings like a wasp every time you piss. I can addle your brain, what there is of it, and I can make your manhood,' the staff suddenly quivered at Mordred's groin, 'shrivel to the size of a dried bean. All that I can do, Mordred, and all that I will do unless you tell me the truth.' He smiled, and there was more threat in that smile than in the poised staff. 'Tell me, dear boy, why you sent Arthur and Derfel to Cadoc's camp?'

Mordred's lower lip was trembling. 'Because Sansum told me to.'

'The mouse-lord!' Merlin exclaimed as though the answer surprised him. He smiled again, or at least he bared his teeth. 'I have another question, Mordred,' he continued, 'and if you do not give me the truth then your bowels will disgorge toads in slime, your belly will be a nest of worms and your throat will brim with their bile. I will make you shake incessantly, so that all your life, all your whole life, you will be a toad-shitting, worm-eaten, bile-spitting shudderer. I will make you,' he paused and lowered his voice, 'even more horrible than your mother did. So, Mordred, tell me what the mouse-lord promised would happen if you sent Arthur and Derfel away.'

Mordred stared in terror at Merlin's face.

Merlin waited. No answer came so he raised the staff towards the hall's high roof. 'In the name of Bel,' he intoned sonorously, 'and his toad-Lord Callyc, and in the name of Sucellos and his worm-master Horfael, and in the name of . . .'

'They would be killed!' Mordred squealed desperately.

413

The staff was slowly lowered so that it pointed again at Mordred's face. 'He promised you what, dear boy?' Merlin asked.

Mordred squirmed in his chair, but there was no escape from that staff. He swallowed, looked left and right, but there was no help for him in the hall. 'That they would be killed,' Mordred admitted, 'by the Christians.'

'And why would you want that?' Merlin inquired.

Mordred hesitated, but Merlin raised the staff high again and the boy blurted out his confession. 'Because I can't be King while he lives!'

'You thought Arthur's death would free you to behave as you like?'

'Yes!'

'And you believed Sansum was your friend?'

'Yes.'

'And you never once thought that Sansum might want you dead, too?' Merlin shook his head. 'What a silly boy you are. Don't you know that Christians never do anything right? Even their first one got himself nailed to a cross. That's not the way efficient Gods behave, not at all. Thank you, Mordred, for our conversation.' He smiled, shrugged and walked away. 'Just trying to help,' he said as he went past Arthur.

Mordred appeared as if he already had the shakes threatened by Merlin. He clung to the arms of the chair, quivering, and tears showed at his eyes for the humiliations he had just suffered. He did try to recover some of his pride by pointing at me and demanding that Arthur arrest me.

'Don't be a fool!' Arthur turned on him angrily. 'You think we can regain your throne without Derfel's men?' Mordred said nothing, and that petulant silence goaded Arthur into a fury like the one which had caused me to hit my King. 'It can be done without you!' he snarled at Mordred, 'and whatever is done, you will stay here, under guard!' Mordred gaped up at him and a tear fell to dilute the tiny trace of blood. 'Not as a prisoner, Lord King,' Arthur explained wearily, 'but to preserve your life from the hundreds of men who would like to take it.'

'So what will you do?' Mordred asked, utterly pathetic now.

'As I told you,' Arthur said scornfully, 'I will give the matter thought.' And he would say no more.

The shape of Lancelot's design was at least plain now. Sansum had plotted Arthur's death, Lancelot had sent men to procure Mordred's death and then followed with his army in the belief that every obstacle to Dumnonia's throne had been eliminated and that the Christians, whipped to fury by Sansum's busy missionaries, would kill any remaining enemies while Cerdic held Sagramor's men at bay.

But Arthur lived, and Mordred lived too, and so long as Mordred lived Arthur had an oath to keep and that oath meant we had to go to war. It did not matter that the war might open Severn's valley to the Saxons, we had to fight Lancelot. We were oath-locked.

Meurig would commit no spearmen to the fight against Lancelot. He claimed he needed all his men to guard his own frontiers against a possible attack from Cerdic or Aelle and nothing anyone said could dissuade him. He did agree to leave his garrison in Glevum, thus freeing its Dumnonian garrison to join Arthur's troops, but he would give nothing more. 'He's a yellow little bastard,' Culhwch growled.

'He's a sensible young man,' Arthur said. 'His aim is to preserve his kingdom.' He spoke to us, his war commanders, in a hall at Glevum's Roman baths. The room had a tiled floor and an arched ceiling where the painted remnants of naked nymphs were being chased by a faun through swirls of leaves and flowers.

Cuneglas was generous. The spearmen he had brought from Caer Sws would be sent under Culhwch's command to help Sagramor's men. Culhwch swore he would do nothing to aid Mordred's restoration, but he had no qualms about fighting Cerdic's warriors and that was still Sagramor's task. Once the Numidian was reinforced by the men from Powys he would drive south, cut off the Saxons who were besieging Corinium and so embroil Cerdic's men in a campaign that would keep them from helping Lancelot in Dumnonia's heartland. Cuneglas promised us all the help he could, but said it would take at least two weeks to assemble his full force and bring it south to Glevum.

Arthur had precious few men in Glevum. He had the thirty men who had gone north to arrest Ligessac who now lay in chains in Glevum, and he had my men, and to those he could add the seventy spearmen who had formed Glevum's small garrison. Those numbers were being swollen daily by the refugees who managed to escape the rampaging Christian bands who still hunted down any pagans left in Dumnonia. We heard that many such fugitives were still in Dumnonia, some of them holding out in ancient earth forts or deep in the woodlands, but others came to Glevum and among them was Morfans the Ugly, who had escaped the massacre in Durnovaria's taverns. Arthur put him in charge of the Glevum forces and ordered him to march them south towards Aquae Sulis. Galahad would go with him. 'Don't accept battle,' Arthur warned both men, 'just goad the enemy, harry them, annoy them. Stay in the hills, stay nimble, and keep them looking this way. When my Lord King comes' – he meant Cuneglas – 'you can join his army and march south on Caer Cadarn.'

Arthur declared that he would fight with neither Sagramor nor Morfans, but would instead go to seek Aelle's help. Arthur knew better than anyone that the news of his plans would be carried south. There were plenty enough Christians in Glevum who believed Arthur was the Enemy of God and who saw in Lancelot the heaven-sent forerunner of Christ's return to earth; Arthur wanted those Christians to send their messages south into Dumnonia and he wanted those messages to tell Lancelot that Arthur dared not risk Guinevere's life by marching against him. Instead Arthur was going to beg Aelle to carry his axes and spears against Cerdic's men. 'Derfel will come with me,' he told us now.

I did not want to accompany Arthur. There were other interpreters, I protested, and my only wish was to join Morfans and so march south into Dumnonia. I did not want to face my father, Aelle. I wanted to fight, not to put Mordred back on his throne, but to topple Lancelot and to find Dinas and Lavaine.

Arthur refused me. 'You will come with me, Derfel,' he ordered, 'and we shall take forty men with us.'

'Forty?' Morfans objected. Forty was a large number to strip from his small war-band that had to distract Lancelot.

Arthur shrugged. 'I dare not look weak to Aelle,' he said, 'indeed I should take more, but forty men may be sufficient to convince him that I'm not desperate.' He paused. 'There is one last thing,' he spoke in a heavy voice that caught the attention of men preparing to leave the bath house. 'Some of you are not inclined to fight for Mordred,' Arthur admitted. 'Culhwch has already left Dumnonia, Derfel will doubtless leave when this war is done, and who knows how many others of you will go? Dumnonia cannot afford to lose such men.' He paused. It had begun to rain and water dripped from the bricks that showed between the patches of painted ceiling. 'I have talked to Cuneglas,' Arthur said, acknowledging the King of Powys's presence with an inclination of his head, 'and I have talked with Merlin, and what we talked about are the ancient laws and customs of our people. What I do, I would do within the law, and I cannot free you of Mordred for my oath forbids it and the ancient law of our people cannot condone it.' He paused again, his right hand unconsciously gripping Excalibur's hilt. 'But,' he went on, 'the law does allow one thing. If a king is unfit to rule, then his Council may rule in his stead as long as the king is accorded the honour and privileges of his rank. Merlin assures me this is so, and King Cuneglas affirms that it happened in the reign of his great-grandfather Brychan.'

'Mad as a bat!' Cuneglas put in cheerfully.

Arthur half smiled, then frowned as he gathered his thoughts. 'This is not what I ever wanted,' he protested quietly, his sombre voice echoing in the dripping chamber, 'but I shall propose to the Council of Dumnonia that it should rule in Mordred's place.'

'Yes!' Culhwch shouted.

Arthur hushed him. 'I had hoped,' he said, 'that Mordred would learn responsibility, but he has not. I don't care that he wanted me dead, but I do care that he lost his kingdom. He broke his acclamation oath and I doubt now that he will ever be able to keep that oath.' He paused, and many of us must have reflected on how long it had taken Arthur to understand something that had seemed so obvious to the rest of us. For years he had stubbornly resisted acknowledging Mordred's unfitness to rule, but now, after Mordred had lost his kingdom and, which was much worse in Arthur's eyes, he had failed to protect his subjects, Arthur was at last prepared to face the truth. Water dripped on his bare head, but he seemed oblivious of it. 'Merlin tells me,' he went on in a melancholy voice, 'that Mordred is possessed of an evil spirit. I am not skilled in these things, but that verdict does not seem unlikely and so, if the Council agrees, I shall propose that after we have restored Mordred then we shall pay him all the honours due to our King. He can live in the Winter Palace, he can hunt, he can eat like a king and indulge all his appetites within the law, but he will not govern. I am proposing we give him all the privileges, but none of the duties of his throne.'

We cheered. How we cheered. For now, it seemed, we had something to fight for. Not for Mordred, that wretched toad, but for Arthur, because despite all his fine talk of the Council ruling Dumnonia in Mordred's stead we all knew what his words meant. They meant that Arthur would be Dumnonia's King in all but name and for that good end we would carry our spears to war. We cheered, for now we had a cause to fight and die for. We had Arthur.

Arthur chose twenty of his best horsemen and insisted I choose twenty of my finest spearmen for our embassy to Aelle. 'We must impress your father,' he told me, 'and you don't impress a man by arriving with broken and ageing spearmen. We take our best men.' He also insisted that Nimue accompany us. He would

418

have preferred Merlin's company, but the Druid declared he was too old for the long journey and proposed Nimue instead.

We left Mordred guarded by Meurig's spearmen. Mordred knew of Arthur's plans for him, but he had no allies in Glevum and no defiance in his rotten soul, though he did have the satisfaction of watching Ligessac being strangled in the forum and after that slow death Mordred stood on the terrace of the great hall and made a mumbling speech in which he threatened an equal fate to all the other traitors in Dumnonia, then he went sullenly back to his quarters while we followed Culhwch eastwards. Culhwch had gone to join Sagramor and help launch the attack that we all hoped would save Corinium.

Arthur and I marched into the high fine countryside that was Gwent's rich eastern province. It was a place of lavish villas, vast farms and great wealth, most of it grown on the backs of the sheep that grazed the rolling hills. We marched beneath two banners, Arthur's bear and my own star, and we stayed well north of the Dumnonian frontier so that all the news going to Lancelot would tell him that Arthur was offering his stolen throne no threat. Nimue walked with us. Merlin had somehow persuaded her to wash and find clean clothes, and then, in despair at ever untangling the matted filth of her hair, he had cut it short and burned the dirt-encrusted tresses. The short hair looked good on her, she wore an eyepatch again and carried a staff, but no other baggage. She walked barefoot and she walked reluctantly for she had not wanted to come, but Merlin had persuaded her, though Nimue still claimed her presence was wasteful. 'Any fool can defeat a Saxon wizard,' she told Arthur as we neared the end of the first day's march. 'Just spit on them, roll your eyes and wave a chicken bone. That's all it needs.'

'We won't see any Saxon wizards,' Arthur answered calmly. We were in open country now, far from any villas, and he stopped his horse, raised his hand and waited for the men to gather around him. 'We won't see any wizards,' he told us, 'because we're not going to see Aelle. We're going south into our own country. A long way south.'

'To the sea?' I guessed.

He smiled. 'To the sea.' He folded his hands on his saddle bar. 'We are few,' he told us, 'and Lancelot has many, but Nimue can make us a charm of concealment and we shall march by night and we shall march hard.' He smiled and shrugged. 'I can do nothing while my wife and son are prisoners, but if we free them, then I am free too. And when I am free I can fight against Lancelot, but you should know that we will be far from help and deep in a Dumnonia that is held by our enemies. Once I have Guinevere and Gwydre then I do not know how we shall escape, but Nimue will help us. The Gods will help us, but if any of you fear the task, then you may go back now.'

None did, and he must have known that none would. These forty were our best men and they would have followed Arthur into the serpent's pit. Arthur, of course, had told no one but Merlin what he planned so that no hint of it could reach Lancelot's ears; now he gave me a regretful shrug as though apologizing for deceiving me, but he must have known how pleased I was for we were not just going to where Guinevere and Gwydre were being held hostage, but to where Dian's two killers believed they were safe from all revenge.

'We go tonight,' Arthur said, 'and there'll be no rest till dawn. We go south and by morning I want to be in the hills beyond the Thames.'

We put cloaks over our armour, muffled the horses' hoofs with layers of cloth and then journeyed south through the gathering night. The horsemen led their beasts and Nimue led us, using her strange ability to find her way across unknown country in the darkness.

Sometime in that dark night we crossed into Dumnonia and, as we dropped from the hills down into the valley of the Thames, we saw, far off to our right, a glow in the sky that showed where Cerdic's men were encamped outside Corinium. Once out of the hills our path inevitably took us through small dark villages where dogs barked at our passing, but no one questioned us. The inhabitants were either dead or else they feared

420

we were Saxons, and so, like a band of ghosts, we passed them by. One of Arthur's horsemen was a native of the river lands and he led us to a ford that came up to our chests. We held our weapons and bags of bread high, then forced our way through the strong current and so reached the far bank where Nimue hissed a spell of concealment towards a nearby village. By dawn we were in the southern hills, safe inside one of the Old People's earth fortresses.

We slept under the sun and at dark went south again. Our way led through a fine, rich land where no Saxon had yet set foot, but still no villager challenged us for no one but a fool questioned armed men who travelled by night in times of trouble. By daybreak we had reached the great plain and the rising sun cast the shadows of the Old People's death mounds long across the pale grass. Some of the mounds still had treasures guarded by grave ghouls and those we avoided as we sought a grassy hollow where the horses could eat and we could rest.

In the next moonlight we passed the Stones, that great mysterious ring where Merlin had given Arthur his sword and where, so many years before, we had yielded the gold to Aelle before marching to Lugg Vale. Nimue glided among the great capped pillars, touching them with her staff, then standing in their centre with her eyes staring up at the stars. The moon was almost full and its light gave the Stones a pale luminosity. 'Do they hold magic still?' I asked her when she caught us up.

'Some,' she said, 'but it's fading, Derfel. All our magic is fading. We need the Cauldron.' She smiled in the dark. 'It isn't far away now,' she said, 'I can feel it. It still lives, Derfel, and we're going to find it and restore it to Merlin.' There was a passion in her now, the same passion she had shown as we neared the end of the Dark Road. Arthur marched through the dark for his Guinevere, I for revenge and Nimue to summon the Gods with the Cauldron, but still we were few and the enemy was many.

We were now deep inside Lancelot's new land, yet we saw no evidence of his warriors nor any sign of the rabid Christian bands who were still said to be terrorizing the rural pagans. Lancelot's spearmen had no business in this part of Dumnonia for they were watching the roads from Glevum, while the Christians must have gone to support his army in the belief it did Christ's work, so we walked unmolested as we dropped down from the great plain onto the river lands of Dumnonia's southern coast. We skirted the fortress town of Sorviodunum and smelt the smoke of the houses that had been burned there. Still no one challenged us because we walked beneath the near-full moon and were protected by Nimue's spells.

We reached the sea on the fifth night. We had slipped past the Roman fortress of Vindocladia where Arthur was sure a garrison of Lancelot's troops would be in place, and by dawn we were hidden in the deep woods above the creek where the Sea Palace stood. The palace was just a mile to our west and we had reached it undetected, coming like night ghosts in our own land.

And we would make our attack at night too. Lancelot was using Guinevere as a shield, and we would take his shield away and, thus freed, carry our spears to his treacherous heart. But not for Mordred's sake, for now we fought for Arthur and for the happy realm we saw beyond the war.

As the bards now tell it, we fought for Camelot.

Most of the spearmen slept that day, but Arthur, Issa and I crawled to the edge of the wood and stared across the small valley at the Sea Palace.

It looked so fine with its white stone gleaming in the rising sun. We were gazing at its eastern flank from a crest that was slightly lower than the palace. Its eastern wall was broken by only three small windows so that it looked to us like a great white fortress on a green hill, though that illusion was spoiled somewhat by the great sign of the fish that had been crudely smeared in pitch on the limewashed wall, presumably to guard the palace against the anger of any itinerant Christians. The long southern façade which overlooked the creek and the sea that lay beyond a sandy island on the creek's southern bank was where the Roman builders had put their windows, just as they had relegated the kitchens and slave quarters and granaries to the northern ground behind the villa where Gwenhwyvach's timber house stood. There was now a small village of thatched huts there as well, I guessed for the spearmen and their families, and a tangle of smoke trails rose from the huts' cooking-fires. Beyond the huts were the orchards and vegetable fields, and beyond them again, bordered by the deep woods that grew thick in this part of the country, lay fields of partly cut hay.

In front of the palace, and just as I remembered them from that distant day when I had taken Arthur's precious oath on the Round Table, the two embankments topped by arcades stretched towards the creek. The palace was all sunlit, so white and grand and beautiful. 'If the Romans came back today,' Arthur said proudly, 'they would never know it had been rebuilt.'

'If the Romans came back today,' Issa said, 'they'd have a proper fight on their hands.' I had insisted that he come to the trees' edge for I knew of no one with better eyesight and we needed to spend this day discovering just how many guards Lancelot had put in the Sea Palace.

We counted no more than a dozen guards that morning. Just after dawn two men climbed to a wooden platform that had been built onto the roof's summit and from there they watched the road that led north. Four other spearmen paced up and down the nearest arcade, and it seemed sensible to deduce that four more would be stationed on the western arcade that was hidden from us. The other guards were all on the land that lay between a stone balustraded terrace at the bottom of the gardens and the creek, a patrol that evidently guarded the paths that led along the coast. Issa, divested of his armour and helmet, made a reconnaissance in that direction, creeping through the woods in an attempt to see the villa's façade between the twin arcades.

Arthur gazed fixedly at the palace. He was quietly elated, knowing that he was on the brink of a daring rescue that would send a shock through Lancelot's new kingdom. Indeed, I had rarely seen Arthur so happy as he was that day. By coming deep into Dumnonia he had cut himself off from the responsibilities of government and now, as in the long-ago past, his future depended only on the skill of his sword. 'Do you ever think of marriage, Derfel?' he suddenly asked me.

'No, Lord,' I said. 'Ceinwyn has sworn never to marry, and I see no need to challenge her.' I smiled and touched my lover's ring with its little scrap of the Cauldron's gold. 'Mind you,' I went on, 'I think we're more married than most couples who've ever stood before a Druid or a priest.'

'I don't mean that,' he said. 'Do you ever think about marriage?' He stressed the word 'about'.

'No, Lord,' I said. 'Not really.'

'Dogged Derfel,' he teased me. 'When I die,' he said dreamily, 'I think I want a Christian burial.'

'Why?' I asked, horrified, and touching my mail coat so that its iron would deflect evil.

'Because I shall lie with my Guinevere for all time,' he said, 'she and I, in one tomb, together.'

I thought of Norwenna's flesh hanging off her yellow bones and grimaced. 'You'll be in the Otherworld with her, Lord.'

'Our souls will, yes,' he admitted, 'and our shadowbodies will be there, but why can't these bodies lie hand in hand as well?'

I shook my head. 'Be burned,' I said, 'unless you want your soul to wander lost across Britain.'

'Maybe you're right,' he said lightly. He was lying on his belly, hidden from the villa by a screen of ragwort and cornflowers. Neither of us was in our armour. We would don that war finery at dusk before we came out of the dark to slaughter Lancelot's guards. 'What makes you and Ceinwyn happy?' Arthur asked me. He had not shaved since we had left Glevum and the stubble of his new beard was growing grey.

'Friendship,' I said.

He frowned. 'Just that?'

I thought about it. In the distance the first slaves were going to the hayfields, their sickles catching the morning sun in bright glints. Small boys were running up and down the vegetable gardens to frighten the jays away from the pea plants and the rows of gooseberries, redcurrants and raspberries, while nearer, where some convolvulus trailed pink on brambles, a group of greenfinches quarrelled noisily. It seemed that no Christian rabble had disturbed this place, indeed it seemed impossible that Dumnonia was at war at all. 'I still feel a pang every time I look at her,' I admitted.

'That's it, isn't it?' he said enthusiastically. 'A pang! A quickness in the heart.'

'Love,' I said drily.

'We're lucky, you and I,' he said, smiling. 'It's friendship, it's love, and it's still something more. It's what the Irish call *anmchara*, a soul friend. Who else do you want to talk to at the day's end? I love the evenings when we can just sit and talk and the sun goes down and moths come in to the candles.'

'And we talk of children,' I said, and wished I had not, 'and of servants' quarrels, and whether the cross-eyed kitchen slave is pregnant again, and we wonder who broke the pothook, and whether the thatch needs repair or whether it will last another year, and we try to work out what to do about the old dog that can't walk any more, and what excuse Cadell will conjure up for not paying his rent again, and we discuss whether the flax has steeped enough, and if we should rub butterwort on the cows' udders to improve their yield. That's what we talk of.'

He laughed. 'Guinevere and I talk of Dumnonia. Of Britain. And, of course, about Isis.' Some of his enthusiasm dissipated at the mention of that name, but then he shrugged. 'Not that we're together often enough. That's why I always hoped Mordred would take the burden, then I would be here all my days.'

'Talking of broken pothooks instead of Isis?' I teased him.

'Of those and everything else,' he said warmly. 'I'll farm this land one day, and Guinevere will go on with her work.'

'Her work?'

He smiled wryly. 'To know Isis. She tells me that if she can just make contact with the Goddess then the power will flow

425

back down to the world.' He shrugged, sceptical as always of such extravagant religious claims. Only Arthur would have dared plunge Excalibur into the soil and challenge Gofannon to come to his aid, for he did not really believe Gofannon would ever come. We are to the Gods, he once told me, like mice in a thatch, and we survive only so long as we are not noticed. But love alone demanded that he extend a wry tolerance to Guinevere's passion. 'I wish I could be more convinced of Isis,' he admitted to me now, 'but, of course, men aren't part of her mysteries.' He smiled. 'Guinevere even calls Gwydre Horus.'

'Horus?'

'Isis's son,' he explained. 'Ugly name.'

'Not as bad as Wygga,' I said.

'Who?' he asked, then suddenly stiffened. 'Look!' he said excitedly, 'look!'

I raised my head to peer over the flowery screen and there was Guinevere. Even from a quarter mile away she was unmistakable, for her red hair sprang in an unruly mass above the long blue robe she wore. She was walking along the nearer arcade towards the small open pavilion at its seaward end. Three maidservants walked behind with two of her deerhounds. The guards stepped aside and bowed as she passed. Once at the pavilion Guinevere sat at a stone table and the three maids served her breakfast. 'She'll be eating fruit,' Arthur said fondly. 'In summer she'll eat nothing else in the morning.' He smiled. 'If she just knew how close I was!'

'Tonight, Lord,' I assured him, 'you will be with her.'

He nodded. 'At least they're treating her well.'

'Lancelot fears you too much to treat her badly, Lord.'

A few moments later Dinas and Lavaine appeared on the arcade. They wore their white Druidical robes and I touched Hywelbane's hilt when I saw them and promised my daughter's soul that her killers' screams would make the whole Otherworld cringe in fear. The two Druids reached the pavilion, bowed to Guinevere, then joined her at the table. Gwydre came running a few moments later and we saw Guinevere ruffle his hair, then send him away in a servant's keeping. 'He's a good boy,' Arthur said fondly. 'No deceit in him. Not like Amhar and Loholt. I failed them, didn't I?'

'They're still young, Lord,' I said.

'But they serve my enemy now,' he said bleakly. 'What shall I do with them?'

Culhwch would doubtless have advised that he kill them, but I just shrugged. 'Send them into exile,' I said. The twins could join the unhappy men who had no oath-lord. They could sell their swords until at last they were killed in some unremembered battle against the Saxons or the Irish or the Scots.

More women appeared on the arcade. Some were maids, while others were the attendants who served Guinevere as courtiers. Lunete, my old love, was probably one of those dozen women who were Guinevere's confidantes and also the priestesses of her faith.

Sometime in the middle of the morning I fell asleep with my head cradled in my arms and my body lulled by the warmth of the summer sun. When I woke I found Arthur had gone and that Issa had returned. 'Lord Arthur went back to the spearmen, Lord,' he told me.

I yawned. 'What did you see?'

'Another six men. All Saxon Guards.'

'Lancelot's Saxons?'

He nodded. 'All of them in the big garden, Lord. But only the six. We've seen eighteen men altogether, and some others must stand guard at night, but even so there can't be more than thirty of them altogether.'

I guessed he was right. Thirty men would be sufficient to guard this palace, and more would be superfluous especially when Lancelot needed every spear to guard his stolen kingdom. I raised my head to see the arcade was now empty except for the four guards who looked utterly bored. Two were sitting with their backs to pillars while the other two were chatting on the stone bench where Guinevere had taken her breakfast. Their spears were propped against the table. The two guards on the

427

small roof platform looked equally lazy. The Sea Palace basked under a summer sun and no one there believed an enemy could be within a hundred miles. 'You told Arthur about the Saxons?' I asked Issa.

'Yes, Lord. He said it was only to be expected. Lancelot will want her guarded well.'

'Go and sleep,' I told him. 'I'll watch now.'

He went and, despite my promise, I fell asleep again. I had walked all night and I was weary, and besides, there seemed no danger threatening at the edge of that summer wood. And so I slept only to be abruptly woken by a sudden barking and the scrabble of big paws.

I woke in terror to discover a brace of slavering deerhounds standing over me, one of the two was barking and the other growling. I reached for my knife, but then a woman's voice shouted at the hounds. 'Down!' she called sharply. 'Drudwyn, Gwen, down! Quiet!' The dogs reluctantly lay flat and I turned to see Gwenhwyvach watching me. She was dressed in an old brown gown, had a shawl over her head and a basket in which she had been collecting wild herbs on her arm. Her face was plumper than ever and her hair, where it showed under the scarf, was untidy and tangled. 'The sleeping Lord Derfel,' she said happily.

I touched a finger to my lips and glanced towards the palace.

'They won't watch me,' she said, 'they don't care about me. Besides, I often talk to myself. The mad do, you know.'

'You're not mad, Lady.'

'I should like to be,' she said. 'I can't think why anyone would want to be anything else in this world.' She laughed, hitched up her gown and sat heavily beside me. She turned as the dogs growled at a noise behind me and watched with amusement as Arthur wriggled across the ground to join me. He must have heard the barking. 'On your belly like a snake, Arthur?' she asked.

Arthur, just like me, touched a finger to his lips. 'They don't care about me,' Gwenhwyvach said again. 'Look!' And she vigorously waved her arms towards the guards who simply shook their heads and turned away. 'I don't live,' she said, 'not as far as they're concerned. I'm just the mad fat woman who walks the dogs.' She waved again, and again the sentries ignored her. 'Even Lancelot doesn't notice me,' she added sadly.

'Is he here?' Arthur asked.

'Of course he isn't here. He's a long way away. So are you, I was told. Aren't you supposed to be talking to the Saxons?'

'I'm here to take Guinevere away,' Arthur said, 'and you too,' he added gallantly.

'I don't want to be taken away,' Gwenhwyvach protested. 'And Guinevere doesn't know you're here.'

'No one should know,' Arthur said.

'She should! Guinevere should! She stares into the oil pot. She says she can see the future there! But she didn't see you, did she?' She giggled, then turned and stared at Arthur as though she found his presence amusing. 'You're here to rescue her?'

'Yes.'

'Tonight?' Gwenhwyvach guessed.

'Yes.'

'She won't thank you,' Gwenhwyvach said, 'not tonight. No clouds, you see?' She waved at the almost cloudless sky. 'Can't worship Isis in cloud, you know, because the moon can't get into the temple, and tonight she's expecting the full moon. A big full moon, just like a fresh cheese.' She ruffled the long hair of one of the hounds. 'This one's Drudwyn,' she told us, 'and he's a bad boy. And this one's Gwen. Plop!' she said unexpectedly. 'That's how the moon comes, plop! Right into her temple.' She laughed again. 'Right down the shaft and plop onto the pit.'

'Will Gwydre be in the temple?' Arthur asked her.

'Not Gwydre. Men aren't allowed, that's what I'm told,' Gwenhwyvach said in a sarcastic voice, and she seemed about to say something else, but then just shrugged. 'Gwydre will be put to bed,' she said instead. She stared at the palace and a slow sly smile showed on her round face. 'How will you get in, Arthur?'

she asked. 'There are lots of bars on those doors and all the windows are shuttered.'

'We shall manage,' he said, 'as long as you don't tell anyone that you saw us.'

'As long as you leave me here,' Gwenhwyvach said, 'I won't even tell the bees. And I tell them everything. You have to, otherwise the honey goes sour. Isn't that right, Gwen?' she asked the bitch, ruffling its floppy ears.

'I'll leave you here if that's what you want,' Arthur promised her.

'Just me,' she said, 'just me and the dogs and the bees. That's all I want. Me and the dogs and the bees and the palace. Guinevere can have the moon.' She smiled again, then poked my shoulder with a plump hand. 'You remember that cellar door I took you through, Derfel? The one that leads from the garden?'

'I think so,' I said.

'I'll make sure it's unbarred.' She giggled again, anticipating some enjoyment. 'I'll hide in the cellar and unbar the door when they're all waiting for the moon. There are no guards there at night because the door's too thick. The guards are all in their huts or out the front.' She twisted to look at Arthur. 'You will come?' she asked anxiously.

'I promise,' Arthur replied.

'Guinevere will be pleased,' Gwenhwyvach said. 'And so will I.' She laughed and lumbered to her feet. 'Tonight,' she said, 'when the moon comes plopping in.' And with that she walked away with the two hounds. She chuckled as she walked and even danced a pair of clumsy steps. 'Plop!' she called aloud, and the hounds frisked about her as she capered down the grassy slope.

'Is she mad?' I asked Arthur.

'Bitter, I think.' He watched her rotund figure go clumsily down the hill. 'But she'll let us in, Derfel, she'll let us in.' He smiled, then reached forward and picked a handful of cornflowers from the field's edge. He arranged them into a small bunch then gave me a shy smile. 'For Guinevere,' he explained, 'tonight.'

At dusk the haymakers, their work finished, came back from the fields and the roof guards climbed down their long ladder. The braziers on the arcade were filled with fresh wood that was set alight, but I guessed the fires were meant to illuminate the palace rather than to give warning of any enemy's approach. Gulls were flying to their inland roosts and the setting sun made their wings as pink as the convolvulus entwined among the brambles.

Back in the woods Arthur pulled on his scale armour. He buckled Excalibur over the coat's gleaming shimmer of metal, then draped a black cloak about his shoulders. He rarely wore black cloaks, preferring his white, but at night the dark garment would help to conceal us. He would carry his shining helmet under the cloak to hide its lavish plume of tall white goose feathers.

Ten of his horsemen would stay in the trees. Their task was to wait for the sound of Arthur's silver horn and then make a charge on the spearmen's sleeping-huts. The big horses and their armoured riders, trampling huge and noisy out of the night, should serve to panic any guards who might interfere with our retreat. The horn, Arthur hoped, would not be sounded until we had found both Gwydre and Guinevere and were ready to leave.

The rest of us would make the long journey to the palace's western side, and from there we would creep through the shadows of the kitchen gardens to reach the cellar door. If Gwenhwyvach failed in her promise then we would have to go round to the front of the palace, kill the guards and break through one of the window shutters on the terrace. Once inside the palace we were to kill every spearman we found.

Nimue would come with us. When Arthur had finished speaking she told us that Dinas and Lavaine were not proper Druids, not like Merlin or old Iorweth, but she warned us that the Silurian twins did possess some strange powers and we should

431

expect to face their wizardry. She had spent the afternoon searching the woods and now raised a bundled cloak that seemed to twitch as she held it, and that weird sight made my men touch their spearheads. 'I have things here to check their spells,' she told us, 'but be careful.'

'And I want Dinas and Lavaine alive,' I told my men.

We waited, armoured and armed, forty men in steel and iron and leather. We waited as the sun died and as Isis's full moon crept up from the sea like a great round silver ball. Nimue made her spells and some of us prayed. Arthur sat silent, but watched as I took from my pouch a little tress of golden hair. I kissed the unfaded hair, held it briefly against my cheek, then tied it around Hywelbane's hilt. I felt a tear roll down my face as I thought of my little one in her shadowbody, but tonight, with the help of my Gods, I would give my Dian her peace.

I PULLED ON MY helmet, buckled its chin strap and threw its wolf-hair plume back across my shoulders. We flexed our stiff leather gloves, then thrust our left arms into the shield loops. We drew our swords and held them out for Nimue's touch. For a moment it looked as if Arthur wanted to say something more, but instead he just tucked his little bouquet of cornflowers into the neck of his scale armour, then nodded to Nimue who, cloaked in black and clutching her strange bundle, led us southwards through the trees.

Beyond the trees was a short meadow that sloped down to the creek's bank. We crossed the dark meadow in single file, still out of sight of the palace. Our appearance startled some hares that had been feeding in the moonlight and they raced panicking away as we pushed through some low bushes and scrambled down a steep bank to reach the creek's shingle beach. From there we walked west, hidden from the guards on the palace's arcades by the high bank of the creek. The sea crashed and hissed to the south, its sound drowning out any noise our boots made on the shingle.

I peered over the bank just once to see the Sea Palace poised like a great white wonder in the moonlight above the dark land. Its beauty reminded me of Ynys Trebes, that magical city of the sea that had been ravaged and destroyed by the Franks. This place had the same ethereal beauty for it shimmered above the dark land as though it were built from moonbeams.

Once we were well to the west of the palace we climbed the bank, helping each other up with our spear-staffs, and then followed Nimue northwards through the woods. Enough moonlight filtered through the summer leaves to light our path, but no guards challenged us. The sea's unending sound filled the night, though once a scream sounded very close by and we all froze, then recognized the sound of a hare being killed by a weasel. We breathed our relief and walked on.

We seemed to walk a long way through the trees, but at last Nimue turned east and we followed her to the edge of the wood to see the palace's limewashed walls in front of us. We were not far from the circular timber moon-shaft that ran down into the temple and I could see that it would still be some time before the moon was high enough in the sky to cast its light down the shaft and into the black-walled cellar.

It was while we were at the edge of the wood that the singing began. At first, so soft was the singing, I thought it was the wind moaning, but then the song became louder and I realized that it was a women's choir that chanted some strange, eerie and plangent music like nothing I had ever heard before. The song must have been reaching us through the moon-shaft, for it sounded very far away; a ghost song, like a choir of the dead singing to us from the Otherworld. We could hear no words, but we knew it was a sad song for its tune slid weirdly up and down by half-notes, swelled louder, then sank into a lingering softness that melded with the distant murmur of the breaking sea. The music was very beautiful, but it made me shiver and touch my spearhead.

If we had moved out of the trees then we would have been within sight of the guards who stood on the western arcade, so we moved up the wood a few paces and from there we could make our way towards the palace through a dappled tangle of mooncast shadows. There was an orchard, some rows of fruit bushes and even a high fence that protected a vegetable garden from deer and hares. We moved slowly, one at a time, and all the time that strange song soared and fell and slid and wailed. A shimmer of smoke shivered above the moon-shaft and the smell of it wafted towards us on the night's small wind. The smell was a temple smell; pungent and almost sickly.

We were now within yards of the spearmen's huts. A dog began barking, then another, but no one in the huts thought the barking meant trouble for voices just shouted for quiet and slowly the dogs subsided, to leave only the noise of the wind in the trees, the sea's moan and the song's eerie, thin melody.

I was leading the way, for I was the only one who had been to this small door before and I was worried that I might miss it, but I found it easily enough. I stepped carefully down the old brick steps and pushed gently on the door. It resisted, and for a heartbeat I thought it must still be barred, but then, with a jarring squeal of a metal hinge, it swung open and drenched me in light.

The cellar was lit by candles. I blinked, dazzled, then Gwenhwyvach's sibilant voice sounded. 'Quick! Quick!'

We filed inside; thirty big men with armour and cloaks and spears and helmets. Gwenhwyvach hissed at us to be silent, then closed the door behind us and placed its heavy bar in place. 'The temple's there,' she whispered, pointing down a corridor of rush-light candles that had been placed to illuminate the path to the shrine's door. She was excited and her plump face was flushed. The choir's haunting song was much quieter here for it was muffled by the temple's inner curtains and its heavy outer door.

'Where's Gwydre?' Arthur whispered to Gwenhwyvach.

'In his room,' Gwenhwyvach said.

'Are there guards?' he asked.

'Just servants in the palace at night,' she whispered.

'Are Dinas and Lavaine here?' I asked her.

She smiled. 'You'll see them, I promise you. You'll see them.' She plucked Arthur's cloak to draw him towards the temple. 'Come.'

'I'll fetch Gwydre first,' Arthur insisted, releasing his cloak, then he touched six of his men on the shoulders. 'The rest of you wait here,' he whispered. 'Wait here. Don't go into the temple. We'll let them finish their worship.' Then, treading softly, he led his six men across the cellar floor and up some stone steps.

Gwenhwyvach giggled beside me. 'I said a prayer to Clud,' she murmured to me, 'and she will help us.'

'Good,' I said. Clud is a Goddess of light, and it would be no bad thing to have her help this night.

'Guinevere doesn't like Clud,' Gwenhwyvach said disapprovingly. 'She doesn't like any of the British Gods. Is the moon high?'

'Not yet. But it's climbing.'

'Then it isn't time,' Gwenhwyvach said to me.

'Time for what, Lady?'

'You'll see!' She giggled. 'You'll see,' she said again, then shrank fearfully back as Nimue pushed through the huddle of nervous spearmen. Nimue had taken off her leather eyepatch so that the empty shrivelled socket was like a dark hole in her face and at the sight of that horror Gwenhwyvach whimpered in terror.

Nimue ignored Gwenhwyvach. Instead she looked about the cellar, then sniffed like a hound seeking a scent. I could only see cobwebs and wineskins and mead jars and I could smell only the damp odour of decay, but Nimue scented something hateful. She hissed, then spat towards the shrine. The bundle in her hand shifted slowly.

None of us moved. Indeed a kind of terror overcame us in that rush-lit cellar. Arthur was gone, we were undetected, but the sound of the singing and the stillness of the palace were both chilling. Maybe that terror was caused by a spell cast by Dinas and Lavaine, or maybe it was just that everything here seemed so unnatural. We were used to wood, thatch, earth and grass, and this dank place of brick arches and stone floors was strange and unnerving. One of my men was shaking.

Nimue stroked the man's cheek to restore his courage and then crept on her bare feet towards the temple doors. I went with her, placing my boots carefully to make no noise. I wanted to pull her back. She was plainly intent on disobeying Arthur's orders that we were to wait for the rites to finish, and I feared she would do something rash that would alert the women in the

436

temple and thus provoke them to screams that would bring the guards from their huts, but in my heavy, noisy boots I could not move as fast as Nimue on her bare feet and she ignored my hoarse whisper of warning. Instead she took hold of one of the temple's bronze door handles. She hesitated a heartbeat, then tugged the door open and the plangent ghost song was suddenly much louder.

The door's hinges had been greased and the door opened silently onto an utter blackness. It was a darkness as complete as any I had ever seen and was caused by the heavy curtains that hung just a few feet inside the door. I motioned for my men to stay where they were, then followed Nimue inside. I wanted to draw her back, but she resisted my hand and instead pulled the temple door closed on its greased hinges. The singing was very loud now. I could see nothing and I could hear only the choir, but the smell of the temple was thick and nauseous.

Nimue groped her hand to find me, then pulled my head down towards hers. 'Evil!' she breathed.

'We shouldn't be here,' I whispered.

She ignored that. Instead she groped and discovered the curtain and a moment later a tiny chink of light showed as she found the curtain's edge. I followed her, crouched and looked over her shoulder. At first, so small was the gap she had made that I could see almost nothing, but then, as my eyes made out what lay beyond, I saw too much. I saw the mysteries of Isis.

To make sense of that night I had to know the story of Isis. I learned it later, but at that moment, peering over Nimue's short-cropped hair, I had no idea what the ritual signified. I knew only that Isis was a Goddess and, to many Romans, a Goddess of the highest powers. I knew, too, that she was a protectress of thrones and that explained the low black throne that still stood on its dais at the far end of the cellar, though our view of it was misted by the thick smoke that writhed and drifted through the black room as it sought to escape up the moon-shaft. The smoke came from braziers, and their flames had been enriched by herbs that

437

gave off the pungent, heady scent we had smelt from the edge of the woods.

I could not see the choir that went on singing despite the smoke, but I could see Isis's worshippers and at first I did not believe what I saw. I did not want to believe.

I could see eight worshippers kneeling on the black stone floor, and all eight of them were naked. Their backs were towards us, but even so I could see that some of the naked worshippers were men. No wonder Gwenhwyvach had giggled in anticipation of this moment, for she must have known that secret already. Men, Guinevere always insisted, were not allowed into the temple of Isis, but they were here this night and, I suspected, on every night that the full moon cast its cold light down through the hole in the cellar's roof. The flickering braziers' flames cast their lurid light on the worshippers' backs. They were all naked. Men and women, all naked, just as Morgan had warned me so many years before.

The worshippers were naked, but not the two celebrants. Lavaine was one; he was standing to one side of the low black throne, and my soul exulted when I saw him. It had been Lavaine's sword that had cut Dian's throat and my sword was now just a cellar's length away from him. He stood tall beside the throne, the scar on his cheek lit by the braziers' light and his black hair oiled like Lancelot's to fall down the back of his black robe. He wore no Druid's white robe this night, but just a plain black gown, and in his hand was a slender black staff tipped with a small golden crescent moon. There was no sign of Dinas.

Two flaming torches becketed in iron flanked the throne where Guinevere sat playing the part of Isis. Her hair was coiled on her head and held in place by a ring of gold from which two horns jutted straight up. They were the horns of no beast I had ever seen, and later we discovered they were carved from ivory. Around her neck was a heavy gold torque, but she wore no other jewels, just a vast deep-red cloak that swathed her whole body. I could not see the floor in front of her, but I knew the shallow pit

438

was there and I guessed they were waiting for the moonlight to come down the shaft and touch the pit's black water with silver. The far curtains, behind which Ceinwyn had told me was a bed, were closed.

A flicker of light suddenly shimmered in the drifting smoke and made the naked worshippers gasp with its promise. The little sliver of light was pale and silvery and it showed that the moon had at last climbed high enough to throw its first angled beam down to the cellar floor. Lavaine waited a moment as the light thickened, then beat his staff twice on the floor. 'It is time,' he said in his harsh deep voice, 'it is time.' The choir went silent.

Then nothing happened. They just waited in silence as that smoke-shifting moon-silvered column of light widened and crept across the floor and I remembered that distant night when I had crouched in the summit of the knoll of stones beside Llyn Cerrig Bach and watched the moonlight edge its way towards Merlin's body. Now I watched the moonlight slide and swell in Isis's silent temple. The silence was full of portent. One of the kneeling naked women uttered a low moan, then went quiet again. Another woman rocked to and fro.

The moonbeam widened still further, its reflection casting a pale glimmer on Guinevere's stern and handsome face. The column of light was nearly vertical now. One of the naked women shivered, not with cold, but with the stirrings of ecstasy, and then Lavaine leaned forward to peer up the shaft. The moon lit his big beard and his hard, broad face with its battle scar. He peered upwards for a few heartbeats, then he stepped back and solemnly touched Guinevere's shoulder.

She stood so that the horns on her head almost touched the low arched ceiling of the cellar. Her arms and hands were inside the cloak that fell straight from her shoulders to the floor. She closed her eyes. 'Who is the Goddess?' she asked.

'Isis, Isis, Isis,' the women chanted the name softly, 'Isis, Isis, Isis.' The column of moonlight was almost as wide as the shaft now and it was a great smoky silver pillar of light that glowed and shifted in the cellar's centre. I had thought, when I had first seen this temple, that it was a tawdry place, but at night, lit by that shimmering pillar of white light, it was as eerie and mysterious as any shrine I had ever seen.

'And who is the God?' Guinevere asked, her eyes still closed.

'Osiris,' the naked men answered in low voices, 'Osiris, Osiris, Osiris.'

'And who shall sit on the throne?' Guinevere demanded.

'Lancelot,' both the men and the women answered together, 'Lancelot, Lancelot.'

It was when I heard that name that I knew that nothing would be put right this night. This night would never bring back the old Dumnonia. This night would give us nothing but horror, for I knew that this night would destroy Arthur and I wanted to back away from the curtain and go back into the cellar and take him away into the fresh air and the clean moonlight, then take him back through all the years and all the days and all the hours so that this night would never come to him. But I did not move. Nimue did not move. Neither of us dared to move for Guinevere had reached out with her right hand to take the black staff from Lavaine and the gesture lifted her red cloak from the right side of her body and I saw that under the cloak's heavy folds she was naked.

'Isis, Isis, Isis,' the women sighed.

'Osiris, Osiris, Osiris,' the men breathed.

'Lancelot, Lancelot, Lancelot,' they all chanted together.

Guinevere took the gold-tipped staff and reached forward, the cloak falling again to shadow her right breast, and then, very slowly, with exaggerated gestures, she touched the staff against something that lay in the water pit right beneath the glistening, shimmering shaft of silvered smoke that now came vertically down from the heavens. No one else moved in the cellar. No one even seemed to breathe.

'Rise!' Guinevere commanded, 'rise,' and the choir began to sing their weird, haunting song again. 'Isis, Isis, Isis,' they were singing, and over the heads of the worshippers I saw a man climb up from the pool. It was Dinas, and his tall muscled body and long black hair dripped water as he came slowly upright and as the choir sang the Goddess's name louder and ever louder. 'Isis! Isis! Isis!' they sang until Dinas at last stood upright before Guinevere, his back to us, and he too was naked. He stepped up out of the pool and Guinevere handed the black staff to Lavaine, then raised her hands and unclasped the cloak so that it fell back onto the throne. She stood there, Arthur's wife, naked but for the gold about her neck and the ivory on her head, and she opened her arms so that the naked grandson of Tanaburs could step onto the dais and into her embrace. 'Osiris! Osiris! Osiris!' The women in the cellar called. Some of them writhed to and fro like the Christian worshippers in Isca who had been overcome by a similar ecstasy. The voices in the cellar were becoming ragged now. 'Osiris! Osiris! Osiris!' they chanted, and Guinevere stepped back as the naked Dinas turned round to face the worshippers and lifted his arms in triumph. Thus he displayed his magnificent naked body and there could be no mistaking that he was a man, nor any mistaking what he was supposed to do next as Guinevere, her beautiful, tall, straight body made magically silver-white by the moon's shimmer in the smoke, took his right arm and led him towards the curtain that hung behind the throne. Lavaine went with them as the women writhed in their worship and rocked backwards and forwards and called out the name of their great Goddess. 'Isis! Isis! Isis!'

Guinevere swept the far curtain aside. I had a brief glimpse of the room beyond and it seemed as bright as the sun, and then the ragged chanting rose to a new pitch of excitement as the men in the temple reached for the women beside them, and it was just then that the doors behind me were thrown wide open and Arthur, in all the glory of his war gear, stepped into the temple's lobby. 'No, Lord,' I said to him, 'no, Lord, please!'

'You shouldn't be here, Derfel,' he spoke quietly, but in reproof. In his right hand he held the little bunch of cornflowers he had picked for Guinevere, while in his left he grasped

441

his son's hand. 'Come back out,' he ordered me, but then Nimue snatched the big curtain aside and my Lord's nightmare began.

Isis is a Goddess. The Romans brought her to Britain, but she did not come from Rome itself, but from a distant country far to Rome's east. Mithras is another God who comes from a country east of Rome, though not, I think, the same country. Galahad told me that half the world's religions begin in the east where, I suspect, the men look more like Sagramor than like us. Christianity is another such faith brought from those distant lands where, Galahad assured me, the fields grow nothing but sand, the sun shines fiercer than it ever does in Britain and no snow ever falls.

Isis came from those burning lands. She became a powerful Goddess to the Romans and many women in Britain adopted her religion that stayed on when the Romans left. It was never as popular as Christianity, for the latter threw its doors open to any who wanted to worship its God, while Isis, like Mithras, restricted her followers to those, and those alone, who had been initiated into her mysteries. In some ways, Galahad told me, Isis resembled the Holy Mother of the Christians, for she was reputed to be the perfect mother to her son Horus, but Isis also possessed powers that the Virgin Mary never claimed. Isis, to her adepts, was the Goddess of life and death, of healing, and, of course, of mortal thrones.

She was married, Galahad told me, to a God named Osiris, but in a war between the Gods Osiris was killed and his body was cut into fragments that were scattered into a river. Isis found the scattered flesh and tenderly brought them together again, and then she lay with the fragments to bring her husband back to life. Osiris did live again, revived by Isis's power. Galahad hated the tale, and crossed himself again and again as he told it, and it was that tale, I suppose, of resurrection and of the woman giving life to the man, that Nimue and I watched in that smoky black cellar. We had watched as Isis, the Goddess, the mother, the giver of life, performed the miracle that gave her husband

442

life and turned her into the guardian of the living and the dead and the arbiter of men's thrones. And it was that last power, the power that determined which men should sit on this earth's thrones, that was, for Guinevere, the Goddess's supreme gift. It was for the power of the throne-giver that Guinevere worshipped Isis.

Nimue snatched the curtain aside and the cellar filled with screams.

For one second, for one terrible second, Guinevere hesitated at the far curtain and turned around to see what had disturbed her rites. She stood there, tall and naked and so dreadful in her pale beauty, and beside her was a naked man. At the cellar's door, standing with his son in one hand and with flowers in the other, was her husband. The cheek pieces of Arthur's helmet were open and I saw his face at that terrible moment, and it was as if his soul had just fled.

Guinevere disappeared behind the curtain, dragging Dinas and Lavaine with her, and Arthur uttered an awful sound, half a battle shout and half the cry of a man in utter misery. He pushed Gwydre back, dropped the flowers, then drew Excalibur and charged heedlessly through the screaming, naked worshippers who scrambled desperately out of his way.

'Take them all!' I shouted to the spearmen who followed Arthur, 'don't let them escape! Take them!' Then I ran after Arthur with Nimue beside me. Arthur leapt the black pool, pushed a torch over as he jumped across the dais, then swept the far black curtain aside with Excalibur's blade.

And there he stopped.

I stopped beside him. I had discarded my spear as I charged through the temple and now had Hywelbane bare in my hand. Nimue was with me and she howled in triumph as she gazed into the small, square room that opened up from the arched cellar. This, it seemed, was Isis's inner sanctuary, and here, at the Goddess's service, was the Cauldron of Clyddno Eiddyn.

The Cauldron was the first thing I saw, for it was standing on a black pedestal that stood as high as a man's waist and there

443

were so many candles in the room that the Cauldron seemed to glow silver and gold as it reflected their brilliant light. The light was made even brighter because the room, all but for the curtained wall, was lined with mirrors. There were mirrors on the walls and even on the ceiling, mirrors that multiplied the candles' flames and reflected the nakedness of Guinevere and Dinas. Guinevere, in her terror, had leapt onto the wide bed that filled the room's far end and there she clawed at a fur coverlet in an effort to hide her pale skin. Dinas was beside her, his hands clutched to his groin, while Lavaine faced us defiantly.

He glanced at Arthur, dismissed Nimue with scarce a look, then held his slender black staff towards me. He knew I had come for his death and now he would prevent it with the greatest magic at his disposal. He pointed his staff at me, while in his other hand he held the crystal-encased fragment of the true cross that Bishop Sansum had given to Mordred at his acclamation. He was holding the fragment suspended above the Cauldron, which was filled with some dark aromatic liquid.

'Your other daughters will die too,' he told me. 'I only need to let go.'

Arthur raised Excalibur.

'Your son too!' Lavaine said, and both of us froze. 'You will go now,' he said with calm authority. 'You have invaded the Goddess's sanctuary and will now go and leave us in peace. Or else you, and all you love, will die.'

He waited. Behind him, between the Cauldron and the bed, was Arthur's Round Table with its stone image of the winged horse, and on the horse, I saw, were a drab basket, a common horn, an old halter, a worn knife, a whetstone, a sleeved coat, a cloak, a clay dish, a throwboard, a warrior ring and a heap of decaying broken timbers. Merlin's scrap of beard was also there, still wrapped in its black ribbon. All the power of Britain was in that little room and it was allied to a scrap of the Christian's most powerful magic.

I lifted Hywelbane and Lavaine made as though to drop the

444

piece of the true cross into the liquid and Arthur put a warning hand against my shield.

'You will go,' Lavaine said. Guinevere said nothing, but just watched us, huge-eyed, above the pelt that now half covered her.

Then Nimue smiled. She had been holding the bundled cloak in both her hands, but now she shook it at Lavaine. She screamed as she released the cloak's burden. It was an eldritch shriek that echoed high above the cries of the women behind us.

Vipers flew through the air. There must have been a dozen of the snakes, all found by Nimue that afternoon and hoarded for this moment. They twisted in the air and Guinevere screamed and dragged the fur to cover her face while Lavaine, seeing a snake flying at his eyes, instinctively flinched and crouched. The scrap of true cross skittered across the floor while the snakes, aroused by the heat in the cellar, twisted across the bed and over the Treasures of Britain. I took one pace forward and kicked Lavaine hard in the belly. He fell, then screamed as an adder bit his ankle.

Dinas shrank from the snakes on the bed, then went utterly still as Excalibur touched his throat.

Hywelbane was at Lavaine's throat, and I used the blade to bring his face up towards mine. Then I smiled. 'My daughter,' I said softly, 'watches us from the Otherworld. She sends you greetings, Lavaine.'

He tried to speak, but no words came. A snake slid across his leg.

Arthur stared at where his wife was hidden beneath the fur. Then, almost tenderly, he flicked the snakes off the black pelt with Excalibur's tip, then drew back the fur until he could see Guinevere's face. She stared at him, and all her fine pride had vanished. She was just a terrified woman. 'Do you have any clothes here?' Arthur asked her gently. She shook her head.

'There's a red cloak on the throne,' I told him.

'Would you fetch it, Nimue?' Arthur asked.

Nimue brought the cloak and Arthur held it towards his wife on Excalibur's tip. 'Here,' he said, still speaking softly, 'for you.'

A bare arm emerged from the fur and took the cloak. 'Turn round,' Guinevere said to me in a small, frightened voice.

'Turn, Derfel, please,' Arthur said.

'One thing first, Lord.'

'Turn,' he insisted, still gazing at his wife.

I reached for the Cauldron's edge and tipped it off the pedestal. The precious Cauldron clanged loud on the floor as its liquid spilt in a dark rush across the flagstones. That got his attention. He stared at me and I hardly recognized his face, it was so hard and cold and empty of life, but there was one more thing to be said this night and if my Lord was to sup this dish of horrors, then he might as well drain it to the last bitter drop. I put Hywelbane's tip back under Lavaine's chin. 'Who is the Goddess?' I asked him.

He shook his head and I pushed Hywelbane far enough forward to draw blood from his throat. 'Who is the Goddess?' I asked him again.

'Isis,' he whispered. He was clutching his ankle where the snake had bitten him.

'And who is the God?' I demanded.

'Osiris,' he said in a terrified voice.

'And who,' I asked him, 'shall sit on the throne?' He shivered, and said nothing. 'These, Lord,' I said to Arthur, my sword still on Lavaine's throat, 'are the words you did not hear. But I heard them and Nimue heard them. Who shall sit on the throne?' I asked Lavaine again.

'Lancelot,' he said in a voice so low that it was almost inaudible. But Arthur heard, just as he must have seen the great device that was embroidered white on the lavish black blanket that lay on the bed beneath the bear pelt in this room of mirrors. It was Lancelot's sea-eagle.

I spat at Lavaine, sheathed Hywelbane, then reached forward and took him by his long black hair. Nimue already had hold of Dinas. We dragged them back into the temple, and I swept the black curtain back into place behind me so that Arthur and Guinevere could be alone. Gwenhwyvach had been watching it all and she now cackled with laughter. The worshippers and the choir, all naked, were crouching to one side of the cellar where Arthur's men guarded them with spears. Gwydre was crouching terrified at the cellar door.

Behind us Arthur cried one word. 'Why?'

And I took my daughter's murderers out to the moonlight.

At dawn we were still at the Sea Palace. We should have left, for some of the spearmen had escaped the huts when the horsemen had at last been summoned from the hill by Arthur's horn, and those fugitives would be spreading the alarm north into Dumnonia, but Arthur seemed incapable of decision. He was like a man stunned.

He was still weeping as the dawn edged the world with light.

Dinas and Lavaine died then. They died at the creek's edge. I am not, I think, a cruel man, but their deaths were very cruel and very long. Nimue arranged those deaths, and all the while, as their souls gave up the flesh, she hissed the name Dian in their ears. They were not men by the time they died, and their tongues had gone and they had just one eye apiece, and that small mercy was only given them so that they could see the manner of their next bout of pain, and see they did as they died. The last thing either saw was that bright piece of hair on Hywelbane's hilt as I finished what Nimue had begun. The twins were mere things by then, things of blood and shuddering terror, and when they were dead I kissed the little scrap of hair, then carried it to one of the braziers on the palace's arcades and tossed it into the embers so that no fragment of Dian's soul was left wandering the earth. Nimue did the same with the cut plait of Merlin's beard. We left the twins' bodies lying on their left sides beside the sea and in the rising sun gulls came down to tear at the tortured flesh with their long hooked beaks.

Nimue had rescued the Cauldron and the Treasures. Dinas and Lavaine, before they died, had told her the whole tale, and Nimue had been right all along. It had been Morgan who stole the Treasures and who had taken them as a gift to Sansum so that he would marry her, and Sansum had given them to Guinevere. It was the promise of that great gift which had first reconciled Guinevere to the mouse-lord before Lancelot's baptism in the River Churn. I thought, when I heard the tale, that if only I had allowed Lancelot into the mysteries of Mithras then maybe none of this would have happened. Fate is inexorable.

The shrine's doors were closed now. None of those trapped inside had escaped, and once Guinevere had been brought out and after Arthur had talked with her for a long time, he had gone back into the cellar alone, with just Excalibur in his hand, and he did not emerge for a full hour. When he came out his face was colder than the sea and as grey as Excalibur's blade, except that the precious blade was now red and thick with blood. In one hand he carried the horn-mounted circle of gold that Guinevere had worn as Isis and in the other he carried the sword. 'They're dead,' he told me.

'All?'

'Everyone.' He had seemed oddly unconcerned, though there was blood on his arms and on his scale armour and even spattered on the goose feathers of his helmet.

'The women too?' I asked, for Lunete had been one of Isis's worshippers. I had no love for her now, but she had once been my lover and I felt a pang for her. The men in the temple had been the most handsome of Lancelot's spearmen and the women had been Guinevere's attendants.

'All dead,' said Arthur, almost lightly. He had walked slowly down the pleasure garden's central gravel path. 'This wasn't the first night they did this,' he said, and sounded almost puzzled. 'It seems they did it often. All of them. Whenever the moon was right. And they did it with each other, all of them. Except Guinevere. She just did it with the twins or with Lancelot.' He shuddered then, showing the first emotion since he had come so cold-eyed from the cellar. 'It seems,' he said, 'that she used to do it for my sake. Who shall sit on the throne? Arthur, Arthur, Arthur, but the Goddess can't have approved of me.' He had begun to cry. 'Or else I resisted the Goddess too firmly, and so they changed the name to Lancelot.' He gave the bloody sword a futile swing in the air. 'Lancelot,' he said in a voice filled with agony. 'For years now, Derfel, she's been sleeping with Lancelot, and all for religion, she says! Religion! He was usually Osiris and she was always Isis. What else could she have been?' He reached the terrace and sat on a stone bench from where he could stare at the moon-glossed creek. 'I shouldn't have killed them all,' he said after a long while.

'No, Lord,' I said, 'you shouldn't.'

'But what else could I do? It was filth, Derfel, just filth!' He began to sob then. He said something about shame, about the dead having witnessed his wife's shame and his own dishonour, and when he could say no more, he just sobbed helplessly and I said nothing. He did not seem to care whether I stayed with him or not, but I stayed until it was time to take Dinas and Lavaine down to the sea's edge so that Nimue could draw their souls inch by terrible inch from their bodies.

And now, in a grey dawn, Arthur sat empty and exhausted above the sea. The horns lay at his feet, while his helmet and Excalibur's bare blade rested on the bench beside him. The blood on the sword had dried to a thick brown crust.

'We must leave, Lord,' I said as the dawn turned the sea the colour of a spear blade.

'Love,' he said bitterly.

I thought he had misheard me. 'We must leave, Lord,' I said again.

'For what?' he asked.

'To complete your oath.'

He spat, then sat in silence. The horses had been brought down from the wood and the Cauldron and the Treasures of Britain were packed for their journey. The spearmen watched us and waited. 'Is there any oath,' he asked me bitterly, 'that is unbroken? Just one?'

'We must go, Lord,' I told him, but he neither moved nor

spoke and so I turned on my heel. 'Then we'll go without you,' I said brutally.

'Derfel!' Arthur called, real pain in his voice.

'Lord?' I turned back.

He stared down at his sword and seemed surprised to see it so caked with blood. 'My wife and son are in an upstairs room,' he said. 'Fetch them for me, will you? They can ride on the same horse. Then we can go.' He was struggling so hard to sound normal, to sound as if this was just another dawn.

'Yes, Lord,' I said.

He stood and rammed Excalibur, blood and all, into its scabbard. 'Then, I suppose,' he said sourly, 'we must remake Britain?'

'Yes, Lord,' I said, 'we must.'

He stared at me and I saw he wanted to cry again. 'Do you know something, Derfel?' he asked me.

'Tell me, Lord,' I said.

'My life will never be the same again, will it?'

'I don't know, Lord,' I said. 'I just don't know.'

The tears spilled down his long cheeks. 'I shall love her till the day I die. Every day I live I shall think of her. Every night before I sleep I will see her, and in every dawn I shall turn in my bed to find that she has gone. Every day, Derfel, and every night and every dawn until the moment that I die.'

He picked up his helmet with its blood-draggled plume, left the ivory horns, and walked with me. I fetched Guinevere and her son down from the bed-chamber and then we left.

Gwenhwyvach had the Sea Palace then. She lived in it alone, her wits wandering, and surrounded by hounds and by the gorgeous treasures that decayed all about her. She would watch from a window for Lancelot's coming, for she was sure that one day her Lord would come to live with her beside the sea in her sister's palace, but her Lord never did come, and the treasures were stolen, the palace crumbled and Gwenhwyvach died there, or so we heard. Or maybe she lives there still, waiting beside the creek for the man who never comes.

We went away. And on the creek's muddy banks the gulls tore at offal.

Guinevere, in a long black dress that was covered by a dark green cloak, and with her red hair combed severely back and tied with a black ribbon, rode Arthur's mare, Llamrei. She sat side-saddle, gripping the saddle bar with her right hand and keeping her left arm about the waist of her frightened and tearful son who kept glancing at his father who was walking doggedly behind the horse. 'I suppose I am his father?' Arthur spat at her once.

Guinevere, her eyes reddened by tears, just looked away. The motion of the horse rocked her back and forth and back and forth, yet she managed to look graceful all the same. 'No one else, Lord Prince,' she said after a long time. 'No one else.'

Arthur walked in silence after that. He did not want my company, he wanted no company but his own misery, and so I joined Nimue at the head of the procession. The horsemen came next, then Guinevere, and my spearmen escorted the Cauldron at the rear. Nimue was retracing the same road that had led us to the coast and which here was a rough track that climbed onto a bare heath broken by dark stretches of yew and gorse. 'So Gorfyddyd was right,' I said after a while.

'Gorfyddyd?' Nimue asked, astonished that I should have dredged that old King's name from the past.

'At Lugg Vale,' I reminded her, 'he said Guinevere was a whore.'

'And you, Derfel Cadarn,' Nimue said scornfully, 'are an expert on whores?'

'What else is she?' I asked bitterly.

'No whore,' Nimue said. She gestured ahead, pointing at the wisps of smoke above the distant trees that showed where the garrison of Vindocladia were cooking their breakfasts. 'We'll need to avoid them,' Nimue said, and turned off the road to lead us towards a thicker belt of trees that grew to the west. I suspected the garrison had already heard that Arthur had come to

451

the Sea Palace and had no wish to confront him, but I dutifully followed Nimue and the horsemen dutifully followed us. 'What Arthur did,' she said after a while, 'is marry a rival instead of a companion.'

'A rival?'

'Guinevere could rule Dumnonia as well as any man,' Nimue said, 'and better than most. She's cleverer than he is, and every bit as determined. If she'd been born to Uther instead of that fool Leodegan, then everything would have been different. She'd be another Boudicca and there'd be dead Christians from here to the Irish Sea and dead Saxons to the German Sea.'

'Boudicca,' I reminded her, 'lost her war.'

'And so has Guinevere,' Nimue said grimly.

'I don't see that she was Arthur's rival,' I said after a time. 'She had power. I don't suppose he ever made a decision without talking to her.'

'And he talked to the Council, which no woman can join,' Nimue said tartly. 'Put yourself in Guinevere's place, Derfel. She's quicker than all of you put together, but any idea she ever had was put before a pack of dull, ponderous men. You and Bishop Emrys and that fart Cythryn who pretends to be so judicious and fair-minded, then goes home and beats his wife and makes her watch him take a dwarf girl to their bed. Councillors! You think Dumnonia would know the difference if you all drowned?'

'A King must have a Council,' I said indignantly.

'Not if he's clever,' Nimue said. 'Why should he? Does Merlin have a Council? Does Merlin need a room full of pompous fools to tell him what to do? The only purpose a Council serves is to make you all feel important.'

'It does more than that,' I insisted. 'How does a King know what his people are thinking if there's no Council?'

'Who cares what the fools think? Allow the people to think for themselves and half of them become Christians; there's a tribute to their ability to think,' she spat. 'So just what is it that you do in Council, Derfel? Tell Arthur what your shepherds are saying?

And Cythryn, I suppose, represents the dwarf-tupping men of Dumnonia. Is that it?' she laughed. 'The people! The people are idiots, that's why they have a King and why the King has spearmen.'

'Arthur,' I said stoutly, 'has given the country good government, and he did it without using spears on the people.'

'And look what's happened to the country,' Nimue retorted. She walked in silence for a few moments. After a while she sighed. 'Guinevere was right all along, Derfel. Arthur should be King. She knew that. She wanted that. She would even have been happy with that, for with Arthur as King she would have been Queen and that would have given her as much power as she needed. But your precious Arthur wouldn't take the throne. So high-minded! All those sacred oaths! And what did he want instead? To be a farmer. To live like you and Ceinwyn; the happy home, the children, laughter.' She made these things sound risible. 'How content,' she asked me, 'do you think Guinevere would be in that life? The very thought of it bored her! And that's all that Arthur ever wanted. She is a clever, quick-witted lady and he wanted to turn her into a milch cow. Do you wonder she looked for other excitements?'

'Whoredom?'

'Oh, don't be a fool, Derfel. Am I a whore for having bedded you? More fool me.' We had reached the trees and Nimue turned north to walk between the ash and the tall elms. The spearmen followed us dumbly and I think that had we led them in circles they would have followed us without protest, so astonished and numbed were we all by the night's horrors. 'So she broke her marriage oath,' Nimue said, 'do you think she's the first? Or do you think that makes her a whore? In which case Britain's full to the rim with whores. She's no whore, Derfel. She's a strong woman who was born with a quick mind and good looks, and Arthur loved the looks and wouldn't use her mind. He wouldn't let her make him King and so she turned to that ridiculous religion of hers. And all Arthur did was tell her how happy she'd be when he could hang up Excalibur and start breeding cattle!' She laughed at the thought. 'And because it would never occur to Arthur to be unfaithful he never suspected it in Guinevere. The rest of us did, but not Arthur. He kept telling himself the marriage was perfect, and all the while he was miles away and Guinevere's good looks were drawing men like flies to carrion. And they were handsome men, clever men, witty men, men who wanted power, and one was a handsome man who wanted all the power he could get, so Guinevere decided to help him. Arthur wanted a cowshed, but Lancelot wants to be High King of Britain and Guinevere finds that a more interesting challenge than raising cows or mopping up the shit of infants. And that idiotic religion encouraged her. The arbiter of thrones!' She spat. 'She wasn't bedding Lancelot because she was a whore, you great fool, she was bedding him to get her man made High King.'

'And Dinas?' I asked, 'Lavaine?'

'They were her priests. They were helping her, and in some religions, Derfel, men and women couple as part of worship. And why not?' She kicked at a stone and watched it skitter away through a patch of bindweed. 'And believe me, Derfel, those two were beautiful-looking men. I know, because I took that beauty away from them, but not because of what they did with Guinevere. I did it for the insult they gave Merlin and for what they did to your daughter.' She walked in silence for a few yards. 'Don't despise Guinevere,' she told me after a while. 'Don't despise her for being bored. Despise her, if you must, for stealing the Cauldron and be thankful Dinas and Lavaine never unlocked its power. It worked for Guinevere, though. She bathed in it weekly and that's why she never aged a week.' She turned as footsteps sounded behind us. It was Arthur who was running to catch us up. He still looked dazed, but at some time in the last few moments it must have dawned on him that we had diverted from the road. 'Where are we going?' he demanded.

'You want the garrison to see us?' Nimue asked, pointing again to the smoke of their cooking fires.

He said nothing, but just stared at the smoke as if he had never seen such a thing before. Nimue glanced at me and shrugged at his evident befuddlement. 'If they wanted a fight,' Arthur said, 'they'd have been looking for us already.' His eyes were red and puffy, and maybe it was my imagination, but his hair seemed greyer. 'What would you do,' Arthur asked me, 'if you were the enemy?' He did not mean the puny garrison at Vindocladia, but nor would he name Lancelot.

'Try to trap us, Lord,' I said.

'How? Where?' he asked irritably. 'North, yes? That's our fastest route back to friendly spearmen and they'll know that. So we won't go north.' He looked at me, and it was almost as though he did not recognize me. 'We go for their throats instead, Derfel,' he said savagely.

'Their throats, Lord?'

'We'll go to Caer Cadarn.'

I said nothing for a while. He was not thinking straight. Grief and anger had upset him and I wondered how I could steer him away from this suicide. 'There are forty of us, Lord,' I said quietly.

'Caer Cadarn,' he said again, ignoring my objection. 'Who holds the Caer holds Dumnonia, and who holds Dumnonia holds Britain. If you don't want to come, Derfel, then go your own way. I'm going to Caer Cadarn.' He turned away.

'Lord!' I called him back. 'Dunum lies in our path.' That was a major fortress, and though its garrison was doubtless depleted, it could hold more than enough spears to destroy our small force.

'I would not care, Derfel, if every fortress in Britain stood in our path.' Arthur spat the words at me. 'You do what you want, but I'm going to Caer Cadarn.' He walked away, shouting at the horsemen to turn westwards.

I closed my eyes, convinced my Lord wanted to die. Without Guinevere's love, he just wanted to die. He wanted to fall beneath the enemy's spears at the centre of the land for which he had fought so long. I could think of no other explanation why he would lead this small band of tired spear-men to the very heart of the rebellion unless he wanted death beside Dumnonia's royal stone, but then a memory came to me and I opened my eyes. 'A long time ago,' I told Nimue, 'I talked with Ailleann.' She had been an Irish slave, older than Arthur but a loving mistress to him before he met Guinevere, and Amhar and Loholt were her ungrateful sons. She still lived, graceful and grey-haired now, and presumably still under siege in Corinium. And now, standing lost in shattered Dumnonia, I heard her voice across the years. Just watch Arthur, she had told me, because when you think he is doomed, when everything is at its darkest, he will astonish you. He will win. I told that now to Nimue. 'And she also said,' I went on, 'that once he'd won he would make his usual mistake of forgiving his enemies.'

'Not this time,' Nimue said. 'Not this time. The fool has learned his lesson, Derfel. So what will you do?'

'What I always do,' I said. 'Go with him.'

To the enemy's throat. To Caer Cadarn.

That day Arthur was filled with a frenetic, desperate energy as though the answer to all his miseries lay at Caer Cadarn's summit. He made no attempt to hide his small force, but just marched us north and west with his banner of the bear flying above us. He used one of his men's horses and he wore his famous armour so that anyone could see just who it was who rode into the country's heart. He went as fast as my spearmen could walk, and when one of the horses split a hoof he just abandoned the beast and pushed on hard. He wanted to reach the Caer.

We came to Dunum first. The Old People had made a great fort on Dunum's hill, the Romans had added their own wall, and Arthur had repaired the fortifications and kept a strong garrison there. The garrison had never seen battle, but if Cerdic ever did attack west along Dumnonia's coast it would have been Dunum that would have formed one of his first major obstacles and, despite the long years of peace, Arthur had never let the fort decay. A banner flew above the wall and, as we drew closer, I saw it was not the sea-eagle, but the red dragon. Dunum had stayed loyal.

Thirty men remained of the garrison. The rest had either been Christians and had deserted, or else, fearing that Mordred and Arthur were both dead, they had given up their defiance and slipped away, but Lanval, the garrison's commander, had clung on with his shrinking force, hoping against hope that the evil news was wrong. Now Arthur had come, Lanval led his men out of the gate and Arthur slid from the saddle and gave the old warrior an embrace. We were seventy spears now instead of forty and I thought of Ailleann's words. Just when you think he's beaten, she had said, he begins to win.

Lanval walked his horse beside me and told how Lancelot's spearmen had marched past the fort. 'We couldn't stop them,' he said bitterly, 'and they didn't challenge us. They just tried to make me surrender. I told them I would take down Mordred's banner when Arthur ordered me to take it down, and I would not believe Arthur was dead until they brought me his head on a shield.' Arthur must have said something to him about Guinevere for Lanval, despite having once been the commander of her guard, avoided her. I told him a little of what had happened at the Sea Palace and he shook his head sadly. 'She and Lancelot were doing it in Durnovaria,' he said, 'in that temple she made there.'

'You knew that?' I asked, horrified.

'I didn't know it,' he said tiredly, 'but I heard rumours, Derfel, only rumours, and I didn't want to know more.' He spat at the road's verge. 'I was there the day Lancelot came from Ynys Trebes and I remember the two of them couldn't keep their eyes off each other. They hid it after that, of course, and Arthur never suspected a thing. And he made it so easy for them! He trusted her and he was never at home. He was always riding off to inspect a fort or sit in a lawcourt.' Lanval shook his head. 'I don't doubt she calls it a religion,

Derfel, but I tell you, if that lady is in love with anyone, it's Lancelot.'

'I think she loves Arthur,' I said.

'She does, maybe, but he's too straightforward for her. There's no mystery in Arthur's heart, it's all written on his face and she's a lady who likes subtlety. I tell you, it's Lancelot who makes her heart quicken.' And it was Guinevere, I thought sadly, who made Arthur's heart beat faster; I did not even dare to think what was happening to his heart now.

We slept that night in the open. My men guarded Guinevere who busied herself with Gwydre. No word had been said of her fate, and none of us wanted to ask Arthur and so we all treated her with a distant politeness. She treated us in the same manner, asked no favours and avoided Arthur. As night fell she told Gwydre stories, but when he had gone to sleep I saw she was rocking back and forth beside him and crying softly. Arthur saw it too, then he began to weep and walked away to the edge of the wide down so that no one would see his misery.

We marched again at dawn and our road led us down into a lovely landscape that was softly lit by a sun rising into a sky cleared of cloud. This was the Dumnonia for which Arthur fought, a rich fertile land that the Gods had made so beautiful. The villages had thick thatch and deep orchards, though too many of the cottage walls were disfigured with the mark of the fish, while others had been burned, but I noticed how the Christians did not insult Arthur as they might once have done and this made me suspect that the fever which had struck Dumnonia was already fading. Between the villages the road wound between pink bramble blossom and between meadows made gaudy with clover, daisies, buttercups and poppies. Willow-wrens and yellowhammers, the last birds to make their nests, flew with scraps of straw in their beaks, while higher, above some oaks, I saw a hawk take wing, then realized it was no hawk, but a young cuckoo making its first flight. And that, I thought, was a good omen, for Lancelot, like the young cuckoo, only resembled a hawk and was in truth nothing but a usurper.

We stopped a few miles short of Caer Cadarn at a small monastery that had been built where a sacred spring bubbled out of an oak grove. This had once been a Druid shrine and now the Christian God guarded the waters, but the God could not resist my spearmen who, on Arthur's orders, broke down the gate of the palisade and took a dozen of the monks' brown robes. The monastery's bishop refused to take the offered payment and just cursed Arthur instead, and Arthur, his anger ungovernable now, struck the bishop down. We left the bishop bleeding into the sacred spring and marched on west. The bishop was called Carannog and he is now a saint. Arthur, I sometimes think, made more saints than God.

We came to Caer Cadarn across Pen Hill, but stopped beneath the hill's crest before we came in sight of its ramparts. Arthur chose a dozen spearmen and ordered them to cut their hair into the Christian tonsure, then to don the monks' robes. Nimue did the cutting, and she put all the hair into a bag so that it would be safe. I wanted to be one of the twelve, but Arthur refused. Whoever went to Caer Cadarn's gate, he said, must not have a face that could be recognized.

Issa submitted to the knife, grinning at me when his hair was gone from the front of his scalp. 'Do I look like a Christian, Lord?'

'You look like your father,' I said, 'bald and ugly.'

The twelve men wore swords under their robes, but could carry no spears. Instead we knocked their spearheads off their shafts and gave them the bare poles as weapons. Their shaved foreheads looked paler than their faces, but with the cowls of the robes over their heads they would pass as monks. 'Go,' Arthur told them.

Caer Cadarn was of no real military value, but as the symbolic place of Dumnonia's kingship its worth was incalculable. For that reason alone we knew that the old fortress would be heavily guarded and that our twelve false monks would need good luck as well as bravery if they were to trick the garrison into opening the gates. Nimue gave them a blessing and then they scrambled over Pen's crest and filed down the hill. Maybe it was because we carried the Cauldron, or maybe it was Arthur's usual luck in war, but our ruse worked. Arthur and I lay in the summit's warm grass and watched as Issa and his men slipped and stumbled down Pen Hill's precipitous western slope, crossed the wide pastures and then climbed the steep path that led to Caer Cadarn's eastern gate. They claimed to be fugitives running from a raid by Arthur's horsemen and their story convinced the guards, who opened the gate to them. Issa and his men killed those sentries, then snatched up the dead men's spears and shields so that they could defend the precious open gate. The Christians never forgave Arthur for that ruse either.

Arthur scrambled onto Llamrei's back the moment he saw the Caer's gate was captured. 'Come on!' he shouted, and his twenty horsemen kicked their beasts up over Pen's crest and so down the steep grassy slope beyond. Ten men followed Arthur up to the fort itself, while the other ten galloped around the foot of Caer Cadarn's hill to cut off the escape of any of the garrison.

The rest of us followed. Lanval had charge of Guinevere and so came more slowly, but my men ran recklessly down the escarpment and up the Caer's stony path to where Issa and Arthur waited. The garrison, once the gate had fallen, had shown not a scrap of fight. There were fifty spearmen there, mostly maimed veterans or youngsters, but still more than enough to have held the walls against our small force. The handful that tried to escape were easily caught by our horsemen and brought back to the compound, where Issa and I had walked to the rampart over the western gate and there pulled down Lancelot's flag and raised Arthur's bear in its place. Nimue burned the cut hair, then spat at the terrified monks who had been living on the Caer to supervise the building of Sansum's great church.

Those monks, who showed far more defiance than the garrison's spearmen, had already dug the foundations of the church and lined them with rocks from the stone circle that had stood on the Caer's summit. They had pulled down half of the feasting hall's walls and used the timber to begin raising the church walls which stood in the shape of a cross. 'It'll burn nicely,' Issa said cheerfully, rubbing his new bald patch.

Guinevere and her son, denied the use of the hall, were given the largest hut on the Caer. It was home to a spearman's family, but they were turned out and Guinevere was ordered inside. She looked at the rye-straw bedding and the cobwebs in the rafters and shuddered. Lanval put a spearman at the door, then watched as one of Arthur's horsemen dragged in the garrison's commander who was one of the men who had tried to flee.

The defeated commander was Loholt, one of Arthur's sour twin sons who had made his mother Ailleann's life a misery and had ever resented their father. Now Loholt, who had found his Lord in Lancelot, was dragged by the hair to where his father waited.

Loholt fell to his knees. Arthur stared at him for a long time, then turned and walked away. 'Father!' Loholt shouted, but Arthur ignored him.

He walked to the line of prisoners. He recognized some of the men for they had once served him, while others had come from Lancelot's old kingdom of the Belgae. Those men, nineteen of them, were taken to the half-built church and there put to death. It was a harsh punishment, but Arthur was in no mood to give mercy to men who had invaded his country. He ordered my men to kill them, and they did. The monks protested and the prisoners' wives and children screamed at us until I ordered them all to be taken to the east gate and thrown out.

Thirty-one prisoners remained, all Dumnonians, and Arthur counted down their ranks and chose six men: the fifth man, the tenth, the fifteenth, the twentieth, the twenty-fifth and the thirtieth. 'Kill them,' he ordered me coldly, and I marched the six men down to the church and added their corpses to the bloody pile. The rest of the captured prisoners knelt and, one by one, kissed Arthur's sword to renew their oaths, though before each man kissed the blade he was forced to kneel before Nimue who branded his forehead with a spearhead that she kept fired to red heat in a cooking fire. The men were all thus marked as warriors who had rebelled against an oath-lord and the fire-scar on their foreheads meant they would be put to death if they ever proved false again. For now, their foreheads burned and hurting, they made dubious allies, but Arthur still led over eighty men, a small army.

Loholt waited on his knees. He was still very young, fresh-faced and with a skimpy beard that Arthur gripped and used to drag him to the royal stone that was all that remained of the old circle. He threw his son down by the stone. 'Where is your brother?' he demanded.

'With Lancelot, Lord.' Loholt trembled. He was terrified by the stench of burning skin.

'And where is that?'

'They went north, Lord.' Loholt looked up at his father.

'Then you can join them,' Arthur said, and Loholt's face showed utter relief that he was to live. 'But tell me first,' Arthur went on in a voice like ice, 'just why you raised a hand against your father?'

'They said you were dead, Lord.'

'And what did you do, son, to avenge my death?' Arthur asked, then waited for an answer, but Loholt had none. 'And when you heard I was alive,' Arthur went on, 'why did you still oppose me?'

Loholt stared up at his father's implacable face and from somewhere he found his courage. 'You were never a father to us,' he said bitterly.

Arthur's face was wrenched by a spasm and I thought he was about to burst into a terrible rage, but when he spoke again his voice was oddly calm. 'Put your right hand on the stone,' he ordered Loholt.

Loholt believed he was to take an oath and so he obediently placed his hand on the royal stone's centre. Then Arthur drew Excalibur and Loholt understood what his father intended and snatched his hand back. 'No!' he shouted. 'Please! No!'

'Hold it there, Derfel,' Arthur said.

462

Loholt struggled with me, but he was no match for my strength. I slapped his face to subdue him, then bared his right arm to the elbow and forced it flat onto the stone and there held it firm as Arthur raised the blade. Loholt was crying, 'No, father! Please!'

But Arthur had no mercy that day. Not for many a day. 'You raised your hand against your own father, Loholt, and for that you lose both the father and the hand. I disown you.' And with that dreadful curse he slashed the sword down and a jet of blood spurted across the stone as Loholt twisted violently back. He shrieked as he snatched his bloody stump back and gazed in horror at his severed hand, then he whimpered in agony. 'Bind it,' Arthur ordered Nimue, 'then the little fool can go.' He walked away.

I kicked the severed hand with its two pathetic warrior rings off the stone. Arthur had let Excalibur fall onto the grass, so I picked up the blade and laid it reverently across the patch of blood. That, I thought, was proper. The right sword on the right stone, and it had taken so many years to put it there.

'Now we wait,' Arthur said grimly, 'and let the bastard come to us.'

He still could not use Lancelot's name.

Lancelot came two days later.

His rebellion was collapsing, though we did not know that yet. Sagramor, reinforced by the first two contingents of spearmen from Powys, had cut off Cerdic's men at Corinium and the Saxon only escaped by making a desperate night march and still he lost more than fifty men to Sagramor's vengeance. Cerdic's frontier was still much further west than it had been, but the news that Arthur lived and had taken Caer Cadarn, and the threat of Sagramor's implacable hatred, were enough to persuade Cerdic to abandon his ally Lancelot. He retreated to his new frontier and sent men to take what they could of Lancelot's Belgic lands. Cerdic at least had profited from the rebellion.

Lancelot brought his army to Caer Cadarn. The core of that army was Lancelot's Saxon Guard and two hundred Belgic warriors, and they had been reinforced by a levy of hundreds of Christians who believed they were doing God's work by serving Lancelot, but the news that Arthur had taken the Caer and the attacks that Morfans and Galahad were making south of Glevum confused and dispirited them. The Christians began to desert, though at least two hundred were still with Lancelot when he came at dusk two days after we had captured the royal hill. He still possessed a chance of keeping his new kingdom if only he dared to attack Arthur, but he hesitated, and in the next dawn Arthur sent me down with a message. I carried my shield upside down and tied a sprig of oak leaves on my spear to show that I came to talk, not fight, and a Belgic chieftain met me and swore to uphold my truce before leading me to the palace at Lindinis where Lancelot was lodging. I waited in the outer courtyard, watched there by sullen spearmen, while Lancelot tried to decide whether or not he should meet me.

I waited over an hour, but at last Lancelot appeared. He was dressed in his white-enamelled scale armour, carried his gilded helmet under one arm and had the Christ-blade at his hip. Amhar and the bandaged Loholt stood behind him, his Saxon Guard and a dozen chieftains flanked him, and Bors, his champion, stood beside him. All of them reeked of defeat. I could smell it on them like rotting meat. Lancelot could have sealed us up in the Caer, turned and savaged Morfans and Galahad, then come back to starve us out, but he had lost his courage. He just wanted to survive. Sansum, I noted wryly, was nowhere to be seen. The mouse-lord knew when to lie low.

'We meet again, Lord Derfel.' Bors greeted me on his master's behalf.

I ignored Bors. 'Lancelot,' I addressed the King directly, but refused to honour him with his rank, 'my Lord Arthur will grant your men mercy on one condition.' I spoke loudly so that all the spearmen in the courtyard could hear me. Most of the warriors bore Lancelot's sea-eagle on their shields, but some had crosses painted on their shields or else the twin curves of the fish. 'The condition for that mercy,' I went on, 'is that you fight our champion, man on man, sword on sword, and if you live you may go free and your men may go with you, and if you die then your men will still go free. Even if you choose not to fight, then your men will still be pardoned, all but those who were once oath-sworn to our Lord King Mordred. They will be killed.' It was a subtle offer. If Lancelot fought then he saved the lives of the men who had changed sides to support him, while if he backed down from the challenge then he would condemn them to death and his precious reputation would suffer.

Lancelot glanced at Bors, then back at me. I despised him so much at that moment. He should have been fighting us, not shuffling his feet in Lindinis's outer courtyard, but he had been dazzled by Arthur's daring. He did not know how many men we had, he could only see that the Caer's ramparts bristled with spears and so the fight had drained out of him. He leaned close to his cousin and they exchanged words. Lancelot looked back to me after Bors had spoken to him and his face flickered in a half smile. 'My champion, Bors,' he said, 'accepts Arthur's challenge.'

'The offer is for you to fight,' I said, 'not for someone to tie and slaughter your tame hog.'

Bors growled at that, and half drew his sword, but the Belgic chief who had guaranteed my safety stepped forward with a spear and Bors subsided.

'And Arthur's champion,' Lancelot asked, 'would that be Arthur himself?'

'No,' I said, and smiled. 'I begged for that honour,' I told him, 'and I received it. I wanted it for the insult you gave to Ceinwyn. You thought to parade her naked through Ynys Wydryn, but I shall drag your naked corpse through all Dumnonia. And as for my daughter,' I went on, 'her death is already avenged. Your Druids lie dead on their left sides, Lancelot. Their bodies are unburned and their souls wander.'

Lancelot spat at my feet. 'Tell Arthur,' he said, 'that I will send my answer at midday.' He turned away.

'And do you have a message for Guinevere?' I asked him, and the question made him turn back. 'Your lover is on the Caer,' I told him. 'Do you want to know what will happen to her? Arthur has told me her fate.'

He stared at me with loathing, spat again, then just turned and walked away. I did the same.

I went back to the Caer and found Arthur on the rampart above the western gate where, so many years before, he had talked to me of a soldier's duty. That duty, he had said, was to fight battles for those who could not fight for themselves. That was his creed, and through all these years he had fought for the child Mordred and now, at last, he fought for himself, and in so doing he lost all that he had most wanted. I gave him Lancelot's answer and he nodded, said nothing, and waved me away.

Late that morning Guinevere sent Gwydre to summon me. The child climbed the ramparts where I stood with my men and tugged at my cloak. 'Uncle Derfel?' He peered up at me wanly. 'Mother wants you.' He spoke fearfully and there were tears in his eyes.

I glanced at Arthur, but he was taking no interest in any of us and so I went down the steps and walked with Gwydre to the spearman's hut. It must have cut Guinevere's wounded pride to the quick to ask for me, but she wanted to convey a message to Arthur and she knew that no one else in Caer Cadarn was as close to him as I. She stood as I ducked through the door. I bowed to her, then waited as she told Gwydre to go and talk with his father.

The hut was only just high enough for Guinevere to stand upright. Her face was drawn, almost haggard, but somehow that sadness gave her a luminous beauty that her usual look of pride denied her. 'Nimue tells me you saw Lancelot,' she said so softly that I had to lean forward to catch her words.

'Yes, Lady, I did.'

Her right hand was unconsciously fidgeting with the folds of her dress. 'Did he send a message?'

'None, Lady.'

She stared at me with her huge green eyes. 'Please, Derfel,' she said softly.

'I invited him to speak, Lady. He said nothing.'

She crumpled onto a crude bench. She was silent for a while and I watched as a spider dropped out of the thatch and spun its thread closer and closer to her hair. I was transfixed by the insect, wondering if I should sweep it aside or just let it be. 'What did you say to him?' she asked.

'I offered to fight him, Lady, man to man, Hywelbane against the Christ-blade. And then I promised to drag his naked body through all Dumnonia.'

She shook her head savagely. 'Fight,' she said angrily, 'that's all you brutes know how to do!' She closed her eyes for a few seconds. 'I am sorry, Lord Derfel,' she said meekly, 'I should not insult you, not when I need you to ask a favour of Lord Arthur.' She looked up at me and I saw she was every bit as broken as Arthur himself. 'Will you?' she begged me.

'What favour, Lady?'

'Ask him to let me go, Derfel. Tell him I will sail beyond the sea. Tell him he may keep our son, and that he is our son, and that I will go away and he will never see me or hear of me again.'

'I shall ask him, Lady,' I said.

She caught the doubt in my voice and stared sadly at me. The spider had disappeared into her thick red hair. 'You think he will refuse?' she asked in a small frightened voice.

'Lady,' I said, 'he loves you. He loves you so well that I do not think he can ever let you go.'

A tear showed at her eye, then spilled down her cheek. 'So what will he do with me?' she asked, and I gave no answer. 'What will he do, Derfel?' Guinevere demanded again with some of her old energy. 'Tell me!'

'Lady,' I said heavily, 'he will put you somewhere safe and he will keep you there, under guard.' And every day, I thought, he would think of her, and every night he would conjure her in his dreams, and in every dawn he would turn in his bed to find that she was gone. 'You will be well treated, Lady,' I assured her gently.

'No,' she wailed. She could have expected death, but this promise of imprisonment seemed even worse to her. 'Tell him to let me go, Derfel. Just tell him to let me go!'

'I shall ask him,' I promised her, 'but I do not think he will. I do not think he can.'

She was crying hard now, her head in her hands, and though I waited, she said nothing more and so I backed out of the hut. Gwydre had found his father's company too glum and so wanted to go back in to his mother, but I took him away and made him help me clean and re-sharpen Excalibur. Poor Gwydre was frightened, for he did not understand what had happened and neither Guinevere nor Arthur was able to explain. 'Your mother is very sick,' I told him, 'and you know that sick people sometimes have to be on their own.' I smiled at him. 'Maybe you can come and live with Morwenna and Seren.'

'Can I?'

'I think your mother and father will say yes,' I said, 'and I'd like that. Now don't scrub the sword! Sharpen it. Long smooth strokes, like that!'

At midday I went to the western gate and watched for Lancelot's messenger. But none came. No one came. Lancelot's army was just shredding away like sand washed off a stone by rain. A few went south and Lancelot rode with those men and the swan's wings on his helmet showed bright and white as he went away, but most of the men came to the meadow at the foot of the Caer and there they laid down their spears, their shields and their swords and then knelt in the grass for Arthur's mercy.

'You've won, Lord,' I said.

'Yes, Derfel,' he said, still sitting, 'it looks as if I have.' His

468

new beard, so oddly grey, made him look older. Not feebler, but older and harsher. It suited him. Above his head a stir of wind lifted the banner of the bear.

I sat beside him. 'The Princess Guinevere,' I said, watching as the enemy's army laid down their weapons and knelt below us, 'begged me to ask you a favour.' He said nothing. He did not even look at me. 'She wants –'

'To go away,' he interrupted me.

'Yes, Lord.'

'With her sea-eagle,' he said bitterly.

'She did not say that, Lord.'

'Where else would she go?' he asked, then turned his cold eyes on me. 'Did he ask for her?'

'No, Lord. He said nothing.'

Arthur laughed at that, but it was a cruel laugh. 'Poor Guinevere,' he said, 'poor, poor Guinevere. He doesn't love her, does he? She was just something beautiful for him, another mirror in which to stare at his own beauty. That must hurt her, Derfel, that must hurt her.'

'She begs you to free her,' I persevered, as I had promised I would. 'She will leave Gwydre to you, she will go . . .'

'She can make no conditions,' Arthur said angrily. 'None.'

'No, Lord,' I said. I had done my best for her and I had failed.

'She will stay in Dumnonia,' Arthur decreed.

'Yes, Lord.'

'And you will stay here too,' he ordered me harshly. 'Mordred might release you from his oath, but I do not. You are my man, Derfel, you are my councillor and you will stay here with me. From this day on you are my champion.'

I turned to look at where the newly-cleaned and sharpened sword lay on the royal stone. 'Am I still a King's champion, Lord?' I asked.

'We already have a King,' he said, 'and I will not break that oath, but I will rule this country. No one else, Derfel, just me.'

I thought of the bridge at Pontes where we had crossed the river before fighting Aelle. 'If you won't be King, Lord,' I said, 'then you shall be our Emperor. You shall be a Lord of Kings.'

He smiled. It was the first smile I had seen on his face since Nimue had swept aside the black curtain in the Sea Palace. It was a wan smile, but it was there. Nor did he refuse my title. The Emperor Arthur, Lord of Kings.

Lancelot was gone and what had been his army now knelt to us in terror. Their banners were fallen, their spears were grounded and their shields lay flat. The madness had swept across Dumnonia like a thunderstorm, but it had passed and Arthur had won and below us, under a high summer sun, a whole army knelt for his mercy. It was what Guinevere had once dreamed of. It was Dumnonia at Arthur's feet with his sword on its royal stone, but it was too late now. Too late for her.

But for us, who had kept our oaths, it was what we had always wanted, for now, in all but name, Arthur was King.

AUTHOR'S NOTE

Cauldron stories are common in Celtic folk-tales, and their quest was liable to send bands of warriors to dark and dangerous places. Cúchulain, that great Irish hero, is said to have stolen a magic cauldron from a mighty fortress, and similar themes recur in Welsh myth. The source of those myths is now quite impossible to disentangle, but we can be fairly certain that the popular medieval tales of the search for the Holy Grail were merely a Christianized re-working of the much older cauldron myths. One such tale involves the cauldron of Clyddno Eiddyn, which was one of the Thirteen Treasures of Britain. Those treasures have disappeared from the modern re-tellings of the Arthurian saga, but they were firmly there in earlier times. The list of the Treasures varies from source to source, so I compiled a fairly representative sample, though Nimue's explanation of their origins on page 119 is entirely an invention.

Cauldrons and magical treasures tell us that we are in pagan territory, which makes it odd that the later Arthur tales are so heavily Christianized. Was Arthur the 'enemy of God'? Some early tales do indeed suggest that the Celtic church was hostile to Arthur; thus in the *Life of St Padarn* Arthur is said to have stolen the saint's red tunic and only agreed to return it after the saint had buried him up to the neck. Arthur is similarly supposed to have stolen St Carannog's altar to use as a dining table; indeed, in many saints' lives, Arthur is depicted as a tyrant who is only thwarted by the holy man's piety or prayers. St Cadoc was evidently a famous opponent whose *Life* boasts of the number of times he defeated Arthur, including one fairly distasteful story in which Arthur, interrupted during a game of dice by fleeing lovers, attempts to rape the girl. This Arthur, a thief, liar, and would-be rapist, is clearly not the Arthur of modern legend, but the stories do suggest that Arthur had somehow earned the strong dislike of the early church and the simplest explanation of that dislike is that Arthur was a pagan.

We cannot be sure of that, any more than we can guess what kind of pagan he was. The native British religion, Druidism, had been so abraded by four centuries of Roman rule that it was a mere husk by the late fifth century, though doubtless it clung on in the rural parts of Britain. Druidism's 'dolorous blow' was the black year of AD60, when the Romans stormed Ynys Mon (Anglesey) and so destroyed the faith's cultic centre. Llyn Cerrig Bach, the Lake of Little Stones, existed, and archaeology has suggested it was an important place for Druidic rituals, but alas, the lake and its surrounding features were all obliterated during the Second World War when the Valley Airfield was extended.

Druidism's rival faiths were all introduced by the Romans, and for a time Mithraism was a genuine threat to Christianity, while other Gods, like Mercury and Isis, also continued to be worshipped, but Christianity was by far the most successful of the imports. It had even swept through Ireland, carried there by Patrick (Padraig), a British Christian who was supposed to have used the clover-leaf to teach the doctrine of the Trinity. The Saxons extirpated Christianity from the parts of Britain they captured, so the English had to wait another hundred years for St Augustine of Canterbury to reintroduce the faith into Lloegyr (now England). That Augustinian Christianity was different from the earlier Celtic forms; Easter was celebrated on a different day and, instead of using the Druidic tonsure that shaved the front part of the head, the new Christians made the more familiar bald circle on the crown of the head.

As in *The Winter King* I have deliberately introduced some anachronisms. The Arthurian legends are fiendishly complex, mainly because they include all kinds of different stories, many of which, like the tale of Tristan and Iseult, started as quite independent tales and only slowly became incorporated in the much larger Arthurian saga. I did once intend to leave out all the later accretions, but that would have denied me, among many other things, Merlin and Lancelot, so I allowed romanticism to prevail over pedantry. I confess that my inclusion of the word Camelot is a complete historical nonsense, for that name was not invented until the twelfth century so Derfel would never have heard it.

Some characters, like Derfel, Ceinwyn, Culhwch, Gwenhwy-vach, Gwydre, Amhar, Loholt, Dinas and Lavaine, dropped out of the stories over the centuries, to be replaced by new characters like Lancelot. Other names changed over the years; Nimue became Vivien, Cei became Kay, and Peredur Perceval. The earliest names are Welsh and they can be difficult, but, with the exceptions of Excalibur (for Caledfwlch) and Guinevere (for Gwenhwyfar), I have largely preferred them because they reflect the milieu of fifth-century Britain. The Arthurian legends are Welsh tales and Arthur is an ancestor of the Welsh, while his enemies, like Cerdic and Aelle, were the people who would come to be known as the English, and it seemed right to stress the Welsh origins of the stories. Not that I can pretend that the Warlord trilogy is in any way an accurate history of those years; it is not even an attempt at such a history, merely another variation on a fantastic and complicated saga that has come to us from a barbaric age, yet it still enthralls us because it is so replete with heroism, romance and tragedy.

BERNARD CORNWELL

THE WINTER KING

In the Dark Ages, a legendary warrior struggles to unite Britain …

Uther, the High King of Britain, has died, leaving the infant Mordred, as his only heir. His uncle, the loyal and gifted warlord Arthur, now rules as caretaker for a country which has fallen into chaos – threats emerge from within the British kingdoms while vicious Saxon armies stand ready to invade. As he struggles to unite Britain and hold back the Saxon enemy at the gates, Arthur is embroiled in a doomed romance with beautiful Guinevere. Will the old world magic of Merlin be enough to turn the tide of war in his favour?

The first of Bernard Cornwell's Warlord Chronicles, *The Winter King* sheds new light on the Arthurian legend, combining myth with historical accuracy and the brutal action of the battlefield.

BERNARD CORNWELL

EXCALIBUR

Arthur's final test of courage is upon him ...

Arthur has crushed Lancelot's rebellion, but at a cost. Guinevere's betrayal has left him reeling, and his Saxon enemies seek to destroy him while he is weak. Chaos threatens to engulf Britain. Yet Arthur is a military genius and noble leader. As the last battle draws close, he prepares to fight his way to victory at Mount Badon and also win back the woman he lost. But in this final journey of the warlord, the intrigues of Mordred, now the adult heir to the throne of Britain, and the magics of the priestess Nimue could prove to be Arthur's downfall.

Bernard Cornwell concludes The Warlord Chronicles, bringing new life to Arthurian legend, successfully marrying myth with historical fact.

'A powerful and dramatic retelling of the Arthurian legend' Sharon Penman

BERNARD CORNWELL

STORMCHILD

Blood is no protection from terror ...

Tim Blackburn's wife died in a ball of flame in the Channel, victim of a mystery bomber. His son had died years earlier in Northern Ireland, killed in a terrorist attack. And his daughter Nicole had vanished in the North Pacific after joining an outlawed organization called Genesis dedicated to saving the planet, by violence if necessary.

The police think Nicole might have been involved in the death of her mother, but Tim won't believe it. And he means to prove it.

With nothing else to live for, Tim goes in search of Nicole in his yacht *Stormchild*. He hopes to rescue her from the clutches of Genesis. But where would a secretive organization of ruthless environmentalists hide? And even if he does find Nicole, will he be a welcome visitor?

BERNARD CORNWELL

If you enjoyed this book, there are several ways you can read more by the same author and make sure you get the inside track on all Penguin books.

Order any of the following titles direct:

0140174583	STORMCHILD	£7.99
014017723X	WILDTRACK	£7.99
0140177248	SEA LORD	£7.99
0140177256	CRACKDOWN	£7.99
0140177264	SCOUNDREL	£7.99
0140231862	THE WINTER KING	£7.99
0140232478	ENEMY OF GOD	£7.99
0140232877	EXCALIBUR	£7.99

Simply call Penguin c/o Bookpost on **01624 677237** and have your credit/debit card ready. Alternatively e-mail your order to **bookshop@enterprise.net**. Postage and package is free in mainland UK. Overseas customers must add £2 per book. Prices and availability subject to change without notice.

Visit www.penguin.com and find out first about forthcoming titles, read exclusive material and author interviews, and enter exciting competitions. You can also browse through thousands of Penguin books and buy online.

IT'S NEVER BEEN EASIER TO READ MORE WITH PENGUIN

Frustrated by the quality of books available at Exeter station for his journey back to London one day in 1935, Allen Lane decided to do something about it. The Penguin paperback was born that day, and with it first-class writing became available to a mass audience for the very first time. This book is a direct descendant of those original Penguins and Lane's momentous vision. What will you read next?

He just wanted a decent book to read ...

Not too much to ask, is it? It was in 1935 when Allen Lane, Managing Director of Bodley Head Publishers, stood on a platform at Exeter railway station looking for something good to read on his journey back to London. His choice was limited to popular magazines and poor-quality paperbacks – the same choice faced every day by the vast majority of readers, few of whom could afford hardbacks. Lane's disappointment and subsequent anger at the range of books generally available led him to found a company – and change the world.

'We believed in the existence in this country of a vast reading public for intelligent books at a low price, and staked everything on it'
Sir Allen Lane, 1902–1970, founder of Penguin Books

The quality paperback had arrived – and not just in bookshops. Lane was adamant that his Penguins should appear in chain stores and tobacconists, and should cost no more than a packet of cigarettes.

Reading habits (and cigarette prices) have changed since 1935, but Penguin still believes in publishing the best books for everybody to enjoy. We still believe that good design costs no more than bad design, and we still believe that quality books published passionately and responsibly make the world a better place.

So wherever you see the little bird – whether it's on a piece of prize-winning literary fiction or a celebrity autobiography, political tour de force or historical masterpiece, a serial-killer thriller, reference book, world classic or a piece of pure escapism – you can bet that it represents the very best that the genre has to offer.

Whatever you like to read – trust Penguin.